No Amount of Trouble

★ *A Strange Space® Novel* ★

KATIE SILVERWINGS

Memphis, TN

PepTalk Productions, LLC

This is a work of fiction set in a universe created by the author's imagination, curiosity, and the possibilities of what could be. While inspired by real science, history, technology, culture, or human experience, the worlds, characters, and events within these pages are entirely fictional and created from the author's imagination. Any resemblance to actual persons, living or dead, or to real places or events is purely coincidental.

The author and publisher make no claim to the accuracy of historical, scientific, or cultural details, which have been adapted or invented for narrative purposes. This book is intended solely as a work of entertainment. Readers are invited to explore the possibilities and contemplate the unlimited potential of the human spirit, but not to mistake fictional possibilities for fact.

Publisher's Cataloging-in-Publication Data
provided by Five Rainbows Cataloging Services

Names: Silverwings, Katie, 1991- author.
Title: No amount of trouble : a strange space novel / Katie Silverwings.
Description: Memphis, TN : PepTalk Productions, 2025. | Series: Strange space adventures, bk. 7.
Identifiers: LCCN 2025922550 (print) | ISBN 978-1-959922-45-2 (paperback) | ISBN 978-1-959922-46-9 (hardcover) | ISBN 978-1-959922-48-3 (ebook) | ISBN 978-1-959922-47-6 (audiobook)
Subjects: LCSH: Space travelers--Fiction. | Extraterrestrial beings--Fiction. | Families--Fiction. | Science fiction. | Illustrated works. | BISAC: FICTION / Science Fiction / Space Exploration. | GSAFD: Science fiction. | FICTION / Science Fiction / Action &Adventure. | FICTION / Science Fiction / Alien Contact. | FICTION / Family Life / General. | GSAFD: Science fiction.
Classification: LCC PS3619.I58 N63 2025 (print) | LCC PS3619.I58 (ebook) | DDC 813/.6--dc23.

Published by PepTalk Productions, LLC 2025
Memphis, Tennessee, USA
www.PepTalkProductionsLLC.com

Books by Katie Silverwings

FEATHERED FRIENDSHIP
✦ A Strange Space® Novella ✦

CELADON
✦ A Strange Space® Novel ✦

HOW OCEAN MERLANI STOLE THEIR NAVIGATOR
✦ A Strange Space® Novel ✦

WARMTH AND DARKNESS
✦ A Strange Space® Novella ✦

THE GARDEN IN THE DARKNESS
✦ A Strange Space® Novel ✦

TALES OF THE NAVIGATORS: VOLUME 1
✦ Strange Space® Short Stories ✦

ON THE SUBJECT OF KITTENS AND MITTENS
✦ A Strange Space® Novella ✦

NO AMOUNT OF TROUBLE
✦ A Strange Space® Novel ✦

The printing of this edition of *No Amount of Trouble* was made possible through the generous support of the members of the Strange Space® Fan Club, including:

Astral Navigator

Sharon T. Hinton

Galactic Traveller

Isaac Goode

Space Adventurer (1 Year+)

Tabitha

Thank you so much to all of my Fan Club members and supporters! I couldn't do this without you.

To find out more about the Strange Space® Fan Club and join for free, visit:

www.KatieSilverwings.com/Fan-Club

Characters Appearing in this Story

The following list of characters is divided by species and arranged in order of their appearance in the narrative. Only characters with significant "speaking roles" have been detailed here. All others present are listed as a group for the reader's reference; characters who are mentioned but do not appear are not included.

Humans

Pilot-Major Anna Toussaint
She/her. 2nd Darter Squadron pilot, assigned to SCV *Surnia*. Former Project Snail Darter test pilot.

Pilot-Major Penny Albright
She/her. 2nd Darter Squadron pilot, assigned to SCV *Surnia*. Former Project Snail Darter test pilot.

Pilot-Major Abigail Ioane
She/her. 2nd Darter Squadron pilot, assigned to SCV *Surnia*. Former Project Snail Darter test pilot.

Pilot-Sergeant Julian Potts
He/him. Also known as "Sarge." 2nd Darter Squadron pilot, assigned to SCV *Surnia*.

Petty Officer 3rd Class Elias Rudolph
He/him. Also known as "Rudy." Darter Maintenance Technician, 2nd Darter Squadron, assigned to SCV *Surnia*.

Florivans

IOLITE MEREDAY

They/them. Primary Quantum Space Drive Engineer, MSS *Equinox*. Counterpart to **Scott Walton**. Parent of **Mirawynd.**

MIRAWYND

They/them. Also known as "Wyndi." A survivor-smallest kitten. Child of **Iolite Mereday.**

DR. STAR SAPPHIRE AYRNYI

They/them. Head of the Sol Coalition Defense Fleet's Medical Division, Captain of SCV *Asio*. A member of the household of **Elder Celadon.**

ELDER CELADON TOREVAL

They/them. Primary Quantum Space Drive Engineer, SCV *Aegolius*. Youngest of the Florivan Council of Elders; Defense Fleet Elder. Counterpart to **Lt. Hsu Li.**

Prelvee

"DOC"

He/Him. Physician, Prelvee starship *Song-of-the-Midnight-Frog*.

"EMERALD"

She/Her. Communications Officer, Prelvee starship *Song-of-the-Midnight-Frog*. Formerly stationed at the Defense Fleet's Shell Island Base.

"FROG'S CAPTAIN"

She/Her. Captain, Prelvee starship *Song-of-the-Midnight-Frog*.

"DUSTY"

She/Her. Engineer's Assistant, Prelvee starship *Song-of-the-Midnight-Frog*. Younger sister of **Dr. Goldie**.

"DR. GOLDIE"

She/Her. Physician, Prelvee starship *My-Love-is-the-Stars*. Elder sister of **Dusty**.

T'irsh-fel

CAPTAIN ZYZYK

He/Him. Captain of the T'irsh-fel battleship *R'zyll*. A friend of *Frog's* **Captain**.

PROFESSOR ZYNN

He/Him. Head of the xenoarchaeological research project at the City of Caves outpost on the planet Jewel-Eye. A friend of *Dr. Goldie*.

"LILY"

She/Her. A "severed" individual, formerly of the xenoarchaeological research project at the City of Caves outpost on the planet Jewel-Eye. A friend of *Dr. Goldie*.

Contents

Contents

CONTENTS

MASTER SERGEANT
POTTS

No Amount of Trouble

★ *A Strange Space® Novel* ★

KATIE SILVERWINGS

Part 1:
Equinox

THE SPACE BETWEEN STARS IS VAST AND LONELY. Untold expanses stretch between the heliopause of one star system and the next, nearly empty save for solar winds and the odd object that's been thrown wide by gravity's slingshot.

To sail these galactic seas takes time and effort. Even the most advanced of humanity's starships must take weeks of slow, carefully-planned travel to go between one of the Sol Coalition's stars and another. If they were limited to the wide, shimmering solar sails and ion thrust engines of the past, it would take decades. As it stands, the gift of the Quantum Space Drive and its perilous shortcuts around physical distance allow shorter journeys.

Each vessel, though, must take care of itself. In the space between stars, much can be made of the courage of the crew of a starship. Beyond the settled regions of a star system, help and resources are never close to hand. A ship must carry all it needs, from food and medical supplies on down to the most basic elements required for survival such as air and water. What can't be carried must be able to be made, or otherwise gone without.

With the onset of the Novan War some three years gone, single cargo vessels passing through the stellar expanses are becoming few and far between, unless they're part of one of the Sol Coalition Defense Fleet's escorted convoys. Civilian ships flying alone are easy targets, and the Novan Imperium's forces have near-light engines of their own which rival QSD tech for speed.

The danger is not unfamiliar to the crew of the Defense Fleet's newest starship, SCV *Surnia*. She's flying alone in the midst of her maiden voyage out from the Teegarden's Star colony's shipyards, but *Surnia* is hardly an appealing target. The first in her class, *Surnia* is well-armed and well-stocked, and carries her own full squadron of the Defense Fleet's newest version of swift little darter craft for extra protection.

Bound for the Defense Fleet's base at the second planet in the Kapteyn star system, at the moment, *Surnia* is in the middle of the 'night' period of her ship-standard day. Aside from the Nav/Quan team running the nightly Quantum Space transit cycle and the small part of her crew assigned to the Evening or Mid watches, most everyone aboard is asleep.

Among those sleepless souls posted to the night watch are a certain set of pilots forming what little remains of the 2nd Darter Squadron. The Musketeers, as they're known, are a single-wing unit that's only recently been attached to *Surnia's* newly-formed 18th. Where a full Darter squadron is composed of sixteen pilots and their support staff, the 2nd only has four. They're the only single-wing unit in the Defense Fleet's ranks, and with good reason: after limping back to Teegarden's Star as the only survivors from SCV *Athene,* the three senior pilots of the 2nd were hardly ready to be separated and assigned to new squadrons of their own.

Instead, the Defense Fleet's staff psychologist helped them find an appropriate fourth pilot to round out their wing and suggested they be paired with *Surnia's* less-experienced collection of young flyers. The ship is more than big enough to house four extra darters, after all, and the Musketeers are in a perfect position to be lent out to whatever ship needs them most at any given time.

As is often the case aboard *Surnia,* the Musketeers have drawn the short straw this week for being on call during the entirety of the night shift. They've not had much to do so far, of course, but it's Fleet protocol to have at least one of the darter wings ready to fly at a moment's notice at all times. Truth be told, they don't mind taking the duty on the whole. The three senior pilots of the 2nd are the sort of people who take the ship's safety seriously, and would rather be on hand to react immediately than have to be roused from their bunks in the middle of an ongoing emergency.

And so it is that three women in ivory-jacketed pilot's uniforms are sitting on stools pulled up around a crate at the back of the hangar that holds their squadron's darters, playing cards. Each of them bears their surname in forest green block-print letters across their back over the squadron's fleur-de-lis and crossed swords insignia.

The first and most senior of the three, Pilot-Major Albright, is a tall, exceedingly pale woman who keeps her shoulder-length mass of ice-white martian curls pulled back at the base of her neck in a pair of poofy ponytails. Her equally pale eyes are almost always partly obscured behind her set of lightly tinted protective lenses. At the moment, she's using that to her advantage as she considers the cards in her hand.

The second, Pilot-Major Toussaint, has a far more deeply tan complexion and keeps all of her hair tucked neatly beneath an ivory headscarf. Her own stack of cards is neatly face-down on the makeshift table. She's the sort of person who memorizes her hand instead of holding it.

Pilot-Major Ioane, the youngest of the three, is more of a tawny-pale in comparison to the other two and a touch shorter, with straight black hair cut just below her chin. She's acting as the dealer tonight, since her usual partner for Snapdragon's Garden is otherwise occupied. Right now, she's drumming her fingers on the edge of the crate and waiting for Albright to declare whether she's taking another card or not.

The fourth member of the wing, nineteen-year-old Pilot-Sergeant Julian Potts, would typically be sitting with the Majors right now, attempting to keep up with Ioane's fast-paced play style. How she ever manages to pull off a win with Potts as her partner, even he couldn't say. It's not that he doesn't know how to play; it's just that the cards never cooperate with him and the Majors as a whole are too good at reading his facial expressions, no matter how hard he tries to bluff.

Tonight, though, Potts has found himself up in the cockpit of his darter with its canopy open, following half-shouted directions from the 2nd's cantankerous maintenance technician and *deeply* regretting several choices he's made this evening—not the least of which was being so foolish as to let said mechanic hear him say that he was bored.

"Try 'er now, Sarge!" bellows a muffled, echoing voice from deep inside the small spacecraft's undercarriage. "I think we're ready to try tuning these new relay crystals."

"Okay, Rudy," Potts calls back, rolling his eyes. He flips the switch to activate the darter's primary com link channel and pulls down the microphone bar on his headset. "*Surnia* Comms Control, this is Darter 2-M-4 *again*... Sorry to bother you, but we're ready to run another system test."

Amidst the static on the com link, Potts thinks he hears the on-duty communications officer laugh. Their words are a bit garbled, but he can still make out most of what they're saying. "*Go ahead, Darter—. Want me—call the med team down?*"

"No, Control," Potts replies. He makes a point of pitching his voice loud enough to make sure the man wedged up inside his darter's systems access crawlspace can hear him "I *think* Rudy's got everything fixed so we won't need to bother the medical response team this time."

"I asked you to keep the line active so I could test it, Sarge, not go bloody *gossiping* with whoever's up there on the bridge!" growls the voice from beneath. "*Stars,* a man goes and gets electrocuted *once* trying to sort out one of you pilots' shoddy attempts at repair work and no one ever lets him hear the bloody end of it..."

"*He's grumbling—isn't—yeah?*"

"Yeah. Well, nothing's sparking yet, Control, so I think we're doing pretty well." Potts leans out of the cockpit towards the access port his friend's legs are sticking out of just to make sure of that. "Sounds like the static's clearing up, Rudy," he says to the legs.

"I'll *bet* it is. Just keep the line active and give me a shout when it's clear."

Potts laughs and goes back to the conversation over his headset. "So, Control, how's things up on the bridge tonight?"

"*All's—quiet up here.*" The static is almost gone now. "*Except—you calling in every half-hour. Usually is—during transit.*"

"Well, glad we could keep you amused, at least."

"*You're amusing, all right—*" Just as the signal is starting to clear up, the communications officer takes on a different tone of voice. "*Sergeant, I've got to let you go. Comms Control out.*"

Potts isn't sure what that's about, but at least he heard all of it clearly. "Hey, Rudy," he says, knocking lightly on the side of the darter. "Think you might as well stop there. Control hung up on me."

"Probably because they got sick of listening to you ramble." Potts can hear the teasing smirk that's doubtless on the other man's face. "All right, then, turn it all off and sit tight while I get this backup power supply wired back in."

Potts shakes his head in amusement and does as he's told. He leans back in his pilot's chair, crossing both arms behind his head. Of all the maintenance technicians in the Fleet, he's still amazed that the one who was pulled in to keep the 2nd's darters flying is the same brilliant grouch a paperwork misunderstanding had stuck him with for a roommate while he was in the Fleet's Darter Trainee Corps at Teegarden's Shell Island Base. Potts has known Elias Rudolph for a little more than a year now, and even being promoted to Petty Officer, Third Class and transferred to a unit whose officers genuinely like having him around has done *nothing* to tame the man's temper.

The fact that the two of them still wound up sharing a cabin after *Surnia's* Captain Brentwood helped the Majors steal Rudy away from the Shipyards is another thing altogether. They're used to the arrangement by now, but some days Potts wishes he could look forward to being *alone* for a while after his shift. This is one of those days, if only because Potts knows how slim the chances are of his best friend being in a good mood once he's done sorting out all the repairs the darter needed.

Potts glances over at the three women sitting around the crate. It's not much of a mystery just why exactly the Majors would be so pleased to take Rudy on—the man's *skilled*, in spite of his temper, and far beyond what a simple relay technician like he'd been serving as back at Teegarden should be.

Why the Majors had chosen Potts *himself*, on the other hand, he still hasn't quite figured out.

Potts has only known the Majors for two months. Like most young darter pilots, though, he'd heard the legends about them on his first day in the Trainee Corps. One of his instructors at Shell Island had been a test pilot alongside the three of them at the very beginning of Project Snail Darter, and made a point of telling tall tales about them at every opportunity. At this point, the Musketeers are legends even outside the Fleet.

By all accounts, Albright, Ioane, and Toussaint have been inseparable ever since they started flying together—and that was *years* ago, even before the Defense Fleet was called upon to defend humanity's systems from the Novan Imperium. Until SCV *Athene* fell, the rest of the 2nd's original four wings were made up of folks from the first generation of pilots trained at Shell Island after the testing phase of the project ended. The Majors have been the heart of the squadron since the beginning.

For whatever reason, Potts is the one they chose to be their new fourth. Despite the fact that there were scores of pilots more experienced than him available, *he* was the one they picked. Whenever he's asked about it, they've taken great delight in giving him contradictory answers. His instinct is that it had something to do with his managing to survive his test flight as Ioane's co-pilot and still be willing to get back into a darter afterwards—especially considering that they crashed through a solar sail and wound up in the Shipyards Orbital's infirmary for two days at the end of that run.

All Potts really knows, in the end, is that they *did* pick him, and that he's glad they did.

As he's considering all of this, Potts sees the 18th's Colonel Bell appear beside the crate where the majors are having their card game. That's not a good omen. The short, golden-blonde woman is notoriously *not* a night owl, and never appears during the late shifts at all unless something's going on. Potts is justifiably intimidated by her forthright, no-nonsense-accepted manner in the daytime; when disturbed from her slumber, the Colonel gives off the vibe of a queen bee preparing to send her swarm on the attack.

From the animated but urgent way the Colonel is quietly talking to the Majors, Potts has no doubt that this is something serious. A few moments later, the Colonel is striding purposefully back out of the hangar and the three of them are scurrying towards their own darters.

Toussaint stops by Potts' darter on her way past. "Sarge! Rudy!" She calls, waving to catch their attention. "Better finish up now! We're launching in twenty!"

"What in the bloody *stars* are you on about, Toussaint?" Rudy shouts back from inside the darter's belly. "We just heard the jump call—you can't bloody well launch this bird into Quantum Space! Especially not when I'm still working on her!"

"Captain's orders, Rudy!" Toussaint looks up to the open cockpit where Potts is shaking his head and trying to hold in laughter. "We're going off course to answer a distress call that came in between the jumps—and our lot's doing the answering. If you don't want to come along, get out of the bird!"

"Distress call?" Potts asks, leaning down from his cockpit.

"Freighter of some sort. Colonel said there's a good chance of Novans waiting for us."

"All right, Major!" Potts salutes for punctuation as he nods his understanding. "I'll be ready to fly as soon as Rudy gets her closed up."

Toussaint nods to him and then hurries off to the other side of the hangar where her own darter is waiting.

"Well, then!" Potts reaches over the side of the cockpit opening to knock on the darter's metal shell. "Better leave off replacing that other thingamabob for now, Rudy. Your farm-rigging should hold me for one flight."

"I *heard* her, Sarge. I was just sealing it all off, if you must know." The other man slides himself out of the maintenance access port and onto the wing, halfway glaring up at Potts. His pinkish-pale face is lightly smeared with a shimmer of non-conductive grease, and his golden-brown hair has fallen into his face again. Rudy pushes the offending lock back behind his ear and then wipes his hands on a rag that's tucked into one of the many pockets of his ivory maintenance tech vest. The green shirt underneath the vest is halfway unbuttoned. Rudy's one of the few people on *Surnia* who could get away with that.

"What, you don't fancy going out for a flight today?"

"Not if I can help it, Sarge. You *know* how I feel about micro-gravity." Rudy fixes Potts with an eye-roll of some magnitude. "Try not to get too fancy flying out there, though. If you jostle it up again and break everything I just put back together, don't go blaming *me* when the girls can't read you."

"Warning received, loud and clear."

"Good." Rudy chuckles and sets about closing up and sealing the access port. "Try to bring the bloody bird back in one piece this time, will you?"

"You worry too much, my friend," Potts laughs. "I promise I'll be back as soon as I can so you can finish the repairs."

"I'll hold you to that."

"I know you will."

★

I F THERE WAS EVER A DAY WHERE THINGS DIDN'T GO
as Potts expected, this is it.

"*All right, Sarge,*" says Major Ioane over his flight
headset's short-range radio, "*We just got our last survivor
loaded. All the upper decks are accounted for now. We're
ready to launch as soon as you finish your sweep. Try not to
take too long. There may still be air left, but I don't like the
look of this place structurally.*"

"Got it, Major," Potts replies. "I'm not finding anyone
down here at all—at least not that's alive. It looks like these
folks took too much of a beating during *whatever* it was
that did all that damage to the hull and took out the arti-
grav system."

Potts himself is currently floating along the corridor of
the last intact deck of the freighter MSS *Equinox's* interior

with only the light of his headset's built-in emergency lamp shining the way, carefully dodging debris and the occasional still forms of the remainder of the crew. He stops at each body to check for signs of life. He and Major Ioane had landed in *Equinox's* shuttle bay with the rescue shuttle from *Surnia* to assist; Albright and Toussaint are flying patrol around the freighter as a precaution. One can never be too careful when Novans might be involved.

He's disturbed by the sight of all this and the work he has to do, but this isn't the first time Potts has been involved in a search-and-rescue effort. He earned his pilot's wings as a volunteer for Teegarden-Millefleur's emergency medical evacuation services before he signed up for the Fleet, flying shuttles with his uncles between the six smaller colony moons and Millefleur Prime itself whenever he wasn't in school. His first solo flight as a preteen, even, had been unscheduled and part of a mass rescue effort from a series of devastating seismic events and subsequent mine collapses at the now-abandoned Moon 3.

He'd made more than one flippant remark about that during his first month in the Trainee Corps going through their required emergency response and search and rescue classes. Trying to impress his classmates with how much he'd already learned and seen and how tame the simulations they were being put through were in comparison didn't work too well, in the end—and in hindsight, he's glad it didn't. He's matured enough since then to be embarrassed by the memory.

Still, Potts knows that he will never *fully* be prepared for days like this, where he has to go through the old routine of checking for pulses and keeping count of the unfortunate people he has to leave where they've fallen. He's looking forward to being done and back in his bunk with a blanket or two pulled over his head so he can try to sleep deeply enough to forget all of what he's seen.

So far, ever since Potts came down to this deck, he hasn't found any survivors. Even so, it's procedure to check everywhere he can reach that might have someone left. It's taken the rescue team four hours already to locate all of the people who *did* survive from the upper decks and get them safely loaded into the shuttlecraft. The task would have been far easier if the freighter's artificial gravity system had still been functioning. Unfortunately, that's completely gone, just like the lights and climate controls.

A few minutes later, Potts comes to the end of the corridor—or at least, what's now the end, as everything that lies beyond has been fully sealed off by debris. To one side, almost fully obscured by the mess, Potts finds a door that's jammed halfway open and broken out of its sliding tracks. Shining the light from his headset toward the label on the wall, he learns that it's the antechamber to the ship's Quantum Space Drive bay.

Moving so the light shines through the door, Potts sees a mass of debris that's almost completely filling the space from the collapsed-in parts of the deck above. From the look of it, the damage to the decks happened before the gravity system was shut off. As his light passes over the debris, he sees what looks like the silver-tufted end of a long blue tail snaking out through the floating pile.

As Potts slips in through the broken door and starts carefully moving bits of rubble aside from around the tail, he's certain he hears a groan of some kind coming from the person underneath all of it.

"Major," he calls over the radio, "I think I might have someone! I'm just outside *Equinox's* Drive bay, and I think I've found her jumper. They're surrounded by a lot of debris, though—not sure how long it'll take me to dig them out."

"Oh? Okay, Sarge, see what you can—we'll wait—"

"I'm getting static, Major, but I hear you. Won't take me two shakes." Potts turns his attention to his work.

Ten minutes or so later, he's safely cleared a path through the debris and uncovered the rest of the Florivan's body. They're a dark, inky sort of blue, dressed in a dusty red button-front tunic and loose trousers, all of which are torn and darkened with ice-blue blood from their wounds. All four arms and both their legs are loosely pulled inward, as if they'd tried to protect themself from the initial impact by curling up into a ball. They're covered in bruises and cuts, and their long silver hair is a mess of tangles that floats wildly around them and obscures most of their face.

When Potts moves their hair to check for a pulse, the Florivan takes in a sharp, raspy breath. The sudden movement from such a still body almost shocks him out of his skin. Somehow, though, despite whatever hurricane hit this compartment, they *are* still alive.

"Easy," Potts says, taking in a breath himself to regain his composure, "It's okay. I'm a friend. I'm here to help you."

A moment passes, and then the lid of the third eye in the center of the Florivan's forehead cracks open a bit, trying to focus on his face. One of their upper arms shakily uncurls and reaches up to touch his hand where it's resting on their shoulder.

"Warm... human?" the Florivan whispers, still rasping each breath.

"Yes. I'm from SCV *Surnia*." Potts does his best to keep his tone calm and reassuring. "We got your distress call. The other survivors are already on our shuttle, I just need to get you there now."

The Florivan weakly wraps their four long, ice-cold fingers around Potts' own.

Potts gives their hand a gentle squeeze in return.

"...Warm... you—" The Florivan starts to say something else, but they fall into a pained fit of coughing instead.

Potts does his best to hold the Florivan steady so the momentum of their coughs doesn't drive the two of them back into the sharper bits of floating debris. He realizes now that only their upper body is able to move. Everything below their first pair of arms is paralyzed and only limply placed in the curled-up position he'd found them in. Potts has had his share of first aid training. He knows how dangerous it would be to move them at all if the artificial gravity was working. Fortunately for him, though, it's not. He'll have to be careful and slow about it, but he should be able to get them to the shuttle without injuring them further.

"Easy," Potts says again once the Florivan's breathing steadies, "don't try to talk too much. You don't have to tell me what happened until you're safe in *Surnia's* sickbay."

"No... you're *warm*." The Florivan fixes him with a look of all three eyes now, as if this is something incredibly important, and then tugs on the hand they're holding.

They seem to be coming around a little more, even if they're still struggling even to breathe and whisper to him at the same time.

"I don't understand."

They tug on his hand again, trying to move it off their shoulder.

Potts doesn't resist. He's still trying to think through the shortest path to the shuttlecraft and how long it might take to get there. At the same time, he can't deny being curious about what they're doing.

The Florivan pulls his hand down underneath the tangle of the rest of their limbs and rests it on their abdomen. He thinks at first that they're trying to show him some sort of a wound, and moves his light to look for it. Surprisingly, that seems to be the one spot where their clothing is intact and mostly clean.

Potts moves his hand briefly to try to inspect further, but the Florivan moves it back, trying to push it under the hem of their tunic.

"There's still... a chance... Please."

Potts has no idea what they're asking of him, but he lets them guide his hand back into place. This time they manage to leave it resting underneath the fabric, directly against their chilly skin. He's always heard that Florivans aren't really a warm-blooded species, but even though this is the first time he's ever touched one, Potts is certain that they're far colder than they should be.

A minute passes, then two, then three—all silent save for the pained sound of the Florivan's breathing.

Suddenly, Potts feels a flutter of movement under his hand. "What in the *stars*?"

"I... held on... long as I could... for them." There's a relieved tone underneath the Florivan's raspy whisper.

Under Potts' hand, the flutter turns to a small wriggling. He moves the hem of the tunic aside with his other hand just in time to see a fuzzy little silver head with three small golden eyes and large catlike ears peek out from a scar-like slit that runs across the upper part of the Florivan's belly just above the place where a human's navel would be.

Before Potts can say anything, the little creature has fully emerged and is nuzzling themself into the space between his hand and the Florivan's body. They shiver and wrap all six of their tiny limbs around the side of his palm. Their long, fluffy tail coils up around his wrist.

Potts has absolutely no idea how he's supposed to react to this. He doesn't know enough about the species to know if any of this is normal or not. This is only the third Florivan he's even *talked* to. He didn't know that they carried their offspring in a pouch like a possum in the first place.

After a moment or two of stunned silence, Potts carefully pulls his hand back up to show the little creature to the injured Florivan. "This is your child?"

"One of them... my survivor-smallest kitten... their littermates are with my Navigator." The Florivan weakly reaches up to rub the little creature behind the ears with two fingers. The kitten responds to their touch with a soft bell-toned purring sound, but then shivers and nuzzles closer into Potts' hand.

Potts wonders briefly how many more of these little fuzzy things there were before *Equinox* was attacked. He knows all too well that the Navigator's station would be up near the ship's command bridge, which doesn't exist anymore. All the same, he feels like it'd be better not to say anything about that until he gets the Florivan back to *Surnia*.

"Please…" The Florivan pushes Potts' hand back towards his own body. "Keep Mirawynd warm?"

Potts nods and tucks the kitten into one of the inner pockets of his jacket, close to his body. Little Mirawynd resists letting go at first, but the warmth seems to convince them that the pocket is an acceptable pouch and they're soon curled up in the bottom of it. He fastens the jacket back to hold in more of his body heat for them and then turns his attention back to the kitten's injured parent.

"I'll keep them safe, I promise. Now, let's get you to the shuttle so you can warm up too."

The Florivan halfway smiles at him, and then nods weakly. They seem to have just enough strength in their upper pair of arms to hold on to Potts. He steadies them against his chest with one arm as well and focuses on maneuvering as safely and gently as he can while he floats back through the corridors.

Potts tries to radio back that he has the last survivors, but the static has gotten worse and no one responds. He chalks that up to the amount of metallic debris around him. With luck, he'll get back to the shuttle bay before anyone needs to get in touch with him again.

Inside his jacket, the kitten begins making a soft, contented purring sound.

★

"*S*ARGE? WHERE—YOU? GET YOUR—IN GEAR! *We've got—*"

Potts reaches up to tap on his radio headset's receiver with his free hand. "What's going on, Major? I only caught a few words of that."

"*Launching now—try—outrun them—catch up—*" The static only gets worse with every word.

"Major? Can you read me?"

He hears nothing but static in response.

"Something's wrong?" asks the Florivan, still in that weak raspy voice. They've been struggling the whole time to stay conscious, as far as Potts can tell, but this is the first they've spoken since giving him the kitten they called Mirawynd. For once, having to work without gravity is turning to Potts' benefit: it's been a much gentler journey up to this point for his injured companion than it would have been otherwise.

"I'm not sure. Don't worry," he says, putting on his most reassuring tone, "I'm sure it's just a comm glitch because this radio's routed through my darter's mains instead of the shuttle's."

A sudden impact and explosion elsewhere on the wrecked ship makes everything shake around Potts and his injured companion. He narrowly misses colliding with a bit of debris that's broken off of something down a side corridor as it comes flying through the air.

Potts holds the injured Florivan a bit tighter and kicks off of the nearest wall to propel them both down the last stretch of hallway before the open door to the shuttle bay. When he reaches the door, it's already too late. He sees both the shuttlecraft and Ioane's darter launch through the soap-bubble-like shimmer of the atmosphere-containment field they'd set up in the bay's open space doors when they first arrived. Without that, they wouldn't have had enough air in the shuttle bay to safely move the survivors from the sealed parts of the ship into the shuttle.

"Major!" Potts calls over the radio, "What the—"

"Sarge! There you—jamming—get—"

The sight of a bright yellow Novan striker zipping along out beyond the containment field with a pair of darters on its tail is all the answer Potts needs to put together what's going on. This was a trap, then—and he's sitting right in the middle of it.

He curses under his breath and then launches himself and the injured Florivan from the door frame on a trajectory towards his own darter. When he reaches it, he catches on to the open canopy with his free hand and steadies the two of them. Luckily, the darter's magnetic clamps are still active, holding it firmly against the deck of the shuttle bay.

The slight impact elicits a pained groan from the Florivan.

"Ah! Sorry about that."

"What..." The Florivan is a bit more alert now, although their mind seems scattered. "Where... where's Scott? What's going on?" They fall into a fit of coughing again.

Potts doesn't like the sound of it at all. There's a wetness under the rasping in their breaths now. He wouldn't be surprised if at least one of their lungs is damaged. To his alarm, he can't remember how *many* lungs Florivans are supposed to have in the first place.

"Easy." Potts holds the injured Florivan steady while they catch their breath. "I'm here to help you, remember? You and Mirawynd get to fly with me instead of in the shuttle, that's all. Just a bit of a change of plans."

Potts carefully guides the Florivan's paralyzed body into the vacant copilot's chair behind his own seat. He's glad to at least have somewhere to put them. Darters are built for speed and efficiency, but the designers left room for the option of a second person. Usually the back chair is used for the training of new pilots and the like, or so there's a second pair of hands to operate the craft's collection of laser guns during a battle so the pilot can focus on flying.

The Florivan winces when Potts does up the safety straps over their chest and waist to secure them into the seat. "What's going on?" they ask again.

"Sorry," Potts says reflexively, knowing he doesn't have time now to try to explain. "Just try to hold on. I'll have you and Mirawynd safely aboard *Surnia* before you know it."

Potts maneuvers himself around into his own seat and pulls the thick shielded poly-glass canopy bubble down, locking it into position and engaging the air pressure seals. He's careful as he straps himself in to arrange his jacket so the safety restraints sit around the pocket holding the kitten rather than over the top of them.

He can still feel the little Florivan's soft purring from within his jacket. At least *they* don't seem to be worried. If anything, he has the impression they've gone to sleep.

While the darter's engines are running through their warming cycle, Potts tries his main radio. "*Surnia* Flight Control, this is Darter 2-M-4, can you read me?"

"*Read—bad static—where are you?*"

"About to launch out of *Equinox* and head home, Control. What's going on out there?"

Another impact and explosion elsewhere on the remains of the ship shakes the darter violently through its magnetic attachment to the shuttle bay's floor.

"*Novans—surrounded—ready to jump—retreat as soon as—*"

"Control, you're breaking up, but I read you. I'm on my way."

"They... came back?" The Florivan behind him groans.

"Looks like it—but don't worry, I can outrun a couple of strikers. No problem!" Potts flips through his switches to free the magnetic clamps and launches out of the shuttle bay. Fortunately, his nav computer is giving him a clear reading on everything it sees around him. Through the canopy, he can see *Surnia* holding her position relative to the crippled remains of *Equinox*, right where he remembered she'd be.

Unfortunately, the nav computer is now also giving him a clear reading on a dozen or so Novan strikers that are already making a beeline for him.

"Just hang on!" Potts calls back to his injured passenger. "This might get a bit rough."

★

FIVE MINUTES AFTER LAUNCHING FROM *EQUINOX'S* shuttle bay, Potts is wondering just what he did to deserve a day like this.

His radio's nothing but static now. While Potts can see on his nav readout that the Majors and the 18th's darters are trying to keep a path open for him back to *Surnia*, the Novan strikers on his tail are making it nigh impossible to get there. Every time he glances over to check, it looks like another wave of them has manifested right between him and where he was trying to go. Even Major Ioane hadn't been able to zip around and take up position with him after the shuttle was safely docked. She's tried several times, but the Novans seem to be making a concerted effort to keep Potts cut off from the rest of the darters.

Finally, Potts settles on a desperate angle of thought that might be his only chance to get his two passengers to safety. It's a Musketeer plan if ever there was one: dangerous, but with just enough of a chance of success that he might as well try. It beats letting the strikers keep piling on his tail, at any rate.

"Brace yourself!" Potts shouts, louder than he intended.

"Why?" rasps the injured Florivan in the co-pilot's seat.

Potts glances at their reflection in the canopy's polyglass just long enough to see three very concerned golden eyes staring at him. He's not sure if it's a good thing or not that they're awake and aware enough of what's going on to ask the question. If what he's planning fails? Well, better they'd not woken up at all, if that happens.

"I'm going to try something *incredibly* stupid," Potts tells the injured Florivan, turning his full attention back to the darter's controls, "but it just might do the trick. Trust me."

The strikers on his tail are speeding up, and one on either wing is starting to close in.

Potts knows he only has one chance to pull this off. He pushes his own throttle to the max and aims his darter directly at the densest portion of what remains of MSS *Equinox*. As long as he times everything right, he *should* be able to pull up just before the point of no return. If he's right about the strikers being too fast-moving and slow-reacting to pull out, it'll take enough of them off his tail that he can zip back over towards *Surnia* and safety before they re-form their ranks around him.

The Novans keep pace with Potts as his darter charges forward, matching his speed and inching ever closer.

Just as Potts allows himself to think his plan is going to work, the striker directly on his tail finally gets close enough to open fire. The first shot hits his left wing dead on, shattering it and sending the darter into an uncontrollable spiral.

Potts tries to recover and pull away, but the darter's controls are frozen. If it weren't for the redundancies in the automatic inertia compensation systems, he knows they'd already be dead—not that it matters much right now.

Potts starts to speak, to apologize to the Florivan for getting their hopes up that he could save them. He can't get the words out. He almost thinks he hears them say something, but the roar of blood in his ears as his darter spirals towards certain death is too loud.

Suddenly, just before the inevitable impact, he feels a hand settle onto his shoulder.

Flash!

Painful, iridescent light bursts behind his eyes.

Potts feels himself still secured in the pilot's seat, but all motion and other frame of reference is gone save one thing: under his jacket, the Florivan kitten is *vibrating* as that same purring sound grows louder, echoing all around him.

His whole field of vision is *bright* and *colors* all at once. Light of every color, *flashing,* washing over him in waves of painful, impossible combinations so bright he can *taste* them.

He can't tell if his eyes are open, but they do feel like they close when he tries to reach up and cover them. It barely helps. Either way, they're burning from the brightness.

The colors have already made it in behind his eyelids.
Finally, his nerves have had too much.
He passes out.

★

A dream.

A field of golden grain, an impossibly blue sky, two suns of different colors.

The Florivan floats beside him, shimmering and translucent. One of their upper hands is resting on his shoulder.

The kitten is on his shoulder too, trying to hold onto their parent's hand.

"You're going to be okay," says their voice all around him, all wind chimes and softness and free of pain. "My Mirawynd will protect you. Keep them warm?"

He doesn't understand, but he nods. "I... I will."

The hand slips off of his shoulder.

The Florivan is gone. Only a soft shimmer remains, and that only for a moment.

The kitten clinging to his shoulder calls out to their absence like a plaintive, pleading bell...

★

WHEN POTTS REGAINS CONSCIOUSNESS, HE'S aware of two things almost immediately.

The first is that he has the worst migraine of his *life*. His eyes feel like they've been rubbed with pickled gravel. No hangover he's ever endured has approached this.

The second is that there's something small and fuzzy nuzzling the side of his neck from underneath his flight jacket's tall collar and making bell-like little squeaking sounds right into his ear.

It takes Potts a few minutes to remember anything that led up to the crash he's *sure* must have happened. It takes a minute or two more to get up the motivation to open his eyes. When he does, he's staring up out of the poly-glass of the darter canopy. Even the small points of light from the distant stars are painful, but not nearly as much as the dim red glow of the darter's emergency illumination on the control panels around him.

He reaches up and gives the little creature who's still snuggling his neck a small pat behind their ears. "Yeah, yeah, I'm awake... why are you out of my pocket?"

Potts is rewarded for his question with a purr and a soft, self-satisfied squeak. If the kitten was actually trying to wake him, they seem to be pleased that they succeeded.

After a moment, he catches the little fuzzball up in his hand and tucks them back inside his jacket. The warmth of his body must have been enough to fully revive them now. Even if they're feeling better, he *certainly* doesn't want to have them floating around in the microgravity of the darter's cockpit—or worse, to get themself wedged into some small space he can't reach.

Little Mirawynd makes a squeak of protest, but stays put in his pocket once he gets them back in there. They seem to have *opinions* about everything, even if they're only expressed in small bell-like squeaks

Potts turns around now to check on the kitten's parent, still trying to squint the sand feeling out of his eyes. He's shocked by what he sees—or rather, what he *doesn't* see. The straps are still buckled together over the co-pilot's seat, but the chair itself is empty save for a couple of oxidized blue bloodstains.

Potts stares at the empty seat for a while and then groans and turns back around. Staring hurts too much to be worth the trouble, and it's hardly helping him solve the mystery. He shifts his jacket around so he can look down into his pocket. Three curious golden eyes peer back up at him.

"Okay, I know *you're* real. Now, where'd your parent go?

If the kitten knows, they certainly don't have the words to say. They just nuzzle against the side of the pocket that's closer to Potts' chest and then curl up in the bottom of it with a satisfied squeak. For all the world, it seems as if they're content with the situation and have settled on going back to sleep now that Potts is awake to handle things.

"Right... Okay, then, Mirawynd," Potts says with a sigh. "Next question. Where the *hell* are we?"

Looking up out through the canopy, all Potts can see are faraway stars. There are no planets, or, at least, none near enough for his pained eyes to spot. There's no wreckage from *Equinox*, either, and no trace of *Surnia* or the Novans. Of that list, only the last item is comforting. At least if he's lost in unknown space in a crippled darter, there aren't any strikers around to finish him off.

Potts turns his attention to the darter's control console. Thankfully, aside from the engines and the laser guns, most of the other systems seem to be functioning. The craft's chronometer shows that he's been unconscious for three and a half hours, but his nav computer is out completely. He taps through the menus to restart it and then tries for the radio.

"This is Darter 2-M-4 with SCV *Surnia* calling any friendly ship within range. I'm stranded without engines and I don't know my position just yet... but if anyone happens to hear this and be in the neighborhood, I could *really* use an assist."

There's no immediate response on the radio, but Potts holds out hope that the repairs his grouch of a best friend made earlier that night are holding. He sets the darter's automated distress beacon up and then sighs and leans back in his chair, closing his eyes again. They still feel like they're full of gravel, and his sinuses are pounding with the headache of the century. He reaches up a hand and rubs at his temple.

He has a dim memory of bright lights and almost crashing into *Equinox*, but he doesn't remember anything after that. It's almost as bothersome a problem as the headache and the disappearance of the injured Florivan he *knows* he strapped into the co-pilot's chair before he launched.

"Really, now, Mirawynd, what's going on here?"

The kitten only responds by increasing the volume of the contented purring sound down in the bottom of his pocket. Potts assumes they must be too young to be able to understand him.

Odd as it is, he's grateful for the company. It means that he won't have to feel like an idiot talking to himself while he waits to see if a miracle will happen before the darter's emergency reserve power supply runs out and they both freeze to death in the void.

A chime from the restarted nav computer catches his attention. When he looks, a new layer is added to his collection of mysteries. According to the positioning readouts, he's nowhere near where he should be. In fact, he's something like three *light-years* deeper into Alliance territory than the Teegarden-Kapteyn passage where he started. That shouldn't be physically possible for a darter flying alone to cover in three decades with working engines, much less for a crippled bird like his to cross in three *hours*.

"Okay, Mirawynd," he says, shaking his head and immediately regretting the motion. "If this is right, then we're *definitely* lost. Either that, or I'm dead and this is what purgatory looks like for stray darter pilots… although in that case, I'm not sure why *you're* here."

Potts reaches down into one of the cockpit's side compartments where he keeps his emergency ration pack, med kit, and other things a pilot seldom thinks they'll need. Pulling out a protein stick, he unwraps the end of it and takes a bite or two. Fruit-flavored compressed calories aren't the tastiest thing in the galaxy by any means, but for a man who's been floating in space for who knows how long and missed at *least* two meals in the meantime, it's not too bad.

A thought occurs to him. Potts checks the label on the wrapper and then pinches off a bit of the protein stick. He holds it over the opening of his jacket pocket. "Say, Mirawynd," he says, looking in at the ball of purring silver kitten fluff, "are you hungry? I can't say I know what you eat, but these are supposed to be safe for Florivans."

The kitten opens their eyes again and sniffs, and then climbs up halfway out of the pocket to reach for the piece of protein stick. They take it from him with their upper pair of hands while the lower pair hold on to the edge of the pocket's opening. Snack in hand, they set about happily nibbling on it like the pocket-squirrel that Potts' older brother kept when they were kids.

Potts immediately decides that his new friend is both cuter and more polite than Eddie's pocket-squirrel. That little monster always bit at his fingers if he tried to get too close. He somehow doubts that a Florivan of any age would be the biting sort.

"Okay, then. That's good to know. *Wherever* they are, I don't think your parent would be too happy if I accidentally let you starve now that you're flying with me."

The kitten continues munching contentedly. They keep their third eye fixed on Potts' face the whole time.

Potts rubs at his temples. His headache hasn't diminished at all, yet. "I have no idea if anyone's going to come for us, you know?"

Having finished their snack, the kitten makes a happy little squeak at him in response and returns to the depths of the pocket.

"Yeah," Potts says, chuckling, "you've probably got the right idea about that."

He sends out one more message to any friendly craft that might be within range to rescue the two of them, and then he pops a pain-relief pill from the med kit into his mouth and washes it down with a sip of the emergency water out of the other compartment.

Potts reaches in to the pocket to absently stroke his little companion behind the ears for a few minutes while he waits for the medicine to take the edge off his headache. Once again, they contentedly nuzzle against his hand and start purring more loudly than before.

Soon, he's fallen back asleep.

★

When Potts wakes, it's to the sound of a rough alien voice in strangely accented Standard on the radio trying to hail him. Each syllable sounds like it's being scratched out by something that doesn't come naturally to vowel sounds at all.

"*—to Dar-ter 2-M-4, repeat: Gree-tings to the small hu-man in the bro-ken craft. Are you still a-live?*"

Potts scrambles to respond. "Yes! This is Darter 2-M-4. Yes, I'm still here! Who is this?"

"*This is the Al-li-ance ves-sel <u>Song-of-the-Mid-night-Frog</u>. Do you still re-qui-re as-sist-ance?*"

"Yes, I do! My mothership is a long way away and I'm sort of stranded." Potts pauses, remembering the accent now from a briefing he went through with the Musketeers not long after they took him under their wings. "You're a Prelvee ship, right?"

"*Yes. We will be reach-ing your po-si-tion in two of your hou-rs. Is that soon en-ough for you?*"

Potts glances down at his readouts. It should just be within the safety window before his backup power supply starts running low. "That's just peachy, thank you!"

"*Good! We will keep in con-tact with you at reg-u-lar int-erv-als. Please do not die while we are on the way; that would be in-con-ve-ni-ent.*"

"I'll be sure to do that," Potts replies, chuckling in spite of the situation. "Thank you."

Once the radio is switched back to standby mode, Potts pats the little Florivan in his pocket on their head and gives them a scratch behind their ears for good measure.

"Hear that, Mirawynd? We're getting rescued after all! You're one cute little good luck charm, you know that?"

The kitten makes a happy little squeak and climbs up out of the pocket to sit on his shoulder again. They keep their fluffy prehensile tail and one of their lower hands securely anchored to Potts' jacket collar.

"You know what, Mirawynd?" Potts reaches over to break off another piece of protein stick to offer his new copilot. "I think you and me are going to be okay."

★

Part 2:
Song of the Midnight Frog

MIRAWYND HAS ONLY HAD THEIR EYES OPEN for a week. They'd only just started exploring the home their littermates had been telling them stories about for so long. Mirawynd doesn't know why their littermates all opened their eyes first, and nearly a year before, nor why their littermates were nearly twice their size. All that ever mattered to Mirawynd was that the other four kittens who shared their parent's soft, warm pouch were warm and wonderful and *theirs*.

Mirawynd doesn't truly understand what happened on the day their parent had to stay in the shining place. They woke up from their nap *cold*, and then a human was there and he was warm. They were finally cozy in his pocket, and then the world shimmered. Their parent said to stay with the human and protect him. Then, their parent was gone, and Mirawynd was still with their human on the other side of the shining place.

Mirawynd likes their human. They've only had him for half of a day or so, but they like him. He's younger than their parent's human was, and pale and scruffy instead of deep brown primness. They like the scruffy sand-blonde hair, though. It's softer than it looks, and makes for a comfy nest for a kitten to curl up in.

At the moment, he's fallen asleep again, and Mirawynd is comfortably curled up in his hair just in front of the band of his headset, watching the stars. They know their family must be out there somewhere near one of the points of light, but they're too young to understand how to return to them. Stars are shiny, though, and fun to watch. They make for something interesting for a kitten to focus their attention on while standing guard over their human.

Their parent made it clear, after all, that it was *important* for Mirawynd to protect him.

A change in the pattern of lights to one side of the bubble the two of them occupy in the great vastness catches Mirawynd's third eye. They turn their head to focus on it.

The thing disrupting the pattern of stars and galaxy is *big*. It's a shimmery golden-green sphere suspended in a pair of wide rings set at right angles to each other, dotted all over with a seemingly random pattern of colored lights. Brighter gold lines trace around it at even levels and around the darker ovals that mark its surface. The large rods holding the rings to the rest of the object are golden as well.

Clearly, this is something for Mirawynd's human to handle. They might be the protector, but he's the adult.

Mirawynd reaches their tail down and waves it across their human's nose to wake him.

"Hmm-wha?" he brushes the insistent waving of the silver fluff out of his face.

Mirawynd slips down to his shoulder and squeaks pointedly as they tug lightly on their human's ear to try to turn his head in the correct direction.

"Fine, fine, I'm awake—you don't have to..." He finally turns towards the now-closer thing that's looming over them. "Oh. Yeah, that's worth pulling on a man's ear."

Mirawynd squeaks at him again with a self-satisfied wave of their tail. They've clearly done well to notify their human of the big shiny thing, whatever it is.

Their human taps one of the little buttons on the side of his headset. "This is Darter 2-M-4 calling. *Song-of-the-Midnight-Frog* Comms Control, please tell me that the enormous ship coming up on my position is you."

After a moment, Mirawynd hears an answering voice with a halting buzzy-click accent talking on the speaker over their human's other ear. *"This is the Al-li-ance vess-el Song-of-the-Mid-night-Frog. Please main-tain your pos-it-ion, as we are pre-pare-ing to re-trieve you gen-tly."*

"I'll take that as a yes." There's a clear note of relief in his tone. "But be advised, my maneuvering engines are out and I've lost a wing. Not sure I can do much to help on my end."

"Not-ed. We have scanned your craft; re-trie-val will be by co-or-di-nat-ed grav-i-ty scoop in-to our shut-tle main-tain-ance bay. Please stand by. We are mat-ching speed and tra-ject-or-y with you now. You may feel a small thud."

"Acknowledged. Standing by." He reaches up and plucks Mirawynd off his shoulder, holding open the side of his jacket. "Back in the pocket with you, now. I'm guessing we're in for a rough landing."

Mirawynd was hoping to stay on their human's shoulder and watch the growing shiny thing that is apparently a starship some more, and starts to protest. Then, they remember the nice human called Scott who belongs to their parent. Their parent trusts Scott to protect their family and works *with* him; if this younger man is now Mirawynd's, then they should listen to him, too. They nuzzle his hand in acceptance and slip down into the nice warm pocket, but wriggle themself into a position where they can peek out of the open collar and see what's going on.

Unfortunately, most of what Mirawynd can see from their vantage point is the underside of their human's chin. Beyond that, the big golden-green starship is looming ever bigger. The two rings are moving into a different position as the ship nears.

A few minutes later, a wide shimmering door in the outer ring slowly opens as it approaches and envelops them from below. There's a momentary jostling as the damaged darter catches up to the starship's gravity fields, and then it thuds belly-down onto the floor of the chamber. Mirawynd peers up from their pocket-nest to see the doors slipping closed above them.

Their human lets out a sigh of relief. "*Frog* Comms Control, that is one of the softest landings I've ever had. Thank you."

"The Cap-tain prides her-self on pre-cise man-eu-ver-ing and will acc-ept your grat-it-ude in per-son lat-er. Our tech-nic-ians will be en-ter-ing the hang-ar short-ly to ass-ist-you, once the air has been re-turned. Our phy-sic-ian will be with them to trans-late for you."

"Translate? But I've been talking to you in Coalition Standard this whole time."

"This vess-el car-ries two off-ic-ers who are flu-ent spea-kers in your lang-uage. The phy-sic-ian is the sec-ond."

Mirawynd is not as interested in the conversation as they are in trying to see as much as they can without emerging from their nice warm pocket. Aside from the now-closed shimmering doors, the whole hangar seems to be a green-covered grey cavern of a space.

"Noted." Their human flips up the microphone bar on his headset, then unfastens the securing belts holding him to his seat. "Now," he says, looking in at Mirawynd, "you need to stay in there for now, okay? I don't think our rescuers know much about Florivans, and I want you to keep close to me. This is a big ship we're on, and I'd hate for you to get lost."

Mirawynd squeaks an acknowledgment. They hadn't intended to leave their human's side in the first place. If anything, they're worried *he'll* get lost if they leave him alone for too long.

He laughs and stretches as if removing some stiffness from his arms, then goes back to tapping things on his pilot's interface. "Why do I think you can understand me? You're probably too young..."

Soon, the ambient sounds of the darter have quieted. So has the whoosh of air movement from outside.

Mirawynd's ears catch another sound, quiet but distinct, of a big door opening somewhere. After that, they hear lots of clicks and buzzes approaching from the rear of the craft. If their human hadn't just asked them to stay put, they'd have scampered out of his pocket to see what those sounds are.

"And..." Their human starts to speak, just as the sounds get closest and Mirawynd glimpses a dark, iridescent something above them on the other side of the canopy bubble. He falls silent and slumps back in his chair.

Mirawynd hears more clicks and buzzes above them, but their human seems to have fallen asleep again. They squeak to try to get his attention, but he doesn't respond.

Deciding that this means they're now the one in charge again, Mirawynd emerges from his pocket and slips up onto his shoulder to assess the situation. Their human is, indeed, asleep, or possibly unconscious. They're a bit too young and unfamiliar with humans in general to be able to tell the difference. Mirawynd tugs on his ear again to try to wake him, but it doesn't do anything.

They look up, and see that the source of all of the clicking and buzzing sounds is a person of some kind who is draped over the canopy bubble. The person is unlike anyone Mirawynd has ever seen in their short life.

They're long—longer than the whole of the darter, even. Their tube-like body is segmented into many iridescent-brown parts. Each of the lower segments bears several pairs of jointed appendages with small, shiny claws. The appendages on the upper third of the new person's body are more slender, and they have a large armored head at the top of their body. Their face bears one great central square-pupiled eye and five long muscular tentacles hanging down like a moving mustache around the rim of a set of large beak-like mouth-parts.

Mirawynd is fascinated by the new person with the shiny hard-shelled body, and waves excitedly up at them and squeaks a greeting. One of the face tentacles waves back at Mirawynd briefly as the eye considers them for a few moments, then the new person goes back to what they were doing. The person seems to be trying to open the canopy bubble from the outside, since Mirawynd's human has fallen asleep and can't do it himself.

It takes the hard-shelled person a few minutes to find the latch. When the canopy bubble does finally rise, the fresh air filling the space around Mirawynd and their human is warm, damp, and somehow heavy. Mirawynd doesn't know why the fresh air makes them feel like they weigh so much more than they did a moment ago, but their species is one naturally adapted to shifting gravity levels. Being heavier is a little inconvenient, but it's not painful. They wave again at the hard-shelled person and do their best in squeaks to convey that they would like some help waking their human up.

The hard-shelled person gently reaches in with several of their upper appendages and inspects Mirawynd's human, making soft buzzes and clicks with their mouth-parts. He doesn't wake.

From below the darter somewhere, another buzzy-click voice sounds off. It belongs, as it turns out, to a hard-shelled person who's barely a third the size of the first one and more of an iridescent green than brown. This one nudges the first away with one of their face tentacles, then taps on the shoulder of Mirawynd's human with a slender claw.

"Ex-cuse me, hu-man pi-lot?" says the smaller hard-shelled person in strongly accented Coalition Standard language, "You are safe now. Are you in-jured?"

Mirawynd's human doesn't respond. They reach up and tap the appendage nearest to them with one of their upper hands. When the smaller hard-shelled person's eye turns to them, Mirawynd squeaks pointedly and shakes their head.

"Oh? He-llo, lit-tle one... I do not know what you are. Are you the pi-lot's pet?"

Mirawynd doesn't quite know if *pet* is the right word for a human's protector, but they squeak affirmatively anyway.

"I see. He seems to be un-con-cious. We will have to re-move him to the in-fir-ma-ry so I can place him in a less phy-sic-al-ly stress-ful en-vi-ron-ment." The smaller hard-shell offers their claw to Mirawynd. "Do you un-der-stand to come with me so that the en-gin-eer can pick up your mas-ter?"

Mirawynd considers it for a moment, and then climbs up onto the small hard-shell person's appendage. Somehow, they have the instinct that this new person is a friend and can be trusted.

"Ve-ry good." The smaller hard-shell person climbs back down from the darter and holds Mirawynd, absently stroking their fur with a second claw while they say something in the buzzy-click language to the bigger hard-shell person.

After a short reply, the bigger hard-shell person climbs back up onto the darter. Before long, they have carefully lifted Mirawynd's human out and are gently cradling him in most of their upper appendages. He's still asleep.

The smaller hard-shell person clicks out a pleased-toned set of sounds and then turns back towards the big sliding door, gesturing with several face-tentacles for the larger one to follow.

Mirawynd doesn't take their own eyes off their human for the entire trip down the long moss-dotted corridor. They might have decided to trust their new hard-shelled friends, but their human is theirs to protect.

★

THE SMALL HARD-SHELL PERSON'S APPARENT home aboard the big shiny starship is bathed in soft blue-tinted light from large glowing globes that hang from the ceiling. It's just as warm and humid as everywhere else, but after the departure of the larger hard-shelled person, its air doesn't make Mirawynd feel nearly as heavy as they did outside.

They're currently sitting where they have been for the last hour or so: curled up on their human's chest, watching his face closely for signs that he might be waking up. He's laying on a soft cushioned platform in the corner of the room, with some kind of beeping monitor built into the wall above his head. The small hard-shell person had been thoughtful enough to set Mirawynd next to him once he'd been laid there.

Across the room, their new friend is sitting with most of their long segmented body coiled up underneath them at a platform of a desk. They seem to be busy with a monitor screen, either tapping at it with their facial tentacles or using their myriad of upper appendages to manipulate buttons on the interface below it. Mirawynd's not sure what that's about. As shiny as all of the things over there are, they're more interested by far in keeping watch over their human.

Soon, his breathing changes slightly and his eyelids flutter. Mirawynd squeaks softly and moves to nuzzle his cheek.

"Mm? What happened?" He sounds groggy, but then, he's been sleeping for a while.

Mirawynd squeaks at him again, louder this time, and swishes their tail pointedly. He fell asleep when he saw their new hard-shelled friends. That's what happened.

"Hey, Mirawynd..." He absently reaches a hand up to pet Mirawynd's soft silver fur. "Where are we now?"

"Ah," says the small hard-shelled person from across the room, now uncoiling themself and looking away from their monitor screen. "You are a-wake! I have checked you for in-jur-ies, but you seem to on-ly be in a state of shock."

Mirawynd's human is still staring up at the ceiling. "Do headaches count as shock? Still feels like mine's been used for target practice."

"That may be due to the high-er grav-i-ty when you en-tered our ship." The small hard-shelled person approaches the human's soft temporary nest, making light clicking sounds as their feet cross the floor. "Once the hu-man med-ic-al dat-a-base my col-league in your Fleet has sent me fin-ish-es com-pil-ing, I will be a-ble to treat your head-ache ap-pro-pri-ate-ly."

"Looking forward to it." Mirawynd's human turns his head to look at the hard-shelled person. For some unfathomable reason, he immediately passes out again.

Mirawynd taps on his face and tries to wake him up, squeaking loudly. They do not like the thought that their human might be broken. Their parent's human *never* suddenly falls asleep for no reason like this, that's for sure. They fail to rouse him. Displeased with this, they look up to the hard-shelled person with a plaintive squeak.

"That is in-ter-est-ing..." the hard-shelled person reaches out to pluck Mirawynd off of their human again. "Come here, lit-tle one, I need to scan him more tho-rough-ly..."

Mirawynd watches from the hard-shelled person's uppermost set of appendages as their human is once again bathed in shimmery light. The scanning system built into the wall around his nest sings its song of beeps and whirs and computer-generated hard-shell language. It takes longer this time. Once it finally all stops, their new friend gently sets them down on the cushion beside their human's head.

"He still scans as be-ing gen-er-al-ly heal-thy and un-in-jured," says the hard-shelled person, going back over to the monitor screen across the room. "Watch him for me, lit-tle one, I need to make a call."

Mirawynd is content to obey, and settles down right next to their human's ear with a not-quite-pleased-with-the-situation squeak.

On the other side of the room, their new friend coils back up and begins tapping rapidly on the button panel.

After several minutes, they say something in the buzzy-click sounds over an intercom and carry on a short conversation with one of the other hard-shell folk elsewhere on the ship.

Just as Mirawynd themself is fighting the cozy urge to curl up fully beside their human's face and take a nap, they hear a chime from their friend's monitor screen, followed by an oddly familiar voice.

"Your message said you needed more advice on your patient, friend?" says the voice, lightly concerned and terse all at once. The after-tone of wind-chimes reminds Mirawynd of their parent. That alone is cause to perk up their ears and listen more closely.

"Yes, Doc-tor Star. The da-ta-base you for-war-ded a-long with his med-ic-al rec-ords is still com-pil-ing. How-ev-er, he is show-ing an un-ex-pec-ted symp-tom that con-cerns me and is not not-ed on his fi-le."

"Oh?" The wind-chime voice of *family* sounds more concerned now.

"He fell un-con-cious when we re-trieved him from his space-craft, and while he seems un-in-jured, al-be-it some-what de-hy-dra-ted and in a mild state of shock, when he re-vived just now he al-most im-me-di-ate-ly passed out a-gain when I ap-proached to as-sess his con-di-tion. I am trans-fer-ing you the sec-ond scan re-port now."

There's a long pause. Mirawynd takes the opportunity to scamper over to join their hard-shell friend and try to see who it is talking on the monitor that sounds so much like their missing parent.

Their hard-shell friend allows Mirawynd to climb up along their long segmented body and sit perched neatly in their two uppermost appendages. Mirawynd's third eye stays trained on the corner of the room where their human is sleeping, but their lower two are fixed in excited fascination on the image on the screen.

There, sitting at a slightly cluttered desk on a starship like the one their family lived on, is someone who looks like their parent. The only differences in this adult Florivan are minor: They're a brighter, crisper blue, their hair is pulled back into a smart braided bun at the top of their head, and they're wearing an ivory lab coat over a green uniform similar to the ivory one Mirawynd's human wears. Notably, on the Florivan's left cheek, their silver stripes form a unique pattern of lines like a six-pointed star. All three of the Florivan doctor's eyes are focused in a different direction from the camera, looking over something on a holoscreen.

Mirawynd squeaks a greeting to their apparent entile and waves at the screen.

The Florivan on the screen looks up as if startled. After a moment, their expression turns to a curious neutral. *"I... take it that your little friend there was with Sergeant Potts?"*

"Yes, they seem to be his pet. I am not fam-il-iar with the spe-cies."

Mirawynd squeaks happily at their entile on the screen, doing their best to convey the story about their parent leaving them behind as their human's protector, as well as how upset they are that he seems to now be broken.

Their entile makes a soft trilling sound of acknowledgment under their breath, then turns their attention back to the hard-shelled person holding Mirawynd. *"They're not common... but they're not the first*

I've seen as a human's companion. Best you make sure they're able to stay with him."

"I had no in-ten-tions of sep-ar-at-ing them." The hard-shelled person's facial tentacles wave gently for emphasis. "They seem high-ly in-tel-li-gent, and quite con-cerned about his well-be-ing."

"*I'm sure they are. I'll forward you some general notes on taking care of such creatures.*" On the far edge of the screen, Mirawynd catches a glimpse of the fluffy silver tuft at the end of their entile's tail twitching in amusement. "*As for the human's condition, I believe it's a matter of stress and a wayward survival instinct. He should be fine once he has a chance to rest and acclimate to the situation.*"

"I am pleased to hear that, Doc-tor Star."

Over the ship's intercom, Mirawynd hears the other crisp hard-shell voice talking again.

Their new friend makes a disappointed facial tentacle gesture. "It seems that we must end our con-sul-tat-tion here. Thank you for your ass-is-tance."

"Anytime, my friend." Their entile's eyes turn towards where Mirawynd must be on their screen. They make a soft chirruping trill that any ears other than a kitten's would probably miss: a sound that says to stay close to their human and be good for the hard-shelled doctor.

Mirawynd squeaks happily in response and waves a goodbye as the video on the screen winks out. They immediately scamper back over to their human's temporary nest to keep watch over him. The soft, clicking footstep sounds behind them say that their new friend is close behind.

Mirawynd takes up their previous position beside their human's head. He's still asleep, but they have the impression that he's less deeply so than before. On a whim, they lightly wave the fluff of their long prehensile tail across his nose once or twice.

To Mirawynd's delight, he stirs, reaching up to brush the offending appendage out of his face. They squeak happily and turn their third eye up to their hard-shelled friend, waving their tail across their human's nose once more.

"Mhh... quit that..." He groggily nudges Mirawynd away from his face. "Okay," he says, only partly opening his eyes, "Still here, still have the headache... what day is it?"

"The same one on which you were res-cued from deep space," says the hard-shelled person, settling into a half-curled sitting position beside the nest. "Please do not move your head too quick-ly. It seems that while you do not show an-y form of brain in-ju-ry, you are still sen-si-tive to rap-id move-ment. You have lost con-si-ous-ness twice since you ar-rived."

"Great..." He sets a hand over his eyes, but doesn't move or fall asleep again, thankfully. "You're the ship's doctor, then?

Mirawynd squeaks cheerfully, trying to convey how much they like their new hard-shelled friend and that they're certain their human is safe.

"Yes." The hard-shelled person pauses and makes a distinctively whistle-edged series of sounds in their buzzy-click language. "—is my prop-er tit-le and name, but you are wel-come to re-fer to me as Doc-tor or Phy-sic-ian in-stead. I am a-ware that it is phy-sic-al-ly im-pos-si-ble for hu-mans to speak our lan-guage. Also, I am a male of my spe-cies and use mas-cu-line pro-nouns." He pauses, waving several of his facial tentacles thoughtfully. "May I ask for con-fir-mat-ion of yours? I am a-ware that hu-mans are a ra-ther com-plex spe-cies soc-ial-ly, and have been re-fer-ing to you as a male, since that is what is on your med-i-cal rec-ords."

"That I am."

"And to al-so con-firm and check your cog-ni-tion and mem-or-y: Your name is Ju-li-an Potts, ranked Pil-ot-Ser-geant, and you are nine-teen Earth Stan-dard years old?"

"Yes. Twenty in about three months, though."

"Not-ed. And your un-it is?"

"2nd Darter Squadron, with SCV *Surnia*. They call us the Musketeers."

"I have heard of your squad-ron." The Doctor makes an amused gesture with one of his facial tentacles, although Mirawynd's human is still staring up at the ceiling through squinted eyes and thus misses it.

"I'm new to it... but I'm not surprised if you have. The Majors are *infamous*, at least in Fleet circles."

"One of my T'irsh-fel col-leagues was am-ong the ob-ser-vers who flew with your squad-ron and the oth-er test pi-lots when your peo-ple's dart-er craft were dem-on-stra-ted to our joint ad-vi-so-ry group. He has man-y things to say a-bout the por-tion of his ex-per-i-ence that he can re-mem-ber."

Mirawynd's human laughs heartily, then winces and sets a hand over his eyes. "Did he say who he flew with?"

"A Col-o-nel Mor-el-i-a Dar-cy. Do you know her? I would be most in-ter-est-ed to hear her side of the sto-ry."

Mirawynd's human shakes his head, and immediately looks to regret the gesture. "No, she's... well, she *was* the original head of the Musketeers. Fell with *Athene* last year. I only met her once, back when I first joined the darter pilot corps. Nice lady, if a bit intimidating... I'm her wing-partner's new wing-partner, now."

"I see. My con-do-len-ces to your squad-ron as a whole. I had heard of that batt-le, but ov-er-looked the con-text."

Mirawynd's human absently begins petting their soft silver fur as he changes the subject. "You speak Standard quite well, Doctor."

Mirawynd purrs and settles in to cuddle against his chest. The room might be warm, but they like their human's warmth best.

"I have been stu-dy-ing since we first pre-pared to make con-tact with your peo-ple!" The hard-shell doctor waves one of his face tendrils in a gesture that comes across as proud. "I have an in-ter-est in hu-man med-i-cine as an ar-e-a of stu-dy. It is plea-sing to con-verse with my col-leagues in your Fleet with-out nee-ding to use a trans-lat-ion pro-gram to gen-er-ate text for them to read, and to be a-ble to catch the nu-ance of con-ver-sat-ion that our trans-lat-or chips do not pick up."

"I can see how that would help..." Mirawynd's human pauses, as if trying to think through something he wants to say. "Forgive me for asking, Doctor, but do I have a fever, or is it boiling in here?"

"You do not have a fe-ver. My peo-ple keep our en-vi-ron-ment a-board our ships sim-i-lar to that of our or-i-gin plan-et's main hab-i-tats, al-though we are a-dap-ted to man-y oth-er cli-mates. The tem-per-a-ture is rough-ly thir-ty-eight de-grees by your cen-ti-grade mea-sure-ments. I un-der-stood that this was with-in the tol-er-a-ble lev-els for hu-mans?"

"*Tolerable*, but not exactly pleasant." He nudges Mirawynd aside for a moment to try to get his flight jacket off. "Human ships are usually around twenty-four degrees, give or take."

Mirawynd squeaks in protest. After a moment, they decide that the cast-off jacket makes a nice warm nest in itself and set about tugging it into a comfortable arrangement beside their human.

As he's readjusting his clothing, Mirawynd's human turns his head towards the Doctor. After a moment, he blinks and then settles back into his nest. "Is..." he sounds distracted, for some reason. "Is the high humidity a thing on your planet too, then?"

"In our pre-ferred re-gions, yes, al-though I have on-ly vis-it-ed our or-i-gin plan-et once. You should al-so be a-ware that our ar-ti-fi-cial grav-i-ty is high-er than you are used to, and on-ly bare-ly with-in the tol-er-a-ble lim-its of your bod-y. I have ad-jus-ted the in-fir-mar-y to ac-co-mo-date you, but it will be sev-er-al days be-fore a-pro-pri-ate quar-ters have been mod-i-fied for you."

"Good to know... but you don't mind that?"

"My peo-ple are ad-ap-ted to grav-i-ty shifts, and fee-ling rel-a-tive-ly weight-less does not bo-ther me."

Mirawynd's human seems to consider this for a moment, then looks up at the Doctor with a wry grin. "Would it bother you to cool the room off just a bit too?"

The Doctor's facial tentacles wave in his equivalent gesture to a smile. "For the sake of a pat-ient, not at all. Shall we com-pro-mise at twen-ty-nine for now?"

"Twenty-nine works for me."

"It would be best that you ac-li-mate to our ship-board en-vi-ro-ment," the hard-shelled physician remarks as he goes over to a shiny collection of interface buttons on the far wall. "You will be trav-el-ing with us for some time."

Mirawynd's human watches the Doctor walk with some interest, as if trying to count how many clawed feet are attached to him and make sense of their new friend's shape. "How long do you think? I know my squadron's probably keen to get me back..."

"I do not know for sure. I have not been in-formed if the Cap-tain in-tends to re-route us to re-turn you to your peo-ple soon-er. I would doubt that will hap-pen, though. This ship is cur-rent-ly on a mis-sion of some se-cre-cy and im-por-tance, and hea-ding in the op-po-site di-rec-tion from your Co-a-li-tion's ter-ri-tor-y. Like-ly, you will trans-fer to an-oth-er ship when we reach our des-tin-at-ion to be tak-en home."

"Ah..." Mirawynd's human looks over at them and ruffles their ears with a rueful grin. "Looks like we're doing a bit of hitchhiking, then, Mirawynd..."

Mirawynd purrs happily and wraps all six of their tiny limbs and their tail around his hand. They don't care all that much about how long it will take to return to their human's ship. As long as they're with him, they're already home.

★

Mirawynd awakens in the nest they'd made out of their human's jacket to find that he is no longer laying beside them. This is immediately distressing. They squeak loudly, looking all over the corner his nest takes up in the Doctor's room, and then all over the room itself. They find that they're *alone*, and they're not happy about it.

In fact, Mirawynd is frightened. They're supposed to be protecting their human. What if something's happened to him? What if he's gone like their family is, and they're all alone forever?

Mirawynd squeaks plaintively again and burrows back under their human's jacket, holding their fluffy silver tail close for comfort. Surely he won't have left them. He's *theirs*, isn't he? But where has he gone?

Amid their frantic squeaking, Mirawynd finally hears their human's voice coming from the other side of a small translucent door in the far wall that they hadn't noticed before. They immediately scamper over towards it, dragging their jacket-nest along with them just in case their ears have been mistaken. They squeak again, louder this time, calling for their human as best as they can without the words that grown-ups have.

The little door slides open, and Mirawynd's human is standing on the other side of it. There's another small room beyond, where the hard-shelled doctor is sitting at a table.

"I'm right here, Mirawynd," he says, sounding confused. "What are you squeaking about?"

Mirawynd leaps up into his arms and clings tight to him, leaving the jacket at his feet. They squeak plaintively into their human's neck, trying to tell him just how scary it was to think that he'd never come back.

Their human gently pats them on the head, still sounding confused as he bends down and takes back custody of his flight jacket. He slings it over his unoccupied shoulder. "You were just so cute sleeping, 'Wyndi, and I didn't want to disturb you... but I'm sorry I left you alone."

Mirawynd looks up into his two big, hazel human eyes with a curiosity that almost makes up for their distress. No one's ever called them something shorter than their full name before. They like it, though, because it's their human saying it.

"See? You're okay." Their human strokes their fur gently and carries them over to the low metal table where the hard-shelled doctor is using his uppermost clawed appendages to carefully pour something translucent and viscously pink into a pair of large bowls from a bright yellow jug.

"Is your pet un-harmed?"

"Yeah, Doctor, I think they were just confused because we weren't easy to find. Mirawynd here was orphaned recently and sort of took on with me... I guess waking up alone scares them."

Mirawynd is too interested in the shimmer on the surface of the bowl in front of their human's green-cushioned seat at the table to think too much about what the two adults are saying. It's shiny and smells sour-sweet. They consider getting down from their human's shoulder and trying to poke it, but at the same time they don't know if they want to get that sour-sweet smell on the finer fur of their hands. Besides, they just found their human again. They're not ready to leave the warm, cozy spot on his shoulder where they know they're meant to be.

"I see. I am glad they have you for a care-tak-er, then." The Doctor finishes filling the bowl in front of his own place and sets the jug down on the table. He then goes over to open a cabinet door at the far side of the room and retrieves a tray filled with steaming spheres of different bright colors and two pairs of long silver sticks with hooked ends from a nearby drawer.

Mirawynd watches him with great interest. The silver sticks are *shiny*, and immediately fascinate them, but it's the warm spiced food smells coming from the tray that catch their attention the most. They don't know how long ago they last ate, and they're reminded now that growing kittens are usually hungry.

"These steamed fruit buns are com-pat-i-ble with your phy-si-o-lo-gy, Ju-li-an," the Doctor says, using the long utensils to deftly hook several of the spheres out of the tray and set them on a smaller bowl in front of Mirawynd's human. "The bev-er-age is sim-i-lar-ly safe. Your Fleet's Doc-tor Star Sa-pphire gave me par-am-e-ters for nu-tri-tion as well as di-et-ar-y safe-ty guide-lines for foods which were mut-u-al-ly safe for both hu-mans and Flor-i-vans some time a-go, so that I could be pre-pared for host-ing them for a meal when our ships met."

"I still can't believe that you're friends with the head of Fleet Medical," Mirawynd's human muses, looking askance at the bowl and the bright-colored spheres. He glances at Mirawynd and smiles. "But I'm glad you could get in touch with them." He experimentally picks up the pair of silver hooked utensils the Doctor had set in front of him, one grasped uncertainly in each hand. "Now, how do I use these, exactly?"

The Doctor demonstrates, holding one silver stick on each side of his body with several of his upper claws. He uses them to gently catch one of the fruit spheres with the two hooked ends and lifts it up to his beak-like mouth-parts. "Like so," he says, after having swallowed the morsel. "If it is too dif-fi-cult for you, I will not be of-fen-ded if you eat with your fin-gers. Doc-tor Star Sapphire's hu-man coun-ter-part had to do that in the end. I will ask the ship's com-mis-sar-y to have a smal-ler set of u-ten-sils made for you lat-er. I can see that e-ven the ones we males use will be too long."

Giving it his best attempt, after some difficulty in keeping the fruit bun from escaping his grasp, Mirawynd's human is successful in spearing one of the fruit spheres on the two hooked ends of his shiny eating sticks. He has to slide his grip down more than half-way to be able to get the ball of alien fruit into his mouth, though. He chews experimentally for a few moments, then swallows. "These are tastier than I expected. Thanks, Doctor."

"They are a fav-or-ite of mine. I am glad you en-joy them."

Mirawynd's human manages to spear a second fruit bun on his eating sticks and holds it over towards their perch on his shoulder. "Here, Wyndi, I'm sure you're hungry by now."

Mirawynd takes the warm sphere in all four of their hands and begins nibbling along its edges. The treat is nearly as big as their head, after all. The fruit inside the lightly bouncy wrapping dough is soft and mildly sweet, with a very *green* flavor to go with its color and a touch of warming spice. They think it's their new favorite food, at least for today. The fruity compressed calorie stick they shared with their human in the darter was both a long time ago and not nearly as nice.

"I hope you don't mind me sharing with them at the table, Doctor," says their human, trying to catch another of the spheres for himself. "You'll have to explain the etiquette to me if I ever eat around the rest of your people... I'd hate to have them see their first impression of a human as... well, rude or unhygienic."

"You are han-dl-ing quite well, com-pared to the last hu-man I at-tempt-ed to teach... sim-i-lar to a nymph of the first mol-ting. As far as the et-i-quette... you are meant to grip with the din-ing hooks, rather than im-pale. Pol-iteness is to not speak with one's mouth full, and to al-low the high-est rank-ing fe-male to sample first from the com-mu-nal dish-es." The doctor pauses to deftly catch another fruit sphere from the still-steaming bowl in the center of the low table. "As for your pet... as you treat them as a per-son ra-ther than an an-i-mal, if they keep to your side or shoul-der and only take of-fered mor-sels so their fur will not con-tam-in-ate the tab-le, it will not be an issue. Pre-mol-ting nymphs are often fed thus-ly by their cho-sen care-take-ers until they de-vel-op their grasp-ing ap-pen-dag-es en-ough to learn the use of din-ing sticks." He waves one of his facial tentacles for emphasis.

"Good to know." Mirawynd's human looks back at the large bowl of shimmering pink liquid. "And this is...?"

"An up-lift-ing bev-er-age. Sus-tain-ing, and sim-i-lar to your peo-ple's cof-fee or tea."

"Right..." He seems unconvinced.

"One lifts the bowl thusly:" The Doctor leans down and grips the bowl with his facial tentacles, balancing it so that his beak-like mouth-parts can immerse themselves in the liquid. Setting his partly-drained bowl down, his large eye turns to Mirawynd's human. After a moment, he makes a few sounds in his own language, and then says, "Par-don, I can see that would be im-pos-si-ble. In-stead, you can raise the bowl in both hands and sip from the rim clos-est to you. No sounds, if poss-i-ble."

Mirawynd's human does this, although the bowl is huge in his small human hands. After successfully taking a quiet sip, he sets it back down with a thoughtful grimace. "Well... it's *nothing* like coffee... but thank you. I'll get used to it."

"I will have a small-er drink-ing bowl pro-cured for you as well. That will make things eas-i-er."

Mirawynd's human takes another sip, clearly trying to be polite about some natural revulsion to the flavor or texture. When he's done, Mirawynd squeaks politely and offers him the remaining bit of fruit bun they weren't able to finish.

He takes it and sets it on the edge of his dish, then holds the bowl up for them. "Thirsty, Mirawynd? Just... try not to fall in."

Mirawynd delicately leans over and slurps up a small mouthful of the shimmery pink stuff. It's just as sour-sweet as it had smelled, with a texture that's a bit slimy and just barely like a liquid going down. They swallow, then look up at their human with the sort of utterly confused grimace he was trying to hide. The shiny drink tasted okay enough, but it felt *weird* to drink.

Mirawynd's human laughs as he sets down the bowl. "Say, Doctor, could I get some water for my friend here to drink instead? I don't think they're quite ready for this stuff."

"Of course," says the Doctor, uncoiling himself and going over to one of the little interfaces near where he had retrieved the food. "Would you like some wa-ter for your-self? I am a-ware it will be ea-si-er for you to be-come de-hy-drat-ed in our en-vi-ro-nment."

"Yes, please, if you don't mind."

Soon, the hardshell doctor has returned and placed a similar-sized bowl of clear water next to the one of pink liquid in front of Mirawynd's human. "I will see if I have a small-er dish of some kind in the med-i-cal sup-plies for your pet..."

"Oh, I don't mind sharing with them." Mirawynd's human lifts the water bowl up as far as his shoulder. "Here, Mirawynd, how about some water instead?"

Mirawynd happily takes a few sips of the more neutral-tasting drink, then makes a show of nuzzling their human's cheek with a squeak of thanks.

Suitably fed and watered, they slip down from his shoulder into the conveniently placed pocket on the breast of his uniform shirt under the embroidered version of his pilot's wings insignia.

This is as good as any time for a nap, now that they're sure their human can't get lost again. Mirawynd falls asleep to the sound of his heartbeat and the gentle tones of the continuing conversation around them. If their parent had to ask them to protect a human, they're glad that it's this one.

★

It's been almost a full day since Potts and his newly-acquired little Florivan co-pilot arrived on the Prelvee starship *Song-of-the-Midnight-Frog*.

Potts has spent most of that time either asleep or waiting for the weirdly persistent headache he'd had from *whatever* it was that sent his darter three light-years out from where it was supposed to be to go away. He refuses to admit to himself that he'd been unconscious for part of the day. Passing out at the sight of one's new alien allies is not something he'd ever confess—especially not when he someday tells this story to the Majors.

Is it his fault that Prelvee are both huge and startlingly like the insects that plagued his childhood nightmares? Even if it is, he's content to let *Frog's* physician assume the fainting was from his misadventure in the darter.

His new Prelvee friend reminds him far too much of home and another doctor he knows who's probably wondering just what sort of trouble he's gotten into by now. "Doc," as Potts has now settled into calling him, is incredibly intelligent and curious about everything—but also, even in his overly-polite conversational tones, still has the trademark physician's sass that Potts associates with doctors who know their business. He's not nearly as pleasant to look at as Potts' favorite human doctor, but that's hardly the point.

At the moment, Doc is measuring him for a set of limb braces. Theoretically, those will prevent Potts from being injured as easily in the higher-gravity environment outside *Frog's* infirmary.

"Now, if you will bend your el-bow for me so that I can note the range of mo-tion?" Doc extends one of his uppermost clawed legs to nudge Potts' arm into place under the odd organic-looking metal thing attached to one of the walls which he insists is a high-tech tape measure.

"Is this far enough?"

"Yes. And now if you will ex-tend it once more?"

Potts does as he's told. He's doing his best to stay focused, but it's hard to keep a straight face when there's an equally curious Florivan kitten perched on top of Doc's head mimicking his movements. It'd be easier to ignore little Mirawynd's performance if it wasn't accompanied by a running commentary of interested squeaks and chittering trills.

"And now your knee, please? Bend and raise it as high as you can." Doc gestures expressively with his facial tentacles as he talks. It's still a touch unsettling to be looking into his large central eye, but Potts is getting used to it. The physician's cheerful manner makes it easier, for sure.

Potts slowly bends his knee and lifts his whole leg up, resting one hand on the nearest wall to balance himself. On top of Doc's head, little Mirawynd does the same. They lose their balance on the smooth surface of the Prelvee's carapace and nearly fall off, but somehow one of Doc's facial tentacles reaches out at the precise moment to catch them around their waist and gently lift them back up to their perch. Potts is impressed more by the fact that Doc shows no sign of losing concentration than the catch—although that's certainly something in itself.

Mirawynd squeaks softly as if in embarrassment and settles down to sit on Doc's head like a little silver dust bunny.

Potts doesn't know for sure whether the physician suspects that Mirawynd is more than a pet, or what species they really are. Doc seems to find his little ward charming, in any case. Potts also doesn't know why he's reluctant to mention the fact that Mirawynd is really a baby Florivan. It might be because he's always heard that Florivans are incredibly private about their biology and such, or because he'd never known that their offspring started out so small and vulnerable. It might also be because he knows that Doc is friends with the head of Defense Fleet Medical, who's Florivan themself and clearly *didn't* say anything about what Mirawynd is when the two of them were discussing his situation earlier.

In any case, Potts knows that it's his responsibility to keep little Mirawynd safe until he can get back to the Fleet and pass them on to a Florivan like *Surnia's* jumper, Indigo, so they can be reunited with whatever family they might have left. The kitten's a sweet little scamp, for sure, and Potts is already growing to enjoy their constant company.

A soft chime sounds from the main door to the Infirmary. At a statement of buzzes and clicks from Doc, the door slides open. One of the far larger Prelvee females enters, taking a minute or so to fully clear the doorway because her green-toned segmented body is so long. She approaches and waves one of her facial tentacles at Doc with a crisp set of words in their language, and then turns her large green eye towards Potts.

"Hel-lo, hu-man pi-lot!" she says, in a voice that's oddly familiar to him, "It is plea-sing to meet you in per-son." Now in front of Potts and Doc, she towers over both of them without even trying to. The third of her body that's lifted up off the ground in the Prelvee version of 'standing up' is nearly two heads taller than Potts himself.

It takes a moment for Potts to connect the facts. He's still instinctively frightened of the Prelvee's odd combination of bug and cephalopod features, even though he knows that they're friendly. He only *just* manages not to faint this time. After he processes what she's actually said, though, he smiles at the still-somewhat-imposing figure. "Ah! You're the communications officer from yesterday, aren't you?"

"I am. The Cap-tain has giv-en me an ass-ign-ment to ass-ist the phy-sic-ian with help-ing you ad-just to the ship, since I am the on-ly other crew mem-ber who speaks your lan-guage with an-y flu-en-cy."

"Nice to meet you in person too, then, ma'am. I don't remember if I introduced myself when we were talking before, but I'm Julian Potts—Pilot-Sergeant with the 2nd Darter Squadron, SCV *Surnia*." Potts holds out a hand reflexively as he introduces himself, then looks at it and stifles a self-deprecating laugh. "I have no idea what the Prelvee equivalent of a handshake is. Sorry about that."

She laughs—or, at least, Potts *hopes* the rhythmic buzzing sound is something like a laugh. "I am fam-il-iar with the hu-man cus-tom!" She reaches down with one of her upper claws and taps his hand gently. "It is good to meet you, Ser-geant. You may con-tin-ue to call me Comms Con-trol or Comm-un-i-cat-ions Off-i-cer if you wish, but the hu-mans I worked with on up-dat-ing your en-cryp-ted con-nec-tions to the Al-li-ance com-mu-ni-cat-ion net-work when I vis-it-ed your Shell Is-land base sev-er-al years a-go gave me the name Em-er-ald."

"Emerald suits you, ma'am." Potts nods. He can't help wondering just how long ago she might have been out at the Fleet's main base at Teegarden's Star. No one he knew back in his Trainee Corps days ever mentioned Prelvee visitors past the Alliance's initial contact phase with the Fleet, at least. Then again, if it was the Fleet communications department she was working with, would any of the darter pilots even know she was there? A thought flashes through his mind that is too much not to ask. "I don't suppose one of those humans you knew was a fellow about my size... maybe a little taller... blonde hair, grouchy—"

"You know my friend Ru-dy?" She asks before Potts can even finish his description, waving her facial tentacles with a clear excitement.

Potts laughs, unable to hold it in any longer. "Well, he's hardly the only mechanic in the Fleet that would fit that list, but yes, that's the one I meant. Small galaxy we have here... I guess you could call him my best friend, ma'am. We've been bunkmates almost since I joined the Fleet—we share a cabin, I mean."

"I see! I have been out of con-tact with him since I was re-ass-signed to this ship, but it plea-ses me that we have a friend in com-mon!" She clicks her top few sets of claws together in a gesture that comes across as happy clapping. "I trust he fares well?"

"Well enough, I suppose, assuming *Surnia* got away from the Novans all right yesterday."

"We re-ceived con-fir-mat-ion that your ship is in-tact when we con-tac-ted your Fleet about hav-ing found you," says Emerald. "Had the phys-ic-ian ne-gle-cted to in-form you?"

Doc looks up at her with an almost sheepish wave of two of his facial tentacles. He clicks out something in their language that Potts is almost *certain* must be along the lines of "it didn't come up while we were talking before" or something like that.

"To be fair, I wasn't in the right frame of mind to ask him, but I'm glad *Surnia* got away safe." Potts pauses to catch Mirawynd as they leap from the top of Doc's head towards his own and help them to their usual perch on his shoulder. The kitten begins squeaking quietly but curiously towards his ear almost immediately. He can feel their swishing tail brush against his neck. "Going back to our mutual friend... I think Rudy's happier with the Musketeers than he was out at the shipyards. He doesn't grouse about my socks finding their way onto his side of the cabin as much, at least."

"I am pleased he is well. When you are re-turned to your ship, please re-mem-ber to give him my fond gree-tings." Emerald tilts her head a little closer down towards Potts, clearly looking at Mirawynd. "And this is your pet? I was not a-ware your Fleet a-lowed pi-lots to keep an-i-mals."

"Oh, 'Wyndi here's a bit more intelligent than the average animal..." Potts pats his little friend's head in hopes of settling them down a touch, since they're still curiously squeaking at him and swishing their tail. "It's a bit of a special case, ma'am. I promised someone I'd look after Mirawynd right before I got stranded out here, so they're sort of stuck flying with me for now."

"They are a ver-y soft and well-man-nered crea-ture," Doc interjects. "Doc-tor Star Sa-pphire sug-gest-ed that they be kept close to Ju-li-an for his well-be-ing."

"I see." Emerald waves one of her facial tentacles at little Mirawynd and holds out one of her upper claws. "It is nice to meet you too, lit-tle one."

This is enough to encourage the kitten to leap from Potts' shoulder onto the large clawed arm and climb up to the top of Emerald's head. They squeak excitedly the whole time, although it's anyone's guess what they're trying to say.

"I... should probably apologize for that." Potts shakes his head. "They're too friendly for their own good."

Emerald is doing her best to turn her large green eye upwards to look at the kitten who is leaning over from their perch on top of her head. She reaches up one of her facial tentacles to gently ruffle the fur between their ears. "Your lit-tle friend is ver-y sweet."

For their part, Mirawynd seems content to perch on Emerald's head and allow themself to be petted while they look around the room. In the short time Potts has known his Florivan companion, he's learned already that they seem to like having a high vantage point. He's not sure why that is, but at least it keeps Mirawynd from getting underfoot.

Potts stretches his hand up as far as he can reach and holds it out like a platform. "Come back down, 'Wyndi, you can't go climbing on people without permission."

The kitten stares down at him with the saddest look he's seen in their three golden eyes and makes a reluctant squeak. After a moment, they hop down onto Potts' hand and scamper back to his shoulder, although their attention is still fixed on Emerald.

"I do not mind, Ser-geant. I like in-ter-ac-ting with small fur-ry creat-ures." Emerald pauses to wave one of her facial tentacles in a gesture that comes across as vaguely the equivalent of a human resting their chin on their hand. "Al-though we will need to try to teach them some man-ners be-fore you are in-tro-duced to the Cap-tain, I think."

"Probably so," says Potts, making a point of gently stroking Mirawynd's soft silver fur to help encourage them to settle down. They respond with a light bell-like trill and the start of a rumbling purr as they snuggle up against his hand.

"Speak-ing of the Cap-tain, she has con-firmed that we have au-thor-iz-a-tion to iss-ue you an in-tra-aur-al trans-lat-or chip of the kind our peo-ple wear to help you com-mu-ni-cate with oth-er mem-bers of our crew." Emerald turns her eye towards Doc. "I can make ap-pro-pri-ate ad-just-ments too the chip it-self once you lo-cate the cor-rect place-ment for his an-at-o-my and give me the rel-at-ive mea-sure-ments."

"Translator chip?" Potts asks, looking between the two Prelvee. "I didn't know things like that even existed outside of stories."

"We use one of our own de-sign when dea-ling with spe-cies who are not cap-a-ble of lear-ning to speak our lan-guage, such as your peo-ple and our peers in the Grea-ter Gal-ac-tic Com-mons," Doc explains, already skittering across the room towards his viewscreen. "It al-lows for real-time trans-lat-ion of the au-di-ble com-mu-ni-cat-ion of most sap-i-ent spe-cies with-in the wear-er's au-ral pro-cess-ing or-gans. For us, im-plan-tat-ion is sim-ple, as our 'ears' are just here, at the join-ing of the first ma-jor car-a-pace seg-ment to the head." He gestures with two of his facial tentacles to a small round spot on either side of his large central eye, just ahead of where the fleshy parts of his body join onto the smooth buglike ones. "It is stan-dard for all space ser-vice in-di-vid-u-als to re-ceive such a chip."

Emerald makes an odd clicking sound and then shifts her body to follow Doc to the viewscreen. "You will be the first hu-man to be al-lowed to use this piece of our tech-no-lo-gy! It is quite ex-ci-ting to fin-al-ly have a rea-son to de-vel-op a ver-sion for your spe-cies."

Potts takes the opportunity to hop up onto the bed built into the wall so he can sit somewhere comfortable while the Prelvee are staring at Doc's collection of anatomical charts. Mirawynd seems to think that's their cue to climb into the pocket of his shirt for a nap. "I'm honored, then," he says, not sure what else would be appropriate. He's well aware just how cagy all of the Coalition's alien allies are with their advanced technology. That's why darter pilots like him exist in the first place.

"Do not wor-ry, Ju-li-an," says Doc, looking back to him, "I will en-sure that the im-plan-ta-tion pro-cess is as swift and pain-less as pos-si-ble."

"Thanks, Doc... I appreciate that." He hadn't considered how ominous the word 'implantation' was until just this moment.

There's part of him that's suddenly wondering just why and how the universe settled on it being him that wound up in this situation. Two days ago, he was playing cards with the Majors and complaining about the boredom of the night shift. Now, he's hanging out in the infirmary of a Prelvee ship with an orphaned Florivan kitten sleeping in his shirt pocket while his new friends chatter on in their odd language of buzzes and clicks about performing experimental surgery on him so he can understand what they're all saying.

The universe, he decides, has a very strange sense of humor.

★

POTTS WAKES UP IN THE MIDDLE OF THE SHIP'S night, sweaty from both the heat and half-remembered terror. The soft blue bioluminescent glow of the dimmed-down infirmary lights and the traces of what must be a soft green moss on the ceiling above him remind him where he is. It's nowhere like the horror of the dream that came before—no swarms of bees, no endless running from crunching crawling things.

Instead, a soft sound from just below his chin catches his ears. When he turns his head to look, there's a rather concerned-looking Florivan kitten perched on his chest. Little Mirawynd reaches out again to tap his cheek with one of their upper hands. He dimly realizes that this is the sensation that woke him. All three of their bright golden eyes seem to glow in the half-light as they stare worryingly at him.

"Mm? Something wrong, 'Wyndi?" He reaches out with his right hand and strokes their soft silver fur. The lack of pain surprises him, for some reason. He hasn't had that dream so vividly in years. The only thing that remains of its origins in the waking world is the fine scar running along the back of his hand.

Little Mirawynd replies in a long string of squeaks and soft trilling sounds that Potts has no hope of understanding. He gets the impression that they're scared or upset, but he has no idea why. After they've said whatever it was they were trying to say, the kitten lets out a yawn that's nearly as big as themself and nuzzles into Potts' hand. Their soft rumbling purr returns.

"Had a bad dream or something?" Potts is too tired to try to remember what the thing is about Florivans and dreams. He can't quite recall whether they're supposed to have them at all. "Well, you woke me up right when mine was getting pretty bad..."

Mirawynd squeaks at him again, although they're already settling down under his hand like a contented little furry ball. Their upper pair of arms, however, are securely wrapped around Potts' wrist.

"That's right," Potts says, stifling a yawn of his own with his free hand, "go back to sleep. You're safe with me, Wyndi."

As he drifts back off to sleep, the kitten's purring surrounds him. With that gentle sound anchoring him, he's soon dreaming once again. If Little Mirawynd is there on his shoulder in his dreams, still watching over him and letting their loud purr chase away any stray nightmares, he doesn't notice nor remember.

★

He's lost again.

He just stepped away from Uncle Sean's shuttle for a moment to try to figure out where the odd sound he heard was coming from, and now the ruins of the formerly tall buildings of Millefleur Moon Three all look the same and he has no idea where his feet have taken him.

Somewhere in the distance, he can hear his big brother calling for him, but the sounds all echo strangely off the piles of rubble and he can't tell where Eddie's voice really is.

He decides to try to climb the nearest pile of bashed concrete and metal to get his bearings from higher up. This is a terrible mistake.

He reaches the top of the pile, yes, and for a moment he spots the distinct 'green fairy' design painted on the shuttle's side. Just as he's waving to his brother and shouting to let Eddie know where he is, the rubble under his feet gives way. Before he knows it, he's sliding down the other side. He can't get a firm grip on anything around him, because everything he touches is sliding too.

He falls with the debris down the chasm he didn't know was on the other side of the hill.

At the bottom, he's sprawled in the only pool of light to be found. His right arm aches, broken at the elbow from where his whole weight had struck it against the ground. He calls out for Eddie, hoping that he'll be heard.

There's no response from his brother, not even after several minutes of shouting.

From the darkness to one side of him, though, he catches a glimpse of movement. He turns abruptly, and immediately wishes he hadn't from the swirling pain in his head. "Is someone there?"

A strongly accented girl's voice replies, hesitant but somehow snarky. "Ye don't watch where ye be walking, do ye?"

The girl the voice is attached to is his age, or maybe a touch younger. Her hair is deeply red, and her pale skin nearly hidden by a coating of dust and muck that matches the debris around him. The cleaner spots of her overdress and leggings are a bright green that matches the eyes that are staring at him.

"I..." He pauses, then forces a grin despite the pain in his arm. "I believe I'm here to rescue you, miss!"

"Ye don't look like ye're doing well at not needing to be rescued ye'self," says the girl, flatly. She picks up a stick from the debris pile and produces a large, marginally clean handkerchief from one of her pockets. "Here, ye arm's clearly broken. Let me splint it and then ye can get back to the rescuing."

He tries to hide the wince when she touches his arm. "Thanks, miss. Don't worry, Eddie probably saw me fall— he'll be over to drop a rope for us or something any minute now."

"If ye say so, boy."

"It's Julian," he says, through gritted teeth. Every movement of even a fingertip sends lightning up the nerves of his arm.

"Reba," the girl replies, seeming not to notice the contortions of his face. "Welcome to me bedroom. I'd ask ye to wipe ye feet, but the rug's under the dirt here anyway..."

★

Potts wakes properly when the infirmary's light orbs begin to glow at their usual brightness, roused in part by the distinctive clicking footsteps of the Prelvee doctor.

"G'Morning," he says, stifling a yawn halfway through the statement. The vestiges of dimly-remembered dreams are still fogging up his brain. He's not sure when the last time he endured that particular recurring nightmare, nor when he's had such a vivid dream return him the time on Millefleur Moon 3 when he first met his childhood best friend. Potts hasn't even thought about that day in his waking hours in years. He dimly wonders if it must have been the combination of *Equinox* bringing up old memories and his new friend being a physician who reminds him far too much of Reba.

"Pleas-ant mor-ning to you, Ju-li-an!" Doc skitters past the bunk Potts occupies, carrying a domed tray toward the side chamber of the infirmary that serves as his office. "I have brought a dif-fer-ent kind of fruit bun for you to try once you have fin-ished your mor-ning cleans-ing."

Potts yawns again and carefully lifts the still-sleeping silver fur-ball that is Mirawynd off of his chest so he can get up. He sets them back down on the silky cushion he's been using for a pillow and tucks his pilot's jacket over the top of them. This is quickly becoming part of his daily routine, as is leaving the door to the infirmary's washroom slightly ajar while he's freshening up so that Mirawynd doesn't make a fuss about not being able to find him if they wake up before he returns.

The washroom itself has taken some getting used to, for sure. Everything is to Prelvee scale, and set up to accommodate their biology. The sink and tap, at least, were familiar, although it took far longer than Potts would be willing to admit for him to recognize why there were two spigots, one set above his head and one at what seems to him a more normal hand-washing height, over the same low, wide trough of a basin. Hand-washing, or rather, claw-washing, is apparently a high priority in Prelvee culture, and takes a bit longer because of the sheer number of hand-analogue appendages each one of them has to wash. The higher spigot, which for Potts also serves as a suitable shower, is intended for the larger female Prelvee's use.

As he rinses off the layer of night sweat and general human grime in the just-warm-enough water, Potts is once again grateful that Doc was already somewhat familiar with human hygiene practices. How to politely to explain to the nice alien why you'd like permission to splash around in their equivalent of a sink isn't exactly top of the list of things pilots are prepared for in flight school, after all.

The flash-drying system the Prelvee use after washing is another thing that's going to take a while for Potts to get used to. In theory, it's similar to the sort of air dryers he's used all his life, where one inserts their hands and lets jets of hot air blast the water away and a disinfectant light shines to kill off any lingering germs. In practice, the thing is the entire floor in front of the long, low basin of the sink, and shoots out a gust of wind strong enough to nearly lift Mirawynd off the ground. It dries a body off, sure, but it feels like stepping on an angry desert tornado. Potts' first encounter with the flash-dryer was an unexpected shock, to say the least.

As for waste removal? That, at least, is somewhat straightforward. A second low trough at the back of the room with a retractable lid, sized to fit both standard sizes of Prelvee anatomy, handles all possible needs. Once again, the Prelvee male accommodations suffice for a human with a decent sense of balance. Potts has dealt with far worse in his time, between camping trips with his uncles and "survival strategy week" back in the Trainee Corps. He's only grateful that this is the one place Mirawynd has shown absolutely no interest in exploring, considering how *strong* the vacuum is which removes all deposits once the lid slides shut.

A small squeak from the other side of the flash dryer plates near the door catches Potts' attention while he's dressing. He looks over to see a curious kitten peeking through the gap he'd left open.

"Good morning, Wyndi." Potts finishes pulling his trousers on and steps around the flash dryer to pick them up. "Fancy a wash before breakfast?"

Mirawynd purrs softly and nuzzles into his hands, then squeaks and twitches their ears toward the sink.

"I'll take that as a yes." Potts crosses back to the easier-to-reach of the water spigots and taps the control button on the floor in front of it with his foot. Once the stream of water begins, he holds his little co-pilot out towards it with both hands serving as a platform.

For their part, little Mirawynd happily splashes all four of their hands in the water for a while, followed by both of their feet. They giggle and squeak at him the whole time. This seems to be one of their current favorite games.

"Good job," Potts says when they seem to be finished. "I'll see about giving you a full bath another day... but hands are good for now. Ready to dry?"

Mirawynd looks up at him with a somewhat hesitant expression, then wraps their tail tightly around his wrist and flips over onto their belly, holding all four hands and both feet straight down off the side of his fingers. This, Potts has learned, is the only way they're willing to go any where near the flash dryer. He has an impression that they don't like the sound the thing makes.

Potts gently triggers the flash dryer, then holds his hand over it at just the right angle so that the hot air hits only the wet parts of his little companion. It only takes a few seconds to get Mirawynd's furry hands and feet dry enough that they won't go leaving soggy kitten-prints all over the place.

"Good." Potts strokes Mirawynd's head gently as he carries them out of the lavatory and makes sure the door shuts behind him to prevent any kitten explorations that might lead to trouble. "So, Doc said there were fruit buns..."

Within seconds, Wyndi has scampered off ahead of him towards Doc's office. If there's one thing Potts has learned about Florivan kittens in the last few days, it's that they're fuzzy little bottomless pits. He follows the streak of silver fur, laughing heartily.

"Oh, come on, Wyndi! Save some breakfast for me..."

★

IRAWYND IS ADJUSTING TO LIFE ON THE Prelvee ship far faster than their human. That might be simply because they're so much younger. After all, they've only had their eyes open for a week and a half now. As far as Mirawynd's concerned, their current situation might as well be normal for them. Another few days, and they'll have spent more time with their human and Doc than they did exploring the world outside their parent's pouch with their siblings back on *Equinox*.

At the moment, they're playing a game of 'chase the shiny thing' with the exceptionally large Prelvee communications officer who's come to visit while Doc is fitting their human for something called an "embedded aural translation chip" that's had to be specially made for him.

"Here, lit-tle one," Miss Emerald says, tossing the little ball she'd brought with her to the other side of the room, "see if you can catch it this time!"

Mirawynd scampers after the lightweight silver-green sphere as it bounces and does their best to leap up into the air to catch it in their upper arms before it has a chance to go further. This time, they manage it and do a bit of a somersault holding the thing when they land. With a triumphant squeak, they skitter back over to their new friend with their prize. They have to scamper a long way up her segmented carapace to reach her upper segments and return it. Miss Emerald is nearly three times as long as their friend the Doctor.

She takes the ball with one of her upper claws, lightly patting Mirawynd's head with a gentle facial tentacle. "You are good at this game, lit-tle one. Do you want to try ag-ain?"

Mirawynd squeaks happily in the affirmative. This game is fun, and they can't wait until their human is done being very, very still on the platform on the other side of the room so they can teach it to him.

"Now," they hear the Doctor say, "you should not feel an-y dis-com-fort as I in-sert the place-ment probe, but if you do, please in-di-cate this by rai-sing your hand..."

"Got it, Doc." There's a hesitation in their human's voice, but he doesn't sound scared, so Mirawynd assumes that he's okay with what Doc is doing. From their vantage point, it looks rather boring and a lot like staring at their human's ear through a set of tubes for a long time.

The only thing Mirawynd finds interesting about their human's ears is how small and rounded those are, and how bad he seems to be at hearing small sounds. Their game with Miss Emerald is far more worthy of their attention at the moment.

Miss Emerald tosses the ball artfully between her facial tentacles and uppermost clawed appendages for a while. "Now, get rea-dy, lit-tle one, so you can catch it be-fore it hits the ground..."

Mirawynd waggles their long fluffy tail in anticipation and scampers down to the floor to stand ready.

"And... there! Go and re-trieve the ball!"

Wyndi leaps after the shining silver ball, only barely missing it this time. They catch it easily on the second bounce, then happily scamper back to Miss Emerald so they can try again.

Before she can throw the ball for them, the Doctor is making pleased clicking sounds and beckoning the two of them over with his facial tentacles. "There, the pro-ce-dure is com-plete. You sat ver-y well for it, Jul-i-an."

Mirawynd's human slowly begins to sit up just as Mirawynd bounces into his lap to show him the shiny ball they've captured. "I'll admit, Doctor, whatever you did to numb that ear is *powerful*. How long did you say it'd take to wear off? It feels like that little area of my skull behind my ear is missing or something."

"Not pain-ful, I trust?" Doc makes a mildly concerned gesture with one of his facial tentacles.

"No, just... Well. I'm not used to being aware of my ears at all, and now not being able to feel that one is *weird*."

"Good. You will re-cov-er sen-sa-tion in ap-prox-im-ate-ly twen-ty min-utes. By then, the caut-er-y ser-um will have done its job and there will be ver-y lit-tle of a wound for you to feel. Are you rea-dy to test the chip?"

Mirawynd squeaks up at their human curiously.

He pats their head and allows them to stash their shiny ball in his shirt pocket for safekeeping, since the game is clearly over now. "Yeah, might as well, if it's already going to work."

Miss Emerald comes over to join the rest of them now and makes a series of curious clicking and buzzing sounds.

Their human looks up at her, clearly puzzled. "Um... no, I'm not hearing any static on that side." He pauses, eyes going wide. "Wait. I could have *sworn* you asked that in Standard."

"Ex-ce-lent!" Doc clicks several rows of his claws together in his version of happy clapping. He says something in clicks and buzzes, then, and makes a vague gesture with one of his facial tentacles towards the door to his office.

"Yeah," says their human, still sounding surprised, "something to drink would be nice right about now."

Mirawynd taps his hand to catch his attention and then squeaks politely, meaning to ask if their human would also be interested in snacks. Chasing their new favorite toy has left them hungry, after all.

He looks down at them, then back up at Doc. "This chip of yours... Does it just work with Prelvee languages?"

Miss Emerald makes a small, pleased sounding series of clicks and then shifts back into the language Mirawynd's human speaks. "I mo-di-fied a stan-dard iss-ue chip for you. Its pro-gram-ming in-cludes most di-al-ects from the Grea-ter Gal-ac-tic Com-mons worlds, as well as a function for ad-ap-ting to new spo-ken lan-gua-ges the ow-ner en-coun-ters. It was sim-pl-er to leave that all in than to pro-duce a new chip with on-ly our spe-cies' lan-guag-es."

Mirawynd's human nods slowly and then looks down at them, chuckles softly, and ruffles the fluff of silver fur behind their ears with one hand. "Okay, then. Good to know. think we could get a few of those fruit buns to share while we make sure this thing's working correctly too? I get the impression my little copilot here's running on empty..."

Later that day, after Mirawynd's post-snack-time nap, they emerge from the warm snugness of their human's shirt pocket to find that he is no longer *wearing* the shirt. He's left it, and Mirawynd, tucked into a neat little nest made of his pilot's jacket and the pillow on his bunk. Mirawynd's initial sleepy confusion doesn't turn into alarm this time, though. They can hear their human's voice clearly on the other side of the room.

"I can't say it's the most comfortable thing in the galaxy, Doc, but at least it's not pinching anymore."

"I will re-fine the de-sign fur-ther for your com-fort, Ju-li-an. It needs more pad-ding at your joints, for cer-tain."

Mirawynd pops their head up out of the layers of fabric of their nest to see their human standing with his arms and legs spread out while the Prelvee physician adjusts some of the glistening yellow ties holding a shiny set of metallic rods in place. Each rod connects to the next, forming lines that run along each of his limbs and down his spine. Aside from the set of rods, he's only wearing his undershorts. His trousers, Mirawynd realizes, are neatly folded next to their nest.

"Padding would be nice." Mirawynd's human looks down at one of the bands of neatly wrapped yellow cloth with an odd expression on his face. "Is that going to be from this stuff too?"

"Of course, al-though I will re-quest some-thing more re-fined for the pad-ding lay-er. Thank-ful-ly, our Quar-ter-mas-ter is most skilled at spin-ning dif-fer-ent forms with her silk." Doc makes the soft clicking sounds that are his version of laughter. "As you can see, I am not all that skilled with an-y-thing oth-er than ban-dag-es."

Mirawynd's human nods slowly. "Ah. I can see how being able to spin bandages like that is helpful, though..." There's a hesitation in his voice that Mirawynd doesn't understand.

Curious kitten that they are, Mirawynd hops down from their nest on the bunk and scampers over to their human's feet. Tapping lightly on one of these, they look up at him with a squeak of greeting.

"Oh, hey, Wyndi. Have a nice nap?" Their human glances down, but seems to be doing his best to stay still.

Mirawynd squeaks happily and waves their tail for emphasis.

"Please do not try to climb him, lit-tle one," says Doc, gesturing with one of his facial tentacles as he leans down towards Mirawynd. "Some of the silk has not yet set, and I doubt you would en-joy hav-ing it stuck to your fur." He turns his eye to inspect their human's right upper arm, which does not yet have a band of yellow cloth holding the rod at the back of it in place like his left one does. "And I still have one se-cur-ing strap to spin."

Mirawynd tilts their head at their Prelvee friend and looks closely into the square pupil of his massive eye. They have no idea what he's talking about.

"Here," says Doc, extending a pair of his claws toward them. "You like to sit on his head. I will help you up where you can watch with-out be-com-ing en-tan-gled."

Mirawynd clambers up onto his offered appendages. They're confused, but he's right. They *do* like to sit on their human's head where it's warm and they can still see everything going on around them.

"I was hoping I could train them *not* to do that," their human teases as Doc gently sets Mirawynd in place. "But fine. Better than having to figure out how to clean the stuff off of them."

Doc buzzes something in the Prelvee language that makes Mirawynd's human laugh, then leans down towards his arm. Mirawynd adjusts their perching position so they can see what's going on better, although they notice their human's eyes turn pointedly up towards the ceiling.

After a moment or two of careful consideration and a gentle touch with one of his facial tentacles, Doc begins making a different sort of soft, rhythmic humming sound. Slowly, each of his five facial tentacles reaches back to touch a spot somewhere just behind his beak where the fleshy parts of his face connect with the armored first segment of his long body. As his tentacles move forward again, each one holds a shimmering strand of yellow that glints like a long golden hair in the light.

Doc deftly touches these strands' ends to the metal bar at the back of Mirawynd's human's upper arm. With a practiced swiftness, he draws his facial tentacles back and forth to pull the strands of silk and form them together into the same sort of tightly meshed fabric band as the others. From a fine gossamer layer to a thicker cloth, he spins the silk in little more than a few minutes.

When he finishes, Doc stretches back up to his usual posture and offers his claws to Mirawynd again. "Thank you for your pat-ience, lit-tle one. You may sit on my head now while the last of the silk hold-ing your mas-ter's tem-por-ar-y ex-o-skel-et-on in place sets."

Mirawynd contentedly makes the leap. Their Prelvee friend's head isn't as cozy and soft as their human's hair, but they like the vantage point he offers.

Their human looks back down from the ceiling now, either marveling at the band of yellow silk Doc has placed on his arm or trying not to be spacesick. For some reason, Mirawynd can't tell which it is—his expression is still odd. "So, Doc... you really think this contraption is going to help?"

"It is on-ly a tem-por-ar-y vers-ion, but yes. The rods will help to sup-port your limbs and dis-tri-bute the un-acc-ust-omed weight when you en-ter our nor-mal ar-ti-fi-cial grav-i-ty field."

"Okay... and I can wear my clothes over this, right?" Mirawynd's human glances over towards the bunk where all of his outer garments are piled. "It's not exactly polite to meet your Captain in nothing but my skivvies."

"Once the silk has had a few more mo-ments to set, yes, al-though you would prob-a-bly be more com-for-ta-ble if you re-mained as you are." Doc lets out another soft clicking equivalent of a laugh. "Af-ter all, I will re-mind you that my spe-cies is not bo-thered by ques-tions of clo-thing."

"Mine is." Mirawynd's human flushes slightly pink. "Standing around like this in front of you is one thing. You're a *doctor*. But your Captain? I need to be wearing pants for that."

Mirawynd squeaks at him with a curious flick of their tail. They're not sure they understand the problem any more than Doc does. It's nice and warm on the Prelvee ship, after all, and as far as they understand, adults wear clothes to keep from getting cold, since they don't have fur.

Their human rolls his eyes lightly, but his good humor seems to have returned. "Wyndi, trust me, pants are *important*." He looks to Doc now, taking on a more lighthearted tone. "Consider it a sign of respect for a powerful female? It might not matter to her, but if it ever got back to the Musketeers or *my* Captain that I'd made my first impression on yours practically naked, they'd never let me hear the end of it."

"I see." Doc makes a thoughtful gesture with several of his facial tentacles. "I will al-so ask our Quar-ter-mas-ter if she can re-cre-ate your gar-ments as well, then. A more light-weight und-er-lay-er will be bet-ter sui-ted for the fin-al ver-sion of your ex-o-skel-e-ton."

Mirawynd's human hesitates, then nods. "Thanks, Doc... I wouldn't mind having a change of clothes, if I'm going to be here for as long as you say."

"I will see to it." Doc leans over and lightly taps the newest band of yellow silk with one of his upper claws.

"The se-cur-ing straps are set now. You may re-trieve your pants."

Mirawynd's human wastes no time going over to dress himself. "You have no idea what a relief that is."

★

J ULIAN POTTS IS HAVING YET ANOTHER IN A LONG series of very strange days. Between having a bit of alien technology embedded somewhere between his ear and his brain and standing practically naked while his Prelvee friend exuded and wove silk to attach a support structure directly to his body, it's been particularly odd and somewhat disturbing. The realization of where all of the textiles he's seen so far on the ship must have come from is equally unsettling. It's taken all of his willpower today not to show just how grossed out he is by the idea of it.

Then again, the silk thing probably wouldn't have been as shocking if it weren't for the memories from his childhood of his older brother's orb weaver collection escaping from their enclosure. Even if Eddie was dating a textile artisan at the time and had designed one of his term projects around collaborating with her, and she was practically part of the family by then, no amount of apology treats from the two of them had ever quite made up for the shock of waking up to a shimmering golden web suspended directly above his bed with its maker staring down like she was calculating how big of a net it would take to catch him.

Why the universe had to put him on a ship full of incredibly friendly aliens who just happen to also be embodiments of all of Potts' deepest fears, he still doesn't know. It seems like every time he begins to settle in and adjust to the reality of things, the Prelvee show up with something even more distressingly bug-like and catch him off-guard again.

Not that he would *ever* say anything about any of that to Doc or Emerald. The two of them are kind, but trying to explain one's instinctive yet completely irrational dread of certain aspects of their species is entirely too embarrassing. If it weren't for little Mirawynd's presence and perfect timing at diffusing most situations, he'd probably have had more trouble keeping it together. As it is, remembering that Florivans are well-known for their good instincts about folks and seeing how much Wyndi already adores their Prelvee hosts helps keep him grounded.

Potts is certain that he'll get used to the clicking, skittering, insect-like bodies and the concept of a sapient, polite species weaving silk from their bodily excretions eventually. He doesn't have much of a choice, after all. It's supposedly going to be a month or two before he and Mirawynd are back with *Surnia*. Besides, he's sure that he's just as unusual and icky to his alien friends, in some way or another. Humans are pretty gross in their own right.

At the moment, though, all he can do is be grateful that the Prelvee *are* friendly. He'd never have survived if *Frog* hadn't come along when she did.

"Now," says Doc, gently guiding him forward through the infirmary's doorway towards where Emerald is waiting for them in the corridor with Wyndi perched happily atop her head, "the art-i-grav trans-it-ion point is at the thre-shold. You will feel your weight in-crease, but your temp-or-ar-y sup-port frame should help comp-en-sate."

Potts takes a breath just before the fateful step through the transition between the two fields. He doesn't know how arti-grav on his *own* people's ships works, much less the Prelvee's more advanced and customizable version. All he knows is that it *does* work, and that the immediate sensation of pulling an extra half-g as his foot lands on the lightly moss-covered floor of the corridor is more sudden even than he expected.

Before he has time to realize that he's nearly fallen, Doc has shifted position to catch him in several gentle but firmly-held claws. "Slow-ly, Ju-li-an. We do not have far to walk, but I know this is a strain on your bod-y. Take your time."

Potts takes another breath, which is harder than he expected. Having extra weight on one's lungs and diaphragm is more of a struggle when it's not just for one thrilling aerial acrobatic moment. He slowly lets it out and does his best to focus on all of his training from flight school. Darters might be equipped with arti-grav tech to compensate for inertia and excess g-forces from sudden maneuvers in space, but pilots like him still have to learn how to fly within planet atmospheres and their accompanying gravity wells.

He was never trained for the heat, though. Even just in his trousers and undershirt, it feels like he's already soaked with sweat. Potts can even pick out the sensation of a heavy droplet tracing down the support bar along his spine. How anyone can stand an environment like this, he'll never know. Hot, heavy, humid—it's nearly unbearable, and he's only taken his first step into it.

Potts forces a small laugh anyway. He can't let himself show too much weakness; he's a pilot, after all, and he'd never hear the end of it if he left a bad impression on the Prelvee. "This is starting to remind me of being put through g-force sims back in the Trainee Corps... but without the spinning."

From their perch atop Emerald's head, little Mirawynd waves and offers him an encouraging, if lightly concerned squeak.

"I'm fine, Wyndi." Potts manages to get his other leg to cooperate as he takes his next step. He pauses afterwards to catch his breath for a moment before looking back up at them. "Just don't jump on me until I get used to this. Walking's hard enough without a heavier version of you to carry."

Mirawynd squeaks again, in a way that Potts can't help but interpret as an adorable affirmative. They curl up into a comfortable-looking position and wrap their long fluffy tail around themself. Their eyes, he notices, remain fixed on him.

Emerald shifts position to fall into step beside him and Doc, although the pace is so slow she doesn't actually have to move forward yet. "If you be-come ex-hau-sted," she says, "it will not of-fend me to car-ry you." Like Doc, even though Potts is now able to understand Prelvee speech, she seems to prefer talking to him in Coalition Standard. According to Doc, both of them like having a human to practice their language skills with in person.

Potts shakes his head lightly, and somewhat regrets the impulse as he realizes just how heavy his head is at the moment. "I'm fine, but thanks." He pauses to catch his breath after another three laborious steps and finds himself lightly leaning against Doc's side for support. He's fighting through the sensation of grayness and sparks at the edges of his vision already, doing all that he can to keep his head clear. It's not easy when the feeling—and reality—of all of his blood trying its hardest to stay in his legs is sustained rather than just a momentary rush from a flight maneuver. Of course, his darter's *designed* to ease the effects of g-forces. So are the compression layers pilots wear under their uniforms, for that matter.

Not that Potts had thought to put his back on today. It's been too warm even in the infirmary to wear them, especially since he hasn't exactly needed to be flying. Even if the pressure from his compression leggings would help keep his blood from pooling where it shouldn't, in this heat he's not sure it would have done much good. A pilot's under-layer is also supposed to keep them *warm*, and that's the last thing he needs right now.

"I'm trained for sitting through g-shifts when I'm flying," he begins again once he's caught enough air to say it. "I can handle this..."

Doc looks over to him with a somewhat doubtful expression in the pose of his facial tentacles. "Your heart rate is al-rea-dy el-e-vat-ed," he says, glancing down at the tiny monitor screen in one of his upper claws that's connected to a sticker-thin sensor he'd placed on Potts' chest earlier. "As is your core temp-er-at-ure. It would be best to al-low your-self to be car-ried the rest of the way. If you lose cons-ious-ness, we will have to re-turn to the in-firm-ar-y."

Potts hesitates, but even his practiced pilot's bravado can't stand long in the face of such high arti-grav fields and all-encompassing, oppressive heat. "Okay, then. If you don't mind, Emerald?"

"Not at all." She gestures with her facial tentacles towards the first of her body segments which have their clawed appendages on the ground. "You may ride on my back, Ju-li-an. I expect you would pre-fer that to being car-ried in my claws like a lar-va?"

Potts' shoulder muscles are too tired already to allow the shudder that wants to run across them from that image. He does his best to take a seat gently, although he's certain his Prelvee friend wouldn't have offered if she thought his weight would hurt her. Once he's settled onto her back, Emerald continues walking down the corridor. Doc remains close beside her, where he can make sure that Potts is still securely seated and can be caught if he does pass out from the unaccustomed stress to his body.

Too exhausted already to keep up much of a conversation and too stubborn to admit that the handful of steps he's taken have drained most of his energy, Potts resigns himself to listening to the conversation between his two friends as a focus while he forces himself to stay upright and awake.

"I will have to adjust a pressure field generator for [Pilot-Sergeant]," Doc says in soft clicks and buzzes, seemingly talking to himself under his breath. "The blood distribution factor is more serious than I considered, even reading the recommendations of [Physician Star Sapphire]..."

Potts blinks a few times, both to get the gray lightheaded feeling out of his eyes and to try to process just how odd the translation over his friend's words sounds when it comes to a phrase that has to be changed into a near equivalent. Apparently, names and titles are too complex for the translation chip in his ear to render accurately for him. The sensation of words-and-meaning overlaid in his mind alongside the actual buzzing and clicking is still incredibly weird.

Emerald, it seems, is the sort of person who doesn't understand the concept of talking to oneself. "You should have asked earlier, [Physician]! Would one from an exterior activity suit work? I'm sure I can get my claws on one without much fuss. [Captain] did give orders to provide whatever you considered necessary for our guest's health..."

"Yes, that would do." Doc looks up at her with a brief wave of one of his facial tentacles. "Can you make the necessary adjustments yourself, [Communications Officer], or would we need to involve another technician?"

"I am practiced at such things. It will be my delight to modify the pressure field generator for [Pilot-Sergeant]." Emerald's tone, even in the translated overlay, has a certain conspiratorial note that accompanies the pleased clicking-together of her uppermost claw sets. "It would be a perfectly reasonable sharing of our technology with an individual human who is our guest, and whose life and safety we are obligated to preserve."

"I am glad we agree, [Communications Officer]." Doc mimics the tone and claw-clicking briefly.

In the back of his somewhat light-headed mind, Potts has the distinct impression that the two of them are talking for someone else's benefit. More than that, there seems to be a small conspiracy afoot—or rather, a-*claw*—regarding using his presence as an excuse to test out sharing Prelvee tech with humans beyond what's necessarily allowed by their rules. He's never had reason to consider before whether the refusal of humanity's alien allies to share their advanced technology was just as frustrating to the folks on the Prelvee and T'irsh-fel side of things.

He doesn't have much time to consider the thought now, though.

"Here we are, Ju-li-an," says Doc, gently touching a claw to his arm to catch his attention. "For-tu-nate-ly, we were ab-le to ar-range for your quar-ters to be near to the in-fir-ma-ry." Doc then turns back to the door in front of them and touches an access pad beside it with one of his facial tentacles. The door slides open. "We will pro-gram the door to re-spond to you once you have re-covered from the walk here."

As Emerald follows Doc in, still with Wyndi perched on her head and Potts sitting on her thickly armored back, he glances down the corridor in the direction from which they'd come. It had felt like the journey took forever, thanks to the heat and the exhaustion from the few steps he'd managed to take for himself. In reality, the infirmary's door is barely ten meters away. Another shade of embarrassment would be coloring his cheeks, if his blood could manage to get there.

The wave of cooler air and lighter arti-grav fields that hits Potts as Emerald crosses the threshold is almost as overwhelming in its relief as the first step into the corridor had been oppressive. He can breathe easily again, although he's still coated in a layer of sweat and sore from the efforts of his muscles simply to stay upright and conscious.

"Do not att-empt to stand too quickly," Doc cautions as the door slides shut behind the last of Emerald's long segmented body and she comes to a stop beside the large, round cushioned structure in the center of the room. "It will take some time for your bo-dy to re-ad-just."

Potts nods, then slowly eases his way off of his friend's back and over to the oversized pillow of a bunk beside her. "I'll take my time, Doc, don't worry." He's not sure he could stand properly right now without falling over.

Wyndi happily bounces down from their perch on Emerald's head and into his lap, squeaking excitedly the whole time. Potts can't quite tell if these are worried squeaks or "we're somewhere new and I want to explore all of it" ones. Judging by how enthusiastically the Florivan kitten begins inspecting first him and then the rest of the room, it just might be a mix of both. They scamper excitedly between the soft mossy-green pillows and lightweight sheets of the big overstuffed cushion the Prelvee apparently use instead of beds, then over to the open viewport and its view of the stars beyond the outer rings of *Song-of-the-Midnight-Frog's* structure. Wyndi even finds their way into the small attached lavatory, although they immediately scamper back at high speed to hide behind Potts when they accidentally trigger what sounds like a smaller version of the infirmary's flash dryer.

"Settle down, Wyndi," Potts says, lightly patting their head once he can reach the kitten again. "You'll have plenty of time to explore here. I promise."

Wyndi seems to content themself with purring up against his side for a moment, then sets about re-arranging the pillow and sheets to make a nest for themself like they always try to do with his jacket on the infirmary's bunk.

"Your pet seems to ad-just quick-ly to grav-i-ty shifts." Emerald notes, watching them with a curious expression.

Potts shrugs, which hurts far more than he'd expected. "Wyndi's like that... I don't know enough about their species to tell you if it's normal."

"I am glad that they do not al-so re-qui-re as-sis-tance to en-dure our en-vi-ro-ment." Doc comes over now to carefully look Potts over with his large square-pupiled eye. "En-sur-ing that you are not harmed is pro-ving dif-fi-cult en-ough."

"I'm fine, Doc. Just a little sore, that's all."

The expression on the Prelvee physician's face might be alien, but there's something universally recognizable about it as the same sort the other doctors in Potts' life always make when they clearly don't believe him. "For-tu-nate-ly, your quar-ters are ad-jus-ted so that you may rest com-for-ta-bly here. I would pre-fer to ex-am-ine you in the in-fir-ma-ry, but it is clear that your bo-dy needs time to re-co-ver be-fore I take you back there."

Emerald shifts her long segmented body towards the door. "I will go get that press-ure field gen-er-at-or now, while Ju-li-an rests. You will let me know when you are rea-dy to move him ag-ain?"

"Thank you." Doc makes an affirmative clicking sound before turning back to the readout on his little monitor. "Now, it would be best if you lay down and al-low your blood to re-turn to its us-u-al flow pat-tern..."

"Right." Normally, Potts would be a little irritated about having a doctor talking him through the concept of resting. He's sore and exhausted enough at the moment that it doesn't matter.

★

It's been nearly a week since Potts took his first steps into the rest of the Prelvee ship. He's spent most of that in the infirmary, hanging out while Doc and Emerald work on the set of braces and accompanying pressure field generator. In the evenings, though, he's been able to sleep in the relative privacy of his own cabin. The Prelvee-style bed cushion is a bit oversized for him, but it's comfortable. Even with the temperature in his quarters turned down to be more human-friendly, being able to sprawl out makes sleeping far easier than it was when he was bunking in the infirmary.

Wyndi, of course, still insists on being either directly on top of his chest or right beside his head when he's sleeping. Potts isn't entirely sure why they're so clingy, but he's getting used to it. The kitten does like to be in their little nest made of his pilot's jacket and the mossy little pillow Emerald had brought for them, but it seems like they're the only person they think should be allowed to nap alone. Even then, if they have the choice, Wyndi seems to want to take their naps in the pocket of Potts' undershirt, so long as he happens to be wearing it.

He wonders, sometimes, if that's a normal thing for Florivans kittens, or if it's just Wyndi's reaction to the trauma of losing their parent and siblings. Of course, he doesn't know for sure if little Mirawynd even understands that their family is gone forever.

What he does know for absolute certain is that Wyndi trusts *him* to take care of them. He's also starting to believe that his little fuzzy copilot is secretly some kind of black hole with fur, considering how much they eat for such a very small creature. For example, from today's breakfast the two of them are sharing with Emerald and Doc back in his office in the infirmary, one would almost think Wyndi can devour more than Potts himself in a sitting.

"Does your pet want an-oth-er fruit bis-cuit?" Emerald asks, holding one out deftly with her long silver eating hooks. The wafer of pink and green pastry is thin, but nearly as wide as Wyndi's entire head.

"I don't know where they'd have room to put it," Potts laughs, looking down at the happily swishing tail and eager crumb-dotted face of the kitten on his shoulder. "But we'll see. Thank you, ma'am." He does his best to carefully use the pair of human-scaled eating hooks Doc had acquired for him to accept the biscuit from Emerald. She's been joining Potts and Doc for meals over the last few days *specifically* to help him practice his table manners for tonight's dinner with the ship's Captain. Accepting offered morsels without dropping them is an important skill, apparently, and one that hasn't come naturally to him.

This time, luckily, he manages to keep his grip on the treat. He holds it over towards his shoulder, where Wyndi is waiting. They eagerly pluck the biscuit from his eating hooks, then break it in half and offer one of the halves back to him. This, Potts has learned, is what *Wyndi* considers polite.

"Thanks, Wyndi." He takes the half biscuit and pops it into his mouth. The lightly floral fruit flavor reminds him of apples and lavender, and the crunch is a nice change from all of the softer buns and broths Doc has shared with him so far.

"Now, lit-tle one," says Emerald in the tone Potts is beginning to recognize as her teasing conspiratorial one, "can you say 'thank you' too?" She repeats the phrase in Prelvee, a certain buzzing trill followed by a click.

Wyndi responds with a squeaky trill of their own and a happy swish of their tail, then goes back to nibbling down their half of the biscuit.

"I'm not sure they'll ever be able to learn to mimic you," Potts comments. "Wyndi's *smart*, I mean, but they're awfully young..." Of course, he has no idea how long it usually takes Florivan kittens to learn how to speak Standard, much less whether they're physically capable of making sounds like the Prelvee do.

"It is fun to at-tempt to teach them." Emerald returns to her inspection of the various colors of biscuits still on the serving plate in the center of the table.

"I ag-ree," says Doc, setting his own set of eating hooks carefully on the edge of his plate so that the hooked ends point towards his left. Everything about how one handles their utensils matters, even small gestures like that. The left-pointing hooks, Potts has learned, indicate that he's done eating. "It would be use-ful, at least, to train your pet to come and al-ert me if you ex-per-i-ence an-oth-er fain-ting spell, since they can tra-verse the ship's cor-ri-dors with-out in-ju-ry."

Potts holds back an embarrassed grimace. "I... don't think that'll happen again any time soon. I mean, I haven't really *fainted* since I first got here."

"Per-haps." Doc makes a small gesture with one of his facial tentacles. "But it is still a great strain on your fra-gile bo-dy ev-en to go from here to your quar-ters. Even with the ad-just-ments to your bra-cing ex-o-skel-e-ton and the mod-i-fied pres-sure field, I am still con-cerned for your well-be-ing as you be-gin to spend more time else-where on the ship."

Emerald makes an affirmative click. "I will at-tempt to teach your pet to say 'help' too, then. The sound is sim-ple en-ough."

Potts shakes his head and sets his own pair of eating hooks down on his plate, double-checking as he does that they face left. "If you want to try, I guess it's okay. Wyndi likes all of the attention, that's for sure."

"The Cap-tain will sure-ly be charmed by them too," says Doc. "Or at least by their good ta-ble man-ners."

"I'll admit," says Potts, gazing thoughtfully into his water bowl, "I'm not sure how much she'll be charmed by *mine*."

"She will ap-pre-ci-ate the ef-fort you are mak-ing to be po-lite," Doc replies. "It is more than is ex-pec-ted from a hu-man vis-it-or."

Potts pauses to take a sip, doing his best to remember to balance the bowl in the correct way with both hands. It's much easier with a bowl that's scaled for a human, that's for sure. "I'd like to make a good impression on her, either way. It's not exactly *usual* for one of us to spend so much time on a Prelvee ship—especially not some lowly pilot instead of an officer who's trained for diplomacy."

Emerald makes her clicking laughter sounds as she, too, sets her eating hooks aside. "You are a far more po-lite hu-man than some of the dig-ni-tar-ies our Cap-tain has met! She will rec-og-nize your re-spect-ful nat-ure, I am sure."

"Thanks, Emerald. I appreciate that." Potts absently reaches up to rub at the somewhat haphazardly combed locks at the back of his head.

"Now," says Doc, standing and clearing the plates from the table, "shall we get your ex-o-skel-e-ton ad-jus-ted so we can test the pres-sure field tun-ing? I would like to try tak-ing you fur-ther down the cor-ri-dor be-fore it is time to in-tro-duce you to the Cap-tain."

"Sounds good to me." Potts stands and plucks Wyndi off his shoulder, holding them gently out to Emerald. "Here, why don't you two practice... words... while Doc helps me change?"

Wyndi happily hops the short distance to Emerald's waiting claws and gives her one of their nuzzle-hugs before climbing up to their usual perch on her head.

Emerald laughs again, clicking her claws together for emphasis. "You are still shy a-bout me see-ing you un-dressed?"

"It's a human thing, Emerald..." Potts follows Doc into the outer room of the infirmary, glad that his friend never presses the point beyond an initial tease. He has the distinct impression that Emerald knows far more about human things than she lets on, though.

"Well, then, Lit-tle one," he hears her say as the door closes, "let us play a game of words..."

★

That evening, Potts is standing in front of a large door several decks above the level which houses the infirmary and his quarters. Standing, in itself, is a definite improvement. He has no idea how the pressure field generator housed in the thin metallic band around his neck works, nor how it connects to the matching set of bands at his wrists and ankles, but it *does* work. He was even able to walk most of the way through the ship to get to the Captain's common room without passing out. Granted, he had to stop a few times to rest, and once he'd gotten as far as the crew lift he didn't have much farther to walk to the appropriate door on this level, but it's the most physical activity he's been able to manage outside the infirmary or his cabin since he arrived.

Beside him is Doc, who'd made a point of escorting him all the way. On the other side is a female Prelvee from the security team who's serving as his official escort, or possibly Doc's. He's not very clear on the details, even though his intra-aural translator seems to be working fine when the security officer talks.

Wyndi, true to form, is curled up in the breast pocket of his shirt for a nap. They'd tired themself out by scampering back and forth ahead of him to explore all the nooks and crannies of the corridors on the way here.

In answer to the light chime from the security officer's tap of the panel next to the door, it slowly slides open. Within, there's a large, open room with higher ceilings than the infirmary or his own cabin. On one side, the wall curves to match the exterior contour of the ship, and is marked by a set of tall, evenly-spaced curved viewports.

As Potts enters with his two escorts, he experiences the mildly dizzying sensation of returning to a more Earth-like level of artificial gravity. It's a relief, even if he's been better able to withstand the ship's environment today. He takes in the rest of the details of the room as soon as he's caught his breath: there's another large door leading to what he assumes is the Captain's private cabin, and a collection of large seating cushions along the wall beneath the viewports. In the center of the room, a table has been set with a wide variety of bright-colored dishes. Behind this table, with the majority of her extensive segmented body coiled elegantly onto a gold-shaded seating cushion, the Captain is waiting.

She's even longer than Emerald or the security officer, with a striking purple-green shimmer to her carapace. Potts wonders if the lady Prelvee simply never stop growing as they get older, or if there's some other detail he's missing here about how their species works. He's not about to ask at the moment, but it's worth remembering to talk to Doc about later.

"Welcome, guest of my ship," says the Captain, making a sweeping gesture with her facial tentacles towards the smaller cushions arranged around the table, "and to you as well, [Physician]. I am pleased your patient is well enough at last to dine with me." Even with the translated words overlaid over her buzzes and clicks, Potts has the impression she's speaking with a different accent from Doc and Emerald.

Doc makes a little bow as he approaches, then takes his place on the cushion to the Captain's right. "I am pleased about that as well, [Captain]. May I introduce your guest?" He shifts effortlessly from speaking in his own language to Standard at her acknowledging gesture. "This is Ju-li-an Potts, Pil-lot-Ser-geant of the Sol Co-al-it-ion De-fense Fleet's Sec-ond Dar-ter Squad-ron and the ves-sel S-C-V *Sur-ni-a*, un-der the com-mand of Cap-tain I-rene Brent-wood." With another small gesture, he turns to Potts and continues, "Ju-li-an, this is your hos-tess and the Cap-tain of the Al-li-ance ves-sel *Song-of-the-Mid-night-Frog*. Many of her names and ti-tles are un-trans-lat-a-ble with-out giv-ing you an ex-ten-sive ed-u-cat-ion in our so-cial stru-cture and hist-or-y, but in our lan-guage, she is known as:" Doc pauses and switches back into a rapid mix of buzzes and clicks. The translation chip in Potts' ear truncates all of this once again, relating the words as "[Captain]."

Potts makes a mental note to ask Emerald if it's supposed to be doing that.

Setting aside matters of title and translation, he salutes as crisply as he can manage with the support bar attached to his arm. "It's an honor, Ma'am. Thank you for the rescue."

"I am pleased my ship was in a position to help, [Pilot-Sergeant]." The Captain makes a gesture towards the other seating cushion. "Do have a seat. I have directed [Cook] to prepare only dishes which are safe for you to eat."

"Thank you again, Ma'am." Potts takes his place at the table, adding, "and thanks for turning down the arti-grav settings in here, too."

"It would be terribly impolite of me to not ensure my guest's comfort." The Captain deftly picks up her long pair of black-enameled eating hooks. With a practiced grace to the motion, she makes the sweeping circle gesture with her utensils that signifies the meal has begun. She deftly plucks a fruit bun from the serving plate nearest to him. "Please, partake of the offered sustenance before you."

Potts is immediately grateful that he'd spent so much time practicing with Doc and Emerald. He picks up the set of human-scaled eating hooks from beside his plate and does his best imitation of the gesture of gratitude that Doc makes look so easy. As he reaches with his eating hooks to retrieve one of the fruit buns he recognizes from the same serving plate, it only takes him two attempts to catch the morsel.

Possibly from the smell of the food, he feels Wyndi stirring in his pocket. After a moment, the sleepy kitten has emerged and, with an adorable little yawn, takes their place on Potts' shoulder.

Potts sets the fruit bun he was holding carefully down onto his plate, then transfers his right-hand eating hook to his left hand. He reaches up with his now-free hand to pat Wyndi on the head. "I was wondering if you'd wake up sometime soon." He pauses to look up at the Captain. "Ah. This is Mirawynd... they fly with me. I hope you don't mind them joining us?"

The Captain makes a genial gesture with two of her facial tentacles. "Your pet is welcome, [Pilot-Sergeant]. My officers have told me much about them." She deftly picks up a large slice of what looks to be some kind of toasted vegetable pastry roll and holds it out on her eating hooks towards Potts. "Here, I am sure your pet must be hungry. [Communications Officer] tells me that they have excellent table manners."

"Thank you, Ma'am." Potts does his best to show his *own* practiced table manners as he grasps the offered pastry slice with his own eating hooks and accepts it from her. He holds it towards his shoulder where Wyndi is now squeaking curiously. "Yes, Wyndi, this is for you. Now remember to be good, okay?"

True to form, now that they've awakened from their afternoon nap, the kitten is hungry. They excitedly take the treat from Potts' eating hooks, then look over to the Captain and squeak pointedly. They wave their long fluffy silver tail for emphasis.

"That's as close as Wyndi can get to saying 'thanks' themself, Captain." Potts says.

Wyndi squeaks again and goes through their usual routine of breaking the slice of pastry roll in half. Unexpectedly, this sends a shower of crumbs up into the air and all down Potts' shoulder. The kitten doesn't seem to notice, and happily holds half of their snack up for him.

Potts sighs, trying to force himself not to flush with embarrassment, and accepts the morsel from his little copilot. "Thanks, Wyndi... but let's not do that with the crispy ones for the rest of tonight, okay?"

Wyndi's happily waving tail has dusted the majority of the crumbs off of his shoulder by the time Potts even finishes speaking. They're far more interested in nibbling at their snack than paying attention to what he's saying, clearly.

Potts looks up to his hostess sheepishly. "I'm so sorry about that... Wyndi usually doesn't make that much of a mess."

"Think nothing of it, [Pilot-Sergeant]." The Captain makes a small series of what he's begun to recognize as Prelvee laughing sounds. "I think it's charming that your pet insists on sharing their food with you." She pauses thoughtfully, then turns her eye toward Doc. "[Physician], remind me to have a table napkin spread out with a small plate and beverage bowl beside our guest's place the next time he dines with me. That should take care of the crumbs."

"Of course, Cap-tain," says Doc, keeping to his habit of using Standard around Potts. "Would you like a pair of u-ten-siles pre-pared for the lit-tle one as well? I am sure that they are clev-er en-ough to learn to use them."

"That would be highly amusing, [Physician]. Please do." The Captain pauses to eat one of the brighter-colored morsels from the assortment on the serving plate nearest her. "I expect from your reports that the creature can be taught to sit beside their master on a serving cloth to eat and not contaminate the table with their fur."

"I have ob-served that they are an un-us-u-al-ly ti-dy crea-ture, Cap-tain. Ju-li-an has ev-en trained them to wash their ap-pen-dag-es af-ter ea-ting."

Potts occupies himself with eating the other half of the pastry roll slice so he has an excuse to not say anything about just how clever Wyndi really is, or why. It's crisp, as he expected, and the soft orange vegetable filling is mildly spiced in a way that reminds him of the carrot and lentil stew from his childhood. Uncle Steve *always* made that whenever it was his turn in the family meal prep rotation— Potts is still convinced it's the only recipe his eldest uncle ever mastered.

Wyndi, for their part, seems content to sit on his shoulder and nibble down the half-slice of pastry roll. If they're aware that they're being discussed, they don't show it.

"Tell me, [Pilot-Sergeant], for I know some of the details from my officers, but I have been waiting to hear from you: how did you find yourself so far away from your ship?" The Captain looks at him curiously over her drinking bowl as she raises it to her beak.

Potts shrugs lightly, so as not to dislodge his copilot from the gesture. "To be honest, Ma'am? I don't really know..."

He tells what he remembers of the story over the rest of the meal, being sure to leave out the parts about Wyndi's parent. Potts still doesn't know why, but something about the fact that they disappeared altogether out of his darter makes him feel like he needs to discuss their part in his and Wyndi's little adventure with a *Florivan* before he goes telling anyone else. He doesn't like having to halfway lie to his Prelvee hosts, but he feels like he has to. He trusts Doc, and the Captain seems friendly enough, but deep down, he knows that telling them about something that's supposed to be secret could endanger Wyndi—or the rest of their people—it's not worth taking the risk.

"The last thing I remember before I blacked out, I was about to crash into the wreckage," he finishes, after a pause to take a sip of the slightly slimy green beverage in his drinking bowl. Potts carefully sets the bowl down and looks up to Doc and the Captain's curious faces. "Then I woke up where you found me. All I can think of is that I must have impacted directly with *Equinox's* Drive Bay, and there was enough charge left in her to throw my darter."

"I see." The Captain clicks a few sets of her unoccupied upper appendages together for a few moments, similarly to a human drumming their fingers on a table. "I am not familiar with your people's Quantum Space Drive technology, [Pilot-Sergeant], but until I am presented with an alternative explanation, I will accept that it is a possibility."

Potts finds himself lightly relieved. "It's the best one I have, Ma'am. To be fair, I don't know anything for sure about QSD tech myself—that's *far* outside what they teach us darter pilots—but it's the only thing we have that does anything remotely similar. Unless you think it's something the Novans pulled on me?"

"I have not heard of such, but the Novans are..." The Captain looks over to Doc for a moment as if choosing her words carefully for his benefit. "Politely, one could say our enemies are tricky. I will take it under consideration that they could be using something unknown to advance their striker forces."

"Tricky is the word for how they fly, that's for sure." Potts finishes his last fruit bun, then looks over to his shoulder. Wyndi is sitting contentedly, and gives his cheek a nuzzle when they notice his attention. They don't make their usual squeak to ask for more food, so he takes it to mean they're full too. He carefully sets his eating hooks aside on his plate to indicate that he's done eating.

Doc has already set his utensils aside as well. He glances down at a small device in one of his upper claws, and then looks to the Captain. It's pretty clear from his tone that he, for one, is not interested in discussing the Novans right now. "Thank you kindly for the excellent meal, [Captain]," he says in Prelvee, dipping his head. "May I request your indulgence that I take my leave now? I have received notice that there is a minor medical issue waiting for me in the infirmary."

"Of course, [Physician]. Extend my well wishes to the affected crew member." The Captain gestures vaguely towards Potts. "I will see to it that [Pilot-Sergeant] returns to his cabin safely."

With that, it's just Potts, Wyndi, and *Frog's* Captain. She sets her own eating hooks aside and stands, stretching out her long segmented body for a moment before retiring to one of the large seating cushions under the viewports. "Join me, [Pilot-Sergeant]? I would be interested to further discuss your experiences flying in combat against our mutual enemies."

Potts stands to move to one of the cushions on that side of the room. Wyndi immediately bounces down from his shoulder and scampers across to the cushion where the Captain is sitting. "Ah! Wyndi, don't go climbing the Captain without permission," he calls, feeling a slight flush warming his cheeks. "I'm so sorry, Ma'am—we've been able to train them to be good at the table, but they're too curious for their own good sometimes…"

The Captain extends one of her clawed appendages to Wyndi, who happily allows themself to be picked up and petted. "I had been warned that your pet was friendly. It is not often we have small furry creatures on our ships to keep us company. I can see why [Communications Officer] expressed such a fondness for this one. They are quite soft and cute."

Potts plops down on the cushion opposite his hostess with a small sigh of relief. "I'm glad you think so, Ma'am. Just… Emerald warned you that Wyndi likes climbing people, didn't she?"

"I have been suitably warned." The Captain's buzzes and clicks are overlaid with a translated tone that comes across as incredibly amused. "Now, is there an entertainment you prefer alongside after-dinner conversation? I understand from my officers that some sort of game is customary among your people, and I had been looking forward to the experience."

Potts is caught off-guard by the question. After a moment, he smiles. "Well, I left my deck of cards back on *Surnia*… but I guess if you have something I could draw up a board with and some small things we could use as pieces, I could teach you to play checkers? It's pretty easy, and it's not the sort of game that distracts you too much from the conversation. A lot of humans like chess, but I've never been able to get the hang of that one."

"If you can describe the 'board' and 'pieces', I'm sure arrangements can be made."

Potts grins. He hadn't expected this, but at least it's something that's well within a darter pilot's realm of expertise. His squadron might be card-players, but checkers was the first game Eddie ever taught him to play. Perhaps getting to know the Captain of the ship that's rescued him and Wyndi is going to turn out to be fun after all.

★

Part 3:
The Siren's Song

IT'S NOT EVERY DAY THAT A JUNIOR-RANKED HUMAN darter pilot finds himself sitting in on a conversation between two influential alien starship captains. It's not particularly common for a human to be a guest on a Prelvee battle cruiser in the first place. Likewise, it's also not every Prelvee starship captain who has the opportunity to appreciate having a squishy mammal around to observe proceedings for her from a completely alien vantage point.

Potts isn't sure his friends back on *Surnia* will believe him when he someday tells them about this part of his adventure. He's been a guest on the Prelvee ship *Song-of-the-Midnight-Frog* for almost a month now. He feels like it's been a lot longer, somehow.

At present, Potts is sitting on a thick moss-colored silk cushion the size of a large bed beside *Frog's* Captain.

He's not entirely sure why he's there. The two of them had been enjoying their regularly scheduled game of post-dinner checkers when the call came in that her presence was needed, and for whatever reason, the Captain had insisted he accompany her up to the ship's command bridge. All Potts has been able to pick up in passing from the conversations around him the last few days is that *Frog* had intercepted a stolen shuttlecraft of some sort recently.

The Captain herself is now in the middle of a rather drawn-out conversation with her counterpart from the T'irsh-fel ship *R'zyll*, which has come to pick up that shuttlecraft.

"As I said, [Captain Zyzyk], I do apologize—but this matter is not something protocol will allow me to compromise regarding." The Captain makes a genial gesture with two of her facial tentacles. "I will, of course, pass your complaints on to my superiors."

Even with the translation microchip the Prelvee ship's physician has implanted under Potts' right ear converting the Captain's combination of buzzing chirps and clicks into words in a language his brain can process, the conversation still makes very little sense to him. Potts is a skilled pilot, sure, and his childhood classification assessments were high enough to reflect minor aptitudes for both linguistics and astral navigation. Even so, the sheer *scale* of the war that the Alliance's two ancient galactic powers are waging to contain the spread of the Novan Imperium is too much for a young human like him to wrap his mind around. With *that* as the main subject of conversation and an apparently long history of affectionate rivalry between the two captains themselves, it's no wonder he's having trouble following along.

Of course, Potts would probably understand better if he could hear a word of what Captain Zyzyk is saying. He'd always heard that the T'irsh-fel are a line-of-sight telepathic species: they can hear and understand spoken language, but only the people *they* want to hear their thought projections can receive them. No one's ever bothered to explain to Potts how that works, but he knows first-hand now that it *does*, even over the sort of real-time video com-link the two captains are using. As a result, Potts has been utterly perplexed by the whole exchange, since all he's hearing arc *Frog's* Captain's remarks—and she's not one for repeating the things said to her when she answers.

As it is, though, the T'irsh-fel Captain somehow seems like he's fuming. All of his eyes are narrowed to an affronted glare, at least. Whatever his problem is, Potts has the impression that he's not taking kindly to the decision that Frog's Captain is talking about. There's something in the way Captain Zyzyk's ruff of hairy red feathers is positioned that exudes *irritation*. Potts doesn't know if that's his own interpretation, though, or if it's some kind of body language translation the chip in his head is providing. He probably needs to ask Emerald about that.

Potts wonders—since all he can *do* at the moment is quietly wonder about things—if there's some sort of insurmountable cultural and biological communication barrier at work here as well. To his very human eyes, at least, both species seem incredibly different and strange.

The T'irsh-fel gentleman on the viewscreen, after all, looks a bit like a three-foot-long hybrid of a feathered serpent and a banana slug: all thick bony scales and hairy feathers, no limbs to speak of, and four pairs of long eye-stalks waving at the top of his head. He's sitting in a high-backed hemispherical chair against a backdrop of frost-covered metal and moving lights. To signify his importance, Captain Zyzyk is wearing a long golden cloak fastened under the ruff of red feathers which marks the difference between his "head" and the rest of his body. From what Potts has heard, the species is also telekinetic over short distances, although he's not seen it himself. That *would* explain how someone with no hands could fasten the intricate-looking clasp on the Captain's cloak, at least.

The Prelvee Captain sitting beside Potts, on the other hand—or rather, *claws*—is a long coiling creature reminiscent of what would happen if some utterly mad biologist were to successfully breed a nautilus together with a millipede. She utterly towers over Potts even when she's mostly coiled up as she is now. In fact, she remains the largest Prelvee he's encountered among *Frog's* crew.

While the appearance of the much smaller T'irsh-fel Captain is strange, it's somehow still less intimidating to Potts than his Prelvee hosts. For whatever reason, be it sheer scale and alien-ness or insect-adjacent anatomy, Potts' first view of a Prelvee leaning over his darter's transparent poly-glass canopy had been downright terrifying. He'd fainted at the sight and had to be extracted unconscious from his cockpit—only to faint a second time when he woke to the face of the Prelvee physician examining him.

That, however, is something Potts plans to never admit having happened. Luckily for him, the Prelvee have been kind enough to assume it had all been a reaction to the sudden changes in shipboard gravity and atmosphere instead.

Potts has learned to live with the frightening aspects of Prelvee anatomy now, for the most part. It's not like he can really *go* anywhere else, after all, and the Prelvee have been nothing but kind to him. More than that, he knows he'll be traveling on their ships for a long while before he can get back to human-inhabited space and his proper place with the Defense Fleet. Even though the Prelvee use an advanced post-light engine of their own design, it would still be a matter of a few weeks of travel if the ship he was currently on had plans to rendezvous with *Surnia*.

Frog has more important things to be doing than to take a major detour like that just to return one pilot, though. Potts' current plan is to hitchhike his way home aboard any allied ship going the right direction. *Frog's* Captain has assured him that her current destination will not be too far out of his way, at least, and that he should be able to find another ship bound for the human systems there. With luck, he'll be back with his unit in a few months or so.

Potts' contemplation of his situation is interrupted by the voice of *Frog's* Captain replying to yet another long, silent rant from her T'irsh-fel colleague.

"Now, [Captain Zyzyk]," she says, gesturing politely with the uppermost portion of her clawed appendages on one side, "I assure you, my crew is more than capable of handling this situation. We were already on a course to return to our nearest base to exchange crew members, and now that we have returned your stolen shuttle, we will resume this. I know you are aware that Alliance policy regarding these matters leaves me no other choice. There is a reason, after all, that your shuttle was able to be stolen in the first place."

The T'irsh-fel captain huffs, shaking and fluffing out his neck-ruff of feathers. After a few minutes of silence, one of his eye stalks turns to look directly at Potts. *"The young human will be wise to practice caution. The young human's honored hostess is not being entirely open with her guest, even if she does regard him fondly. This humble self is certain it will be ill-fated for all of us if the siren takes the young human's eyes."*

Potts blinks for a moment, then realizes that the voice he's hearing is real. The inaudible sound of it reminds him entirely too much of the man who'd been in charge of Darter Cadets when he was in the Trainee Corps back at Teegarden: firm, self-assured, and with a distinctive air of condescending superiority. Flight Instructor Fagervoll, though, had something resembling a sense of humor—a quality Potts suspects this Captain Zyzyk lacks entirely.

"I thank you for the warning, then, Captain Zyzyk." Not completely sure of what's expected of him, Potts gives the T'irsh-fel captain a salute.

"Hm. The young human is capable of politeness. If the young human survives to rejoin his kindred, he will present this humble self's greetings of approval to his honored Lady the Admiral Marvin as evidence that her officers should not be incapable of improvement."

"I'll... be sure to do that, sir." Potts nods as if he understands what any of that means—which he doesn't. Still, he has the impression that polite agreement is expected.

Captain Zyzyk's eye stalk turns away from him again.

Potts looks up to *Frog's* Captain as subtly as he can manage. She gives him the Prelvee equivalent of a shrug. Potts is reasonably sure she didn't hear what Captain Zyzyk said to him. If she did, she's certainly not acting like it was anything that offends her. After a moment, she reaches over with one of her many nearby appendages to pat him reassuringly on the head, taking care not to accidentally harm him as she does so. Potts allows it, but he has no idea how to feel about the gesture. Head-pats are more of Wyndi's thing. Then again, to the Prelvee, he must appear as just another somewhat furry creature who could do with their "fur" being petted to calm them down.

After another ten minutes or so, the two captains have finished their conversation. Captain Zyzyk gives a little bow with all of his eye-stalks just before the image on the viewscreen dissolves back into a display of the scene outside *Frog's* forward end: void, stars, and the greater galaxy glowing in the distance.

"What's this whole 'beware of sirens' thing?" Potts asks, curiosity finally getting the better of him.

"Is *that* what [Captain Zyzyk] said to you?"

"Pretty much. Well, that and I *think* something about needing to say hi to the Admiral for him and tell her that he thinks her officers are rude?"

"I heard the second statement; that is in character for him. As for his warning, my old friend has a concern that a Novan could do harm to you." The Captain says this as if she thinks it explains everything.

It doesn't.

"Ma'am," says Potts, raising an eyebrow, "the *last* time I ran into a Novan, they shot the wing off my darter. If 'harm' wasn't the intent of that, they have an awfully odd way of saying hello."

Although he's now far more personally familiar with the aliens of the Alliance than the average human, Potts has very little knowledge of the species who *started* the war. All he knows about the Novans is that they have it out for humanity—and any other species who happens to stand in the way of their conquering more planets, for that matter, sapient or not. His personal experience with them is limited to flying against Novan strikers and trying not to get killed.

The Captain seems to notice the look of uncertainty on his face. She gently pats him on the head again. "Do not worry, [Pilot-Sergeant]; I have promised you safe passage. You will *remain* safe on my honor as long as you are a guest aboard my ship."

"Never doubted that, Captain." Potts reaches up to smooth out his hair from where she's ruffled it. It's started to get a bit scruffy as it is without her assistance. So has the patchy stubble on his chin, but he's yet to remember to ask Doc for help finding some safe equivalent of a razor to deal with that.

The Captain makes an appreciative clicking trill sound and stretches her upper segments as she moves into a more comfortable coiled position to face Potts rather than the viewscreen. "Now that my talk with my colleague is completed, I have been meaning to ask you: how are you faring with your exoskeleton? [Physician] mentioned he was planning to revise the design for comfort."

"Oh, it's all working fine—still a bit heavy and hot, though." Potts stretches an arm to demonstrate the movement of the metal support braces he's strapped into. The pressure field surrounding his arm shimmers in reaction to the motion. The latest version of an 'exoskeleton' he's wearing is the only reason he's able to freely move about the ship. Without it, his body couldn't withstand the higher level of artificial gravity the Prelvee keep on their vessels for long. "I'm supposed to see Doc today so he can try his new rig on me."

"Ah! Very good. You must show me when he finishes."

"I'll be sure to do that, Ma'am. He's said it should be cooler, too."

The Prelvee have, in Potts' opinion, a very peculiar idea of a comfortable climate even if gravity isn't taken into account. Their ship's hot, humid air and higher oxygen atmosphere alone are just within the survivable limits for a human—survivable, but not necessarily comfortable. His guest quarters, thankfully, have been set up with a more Earth-like environment so his body can rest and reduce the risk of permanent damage. Usually, when he's socializing with Doc and Emerald or the Captain, they're in a space where the environmental settings can be adjusted to be more human-friendly. The ship's command bridge is *not* one of those places.

Potts is sure that he's going to sweat himself into a puddle one of these days if he keeps on with *Frog* or other Prelvee ships for too long. Aside from the sheer barrier fabric underneath the braces and the pressure field shimmering over his body, he's taken to going around in nothing more than his green undershirt with the sleeves rolled up and a pair of long shorts that *Frog's* Quartermaster had made for him along with the barrier fabric for his braces. She'd been kind enough to dye them to match his undershirt, although Potts hasn't dared to ask for any details about that. It still disturbs Potts a bit if he thinks about *where* the fabric must have come from, but he's grateful to have something less hot than his uniform trousers to wear outside his cabin.

Since the Prelvee themselves don't have a need for clothing and have assured him they won't be offended by the sight of human skin, he's thought about doing away with the shirt altogether. So far, though, he hasn't, if only because Potts is the sort of man who, unlike a certain mechanic he knows, *prefers* having a shirt on. That, and the fact that his traveling companion likes to sleep in the breast pocket.

Said small companion is just now waking up from the long nap they've been taking while Potts was half-listening to the conversation between Frog's Captain and her T'irsh-fel counterpart. One by one, four small silver-furred, four-fingered hands reach up out of Potts' pocket, followed by a fuzzy little head crowned by a pair of tufted catlike ears. The face itself is not that far from human-ish, really, but with a third small golden eye in the center of their forehead. With a small yawn, the kitten climbs out of the pocket and up to their usual place on Potts' shoulder. The little creature's four arms and two long slender legs are all coated in soft silver fur, as is their long, fluffy prehensile tail. Potts still doesn't understand how Wyndi copes with the heat, having all of that fluff.

"Oh, hello, Wyndi. Sleep well?" Potts reaches up and gives his little friend a scratch behind their ears.

Wyndi responds with a series of small happy squeaks over the top of their signature bell-toned purring sound as they nuzzle into his hand.

"I see your pet has not had any interest in diplomacy today," the Captain quips.

"They fell asleep about ten minutes in—that's a new record for them paying attention, I think."

"They were probably wise to go to sleep. I count [Captain Zyzyk] as a friend, but he is *terribly* long-winded at times." The Captain holds one of her clawed appendages down to Wyndi as an invitation.

Wyndi looks at the claw, and then up at Potts.

Potts nods, holding back a chuckle. He can't help thinking it's adorable that they seem to want to ask his permission. It's a distinct improvement over them jumping and trying to climb everyone they meet on impulse, though.

Within moments, Wyndi has excitedly climbed all the way up the Captain's offered leg and onto the back of her upper carapace to get a better view of the whole bridge. The Florivan home planet at Procyon is incredibly Earth-like, as far as Potts has ever heard, but for some reason unknown to him, the higher gravity barely slows Wyndi down at all now that they've had a few weeks to adjust to it. Considering that their parent's last request to him was to keep them warm, though, Potts is sure that the rest of the climate on this ship agrees with Wyndi too.

Wyndi makes a curious squeak and leans over upside-down to look into the Captain's eye for a few moments before giving her nearest facial tentacle a curious poke.

"Hello to you too, little one." The Captain waves the rest of her facial tentacles at them playfully. *Frog's* Captain seems to have become rather fond of Wyndi, just as she seems to be fond of Potts himself. From what she's said, the novelty of having aliens as guests on her ship appeals to her. From what Potts has observed, though, Prelvee are just as easily charmed by small furry creatures as humans are. He hasn't met one on the ship yet who didn't seem happy about having the opportunity to pet the little Florivan kitten.

Wyndi squeaks again happily and scampers back upright to stare out the viewscreen at the stars.

"If they ever bother you, Captain..."

"They do not. Your pet is quite entertaining."

A chime from a nearby console alerts the Captain's assistant to an intra-ship message. "[Captain]," the assistant says with what Potts has learned to recognize as an amused tone in the clicks and buzzes he hears under her translated words, "[Physician] asks if you are done with his patient for the day."

"Of course." The Captain lightly nudges Potts' shoulder with one of her claws, taking on the same tone. "You had better go before he comes looking for you, [Pilot-Sergeant]."

"Yes, Ma'am." With a grunt of effort, Potts pulls himself up out of the soft mossy cushion and gives the Captain a small salute. He whistles up at his fuzzy little copilot and nods his head towards the door. "Come on, Wyndi, let's not leave Doc waiting."

Wyndi looks down at him curiously. After a moment, they gracefully hop over to sit atop his head. In the short time he's been caring for the kitten, Potts has learned that their two favorite places to be are down in his shirt-pocket sleeping or up in a high place where they can see everything. Usually, they settle down to contentedly sit on his shoulder once they've seen whatever it is they want to see of their surroundings. He's grateful Wyndi isn't any bigger or heavier than they are. Even with the assistance of the pressure field and support braces, the weight of anything larger than their tiny self impacting him would probably be enough to knock him over.

"We're still on for finishing that game of checkers tomorrow, ma'am?"

"Of course," the Captain calls after him, "I enjoy the simplicity of your human game."

Potts chuckles and leaves the room, still with the kitten surveying everything around him from their perch in his hair.

★

*F*ROG'S INFIRMARY IS A FAMILIAR PLACE TO POTTS by this point. He's even come to think of it as cozy, with its general aesthetic of a large mossy cavern with platforms that can be summoned up out of the middle of the floor and small shelves and glass-doored cupboards lining all of the walls. A metal chandelier holding large glowing spheres in the center of the ceiling provides illumination, along with a few additional smaller spheres sitting at regular distances along the walls in matching sconces. The design is otherwise similar to the rest of *Frog's* corridors and rooms—all gentle organic curves and moss-highlighted engraved details—but with more blue-toned lighting than elsewhere in the ship.

While he's not living there on the bunk built into the wall of the back corner anymore, now that he's been given his own cabin, Potts still spends a good amount of his time in the infirmary. Usually, it's to hang out with the first Prelvee friend he and Wyndi made, but today it's for a general check-up and the final fitting of Doc's latest version of his support gear.

Potts is dwarfed by the examination platform he's sitting on, but he's gotten used to that sensation by now. The whole ship is designed to accommodate people several times his size, after all.

"Now, Ju-li-an, how does this feel?" The Prelvee physician's multitude of nimble claws finish fastening the straps securing Potts' left arm into the new version of the braces. "Not too tight?"

"No, that feels fine, Doc," says Potts. He's grateful that Doc went with the idea of having straps that he could tie on himself instead of extruded silk fastenings that needed to be cut to be removed. With the new straps, it means he'll be able to take this set of braces *off* himself, which he hopes will make it easier to sleep.

"I have carved your new sup-port pie-ces from a light-er and more ro-bust mat-er-i-al; they should still be strong and pro-tect you from dam-age, but will not add as much to your to-tal bo-dy weight."

"That'll be nice." Even with the earlier versions of the braces and pressure field helping to support his unaccustomed weight and assisting his organs and bodily fluids to function just as they would in an Earth-normal environment, he's still found it tiring to be up and about for more than an hour or so at a time. The added weight of the metal braces didn't exactly help.

Potts makes an experimental motion with his left arm, turning his elbow and wrist over a few times. A curved, two-inch wide segmented bar of iridescent purple-green material extends over the fine tubes running down the length of his arm which hold all of the mechanical elements that allow him such a full range of motion. A soft padded silk under-layer on each segment cushions his arm and prevents the straps from chafing.

The new brace is far less restrictive than any of the previous versions he's worn. With this edition, a second spine flows down his back and connects to the segmented supports along his limbs. Electrical impulses from his brain are gathered with a sensor in the section supporting his head to control the intricate micro-mechanical system held inside the carved supports. The whole of his weight is redistributed through the rig to give him greater ease of movement without putting as much strain on his joints.

The pressure field has also been improved. Now, instead of a set of metal bands attached to the brace rig itself, Potts is wearing a slim collar of a lightweight metallic textile which houses the streamlined projector matrix Doc and Emerald have been modifying. Matching bracelets and anklets made out of the same thin material complete the set as refinement points for the skin-tight pressure field. According to Emerald, all of this is designed so that unlike the braces, he can keep it on at all times comfortably. The "pressure jewelry" is all waterproof and programmed to notice changes in the atmosphere and gravity conditions around him and make adjustments to the projected field accordingly.

"Yeah, this is great, Doc," Potts says, once he's gotten a feel for the brace's range of movement. The infirmary's arti-grav settings are still turned down to Earth-like at the moment, but he can feel the light assistive pressure as he moves his arm. "What's this new material you used? It's certainly lighter than the last rig. I think once I get used to it, I won't even notice it's there"

Doc makes a few untranslatable self-congratulatory clicks before he answers. "The Cap-tain all-owed me to use some of her re-cent ex-o-ske-le-ton moul-tings. They have the ex-act mat-er-i-al strength and qual-i-ties need-ed for this—af-ter all, we have ad-ap-ted for mil-li-ons of years to with-stand our lev-el of grav-i-ty."

Initially, the idea that he's wearing what amounts to a partial suit of armor made from a shed part of his hostess's *body* is the most bizarre and gross thing Potts has encountered yet. He'd only just gotten used to the idea that all of the textiles he's seen on this ship are spun from the Prelvee's own silk.

"I'm... honored." Potts makes a mental note that he'll have to thank the Captain personally the next time he sees her. No wonder she'd asked about the braces earlier— she'd probably been looking forward to hearing what he thought of her gift. "And it does seem more comfortable overall—not as sweaty and chafe-y as before."

"I am glad!" Doc claps happily with most of his upper claws. "I was not con-tent that the pre-vi-ous de-sign was en-ough to pro-vide the sup-port you need for your en-do-skel-e-ton and fra-gile or-gans. This ver-sion should al-so pro-tect you from o-ther in-jur-ies if you hap-pen to fall."

"That's nice to know." Potts tries moving around a bit more, slowly clambering down from the platform. "Ah, yeah, this is *definitely* an improvement. Thanks, Doc."

"It has been a pleas-ant di-ver-sion from my us-u-al du-ties." Doc's single large eye watches closely as Potts continues to test out his range of motion and settle into his new braces. "I do not get to work with spe-cies outside the All-i-ance first claw as of-ten as I would like."

"Well, if this brace design works for *me*, maybe you'll be able to have more humans around?" Potts makes a small adjustment to the way the fabric of his shorts is lying under the brace junction near his lower spine. It's a definite relief that this version can be worn *over* his clothes.

"Per-haps! I would be in-ter-es-ted to see more of your peo-ple!" Doc leans casually against the examination platform and gestures with several of the clawed appendages on the upper right side of his body. "I as-pi-red to serve in a med-i-cal ex-change po-sit-ion be-fore I was as-signed to this ship. Per-haps, af-ter the war is o-ver, I will be a-ble to gain per-miss-ion."

"I can think of a few human ships that'd be grateful to have you," Potts replies. Doc has often mentioned his interest in human medicine and cultures. "You certainly have a better bedside manner than at least *one* doctor I know."

"Is that so?"

"Yeah." Potts chuckles at the memory of the last time the doctor he's thinking of had an occasion to chastise him. "Then again, maybe it's just me she's hard on?"

Doc waves his facial tentacles in a way Potts has learned indicates amused confusion. "Why would the she be more harsh with you than her oth-er pat-ients?"

"Eh…" Potts absently rubs at the back of his hair. He's been thinking about that particular doctor a lot lately, even more than he had after she left to help with some civilian hospital station or other that's being set up for the Fleet's use out at Kapteyn. "We knew each other as kids? And she was at Teegarden's Medical Academy while I was in the Trainee Corps… and I *maybe* came in injured once too often while she was doing her residency at Shell Island?"

"I am not sure I un-der-stand."

"You would if you ever met Reba—I have a feeling the two of you would get along, too." Potts chuckles again and then glances around. "Say, Doc, did you see where Wyndi went?"

"No. How-ev-er, I am sure your pet is here some-where."

Potts whistles, but Wyndi doesn't appear immediately. That's not entirely unexpected, since now that they've fully adjusted to the ship's environment, the kitten does this explore and hide routine at least twice a day. After a few minutes of searching, Potts realizes that Wyndi must have left the room—they're certainly not lurking in any of their usual hiding places around the infirmary.

"Well, Doc," he says, sighing, "looks like I'm going to have to go play hide and seek around the ship again."

"Would you like as-sist-ance?"

"Yeah, if you're not busy. Just my luck they'll have wandered in somewhere off-limits again."

"I am sure your pet has not gone far."

"Knowing Wyndi? They're probably sleeping in the least convenient place for me that they could possibly find."

It's right as he says this that Potts hears a curious little squeak above him. He looks up, only to see that Wyndi has *somehow* managed to get all the way up into the infirmary's chandelier and is staring down at him from between two of the glowing blue spheres.

"Well, now," Doc says, also looking up, "that *is* a new place for your pet to hide."

"Doc, I don't even *want* to think through how they could have gotten all the way up there." Potts whistles pointedly and gestures for them to come down.

With another happy little squeak, Wyndi drops down into Potts' waiting hands. They quickly scamper up to their usual place on his shoulder and begin inspecting the new braces and field-projecting jewelry he's wearing. Judging by the tone of their squeaking, Wyndi approves of the design. He's not surprised. One of the things Potts has learned about Florivan kittens in the short time he's known his little copilot is simply that if there's something with a shine or a sparkle to it, Wyndi is interested.

"Well, Wyndi, at least you still haven't figured out how to get into the air vents..." Potts shakes his head even as he gives the kitten a scratch or two behind their ears.

"That would be a prob-lem, yes. The vent sys-tem runs through the whole ship." Doc pulls a nutrient stick out of one of the pockets of his tool sash and breaks a piece off, offering it to the kitten. "Thank you for your pat-i-ence while I was as-sist-ing your mas-ter with his bra-ces, lit-tle one."

Wyndi happily accepts the bribe and makes a bright little bell-like half-chirp at Doc before they start nibbling away.

"Such a re-mark-a-ble lit-tle crea-ture, your pet." Doc smiles at the kitten as much as any Prelvee could be said to smile, with a slow wave of his facial tentacles. "They seem to be high-ly in-tel-i-gent."

Potts looks down at his fuzzy little copilot.

Wyndi turns their third golden eye to him in response. He's *certain* sometimes that they understand what he's saying, even though they don't seem to be old enough to talk yet.

"They're smarter than they let on." Potts lets out a laugh. "Probably smarter than me, even."

"Then you should be hon-ored, Ju-li-an," Doc says with an amused wave of his facial tentacles, "to have had such an in-tel-i-gent lit-tle life form choose you for their com-pan-i-on."

Having finished nibbling down the nutrient stick, Wyndi makes another of their happy bell-like squeaks and climbs back down into Potts' shirt pocket. They curl up into a fluffy silver ball like they always do to take a nap. Within moments, he can feel the tiny vibrations of their contented purr.

Potts chuckles again. "Yeah, Doc... I'm awful lucky they decided to stick around with me."

★

IRAWYND IS STILL TOO YOUNG TO REALLY form thoughts in the shapes of words.

They spend most of their time either snuggled down into their human's warm pocket-pouch sleeping or riding around on his shoulder where they can observe everything going on around him.

Mirawynd likes the human their parent gave them to protect. He's *warm*. They never really feel cold in the new ship, but his warmth is still comforting. He smells a bit like their parent's human, too, even though he looks nothing like Scott.

Mirawynd also likes the hard-shell people their human is living with. They're very fond of both Miss Emerald and the Captain. Both of them are the Prelvee version of *tall*, and are happy to give a good ear-scratching if

Mirawynd offers them an opportunity for snuggles. Miss Emerald is also good at finding new shiny toys for them to play with, and lets them ride on her head whenever she's accompanying their human to different places on the ship. The Captain, meanwhile, always lets Mirawynd guard her collection of captured checkers when she's playing with their human, and is happy to share all sorts of tasty snacks with them too.

The smaller one their human calls Doc is their favorite, though. He always has a treat for Mirawynd somewhere in the pockets of his carry-pouch. They've hidden in Doc's pouch before, but ultimately decided it wasn't a comfortable napping place because of all of the other things he keeps in there.

Their human's shirt pocket is much nicer, especially because Mirawynd can hear his heart beating when they sleep there. It's not quite the same as their parent's purring, but it's close enough for Mirawynd. Even though their human isn't their parent or littermates, he's still very much *theirs*. They know they're safe with him.

Mirawynd doesn't understand at all why their parent didn't come with them and their human to the new ship, nor why their littermates and their parent's human aren't there. They only know that their parent picked a nice human for them to stay with and protect while they wait for their family to come back. They've already decided they're going to keep their human forever, because he is *warm* and wonderful and has a nice voice. They just *know* their family will want to keep him too.

Right now, Mirawynd is playing their favorite game with their human. It's the one that, if they had the words for it, they'd call "explore and hide and see how long it takes my human to find me."

It's a good game, too. Mirawynd's littermates used to play something like it, but the old ship was *cold*. Mirawynd could never go far before they started to get chilled and couldn't keep up with their littermates anymore because they were so much smaller than the rest. That was usually when Mirawynd would retreat to their parent's pouch and leave their bigger, stronger littermates to the games they liked to play with their parent's human. They've always been the smallest, though, and they were the last to have their eyes open and be given their name and be allowed out of the pouch in the first place. That only happened a few days before their parent left Mirawynd with their human, even though their littermates have been seeing and exploring the world for *months* now without them.

In any case, the new ship is nice and warm, even if the air in most of it makes Mirawynd feel heavier than they used to be. They can explore all over the place and never have to worry about getting cold at all. The only thing they have to watch out for are the many, many clawed feet of the nice hard-shell people. Mirawynd knows they are a very small person in comparison and could accidentally get stepped on, and so should be careful.

Mirawynd knows too that if one of the hard-shell people notices them while they're playing the explore-and-hide game, they'll be captured and returned to their human. They do their best to avoid this. It's not *nearly* as much fun if someone other than their human finds them first—although if the finder has treats for them, Mirawynd doesn't mind the defeat as much. Ever since they came up with the game, they've been finding that more and more of their hard-shell friends are keen to give them a snack before returning them to their human, too. They're not sure why, but they like the attention.

Today, Mirawynd has found their way up one of the damp mossy walls and into the maze of caves that carry the nice warm air all over the ship. They're excited to scamper and explore all through the warm caves. Eventually, they know that their human will realize that it's his turn and come find them.

So far, Mirawynd's human seems to think they're still somewhere nearby in the big room where Miss Emerald and one of the other larger hard-shell people are helping him try to repair the broken parts of his small ship. Mirawynd has spent most of the morning delightedly exploring all of the interesting things in the hard-shell person's tool boxes. They *do* like shiny metal bits and tools and things, but they like exploring even better.

Mirawynd takes another look down from the little grated vent to see that their human is still busy and then goes off down the warm cave to see where it can take them.

The small cave leads into a long network of warm, damp tunnels spreading up and down and all around the ship. Mirawynd scampers excitedly across the soft bed of moss growing on the floor of the caves. The moss is nice to grab onto for climbing, too; it grows in patches all over the ship, but it seems to make a particularly thick carpet here in the tunnels. The moss makes the air cleaner and nicer smelling, although Mirawynd themself doesn't understand how and why it's there.

Every now and then, Mirawynd stops at one of the grated vents to peer out and see who's down below them. Most of the time it's either no one or a few of the hard-shell people talking in their click-and-buzz language and going about their business. Mirawynd can't understand much the hard-shell language yet, although they're already getting an instinctive feel for it just like they have for the language their parent and the humans use. Miss Emerald has taught them to recognize a few words, even if they can't mimic any of them properly yet: "thank you," "please," "snack," "water," and "help." The first four are to do with mealtime, which is one of Mirawynd's favorite things. The last one, according to Miss Emerald, is for them to learn in case their human gets into trouble. Luckily, he's not falling asleep for no reason any more, and Mirawynd is happy to let their hard-shell friends help them take care of him.

As they continue exploring, Mirawynd keeps thinking they'll look down one of the vents and see their human, but he doesn't seem to have noticed their absence yet. That's just as well, though. They know he's safe where they left him, and they're hardly done exploring.

They go further into the caves and deeper down. At one point, they think they hear a sound for a moment or two. It sounds like something they remember, but they don't know what it is. It's almost like singing, somewhere far down in the belly of the warm ship.

Mirawynd is a curious creature by nature. They can't help but want to follow the sound and see whatever might be making it. Eventually, they find themself in one of the dead ends of the cave system, where a grate with mesh instead of wide bars blocks off the place where they could have slipped back out into the room below. They peek through the mesh anyway, still curious.

On the other side, Mirawynd sees a room with rows of big shiny-walled boxes suspended along each side of a center aisle. The shiny walls glow orange and yellow, shifting with a buzz as the colors pass over the emptiness of the boxes. In the middle of the last shining box—the one closest to them—there's something other than emptiness. Mirawynd looks more intently, focusing all three of their eyes on the form in the shadows.

It's some sort of a person, floating in a bored-looking seated position with flowing layers of pink fabric draped all around their body. For a moment, they think they see their parent's human there, under all the pink.

Mirawynd places the upper pair of their hands on the grate and tilts their head to refocus their three eyes on the person, then makes a small questioning squeak of greeting.

The *thing* that looks up at them is not their parent's human.

It's not anyone.

It's too many faces in one face and it's looking right at them and smiling a smile with too many teeth.

Mirawynd squeaks in alarm and runs back down the tunnel as fast as they can, as far away from the monster as their six tiny limbs can carry them.

Exploring isn't fun anymore when there are scary things lurking in the dark. The only thought in Mirawynd's mind now is that they need to find their human. Instinct carries them forward through the caves, retracing their path back to the place where they left him. Luckily for Mirawynd, although they're not aware of it, their species has a good innate sense of direction. They don't get lost at all trying to find their way back to the place where they left their human.

The only problem is that once they get there, their human is not where they left him.

He's *gone*.

Mirawynd squeaks unhappily when they see nothing but hard-shell people down below them. They sit at the grate for a while, holding their long fluffy tail for security between their lower set of hands while they try to figure out where their human has gone.

They are at a complete loss for what to do.

The feeling, rather than the thought, overwhelms Mirawynd that maybe they've left their human alone for too long this time.

Maybe he's forgotten them.

Maybe they're going to be all by themself forever now, and their family will never come back for them either.

Then, when Mirawynd has just about decided the only thing they *can* do is curl up in the moss at the grate and take a sad nap while they wait for their human to hopefully return and look for them, their large tuft-tipped ears swivel at a familiar sound echoing through the cave behind them.

A whistle!

Their human *always* makes that sound when he's looking for them.

In a flash, Mirawynd releases their tail and scampers down through the tunnels in the direction of the whistling.

With their keen hearing and the magnifying echo of the caves, it's not hard now for Mirawynd to find their human. He's talking to Miss Emerald as the two of them walk down one of the ship's lower corridors.

"You're sure you heard them, Emerald?"

"I am. Your pet has a ver-y dis-tinc-tive sound pro-file."

"I just don't get why they'd have come all the way down here."

"Per-haps they were just cur-i-ous a-bout where the air vents lead?"

"Knowing Wyndi... that's not too bad of a guess." Mirawynd's human whistles again, pausing for a moment in the corridor.

Mirawynd slips out of the grate closest to him and scampers down the mossy wall, since he's not standing close enough for them to leap onto his shoulder like they usually do. They reach their human's foot and pat his leg with both upper hands, squeaking excitedly to get his attention.

"Ah! There you are, Wyndi!" Their human leans down and picks them up, almost laughing. "I was wondering when you'd reappear. Did you have a good wander?"

Mirawynd happily accepts their human's affectionate snuggles before slipping down into their place in his pocket and curling up for a nap. The sound of his heartbeat soothes all of the fears they'd had of monsters and of being alone.

They've had enough adventure for one day.

★

POTTS YAWNS BROADLY, HOLDING UP A HAND TO cover his gaping mouth. "I'm sorry, Ma'am," he says, once he has control of his lungs again, "what were you saying?"

The Captain looks between him and the checkerboard she's set up on one of the small tables in her company-hosting area, her facial tentacles making an expression he's started to recognize as amusement. "I was saying that it is your turn, [Pilot-Sergeant], but I think it is probably best we end our visit for tonight sooner so that you can rest."

On the side of the board, amidst the neatly-stacked pile of checkers they're guarding for the Captain, Wyndi waves their tail anxiously and also stares at him.

Potts answers sheepishly. "I'm fine to finish the game… it's just been a long day." He pauses to study the board, then advances one of his few remaining checkers a square. "There, your move."

The Captain clicks a few of her upper claws together rhythmically, as she often seems to do when she's considering something. After a few moments of contemplation, she picks up one of her own pieces and deftly jumps it over the last three of Potts' own, With a triumphant wave of her facial tentacles, she lands it squarely on the final row on his side of the board. This accomplished, the Captain reaches over and gives Wyndi a gentle pat on the head with one of her claws. "Go ahead, little one."

Wyndi knows the signal quite well by this point. They happily bounce up and collect the jumped checkers, moving them to the stacks where all of Potts' other pieces are waiting. With a flourish of their fluffy prehensile tail, the kitten crowns the Captain's king with a second piece from her much smaller pile.

"Good game, Captain." Potts stifles another yawn. "I didn't even see that coming."

"Perhaps you will see my possible moves better tomorrow, when you have had a chance to sleep first." She picks up the box she stores her recently-made checker set in and sets it on the table beside the board.

As they have every night since the ship's quartermaster presented the Captain with the set she'd made to Potts' specifications, Wyndi happily sets about gathering up all of the collected gold and green playing pieces and setting them neatly into their rows in the cushioned interior of the box. Potts has discovered that the kitten likes playing checkers with him just as much as the Captain does— although Wyndi's way of playing is more to snatch away any piece removed from the board so they can stack it into towers.

He's looking forward to introducing his little copilot to the rest of the Musketeers someday and showing Wyndi how much fun *cards* can be to stack.

Potts stands and stretches. He's a little stiff from sitting still, but the stretch is more in preparation for the walk back through the higher-gravity sections of the ship to his cabin. "I might. You're getting good at the game, though, Ma'am—the more we play, the harder it is to keep up with your strategies."

The Captain gives him the Prelvee equivalent of a grin as she shuts the box and turns off the projection of the playing board. With another tap of her claw, the whole table descends into the floor beside her seating cushion and disappears. "I do enjoy the challenge, even if the game is relatively straightforward. You will have to teach some of my officers to play so that I will have an adequate selection of opponents once you leave us."

Potts scoops his little Florivan companion up from the floor, since they're waving their arms and squeaking in the tone he knows means they don't want to bother trying to climb him. Even Wyndi's tuckered out, it seems. As soon as he has them up to chest height, they slip down into his shirt pocket with a squeaky yawn.

"Sounds good to me, Ma'am." He makes his usual salute before turning to leave. "Goodnight, Captain."

"Goodnight, [Pilot-Sergeant]."

As he walks down the corridor from her quarters to the lift that will take him to the level of *Frog's* infirmary and his quarters, he feels the near-doubled weight of his body with every step. He's gotten more accustomed to walking with his braces on, which combined with the pressure field do make it a lot less uncomfortable—but when he's already more tired than he realized, it's still a considerable strain. He pauses to rest beside the crew lift for a few moments, leaning against the wall.

He'd only thought he closed his eyes for a moment to take a breath, but it's clear several minutes have passed when he opens them in response to a gentle tapping on his shoulder. One of the younger—or, at least, slightly less lengthy—female Prelvee is waiting on the other side of his eyelids.

"Are you well, [Pilot-Sergeant]?" she asks, waving a concerned facial tentacle. "Would you like me to summon [Physician]?"

Potts does his best to hide the instinctive startle reaction from the unexpected massive eye mere inches away from his face. "I'm okay..." he straightens up against the wall, awkwardly trying to regain his composure. He knows this is one of the engineer's assistants he was talking to earlier in the day—she's got a distinct golden speckling on her body segments and facial tentacles that's unique among *Frog's* crew. "I just must have dozed off. Thanks for waking me, Miss."

She looks at him silently for a few moments, then shifts herself towards the crew lift door and taps the button to summon it. "Please, allow me to escort you the rest of the way to your quarters. [Communications Officer] mentioned that you sometimes lose consciousness from strain; it is clear you are over-tired from helping us with your spacecraft and searching for your pet."

Potts finds himself too tired to even try to turn her down. "Thanks. I'd appreciate that."

As his self-described escort guides him into the lift, she makes idle chatter about his darter and how pleased she is to be assigned to help reconstruct its missing wing. Potts is grateful for the running conversation, if only because it's something to focus on to keep himself awake and moving forward. He likes the chipper young Prelvee engineer—she reminds him in a way of a sweeter version of Rudy.

"Here we are," she says before Potts has even noticed they've walked that far, nudging him towards his cabin door. "Thank you for entertaining my thoughts, [Pilot-Sergeant]. I hope that you are able to rest well so that we can work together more tomorrow." She pauses, running a thoughtful facial tentacle across the rim of her beak. "If you allow it, I will speak to [Head Engineer] about adjusting the environmental settings in the repair bay temporarily so that you will not be so drained from working with us."

Potts turns and looks up at her with a mix of surprise and appreciation as he catches his breath from the shift into the Earth-normal gravity field of his cabin. "I'd…" he stifles a yawn. "I'd be grateful if you did, actually. Thank you."

As he removes Wyndi from his shirt pocket and sets them still-sleeping onto the pillow beside his own, Potts can't focus his thoughts enough to wonder just why today has been so much more exhausting than all the others since he arrived on *Song-of-the-Midnight-Frog*. Probably, he muses between washroom and bed, it was hunting Wyndi through the ship's air vents for so long that tired him out in the end.

Without ceremony, he flops down onto his massive Prelvee-style bed, still dressed and wearing his new braces. Just a few minutes to rest his eyes, he assures himself, and then he'll properly get ready for bed.

★

A song filters through his dreams.

From the rubble of the hole that was once Reba's childhood bedroom, to the tree house Eddie and his uncles built in the woods behind the rescue station where they all lived, to the classrooms of his Academy days, the haunting melody pursues him through one half-remembered scene of mixed-up images and people to another.

"Darling, I know you're there now..."

No song he's ever heard before—it resonates deep in his bones like a call ancestral to his being.

Melody changing faces, calling, pulling him through the mists of dream to dream.

"Darling, can't you hear me?"

The song's pull anchors deep, calls on instincts, calls him forward.

A face in the mist, a melody of longing, of desire.

"This way, darling, that's right."

He's walking unfamiliar paths, following the song...

★

EEP INTO THE SHIP'S NIGHT, MIRAWYND IS IN
their usual place on their human's mossy pillow in
the comfortable nest the hard-shell people have given him.
They've been sleeping peacefully, curled up against his
neck and floating right on the edges of one of his dreams.
They're too young to be conscious of the fact that they
only experience sleep-images like that when they're sharing
his, of course, or to understand what those are.

They only know that snuggling with their human is
warm and comforting and drifting into the place he goes
when he's sleeping feels like being in the warm colorful
floaty place their parent used to take them and their
littermates—the place their parent stayed when they sent
Mirawynd and their human back into the stars in his
broken darter.

When Mirawynd wakes up, they're not sure at first why they've woken up.

As they open their eyes, they recognize the problem. Their human is no longer sleeping where they left him. They've woken up because his warmth is gone—because they're alone.

This is not something Mirawynd likes at all.

They make a displeased squeak, hoping to call their human out from wherever he's hiding.

This is not how the game is supposed to go. *He's* supposed to be the one looking for *them*.

He doesn't reappear.

Mirawynd looks all over the nest room for their human. He's not anywhere at all. This is even more distressing than the initial realization that he was gone: the thought that he might never come *back*.

Mirawynd scampers over towards the door, but finds that they're too small for it to notice and open for them like it does for their human and the hard-shell people.

They think for a moment that they hear their human's voice, but it's only an echo through the ceiling caves. Then, Mirawynd remembers that there are ceiling caves, and that they can escape from the room that way to continue their search.

Climbing up the trail of moss on the wall, Mirawynd quickly reaches the grate and slips in. Tail waving determinedly behind them, they scurry onwards in the direction of another echo of their human's voice.

They don't want their human to stay lost. He's *theirs*. They don't want him to go away like their family has.

Mirawynd doesn't take note of how long they're racing around through the caverns. They aren't very good at understanding the passage of time. All they know is that it's been too long since they last saw their human and they can't see him through any of the grates leading out of the caves.

They think they hear his voice again.

They stop where they are in the mossy cavern and swivel their ears around until they can pinpoint the direction. After a few moments, they have it—although they don't know why their human's voice sounds like someone's singing near him.

Mirawynd scampers off towards the echoes.

The singing sounds grow more distinct the closer they get to their human's voice.

Mirawynd isn't sure why, but they don't like the singing voice at all. It makes the soft silver fur along their spine itch just to hear it.

Soon, they find their human.

"No, really?" they hear his voice say as they peer out the nearest grate to look for him, "You're all the way down here? But why?"

Mirawynd's human is slowly walking along the corridor below, almost in a daze, talking to someone who isn't there. They can't see another person around anywhere for him to talk to. Their human *never* goes so far from his nest alone like this.

Mirawynd squeaks down at their human, but he doesn't stop beneath the grate to look up at them. He just keeps staggering along.

They try again at each of the next grates. Not even their loudest and most direct squeaks seem to catch their human's attention.

Needless to say, Mirawynd *doesn't* like this.

They continue following their human from above.

When he stops at the door to one of the swift tunnels leading between decks, they have their chance to slip out of the grating above him and hop down onto his head.

Their human doesn't react to this at all, even though the impact makes him stumble for a moment.

Mirawynd climbs down to their human's shoulder just as the door opens for him and he steps onto the platform that will carry him down further into the ship. They squeak at him again and nuzzle against his neck, but he still doesn't react.

On closer inspection, they find that his eyes are barely open at all.

He almost seems to be dreaming, although Mirawynd doesn't have the words to call it that. All they know is that it feels the same sitting on their human's shoulder now as it does when he's sleeping and they drift into the edges of him—and somehow, that is something very *wrong*.

The singing sounds are louder now, and grow louder still as their human lurches off of the platform and into the corridor.

Mirawynd doesn't like the sound of the singing any more than they like the sensation of this walking dream their human is having. They reach up with all four hands and pull on their human's ear, making the loudest squeaking sounds their tiny voice can produce.

"What the—*Wyndi*!"

Even though his reaction includes almost knocking them off his shoulder before correcting his aim and just gently plucking them off of it, Mirawynd is content with the result.

"What in the *stars* was that for?" Their human asks this knowing they can't actually answer him, holding them gently in one hand up to his face. He does this sometimes, when he thinks Mirawynd needs scolding after they've done something that doesn't meet with his approval.

Mirawynd meets his now-very-awake pair of hazel eyes with a pointed look of all three of theirs and squeaks happily at him.

"You know how I feel about being... woken up... before..." their human trails off and looks around, then sighs. "This isn't our cabin, is it?"

Mirawynd is rewarded for their efforts with a gentle rub behind their ears while their human starts slowly making his way back to where the two of them *should* be.

For their part, Mirawynd is simply pleased to have found their human again. All the worries they might have disappear entirely, if only because he's holding them.

★

Two weeks later, Potts once again finds himself laying on the examination platform in *Frog's* infirmary.

"I tell you, Doc, it's just plain *weird*."

"Then this be-ha-vior is not com-mon for your spe-cies?"

"No—well, I mean, lots of people sleepwalk. *I'm* just not one of them, that's all. Never have been. That's more my Aunt Kit's thing—but as far as I know, we're not bio-related close enough for that to count as a family history."

"Fas-cin-a-ting." Doc's single melon-sized eye is still focused on the information from the scans he's currently taking of Potts' entire body.

Wyndi is quietly sitting on the Prelvee doctor's head, also staring at the scanner's bright-colored interface.

"I do not see an-y an-o-mo-lies com-pared to the ex-am-in-a-tion I made of you when you first came a-board. There is no-thing which would in-di-cate an-y re-cent dam-age to your brain."

"Okay, good to know... So why do I keep waking up in the corridors with no idea how I got there? If it was just once, fine, but it's happening every night now—I've taken to sleeping in my braces, just in case."

"I am not sure." Doc continues his scans, drumming four or five of his lower clawed appendages on the floor as he does. "Per-haps it is re-la-ted to the trou-ble you had sleep-ing when you were first ad-jus-ting to our en-vi-ro-ment?"

"Maybe you're right." Potts sighs, staring up at the lines of moss on the ceiling above him. "It'll probably go away on its own."

Scans completed, Doc looks down to Potts with a curious wave of his face tentacles. "How-ev-er, ev-en if we do not yet know the cause, I be-lieve I can off-er you some op-tions for deal-ing with this while I wait for Doc-tor Star Sap-phire to re-spond to my in-qui-ry."

"Oh?" Potts sits up slowly, tilting his head slightly to one side.

"Yes." Doc helps Pots strap his braces and pressure field bands back on as he explains, since these had been taken off to prevent interference with the scans. "First, I can give you more of the sed-a-tive we used to ease your ear-li-er in-som-ni-a. That may keep you in the deep-er phase of sleep and pre-vent you from wan-der-ing."

"No offense, Doc," Potts says, "but I'd rather not spend the rest of however long I'm here developing a dependency on those things." It was one thing when he'd had a migraine to go along with the insomnia, but Potts has never liked the idea of needing to take any sort of medicine to be able to sleep.

"I re-mem-bered you would have a con-cern re-gar-ding that risk." Doc gestures with a few of his uppermost claws as he says this. "For that rea-son, I would als-o like to off-er to ob-serve your next sleep-walk-ing ep-i-sode and de-ter-mine if there is some oth-er fac-tor in-volved first."

Potts is not sure he's heard this correctly at first. "You mean... you'd *watch* me sleep and somehow that would tell you why this is happening?"

"Po-ten-tial-ly! I have been con-sul-ting the man-y sour-ces Doc-tor Star Sap-phire has sent me re-gar-ding hu-man med-i-cine. If there is a psy-cho-log-i-cal is-sue in-volved, the ob-ser-va-tion notes may give you some in-sight."

"That's... weird, but reasonable, I guess. You'd probably be bored to death watching me sleep, though, Doc."

"Per-haps your pet will keep me com-pa-ny while I ob-serve, then." Doc reaches a claw up and offers the kitten in question their reward for staying out of his way.

Wyndi happily climbs down from Doc's head and onto his upper claws to accept the segment of nutrient stick. After allowing the physician to give them a bit of a scratch behind the ears as well, they squeak happily and make a graceful leap over to Potts' shoulder to consume their treat.

"I wish Wyndi could tell you what *they've* observed," Potts remarks, giving Wyndi's little silver head a bit of a rub behind their catlike ears. "They're the one who keeps waking me up, after all."

"That would be con-ven-i-ent, if they were a-ble to speak."

"It would." Potts thinks it over for a moment or two and then nods. "All right, then. Medically warranted sleepover it is. It beats not knowing at all."

"Sleep-ov-er?"

"It's a human thing. Sort of a social gathering for children that usually involves things like staying up too late and throwing pillows at each other."

"Pil-lows?" Doc makes an amused clicking sound. "Your spe-cies is fas-cin-a-ting, Ju-li-an."

"If you say so, Doc." Potts shakes his head and stretches as he stands up. On his shoulder, Wyndi mimics the motion.

★

MIRAWYND IS HAVING SOMETHING OF AN ODD evening.

In all the time they've had their human, they've *never* seen him bring one of the hard-shell people into his nest room before—especially not when it's "dark time" and he's meant to be sleeping.

And yet tonight, for whatever reason, Mirawynd's favorite hard-shell person is here sitting on one of the bench platforms near their human's nest. His wide square-pupiled eye's gaze alternates between some kind of display screen he's holding in his upper claws and their human's sleeping form.

Mirawynd isn't sure *why* Doc is here, since their human is very boring while he sleeps. Normally, of course, they don't notice just how boring he is, since they're also sleeping and soaking up their human's dream-flavored warmth.

The oddness of it all is enough that for once Mirawynd is not taking the opportunity for sleeping snuggles with their human. Instead, they're playing their new favorite game: "pester the hard-shell friend for attention and treats." So far, it's a good game. Doc seems to enjoy playing with them, too. He's even tied one of the treats on a bit of string for Mirawynd to chase while he makes it jump around in the air. They only ever manage to catch it long enough to take a few nibbles before it escapes. Having to recapture their snack is fun.

Every now and then, Mirawynd bounces back over to see if their human is still in the nest where they left him. After so many times now of him not being there, this has become their greatest insecurity.

Certain that their human is still sleeping and within easy scampering distance, Mirawynd comes back to their hard-shell friend and makes a soft squeak to catch his attention.

"Yes, lit-tle one," Doc says, barely above a whisper, "I see he is still there." He reaches down with a few of his claws to lift them back up to their preferred perch on his carry-pouch's back strap.

Mirawynd makes themself comfortable, still keeping their lower two eyes on their human. Normally, they'd be nestled up beside his head on the pillow and sleeping, but the bigger game tonight seems to be "watch the human snore," so they're trying to play along.

Mirawynd's ears prick up towards the entrance to the warm caves in the ceiling. That singing sound is back again; the same one they always hear when their human tries to leave without them. They make a glaring half-hiss at the cave grating and start to scamper back over to their human to protect him. They don't know what makes that sound, but they have an impression that it wants to take their human away—and they *don't* intend to let it have him.

Doc catches Mirawynd before they can go far and holds them back, even though they squirm in his gentle claws and try to escape.

Mirawynd looks up at his large single eye and makes an annoyed squeak of protest. Normally, he's much more cooperative than this. They don't want to be held right now, they want to wake their human up so the sound will go away.

"Hush, lit-tle one. Your mas-ter will not leave our sight, but you must stay with me so he does not wake."

Mirawynd is very confused, but the soft whispered tone makes them stop wiggling for a few moments. Then, they see their human haltingly rising out of the nest and shuffling towards the door. They make a louder squeak at Doc and try to escape his claws again.

The kind hard-shell tucks them into one of the pockets of his carry-pouch and leaves several of his claws occupied with gently rubbing behind their ears in the same soothing way their human does—the way their parent used to.

"Please, lit-tle one, trust me. I pro-mise I will not let your mas-ter come to harm."

Instinct and kitten reflexes conspire against Mirawynd in response to the stroking of their small ears. They can't help but relax and content themself with riding along in Doc's herbal-smelling pouch while he follows their human out of the room and into the corridor. The only sound he makes is the soft clicking of his many lower foot-claws against the floor. The new game, it seems, is "follow the human so he doesn't get lost."

Their human is doing the thing again now where he babbles nonsense to the person who isn't there. He seems completely unaware that Mirawynd and their hard-shell steed are following him. Even when Doc slips onto the moving platform behind him to be carried lower down into the ship, Mirawynd's human still does not react.

Mirawynd, of course, would rather be sitting on their human's shoulder and waking him up, but their friend is carrying them close enough beside him that they don't feel an urgent need to try to escape just yet. They can still hear the singing, though, growing ever louder and more insistent as they go deeper into the belly of the ship.

The corridors are starting to smell familiar—and they should. Every time Mirawynd's human wanders in his sleep and has to be caught, he's been following the same path. As he turns down a side hallway, Mirawynd sees a dead end up ahead with a door and one of the big hard-shell people standing in front of it. She's a particularly shiny red-brown person whom Mirawynd has never met before.

She says something to Doc in trilling buzzes and clicks.

Mirawynd recognizes the sounds that make the word for "help" somewhere in Doc's quietly-spoken response. They assume now that he must be asking the guard to assist with making sure Mirawynd's human stays safe while he's sleepwalking.

All the while, Mirawynd's human is stumbling closer and closer to the door. The singing sounds are becoming almost constant. Mirawynd now thinks that Doc and their new friend must not be able to hear the singing. Otherwise, wouldn't they do something to make it stop?

After a moment or two more of quiet conversation with Doc, the guard nods and gestures with the long, sharp-ended rod she's holding. This causes the door to open just as Mirawynd's human approaches. He steps into a dimly lit room filled with a long row of large glowing orange boxes. Doc and the guard follow closely behind him.

Mirawynd looks up to the guard and makes a greeting squeak combined with curiosity.

"Do not wor-ry, lit-tle one," whispers Doc in response, "we know what is hap-en-ing now. We will pro-tect your mas-ter."

It's at this point that Mirawynd recognizes the place their human has wandered into. A chill runs all the way down to the tip of their tail.

This is the place where they once found a monster while they were exploring.

Their human is further up ahead, walking along the row of shiny boxes. They hear him speaking to a second voice now—one that's rearranging itself out of the singing sounds.

Mirawynd scampers up out of the pouch and on top of Doc's armored head so they can get a better look at what's happening.

"You're... the most beautiful woman I've ever seen..."

"Oh, really, now, darling?" The voice giggles. "I'm sure you say that to *all* the girls."

Mirawynd does *not* like the voice that's talking to their human at all. It sounds like sweet darkness in the worst way.

"No, I mean it, I... I've never... What in the *stars* is a human doing as prisoner on a Prelvee ship?"

"They took my escape pod and locked me away. They're lying to you if you think you're not their prisoner. I don't know if anyone survived the attack besides me—they said they left my crew for dead."

It's at this point that Mirawynd sees *what* their human is talking to. It's the monster they saw through the mesh-covered vent. It's still all floating layers of pink fabric and too many faces, to their eyes, more or less coalesced now into something human-ish. Somehow, though, despite the scariness, the monster seems to have their human's full attention.

Mirawynd doesn't like the way it's looking at him. It looks *hungry*.

The two hard-shell people have stopped walking just far enough away from the shiny box the monster is in that it seems not to notice either of them. Doc and the guard are just standing there now, watching the exchange. The guard slowly adjusts her grip on the sharp-ended rod she carries, even as Doc sets a few claws on the edge of her upper shell to stop her from moving forward.

"I'm not sure how to get you out..." Mirawynd's human says, holding his hand up towards the wall of the box.

"It's the panel with the buttons by the door over there, darling... destroy that and this shield will drop so we can escape."

"Ah... right..." Mirawynd's human turns away from the monster in the box and starts slowly moving toward the door where he entered. He's still acting the way he does when he's wandering the corridors alone.

Mirawynd is *not* interested in waiting around for the monster to eat their human. They're done with this game. It's not fun anymore now that the monster is playing. They slide down the smooth segments of Doc's back and scamper across the floor towards their human before either hard-shell can move to catch them.

When Mirawynd reaches their human's foot, they squeak pointedly at him in the way that usually convinces him to pick them up. He doesn't respond, so they jump after him and climb up his braces and onto his shoulder. He feels like sleep and singing dreams again.

"That's right, darling, just break that panel and we can be free."

Mirawynd looks back over towards the shining box. The monster is staring at him still, and staring at *them*. They don't like it. They rub their fuzzy silver cheek against their human's soft pinkish one.

He keeps walking, as if he doesn't even know they're there.

Mirawynd squeaks into his ear, taking hold of it like they've done before when he won't pay attrion to them and wake up.

"Mm?" Their human brushes them away from his ear.

Mirawynd slips around to the other side of his neck and does the same thing, only louder. This time, he stops walking and gently removes them from his shoulder.

"Wyndi, stop that... I'm busy."

Mirawynd squeaks at him again in frustration and wriggles out of his hand so they can climb up onto the top of his head. They swish the fluffy tip of their tail in his face as they turn to fix all three of their small golden eyes on the monster in the box. It's still *watching* him.

"What in the *stars* has gotten into you, Mirawynd?" Their human tries to bat their tail away. For a moment, he sounds and feels like himself, like he's waking up.

Then the singing starts again, louder, all around the monster's voice. "Is something wrong, darling? Who are you talking to? Why did you stop?"

"I..." Mirawynd's human turns around, locks eyes with the monster. "You... I... what was I doing?"

"Come back here to me, darling, show me what's bothering you."

Mirawynd doesn't understand why the monster's dark eyes and the singing are enough to put their human back into his wandering dream. Nor do they understand why he now walks back towards the box the monster is in—or, for that matter, why their two hard-shell friends are still watching from a place in the shadows where the monster can't possibly see them.

All Mirawynd knows is that they don't like the monster. Not one bit. They have no intention of letting it get near their human.

They return to the tactic of swishing the fluff of their tail in their human's eyes. This at least gets him to stop walking so he can pluck them off the top of his head. Mirawynd resists being plucked as much as they can, squeaking and batting his hands away and clinging tightly to his hair.

Their human succeeds in catching them anyway and holds them with one hand in front of him. "Now, *really,* Wyndi, I need you to be quiet so I can help our friend..."

Mirawynd swivels around, wrapping both pairs of arms around their human's hand and their tail around his wrist so he can't escape. They glare at the monster in the box, all three eyes focused on it.

The monster looks back at them with too many teeth for Mirawynd's liking flashing across its too-perfect-to-be-real version of a human face. "What is that creature?"

"This? Oh, this is—"

Mirawynd yells at the monster with the loudest, fiercest set of squeaks and hisses they can manage. They may not have words yet, but they *do* have the instinct for how to tell a predator that it will have to find another meal elsewhere.

"What a terrifying little beast! Don't let it bite you, darling!" The monster shifts position, coming all the way up to the shimmering orange wall of the box.

If Mirawynd was old enough to understand exactly what "terrifying little beast" *meant,* they would probably take it as a compliment. As it is, they take a deep breath and then repeat their fiercest sounds. They tighten the grip of their long prehensile tail around their human's wrist. *Nothing* is going to take him away from them without a fight—not even something several times their size with too many teeth.

"They're not usually like this..."

"Get rid of it, darling, it's clearly dangerous! I've been so afraid the little monster would attack me from the air vents again..." The monster sets a hand up right against the wall. It's putting on a tone like it's hurt, under all the singing.

"They're not... not really... Wyndi wouldn't have..."

"I promise, darling, once we're safe I'll get you a nicer pet. Where did you even find that horrid thing?"

"I... they came from *Equinox*..."

"Oh, that can't be. We'd never allow vermin on my ship... please, darling, get rid of it and help me escape. These aliens have brainwashed you, making you think a pest like that was safe to have around."

"...A pest? Mirawynd?" Their human looks down at Mirawynd, turning them so he can see their face.

Mirawynd pauses their ongoing display of ferocity and looks up at their human. There's something strange about his eyes. They're all glassy and dark like the monster's eyes.

But still, this *is* their human. Mirawynd is just happy he's looking at them now instead of the monster in the box.

Mirawynd nuzzles against his hand, squeaking gently and letting their I-trust-you-and-you-are-warm-and-safe sound start up. Their human never purrs back, not like their parent and littermates did, but they know he likes the sound anyway.

"What are you waiting for, darling? It'll bite you! Quickly, before the guard comes back!"

"Oh, they're a *pest*, all right..." Their human raises his other hand close to the one holding Mirawynd and sets it on their head.

After a long moment, he starts absently rubbing Mirawynd's ears.

Mirawynd sees his eyes go back to their normal shiny hazel color. He pulls them in closer and loosens his grip so they can slip out and take their rightful place on his shoulder.

Mirawynd does so happily. Once back in their proper perch, they return to being loudly fierce at the monster in the box.

It doesn't look happy.

"I don't know *why* Wyndi doesn't like you," says their human, looking back to the monster, "but I've never seen them act like this around *anyone*."

"You can't possibly believe that horrid little creature has enough brains to—"

"You're not really *Equinox's* Captain, are you?"

This, for some reason, makes the monster's singing sounds stop completely.

Finally, the two hard-shell friends appear out of the shadows. The guard places the lower two-thirds of her long segmented body as a barrier between Mirawynd's human and the box.

"No, Ju-li-an," says Doc, appearing on their human's other side. "This per-son is not what she app-ears to be. Please come with us now."

"You can't believe—"

Mirawynd cuts the monster off with another pointed hiss.

The guard says something loudly in clicks and buzzes and taps the shining wall with her sharp stick, turning it completely opaque.

"For-give us, Ju-li-an." Doc sets a claw on their human's arm and guides him back towards the door. "We need-ed to see how she was aff-ect-ing your mind so that we could prop-er-ly seal her cell to pro-tect you."

"...Right." Mirawynd's human walks slowly, as if he's suddenly exhausted. He rubs at his temples. "Whatever all of that was, I've got the *worst* headache..."

"I will give you some-thing for the pain and check your health mar-kers be-fore you go to see the Cap-tain a-bout this in-ci-dent."

"...Thanks, Doc."

"It is your pet you should be thank-ing. Their in-ter-rupt-ions may have ul-ti-mate-ly saved your life. They are a rem-ark-a-ble crea-ture." Doc digs around in his pouches until he finds one of the tasty red snacks. He offers it to Mirawynd. "Good work, lit-tle one."

Mirawynd takes the treat happily and spends the rest of the walk back to their nest sitting on their human's shoulders and nibbling on it. They don't hear the singing sounds at all anymore, and their human is acting like himself again. As soon as Doc's done making sure he's not hurt in any way, they contentedly curl up in the bottom of their human's shirt pocket for a well-deserved nap. They're sure their parent would be proud of them for how well they've protected their human from the monster.

The sound of his heartbeat and their own purring lull them to sleep almost immediately.

★

P OTTS LOOKS UP FROM HIS BOWL OF MURKY green liquid. He's gotten used to the taste, but he still hasn't worked up the courage to ask his Prelvee hosts just what the slightly sour nutrient broth they serve instead of coffee actually *is*.

At least his head is clear now. Whatever Doc gave him has certainly taken the edge off of the headache.

"So, Captain... what exactly happened down there?"

"It seems our prisoner was able to affect your mind even though you had not yet seen her and we had ensured that none of her pheromones could be spread through the ship. I apologize for the error, [Pilot-Sergeant]. I am grateful that you were not injured."

Potts takes another cautious sip and then shakes his head. "That's clear as mud, ma'am. I know Doc said she wasn't human... but then what *is* she, even? And how in the *stars* did she have me sleepwalking all over the ship?"

The Captain gestures with her facial tentacles and a few of her upper claws. "She is the Novan spy who stole a shuttle from my friend [Captain Zyzyk]. It is a talent of these sirens to entrance others to do their bidding. Usually, as far as we were aware, they require visual or physical contact first."

"Wait... she's a *Novan*? I always thought they'd be..." Potts trails off, not sure how to even describe the thought of the unseen monster he'd always assumed was in the strikers shooting at him.

The Captain waves her facial tentacles knowingly. "Less beautiful?"

"...Yeah. That."

"They are known as the most attractive species in this galaxy for a reason."

"She looked *human*, though."

"I assure you, she is not. She made you see her as more human-like than she is."

"So the woman I saw... that was just an illusion?"

"Yes, and also no." The Captain doesn't elaborate any further on that point.

"Okay..." Potts still has enough of a headache that he knows he wouldn't understand even if she did try to explain. "Why did she try to get to *me*, though?"

"My species is not as vulnerable to the siren's call as many others are. It is well known in the Alliance that it is safer to have Novan prisoners kept on our ships for that reason. I had her in a shielded cell to protect the susceptible members of my crew..." The Captain pauses to drink from her own bowl of nutrient broth, looking Potts over closely with her single large eye. "...I had not considered that she could target you from a distance."

"She's an opportunist, then? Didn't expect to have a guy like me aboard to exploit?"

"Most likely. We were not aware humans would be so vulnerable."

"How in the *stars* did no one know that? We've been involved in the war for *years* now."

"The Novans do not return prisoners," says the Captain matter-of-fact-ly, "and their ability to deceive others does not work over communication channels or long distances. There has not been another opportunity that I am aware of to learn how vulnerable humans would be."

"They'd have taken most of us by now if they could do that over a radio... or if they'd sent spies like her in to infiltrate us before they attacked." Potts sighs and absently strokes the fuzzy silver head of the Florivan kitten perching on his shoulder. Ever since he found Wyndi's dying parent on *Equinox*, his life has been a series of awkward revelations of facts he would have preferred not to learn. The idea that the Novan Armada is made up of beautiful, mesmerizing creatures like the woman down in *Frog's* brig is just another overwhelming addition to the list of things he doesn't understand about the universe he lives in.

The T'irsh-fel Captain's warning about sirens makes a lot more sense to him now.

Wyndi purrs contentedly. They reach out and take hold of his hand with their upper pair of arms. They've been even more clingy than usual ever since they woke up from their nap. Potts is sure it's because of what went on with the Novan woman earlier—although whether because they're afraid of her or being overprotective of *him*, he doesn't know.

"I am impressed with your pet's performance," says the Captain, after taking another sip from her bowl. "[Physician] tells me they were unaffected by the prisoner?"

Potts chuckles. "Well, unaffected by the illusions, for sure. The way Wyndi was carrying on, it sounded like they hated just to *look* at her."

"Such a perceptive creature could be very useful to the war effort, [Pilot-Sergeant]."

Potts can certainly see her point, but he's certain it's not his place to explain what species Mirawynd really belongs to or speculate on whether an adult Florivan could do the same thing. After all, Florivans are well-known for being a semi-eusocial species of pacifists, and the ones who serve as volunteers with the Defense Fleet have all chosen *exile* in order to help humanity protect its systems and, by extension, theirs. Somehow, he has the feeling Wyndi's parent wouldn't have been happy to see their only surviving kitten drafted as a Novan detector.

"Yeah, I can see that," Potts says at last, "but to tell you the truth, Captain, I think they were only upset because she was after *me*. Wyndi's got a bit of a thing about being left behind—I'm pretty sure they would say I'm more their pet than they are mine, you know?"

The Captain seems amused by that remark. "Perhaps. Still, I would be interested to learn more about your pet's species."

"You and me both, Captain," Potts says, still trying to get his little copilot to let go of his hand. "I don't know much myself—never saw anything like them before they decided to fly with me."

"So you have said. It is a pity. In any case, I am pleased that you will both be with my ship for a while longer."

"Same here, Captain." Potts pauses, looking back to her. "So, do you think I'll stop sleepwalking now that your prisoner knows I have this fierce little fuzzy thing guarding me?"

"I would hope so." The Captain gestures lightly with some of her upper claws. "In any case, now that we are aware of the problem, we can take steps to prevent it from happening again. [Primary Guard] assures me that she has set appropriate sound seals on the prisoner's cell."

The fearsome fuzzy thing in question finally releases Potts' hand and yawns dramatically before slipping back into his shirt pocket.

"Good." Potts can't help having to stifle a yawn of his own. "I don't like waking up in odd corners not knowing what's going on."

"Understandable. Perhaps you should go back to your cabin now and rest?"

"There's a shout." Potts stands and stretches lightly before making the appropriate salute to his hostess. "Goodnight, Captain."

"Pleasant dreams to you, Sergeant. We will speak again tomorrow."

As Potts makes his way back through *Frog's* corridors, he thinks for a moment that he hears a familiar voice singing in the distance, calling his name.

He shakes it off as his tired mind playing tricks.

After all, the sound is quickly drowned out by the purring of the kitten in his pocket. As strange as it might seem, he's glad to know that he can count on Wyndi to wake him from even the most beautiful of nightmares.

★

Part 4:
The City of Caves

SOME WEEKS AFTER THE INCIDENT WITH THE Novan prisoner, Potts finds himself in an amusingly familiar situation: sitting in his darter with his radio headset on, waiting for the person working on the little spacecraft's repairs to need his help for another check of its communications system. Emerald's been overseeing most of the repair work.

Potts counts himself lucky that there was a Prelvee officer on this ship who has experience both with human technology in general and Rudy's way of working on it in specific. It amazes him that Emerald can understand and work with his darter's systems just as well as she does with her own people's technology.

He's never read through the full operations manual for his darter himself, much less all of the addenda his grouchy mechanic friend has made in its margins since Potts was assigned to the Musketeers. It's a bit of a superstition among darter pilots that reading too much of one's darter's documentation is bad luck, though.

Whether Potts believes that or not, even he isn't certain. He knows enough about how his darter works to be able to *fly*, and that's always been enough. Thinking too hard about what's really holding the thing together is a distraction at best. The fact that the standard darter operations manual is the densest piece of technical writing he's ever encountered doesn't help either.

It's different for shuttle pilots, though, and especially for short-range rescue fliers. In Potts' experience, they tend to be the sort of people who not only know how to fly their respective craft, but are doggedly determined to know every detail of its operations and construction backwards, forwards, and upside-down. His uncles are all like that, at least, and so is his Aunt Kit. He's seen *her* take apart the majority of her own shuttle's main engine, clean every single component part, and re-assemble the thing perfectly from memory just because she was bored and felt like it needed doing. Granted, pilots like the folks who raised Potts and his brother tend not to have the luxury of someone like Rudy being around specifically to keep their birds in good order.

Emerald, as it turns out, is more of his Aunt Kit's type of person. She might not be a pilot, but she and the young engineer's assistant who's been most involved with the repairs have been pouring over the manual and repair documentation files for Potts' darter ever since he showed her how to access them. He's sure the two of them could have built a perfect replica of his darter by now if they'd wanted to.

Since the missing wing has now been recreated out of something the Prelvee call "bio-steel," the remaining repairs are all to do with reconnecting the darter's various systems. Today, it's the turn of the communications connections. Emerald is up in her normal position on the bridge to run the tests from that end, while the young engineer's assistant is somewhat precariously wedged into the darter's access port. As it turns out, of all the ship's engineers and technicians, this young lady was assigned to the project specifically because she was the youngest—and therefore, the smallest—crew member with the required skill set. In fact, she's roughly the same age as Potts himself. She might be almost twice as long as Doc, but she's still slender by Prelvee standards and able to slip at least a portion of her body into the darter's already-cramped access ports.

"[Pilot-Sergeant]," she calls, her clicks and buzzes echoing strangely from within the darter's body, "I am now ready to perform the next short-range radio test."

"Got it." Potts flips down his microphone bar and taps the appropriate buttons on his interface. "Darter 2-M-4 calling *Frog* Comms Control for a radio test; please respond."

"*Con-trol here,*" says Emerald's distinctively accented voice over his headset. "*Go a-head, Dar-ter 2-M-4.*" Even if it's only a simple set of tests for the repairs, she's still on duty, and therefore using all of her formal protocols for the call.

"I have Emerald on the line," Potts calls down to the engineer's assistant. "All set for your tests."

"Thank you, [Pilot-Sergeant]. We will begin with the lower band channels…"

After nearly half an hour of cycling through the different com-link modes and channels, and waiting in between for any quick tuning or repairs, Potts is relieved to think they've finally reached the end of the process. He doesn't know how Astral Navigators stand all of the comms checks he's heard they do every night before a jump shift. As far as he's concerned, this is the most tedious aspect of helping with repairs regardless of who's leading.

"Only one more connection to test, [Pilot-Sergeant]," the engineer's assistant calls up to him, "and then we can stop to acquire sustenance."

"There's more? I thought we already did all of them."

"This is the one [Communications Officer] instructed me to install. Please switch to the channel she marked as P-Silent in your system."

Potts does as he's told, confused but curious. "All right, *Frog* Comms Control, this is Darter 2-M-4 calling in again."

There's a momentary high-toned static whine over his headset, and then Emerald's voice comes through, albeit distantly. "*Con-trol here, Dar-ter 2-M-4.*"

"I'm told this is the last test we're doing before lunch. Now, what exactly is it?" At the mention of lunch, he feels the kitten sleeping in his breast pocket stir and cease their gentle purring. Wyndi's been napping for a while now, likely because they'd become bored with waiting for him to be free to play with them. He's just grateful that they've not decided to go exploring in the air vents again today.

"This is the en-cryp-ted chan-nel for ranged con-tact be-tween our ships. Please tell the Eng-in-eer's As-sist-ant to ad-just your fre-quen-cy con-ver-sion re-cei-ver two points low-er."

Potts covers his microphone bar for a moment as he repeats the request. "Check. So you got permission to tie me in to the Alliance comms network directly?"

The tone of Emerald's voice as she replies and the channel clears up to the same perfect reception as all the others is that same conspiratorial one she and Doc used so much when they were discussing the modifications to the pressure field generator set Potts is now wearing. *"The Cap-tain ag-greed with me that it would be wise to en-sure no one could eves-drop when the re-pairs are com-plete and you be-gin flight tests. It would be quite rude of an-y near-by No-vans to in-vite them-selves to help you test your dar-ter's fit-ness."*

"It really would." Potts laughs. It's no wonder to him now that Emerald was friends with Rudy—she's just as sneaky as he can be, but she's better at being subtle about things and getting along with officers. He takes all of that to mean that *technically*, this modification to his darter's systems is another thing that the Prelvee's rules about sharing tech with humans would normally forbid, but she's found a loophole that serves her purposes.

As he signs off of the test call, Wyndi pops their head up out of his pocket and squeaks curiously up at him. They're still blinking the sleep out of their adorable trio of golden eyes.

Potts lightly pets their fuzzy silver head. "Yes, we're done now."

Wyndi purrs happily, nuzzling into his hand.

He takes off his headset and stows it away on its charging dock, then climbs out onto the darter's new wing. The bio-steel construction is the same golden color as *Frog's* own exterior, rather than the Fleet-standard green and ivory of the rest of the craft. Aesthetics aside, though, it's a perfect replica. It even has the same light bounce when Potts is standing on it that he's come to expect. Testing that is a good opportunity to stretch his legs out, too. After dealing with the mild stiffness in his muscles from sitting still for so long, he leans down towards where the engineer's assistant is closing up the access port. "Thanks for your help with all of this."

"It is my delight to assist you, [Pilot-Sergeant]." She waves a friendly facial tentacle at him. "This is a rare opportunity to study your people's technology first-claw."

Potts is puzzled by her interest for a moment, until he remembers that the whole reason the Defense Fleet's Darter Corps is considered important to the war effort and the Alliance's strategy is that neither of their highly advanced alien allies had ever come upon the idea of live-piloted fighter craft. He's never heard all of the details of it, but the Musketeers have told him a few stories from their test pilot days about how shocked the Prelvee and T'irshfel liaisons were to see darters in action.

"Well, you're welcome to study my darter as much as you like, as long as you can get her flying again." Potts helps Wyndi up to their usual perch on his shoulder and then slips down onto the floor. "You're having lunch with us today, right?"

"I would be honored, [Pilot-Sergeant]." She clicks several of her free upper claws together happily. "In fact, now that this task is done, it is the end of my duty shift. Let me put my tools away, and I will join you."

Wyndi waves their fluffy tail with excitement and squeaks towards his ear.

"Yes, I *did* say 'lunch'. Now don't go wandering off before we get there, and I'll let you have first choice of snacks. Okay?"

The Florivan kitten squeaks a cheerful affirmative and does their best to sit still on his shoulder. Their tail never stops swishing against his neck, though. As far as Wyndi is concerned, mealtimes are serious business.

★

As they're nearing the infirmary and thus their lunch destination, a lull in the ongoing conversation about darter flight and the young engineer's assistant's interests in human culture and technology sparks a thought Potts had been meaning to bring up for some time.

"Say," he begins, looking up at the distinctly gold-speckled carapace and face of his companion, "how would you feel if I gave you a nickname? We've spent enough time working together that it feels weird to only call you by your job title."

She clicks most of her upper claws together happily. "I would be honored, [Pilot-Sergeant]. Informal names are a very human thing, but I can see why your people use them, since your language is so limited."

Potts stifles a chuckle. She's right about that last bit. He'd finally had to ask Emerald recently why the translation chip in his ear always seemed to edit names or titles and put emphasis on them. According to her, it's because in the Prelvee language and customs, one's formal title, given name-sound, lineage, gender, and other details are all encapsulated into a specific word-form that's nearly untranslatable in some aspects; for ease of use, she'd programmed his chip to paraphrase all of it into just the title. Otherwise, every single time anyone was referred to by "name", he'd hear something like Emerald's "[untranslatable name], third-ranked un-partnered female of [untranslatable lineage group], belonging to *Song-of-the-Midnight-Frog* as Communications Officer." Emerald had a point about how confusing and repetitive that could get, considering that she was an example of a Prelvee with a *short* "name."

"Well, if you're okay with it, then... how does 'Dusty' sound to you?"

She looks down at him with a curious wave of two facial tentacles. "You wish to nickname me for small particles of airborne detritus?"

Potts runs a hand through the back of his hair sheepishly. "That's what it translated to for you? Ah, sorry... I was thinking of it as a shorter form of 'Gold dust'—I guess 'small particles of gold,' if that doesn't translate clearly—because of your patterning. Kind of on the same theme as Emerald's?"

After a moment, the engineer's assistant clicks her upper claws together again. "I understand, [Pilot-Sergeant].

That translation is much more pleasing. I will happily accept this nickname!”

“I’m glad you like it, Dusty.” Potts grins. They’ve reached the infirmary door now. “Come on, you can tell Doc and Emerald you’re properly a human’s friend now.”

As soon as the door slides open, Wyndi leaps down from his shoulder and scampers towards the lavatory, squeaking excitedly for Potts to follow. They know the routine for mealtimes means washing all of their hands, after all.

Potts chases after his little Florivan copilot, glad to be once again in the lower-gravity environment where he *can* chase after them. Even as he’s negotiating with the flash dryer, he can hear the excited conversation of his newly nicknamed friend with his two older ones.

He chuckles softly to himself. If he’d have known how happy Dusty would be about it, he’d have given her the nickname weeks ago when she helped him back to his quarters and he first thought of it.

★

I T'S A BITTERSWEET DAY FOR POTTS AND HIS LITTLE Florivan companion when the time comes for them to say goodbye to *Song-of-the-Midnight-Frog* and her crew. They've finally arrived at the system known to human astral cartographers as Groombridge 34, just a touch under twelve light years away from Sol.

The system's pair of variable red dwarf stars host five major planets and several dozen planetoids between them. Because Groombridge 34 sits on the edge of the fifty-light-year-wide disputed zone between the Novan Imperium's claims and the T'irsh-fel and Prelvee territories, its singular naturally inhabitable planet in the system is home to the closest Alliance base to humanity's stars.

This "super Earth" type world is tidally locked in orbit of the two stars, securely within their combined habitable zone. Its continents are arranged in such a way that the dark side of the planet is covered in a dense ice sheet, but the ring of land masses around this enjoy a wide range of climates ranging towards hot, dense jungles on the edge where day meets night. If there was ever a world that could comfortably support both member species of the Alliance and their drastically opposite environmental preferences, it's this one. They call it "Jewel-Eye," for the way it looks when seen from space.

Currently, Potts and Wyndi are in a good position to see just how much the planet looks like a massive sapphire eye from above. The central hub of Jewel-Eye's largest orbital spaceport has a high-domed polyglass ceiling, allowing for incredible views whenever one chances to look up. Neither of them are stargazing at the moment, though. They're too busy saying their goodbyes to their friends from *Frog's* crew who've come with them this far.

"Don't worry, [Pilot-Sergeant]," says the Captain, lightly gesturing with her facial tentacles, "I am sure that we will all cross paths again. After all, I believe I owe you a rematch at checkers after our last game."

"I look forward to that, Ma'am." Potts is surprised, in a way, just how much he's realizing that he's going to miss spending his evenings with the Captain. If anyone had told him before he left Teegarden that he'd one day be such good friends with a high-ranking Prelvee officer, he'd have laughed.

Doc sets a gentle claw on his shoulder, not-so-subtly inspecting his support braces one last time. "I will miss hav-ing you a-round, Ju-li-an. The in-fir-ma-ry will be ver-y qui-et with-out you and your pet."

Potts reaches up to pat the claw briefly. "I know we'll miss you, Doc. Wyndi especially..." He looks up to the kitten who's still perching on his friend's head. "I don't think they understand what's going on."

"Your pet is smart, [Pilot-Sergeant]." The Captain leans over to ruffle Wyndi's ears with one of her claws. They happily allow her to pick them up and give them some farewell cuddles. "They will adapt to the change just as you do." She passes the kitten to him with an air of reluctance.

Potts takes his little copilot and tucks them into the breast pocket of his shirt. He makes a point of petting Wyndi's ears to settle them down. The last thing he needs right now is for them to decide to go exploring the orbital station.

"We will keep in touch," says Emerald. Something in the glint of her single large eye tells him that this is a *promise* rather than an empty farewell platitude. If anyone is capable of finding a way to keep in touch across long distances and military protocol barriers, it's her. "Do give my re-gards to Ru-dy when you see him a-gain? I left sev-er-al notes for him in your dar-ter doc-u-men-tat-ion fi-les that I would like to hear his re-sponse to some-day."

Potts grins. "I'll be sure to do that, Emerald. I know he'll be grateful it was you and Dusty mending the bird instead of me."

Dusty lets out a soft version of the Prelvee laughing buzzes. She doesn't talk much when higher-ranked officers are around, especially the Captain. Unlike the other Prelvee from Frog's crew, though, she isn't here to say goodbye. Since there are still repairs to be made on his darter and she's in a position to be temporarily transferred to continue working on that, Dusty is accompanying him and Wyndi for the next leg of their journey.

"Oh!" Doc waves most of his facial tentacles at someone approaching from behind Potts. "My col-league has arrived to collect you, Ju-li-an."

Dusty turns to look, then darts over to greet the new arrival with an excited entwining of upper claws. The older female Prelvee who's just joined them is the same size as Emerald, and displays a striking match in color and patterning to Dusty.

As the two of them finish their personal greetings, the older female bows politely to the Captain. "I am pleased to see you again, [Captain of *Song-of-the-Midnight-Frog*], and honored to be tasked with caring for the young human you've acquired."

The Captain dips her head briefly. "It is equally pleasing to see you, [Physician of *My-Love-is-the-Stars*]."

At an almost imperceptible gesture from the Captain, Doc steps forward with a deep bow. "My dear col-league," he says, indicating Potts with a sweep of his upper claws, "on be-half of my Cap-tain, may I in-tro-duce Ju-li-an Potts, Pil-lot-Ser-geant of the Sol Co-al-it-ion De-fense Fleet's Sec-ond Dar-ter Squad-ron and S-C-V *Sur-ni-a*, un-der the com-mand of Cap-tain I-rene Brent-wood. As his doc-tor, I now give him in-to your care."

Potts forces himself not to break into a laugh. Hearing his full introduction in the Prelvee formal style always amuses him. To hear Doc talk, he must be someone terribly important. Of course, if his name and description were translatable into the Prelvee language properly, it would only take two words at most to say all of that.

The Captain makes a genial gesture with her facial tentacles. "You will find [Pilot-Sergeant] to be a most entertaining companion. Please extend my greetings and compliments to [Captain of *My-Love-is-the-Stars*] when you present him to her."

"I will be sure to." The lady physician offers her claw to Potts. "Forgive me for not being as well-versed in your language as my colleague is, [Pilot-Sergeant]. Perhaps you will help me practice?"

Potts takes the claw with all of the ceremonial politeness he can muster and lightly dips his head. "I'd be glad to, Ma'am." At a small curious squeak from his pocket, he adds, "and this is Mirawynd. They're sort of my traveling companion."

Little Wyndi waves happily to the lady physician. If Potts weren't still stroking their ears to encourage them to stay settled in his pocket, he's sure they'd already be trying to climb up to the top of her head.

"I am pleased to meet you too, little one," she says, waving her facial tentacles genially. "My colleagues have told me about your pet, [Pilot-Sergeant], but I will admit they are far cuter in person."

With one last round of fond farewells, Potts and Dusty follow *Love's* physician out to the docking ring of the orbital station. Once they're walking down a quieter corridor, the physician turns her eye towards Dusty.

"It does please me that you will be with my ship for a time, little sister. I have been too long out in the stars without family close by." The translation voice in Potts' ear is accented differently now than when she was speaking to *Frog's* Captain. He's not sure if it's a completely different dialect she's speaking, or just a change in tone. He almost thinks she's making a light hissing sound along with the buzzes and clicks.

Dusty's response is in the same accent and cadence. "I am most pleased!" she looks to Potts with an excited clicking of her upper claws, switching back into her usual mode of speech. "[Pilot-Sergeant], I doubt you were told, but this is my eldest sister! She left for her journeying studies before I went through my first adult molt. Thank you for giving me an opportunity to spend time with her."

Potts grins. "I thought I saw a family resemblance, Dusty, but I wasn't sure if I should ask."

Before her sister can even finish asking, Dusty has already excitedly explained the correct translation of her nickname. *Love's* physician seems quite pleased by it.

"It suits you," she says to Dusty, with that same hissing accent. Looking back to Potts with a wave of her facial tentacles, she switches to the standard Prelvee tones to add, "As we will be spending a lot of time in each other's company, [Pilot-Sergeant], you are most welcome to choose a nickname for me as well."

Something about her body language tells Potts that she's excited about the notion. He decides he likes this new doctor already. "Well, it's sort of traditional to call a physician 'Doc' if they're the only one around... but since I've already used that with our mutual friend, I'll have to pick something else for you." Looking between the two sisters, he impulsively adds, "Goldie works, since you two are a matched set."

Dusty clicks her claws together happily. "That's the other half of mine, isn't it?"

"That was the thought." Potts nods.

"I like it," says the newly-nicknamed Dr. Goldie, "thank you!" She turns down a side corridor, gesturing for Potts and Dusty to follow. "Now, [Pilot-Sergeant], your quarters aboard *My-Love-Is-The-Stars* are in roughly same position they were on our sister ship *Song-of-the-Midnight-Frog*, near to the infirmary. They have already been prepared to be comfortable for you."

"Good to know," Potts replies.

"Now, as our ship will be docked here for another week while some essential maintenance tasks are completed, I had made arrangements to visit the surface during that time so that I could assist some colleagues of mine who are working there. Would you be interested in joining me?" Dr. Goldie looks down to him curiously.

Potts doesn't hesitate in his answer. What pilot in their right mind could pass up a chance like this? "That'd be stellar—if you don't mind having me along, that is."

"I'd be pleased to bring you." She gives Dusty a light nudge, switching into their hiss-accented dialect. "And you as well, little sister. I will make arrangements for you to join us—there is a proper spring system at the place we will be visiting."

Dusty clicks her upper claws together happily. "Oh, yes, please! It has been too long since I could swim in surface waters."

Potts glances down at his pocket, where Wyndi is still contentedly sitting with their head sticking up to observe the world. He's somehow sure that if they could understand what the two Prelvee are saying, they'd be just as excited as Dusty to join in on this new little tangent of their adventure. Becoming the first human and Florivan to visit one of the Alliance's planets is a milestone he wasn't expecting, but it certainly beats sitting around waiting for a ship to leave port.

★

POTTS HAS BEEN ENJOYING HIMSELF IMMENSELY since his new Prelvee minder took custody of him. Dr. Goldie is a pleasant person to be around, for one. She reminds him more than a little of his dear friend Reba's adoptive mother, Dr. Kiely. Their choice of profession isn't the only similarity; baring a few obvious differences in species and culture, the two women have the same sort of lighthearted spirit and easygoing manner.

More than that, though, for the first time in more than a month, he's had a chance to fly. Or, at least, to hang out with a fellow pilot and chat while they fly. The shuttle he's in now is hardly a darter, but the young Prelvee lady who's flying it is just as sparky as any good pilot Potts has ever encountered. After *Love's* surface transport shuttle took off, she was insistent that Potts join her up in the spherical craft's domed cockpit for the rest of the flight. He was more than happy to take her up on the offer and let Dusty have a chance to catch up with her big sister in the passenger compartment below them.

So it is that for the last few hours, Potts has been sitting beside the neatly coiled sapphire-pink flashed lower segments of his new friend on the edge of her seating cushion, enjoying the view and talking shop. Since it's only him and his companions she's ferrying down to the surface today, the pilot has even been thoughtful enough to set the shuttle's arti-grav to something more comfortable for her human passenger.

"And if you look in this direction," says the pilot, gesturing with one of her facial tentacles towards a particular landmass on the growing planet ahead of them, "Our destination is in view now. It is on the northern side of this continent, at the junction of the two large river systems."

"I see it." Potts tries to focus his eyes on that area. It's a bit difficult, with a long, fluffy silver tail swishing across them every few seconds. Wyndi has been awake and curiously exploring the shuttle for some time now, but they'd just recently returned from playing with Dusty and Dr. Goldie and immediately taken to perching on top of Potts' head. Apparently, his little copilot enjoys stargazing and planet vistas just as much as he does.

Without glancing away from her instruments for more than a moment, the pilot leans over and gently uses two of her upper claws to pick Wyndi up and turn them around to face the same way he is. "There," she says, more to the kitten than to him, "now you can see it."

Wyndi squeaks happily, then leans down to look into Potts' eyes and squeak some more. They point in the general direction with both of their left hands.

"Yes, Wyndi." Potts laughs. "I see it just fine now that your tail isn't in the way." He looks back to his new friend. "So it's in the jungles on the edge of the twilight ring?"

"That is correct. The site is one of the research outposts my people have established supplemental to our military presence. It is called the City of Caves." She pauses to attend to some alert or other on her secondary interface. "The site is quite remote compared to our other bases. Pleasant to visit, but the landing zone is rather small due to the surrounding mountains."

Potts surveys the grand aerial view before him. "Reminds me a bit of home, from this distance."

"Does it?"

"Yeah—I grew up at a wilderness aid station of sorts back at Teegarden-Millefleur Prime. We were right in the middle of three different major nature preserve areas, and one of them has a big river system like that." Potts isn't sure how much his new friend knows about human worlds, so he adds, "Prime is one of Millefleur's moons. It's essentially an Earth-size world with a natural biosphere, so other than the original colony sites, it's been mostly left alone so it can be studied."

The pilot makes a soft clicking with several of her upper claws. "That is similar to the arrangements that have been made for Jewel-Eye. Although we do have a number of significantly developed worlds within our core systems, most of those were adjusted from lifeless ones. Naturally inhabitable planets and moons are the galaxy's rarest treasures, after all. It is a delight of my work that I am able to see them like this."

Potts would nod his agreement, but there's a Florivan kitten perched on his head who he knows will start fussing if he dislodges them unexpectedly. "Well, remind me at some point and I'll give you comm codes so that if you ever wind up out at Teegarden, you can meet up with my family—they're all pilots, so I'd bet you'd hit it off with them. They know Millefleur's moons better than anyone." He doesn't mention that Eddie would certainly be *thrilled* to encounter a Prelvee for himself, entomologist that he is. He'll warn his new friend about that later.

"There is no one better to learn a place from!" She taps a few buttons on her console. "Now, we'll be entering the atmosphere in a few moments, so I need to deploy our wings. If you look over to your right, you'll be able to see them extend."

Potts watches as a large panel on the side of the shuttle's spherical body slides back. Slowly, a segmented two-tiered wing extends out of it, complete with a pair of sleek rotary propellers on the front. When the whole of the structure has emerged, it appears nearly seamless.

"Now that," he says, glancing over at the matching wing on the other side of the shuttle, "is impressive. I'd bet if my darter could stow her wings like that, Rudy wouldn't get onto me nearly as much about tapping them."

"It is convenient to stow them, certainly. Our shuttles take up far less space this way."

Wyndi, apparently fascinated by the shuttle's newly deployed wings, leaps off of Potts' head and scampers over to the rim of the cockpit's translucent polyglass dome.

They squeak excitedly for a few moments, then disappear down the access hatch to the passenger compartment.

"I take it your pet has gone to alert the other passengers that we will be landing soon?"

Potts laughs. "I think so. They like squeaking at Dusty about... well, everything, apparently. I don't think they understand her any more than she understands them, though."

"Cute." She turns to call in to her flight radio and check in with their destination.

Potts enjoys watching the view of the surface growing closer for as long as he can. Ultimately, though, he has to return to the secured seats of the passenger compartment for the shuttle's landing procedure. As much as he'd have liked to see that, he's more than familiar with safety protocols that need to be followed. Even with the Prelvee's advanced technology for arti-grav and inertial stabilization, it's always better to err on the side of caution and make sure that everyone is strapped in for a landing. It's comforting to see that the Prelvee feel the same way about that.

Still, he hopes that his new friend was serious earlier about her offer to show him how to fly the shuttle at some point during the long trip to Kapteyn. It might not be a darter, but the little winged sphere is still fascinating. Whether he'd ever have occasion to actually use such a skill doesn't matter. He's a pilot. Any chance he gets to fly something new, he's taking it.

★

AN HOUR OR SO AFTER THEY LAND, POTTS FINDS himself accompanying his Prelvee friends to dinner with the senior staff of the xenoarchaeological research project which takes up most of the City of Caves outpost. Out of all the unexpected facts of the situation, the most surprising is that there's an archaeological site here in the first place for them to be studying.

The climate at the outpost is more similar than he expected to the conditions on *Song-of-the-Midnight-Frog*. It's humid, for one, and just barely within the levels of heat Potts can personally tolerate. He's glad now that he'd left his pilot's thermal compression layers stashed on the rear seat of his darter before they departed, but he wishes he'd switched back to the shorts he's been in the habit of wearing on the ship. It's nice to have his uniform trousers to protect his legs from brushing against the alien plants growing along the paths, but they're still a bit too warm for his taste. His pilot's jacket, too, is technically unnecessary for these conditions, but he's got *that* slung over one shoulder. Darter pilots don't leave their jackets behind easily.

"So this place really had native sapients once?" Potts looks up to Dr. Goldie with startled wonder. What he's seen of the outpost since they landed has been mostly the Prelvee-style habitation buildings that cluster around the runway and the docks along the stretch of river separating City of Caves from the denser parts of the jungle. He hasn't encountered anything yet that looks like it was made by anyone else.

"It did," she replies, gesturing with several of her right-side upper claws towards the network of large domed tents they're approaching. "The surface ruins are obscured by the protective structures the team has erected."

Wyndi, who's currently perching on top of the doctor's head, squeaks excitedly and leans down towards her large eye's field of view. They point towards something in the trees beyond the path that Potts can't see from his vantage point.

Dr. Goldie turns in that direction, waving a facial tentacle up at the Florivan kitten. "Yes, little one, I see him. That is my friend [Professor Zynn], who leads the project. He is expecting us."

As she leads him and Dusty around a bend in the path and towards what seems to be the entryway to the tent complex, Potts is startled to see a T'irsh-fel gentleman waiting for them. His ruff of feathers separating his eye stalks from the rest of his thick-scaled body is bright yellow, and all but two of his eyes are fixed on the approaching group. Along the mid-line of his back, he's wearing what appears to be an iridescent black backpack of some kind, with three bands running around his belly to secure it.

"Welcome back to City of Caves, friend!" Potts hears the T'irsh-fel's telepathic voice say when they reach him, *"And welcome to your companions. This humble self is called Zynn, Professor of Xenoarchaeology and head of the City of Caves Project. Our team is most pleased to have visitors, including wayward humans."*

Dr. Goldie leans down for a moment to affectionately pat the T'irsh-fel's equivalent of a shoulder with one of her facial tentacles. "It is good to see you too, [Professor Zynn] This young one is my sister, [Engineer's Assistant], and this is our friend [Pilot-Sergeant]."

"Julian Potts, sir," Potts supplies, making a small bow to match Dusty's gesture upon being introduced, "and the little fuzzy critter is Mirawynd. They're sort of my traveling companion."

Wyndi squeaks and waves excitedly when their name is mentioned. Then, for reasons known only to themself, they scamper down Dr. Goldie's back and hop to Potts' shoulder, where they squeak at him some more and gesture to the T'irsh-fel.

The T'irsh-fel professor fluffs his ruff of feathers. *"This humble self is most pleased to meet you, Julian Potts. Our honored friend the doctor has relayed some of your story, but this humble self is not the only member of the team who is eager to hear more of it."*

Potts can't help liking the fellow already. There's something about the warm tone of Professor Zynn's telepathic projection that's immediately endearing. It reminds him a bit of his brother Eddie, although he's not sure why. "I'll be happy to tell you all about it over dinner."

"*Excellent.*" Professor Zynn turns and telekinetically opens the flap of the tent door. "*Come along, friends. This humble self will orient you to the site on our way to the team's eating area.*"

As soon as he passes through the doorway, Potts is struck by how much cooler it is inside. The interior of the tent complex is still well-lit from translucent skylights built into the tops of each tent's domed roof, but the temperature of the lightly shaded area within is far more comfortable by human standards. It's still quite humid, though.

From the entry tent, they follow a well-marked path down the side of a huge area of excavated ruins with terraces of carefully measured dig sites trailing down into a massive sinkhole at the center. Potts catches the flash of light reflecting off water somewhere deep within that. Paths down through the ruins are marked with ropes and brightly colored flags.

"*This is the main above-ground site,*" Professor Zynn explains as he leads them towards another tent-flap door on the other side of the excavated area. "*We believe this was the trading and working hub for the inhabitants. The majority of domestic spaces we have discovered are underground, built as additions to the natural cave network which underlies this region.*"

"It's amazing," says Potts.

"I have seen your images from when you were assigned here," says Dusty, looking up to her sister, "but I do not think I ever recognized just how extensive the site was."

"This is only the main part of it." Dr. Goldie gestures with one of her facial tentacles. "The secondary aboveground site is on the other side of the habitation and laboratory tents."

"This humble self will arrange for a proper tour of the ruins for our visitors tomorrow." Professor Zynn telekinetically raises the next door flap for the four of them to pass under. *"For tonight, our work is concluded, and it is time for companionship and food."*

Potts sits between Dr. Goldie and Dusty at the long, low table on the end reserved for guests. The four other resident members of the xenoarchaeological team are arranged on either side, a colorful even mixture of T'irsh-fel and Prelvee scientists with Professor Zynn at their head. From what he understands, there are a dozen or so others who rotate through the site during the day, but all of them reside at the part of City of Caves which is built up around the landing zone and docks.

Thankfully, most of the dishes laid out for his Prelvee friends are things he recognizes as safe to eat. Dr. Goldie had apparently sent word ahead to her colleagues about human dietary restrictions, since she's made a point of gathering morsels from the more unfamiliar plates for him. The T'irsh-fel food has a stranger appearance by far: it looks like little more than different forms of moss, lichen, or algae artfully arranged onto the plates.

He does his best not to stare too much and to focus on remembering his manners with his small set of Prelvee eating hooks, but watching a T'irsh-fel eat is a peculiar sort of fascinating. Potts still hasn't determined what sort of mouth they really have, or where it would be among all the feathers that obscure the place where their eye stalks meet the rest of their bodies. Still, as the bits of green and grey plant—or whatever it is—float up from their carefully-formed rosettes and wind themselves into bundles before disappearing down into the depths of the feathers is hard not to watch with interest.

Wyndi is clearly fascinated by the dance of food morsels in the air too. It's taken all of Potts' influence with the kitten just to convince them to stay sitting on their mealtime napkin and not bounce around trying to chase after the floating food.

The T'irsh-fel lady with the purple ruff sitting on the other side of Dusty seems to notice this. She turns an eye-stalk towards Potts and floats one of the Prelvee fruit biscuits from a plate nearer to her in his direction, saying, *"would your pet like something more to eat? They are very polite to wait for someone to share with them."*

"Wyndi is an adorable bottomless pit when it comes to snacks. Thank you." Potts moves to set down the root vegetable bun he was eating, but the fruit biscuit continues floating past him and hovers directly in front of Wyndi instead.

The kitten looks over to him and squeaks excitedly.

Potts stifles a laugh. "Yes, Wyndi, that's for you. Go ahead."

With the amount of happy tail-waving and mid-nibble squeaks, it's clear that his little copilot enjoys the novelty of floating food. The T'irsh-fel lady only loosens her telekinetic grip on the fruit biscuit once Wyndi has had an opportunity to bite it in the air a few times. Once they've properly caught their snack, they make a triumphant show of breaking off half of what's left of it and setting it on the edge of Potts' plate. Wyndi looks up to him with an expectant squeak.

Potts carefully lifts the morsel with his eating hooks and pops it into his mouth. "Thank you."

"It's adorable that they insist on sharing their food with you, [Pilot-Sergeant], really," says Dr. Goldie. "Did you train them to do that?"

"Oh, no, Wyndi just started that on their own." Potts pauses to take a sip of water from his drinking bowl. "I don't know why they do it, really. The only time they don't is when someone ties a treat to a string for them to chase."

"*They are a fascinating little creature,*" says the purple-ruffed T'irsh-fel. "*And quite well-mannered.*" A neatly wrapped ball of algae and lichen bits disappears beneath the junction of her feathers.

"Doc spent a lot of time educating both of us on that."

"[Frog's Physician] did an excellent job, then." The small rust-colored Prelvee gentleman on the other side of Dr. Goldie makes a pleased gesture with one of his facial tentacles. "As he did with his work to ensure you could survive visiting us."

Potts glances down at the shimmer of the pressure field over his arm and the iridescent bar of the brace running from his wrist to his elbow. "I'd have to agree with that."

Being on Jewel-Eye's surface is just as severe gravity-wise as anything he had to deal with back on *Frog* or the orbital station. The only difference, really, is that the gravity here is natural.

"This humble self is still amazed that you have survived so much in such a short period of time, honored Pilot-Sergeant," says Professor Zynn from the other end of the table. *"But then, stories have often reached us, even here, about how remarkably resilient humans are despite your obvious frailty."*

Potts shrugs. "I'm just lucky, I guess?" He'd spent the first half of the dinner doing his best to tell a reasonably acceptable version of how he and Wyndi came to be hitchhiking between Prelvee ships. Thankfully, the researchers of the professor's team have been far more interested in the fact that they have a human visitor at all than in picking apart any of the inconsistencies in the story. Still, he's had enough of talking about himself for one day. "Personally, I'm still amazed that there used to be native sapients here."

"Our peoples were surprised too, when we first discovered these ruins," says the rust-colored Prelvee gentleman beside Dr. Goldie. "This remains the only site we know that was built by Jewel-Eye's Diggers."

"Diggers?" Potts echoes.

"It is an affectionate nickname the team here has for the honored subjects of our research," Professor Zynn explains. He pauses thoughtfully while he levitates a mesmerizing sphere of water up from his drinking bowl and slips it towards his hidden mouth. *"While we have found some samples of their writing, there are not enough yet to piece together a translation and determine what they called*

themselves. This humble self hopes that one day we will find enough of their records to better understand what happened to them."

"The Diggers were incredible craftspeople and builders," adds a pink-feathered T'irsh-fel sitting near the Professor. *"It is deeply regrettable that we arrived on their world too late to meet them."*

Potts tilts his head curiously. "How long ago do you think they disappeared, then?"

"At least several centuries. Perhaps considerably longer." The deep copper-green Prelvee lady who's remained silent for most of the meal finally turns her eye toward Potts. "They have been gone long enough that the jungle has completely overgrown and destroyed most of their above-ground structures. If one of the survey teams investigating the geology of this area had not stumbled into the developed portions of the great cave here, we would never have known that the Diggers had existed at all."

"Our purpose now," says Professor Zynn, *"is to learn all that we can about them. It is a unique opportunity. Many of the sites we have investigated in the past were victims of the Novan expansion. To study and record a people who seem to have met a natural end is a gratifying change."*

Potts stares at him incredulously for a minute. "You've had to study civilizations the Novans wiped out?"

"It is an unfortunate reality of the war our Alliance has been fighting for so long." The rust-colored Prelvee gentleman makes a sad gesture with his facial tentacles. "We and our colleagues across the stars are often called in to assess whether the lost cultures found on worlds the Novan Imperium has once claimed were already extinct when they arrived. More often than not, it is clear that the Novans were the cause of their destruction. We do what we can to preserve the memory of the victims."

Potts looks down into his drinking bowl for a long time during the silence that follows. He wonders, for a moment, if the Admiral knows this detail about the people they're trying to keep out of humanity's systems. Then again, maybe knowing the Novan track record for exterminating sapient species is the whole reason the Alliance brought them into the war in the first place.

Beside him, he feels a tiny soft-furred hand tap on his arm. He turns his head to see Wyndi looking up at him with wide, concerned eyes.

Potts reaches over to give the kitten's ears a reassuring scratch. "So," he asks, looking to change the subject to something less ominous, "what were the Diggers like, then?"

"*Well!*" says the purple-ruffed T'irsh-fel beside Dusty, "*for one thing, they were about your size, and we believe they were insectivores!*" The tone of her telepathic voice betrays a relief at the turn of the conversation.

"*Indeed,*" her pink-feathered colleague chimes in, "*we have not yet discovered any physical remains, but the artwork in the less degraded sections of the lower habitation zone gives remarkably clear suggestions as to their forms.*"

"We've even found caches of preserved insects," says the rust-colored Prelvee fellow. "Remarkably, some of the species I've identified among the caches were clearly brought from other regions. There's a rather clear indication that the Diggers had cross-continental trade networks, even if we haven't discovered any of their other cities as yet."

Potts happily passes the time listening to the three more eager members of the research team talk about everything they've come to know about Jewel-Eye's native sapients. He makes a mental note to give the Prelvee he's mentally referring to as "Rusty" his brother's contact codes before he leaves the planet. Hopefully, sometime after the war is over, his new entomologist friend will have a chance to get together with Eddie and talk about bugs and their respective nutritional value all he likes. Potts personally could have done without knowing a few of those details about the things that buzz around the jungle he's in.

As far as the unexpected turns of his and Wyndi's little adventure go, this one is shaping up to be a nice change of pace.

★

MIRAWYND IS AN EXCEPTIONALLY HAPPY Florivan kitten.

They've spent their whole life until now on one starship or another. Over the last few days, though, they've gotten to join their human in exploring a *planet*. Or, at least, a small piece of one, but even this is bigger than anywhere Mirawynd has ever been.

Mirawynd's human has spent his time following Dr. Goldie or the nice Professor Zynn around, seeing all the different parts of the ruins under the research tent. Mirawynd, of course, has been with him. They are curious about everything, and would like to explore into every nook and cranny they come across, but after their encounter with the monster up on the ship that tried to take their human away, they're even more protective of him than ever. They never scamper out of a clear line of sight from him.

Mirawynd is still amazed by the *bigness* of things here. Beyond the tent, the world stretches on for what seems like forever. Above the treetops of the jungle surrounding the outpost, there's a blue expanse of a sky that generally feels like it wants to swallow them. They know there are stars beyond the blue, but they don't understand why they can only feel them. Mirawynd's never been anywhere before that they couldn't see the stars whenever they looked for them.

Today, they and their human are exploring as far as a little clearing outside the cover of the tents where Professor Zynn has been surveying some newly uncovered ruins. Most of the new site is overgrown with plants around the edges of the clearing, but the scattered carved stones from ancient buildings are hard to miss. There's even one building that's half-intact, although it's mostly hidden under the roots of the biggest tree of all the trees Mirawynd has encountered in their short time on the planet.

Dr. Goldie and Dusty have been with them most of the time since they arrived, but today the two of them have gone to explore and swim at a nearby spring. For reasons Mirawynd still doesn't understand, their human was eager to come help Professor Zynn with his survey rather than go swimming with their friends.

Mirawynd's human is being helpful and holding the shiny reflector sphere in the center of the clearing that Professor Zynn's hovering beeping things use to make marks. As far as Mirawynd has been able to gather from their human's side of the conversation, Professor Zynn is measuring the area so that a tent can be erected around it to keep everything safe while the team cleans the dirt and jungle off of the crumbled stones. The tents do something to make it cooler so the feathers-and-eyes people like the Professor can work without getting overheated, but Mirawynd doesn't quite understand what that's about. They've learned that the strange backpacks the Professor and all of his people they've seen wear are *cold*, though, and not fun to try to climb on.

Mirawynd has been amusing themself by scampering back and forth between Professor Zynn and their human. They don't know what the Professor's measurements are saying, but in terms of kitten-scamper paces, the clearing is about twice the size of the hangar on *Frog* where their human's darter lived. They can't hear anything that Professor Zynn is saying to their human, unfortunately. There's only so much Mirawynd can learn from their human's side of the ongoing conversation. They're getting better at understanding the hard-shell people's language of buzzes and clicks, although most of the words they know best are about food. The silent talking the eyes-and-feathers people do is a bit annoying, in comparison, because Mirawynd can't hear any of it unless someone decides to say something directly *to* them.

They'd spent a bit of the morning napping in the little nest their human made for them out of his ever-present jacket in the sheltered area of the intact building. That was nice, but Mirawynd is awake now. There's too much of interest to a kitten for them to nap for very long at a time around here.

As they bounce back towards their human again, a drop of something wet plinks down onto the mossy ground right in front of them. Mirawynd halts in their scampering, trying to find the thing so they can figure out what it is. It seems to be gone altogether.

They start to move towards their human again, only for another drop to brush the fluff on the tip of their long prehensile tail. Mirawynd whirls around to catch it, but it's gone again. As soon as they've turned around, they hear a plink behind them again.

They look over to their human and squeak to get his attention. For some reason, he's *laughing*. Mirawynd barely has a moment to fix all three of their eyes on him in annoyance before their stare is interrupted by a drop going plink right on their nose. This startles them enough to make them leap up as high as they can into the air.

Mirawynd makes a fine game of chasing the drops that are falling from the sky now. If they can only catch one, they can take it to their human and make him explain what it is. That'll show him for laughing at them, for sure.

Catching droplets is harder than they thought. Each one disappears as soon as it plinks on the ground, leaving the fur on their hands damp and empty. They scamper all over the clearing trying to catch just one of the things, but it's all in vain.

The game is fun, though, right up until the point where the drops start coming down in greater numbers. They skitter closer to their human now and squeak at him. Usually, a shower like that is *his* doing, because it's time for cleaning. He doesn't seem to have remembered to turn on the warmth for the water.

"No, Wyndi," he says, "I can't turn the sky off for you. It's just rain."

Mirawynd tries to pounce another drop as it lands. They wind up splashing into the growing puddle at their human's feet instead. They look up to him with a soggy squeak. They've enjoyed chasing the raindrops, but now they're cold and wet.

"It's okay, let's get you dried off." Their human scoops them up out of the puddle just as the sky water starts pouring down. He's all soggy too now. That's mostly the rain's fault, but Mirawynd's efforts to use his shirt as a towel haven't helped matters.

Mirawynd is annoyed to find that even his pocket is soggy. They get into it anyway, since their human is holding his hand over the top of their head to keep more water from pouring down on them.

"Hey, Professor? I'm going to duck out of the rain before Wyndi gets chilled. Let me know when you're ready to head back to the tents?" At some unheard confirmation from Professor Zynn, their human waves to him and starts walking towards the most intact part of the ruined structure they'd measured this morning. It at least has something of a roof left on one side, made of a single slab of stone balanced perfectly on those of the walls around them.

Mirawynd had enjoyed exploring the little building's uncovered parts with their human and Professor Zynn when they first arrived on the site. They even climbed up the tree roots that are really holding everything together and chased a big orange-winged bug thing for a while before their human whistled.

Now, though? They're just glad the mossy inside of the place is *dry*. They squeak up at their human and try to shake the water out of their fur.

"Hey!" He holds his free hand up in front of his face to stop the splash of water. "Wyndi, what have I told you about doing that while I'm holding you?"

Mirawynd looks up at him and squeaks innocently. They set about carefully grooming their fur to squeeze the rest of the water out so they can dry. Their human has apparently not come prepared with a towel for this adventure.

He sets them down on a tree root near the nice round slab of rock on the floor beside the most intact wall where he'd made their jacket-nest earlier. He pulls his shirt off and wrings it out, then drapes that over another tree root. "Well, that *might* dry before the rain stops... Professor Zynn's just going to finish the last of his measurements, since the wet doesn't bother him, and then we'll go back and get something warm to eat." He loosely pulls on his pilot's jacket. "Didn't think I'd actually wear this thing today, but *stars*, that rain is cold."

Mirawynd takes this as the sign that it's time for them to get into the nice dry inner pocket of the jacket and soak up some of their human's warmth. They squeak at him and hold all four of their arms out in the universal gesture of small creatures wanting to be picked up.

"Yeah, I'll bet you're cold too." Mirawynd's human gently picks them up and tucks them into his jacket so they can curl up in their favorite sleeping pocket. "We'll get properly dry once we get back to the tents." They feel and hear him sitting down on the stone, then leaning back against the wall with a contented sigh.

A moment later, there's a rough sound of grating stone on stone. Mirawynd feels the scary weightlessness of falling through the air. There's a heavy thud underneath them as their human lands on a distant floor.

As the stone-on-stone sound rasps again above them, Mirawynd peeks out of the safety of their human's jacket pocket and finds that he, once again, is unconscious.

The world around them is nothing but a big, empty darkness.

★

W HEN POTTS AWAKENS, IT'S WITH THE SECOND-worst headache he's ever had. Every inch of him is sore. He opens his eyes, and sees nothing. He's engulfed in the deepest, blackest darkness he's ever experienced. Somewhere distant, water is dripping slowly into a puddle of some kind, from the sound of the splashes.

A soft, fuzzy something brushing at his cheek and a concerned squeak tell him that once again, Wyndi is doing their best to wake him.

"Wyndi? What happened?" Potts cautiously lifts one hand to where he thinks the Florivan kitten is to try and pat them on the head reassuringly. He's marginally successful at this, but it feels like his arm is bruised all along the places where his support braces run. Bruised, but not broken, which is a distinct win in his world when it comes to waking up in unexpected places.

Wyndi answers with a flurry of squeaks as they catch hold of his hand and nuzzle against it. Unfortunately, Prelvee translator chip or no, he still doesn't understand anything they're saying.

"Okay, slow down, I'm fine—I think." Potts slowly takes stock of his body and does his best to come up to a proper seated position rather than the crumpled mess he'd woken in. Like his arm, everything feels bruised and sore. "Last thing I remember," he says, talking to his little purring companion so he doesn't have to talk to himself, "I sat down on that rock by the wall..."

Potts tries his hardest to remember what came after sitting down. It's a near blank. He carefully turns his head upwards to stare into the darkness. He almost remembers the sensation of falling, but to fall from any real height in near-double Earth's gravity should have killed him. Wyndi squeaking on his shoulder and brushing their fluffy tail against his ear is a definite sign he's alive.

"But then, Doc said something... what was it?" Potts rubs at the sore spot on the base of his skull for a few moments as he tries to remember. "Falling is bad... human bones can't handle the impact... oh!" He tries to give Wyndi another pat on the head, feeling an appreciative twitch of their ears when he finally finds them. "That's why we're alive, then. He said something about the pressure field reacting to cushion impacts, didn't he?"

Wyndi's squeak is either an affirmative or a question about whether he has snacks in his pocket. Potts can't tell either way.

"And from the echo in here... wherever here is, it's big enough that we must have fallen quite a ways..." Potts stares up at the assumed ceiling in the blackness for a while, trying to spot even the smallest fragment of light. "And whatever it was, hole, ancient trap door, or otherwise... it closed off. Just our luck, hey, Wyndi?"

Wyndi remains silent, but their fluffy prehensile tail flicks against his neck as if they're swishing it.

Potts tries to think through the situation. He's glad that his only real phobia is nothing to do with darkness or caves. He forces the thoughts about what sort of horrible alien insects might be lurking in the dark away. He can't let himself get panicky just yet.

"Well," he says at last, patting down the pockets of his jacket and trousers to try and feel for anything that might be a light source, "I'd guess Professor Zynn's noticed we're missing by now, and he knows where we *were*... so it shouldn't take too long for someone to come looking for us. No idea how long I was out, but it's not like we were far from the tents." He does, at last, locate his pocket-com. Unfortunately, he'd stashed the little device in the same hip pocket that he landed on. It won't turn on, and feels like it's been partly crushed. He curses under his breath. A little light to take stock of his surroundings would have been nice.

Just as he's settling in to the idea that he's going to have to sit around in the dark for who knows how many hours, Wyndi squeaks in his ear again. This time, it's the squeak he recognizes as the one they use to get his attention when they have something to show him. They tug on his ear, too, as if trying to turn his head in the direction he should be looking.

Potts turns, if only to humor the kitten. "What is it, Wyndi? Do you see something? I've always heard Florivans could see in—"

He halts mid-sentence. If Wyndi weren't so excited about it, he'd think he was hallucinating. There's a small, dim light of some kind off in the distance. Watching it closely, it seems to be drawing nearer.

"Hello?" Potts calls, waving to the light. His only thought is that it must be someone coming down a path from the surface to rescue them.

The light continues to approach. It's soft and white, and grows larger as it comes closer to them.

In the back of Potts' mind, he has the distinct flash of human instinct that says lights in dark places can also be *dangerous*. A memory of when Eddie showed him what glowworms really are and how they use their lights to catch prey crosses his mind unbidden.

"Say, Wyndi," he whispers, doing his best to shake off the nerves. "You'd tell me if that light wasn't a friend, right? Like you did with the Novan?"

Wyndi squeaks happily and bounces down off of his shoulder and into the darkness.

"That wasn't what I meant!" Potts starts to stand up and chase them, and then realizes he has no idea what lies between him and the light. For all he knows, there's some greater chasm waiting to swallow him if he takes a step in the wrong place. Wyndi, at least, can see where they're going.

A few minutes later, after listening to the echos of a running squeaky commentary from his unseen companion, Wyndi returns. To Potts' amazement, they're riding on the back of the source of the light: a T'irsh-fel with a ruff of white feathers, all of which are giving off a distinct bioluminescence.

"*Greetings,*" says a hesitant feminine voice in his mind. "*This creature belongs to you?*"

"Wyndi belongs to themself, mostly, but we take care of each other." Potts lets the kitten scamper back onto his shoulder before attempting to stand. "You're from the outpost, right? Here for a rescue?"

The T'irsh-fel's eyes furtively glance away from him for a moment or two before she speaks again. "*This lowly one was once a humble helper to respected Professor Zynn's team. You are lost?*" Something about the tone of the telepathic voice makes Potts wonder now if he and Wyndi are the only people here in need of a rescue.

"'Lost' is the word for it, yeah." He looks up. He can just barely see the ceiling in the soft glow from the T'irsh-fel's feathers. "You too?"

"*'Lost' is an inadequate word. This lowly one has been seeking an achievable exit for some weeks, and knows the routes through this level of the honored Diggers' caves. It is unfortunate that the only opening to the surface this lowly one has discovered which is large enough to accommodate her size is also impossible for her to climb.*" There's a pause, and another furtive glance of all her many long-stalked eyes away from Potts before one turns back towards him. "*'Trapped,' perhaps, is the right word.*"

"Well," says Potts, brushing the dirt off of himself now that he can see where it is, "maybe the three of us can find a way to get un-trapped." He starts to extend a hand to his new friend on reflex, then chuckles to himself and settles for a deep nod of his head. "Nice to meet you, friend. I'm Julian Potts, a Pilot-Sergeant with the Defense Fleet—and the little fuzzy critter is Mirawynd."

For their part, the kitten lets out a sleepy squeak, yawns broadly, and then tucks themself back into Potts' inner jacket pocket. Apparently now that he's conscious and has someone to help him get them out of this latest bit of mess, Wyndi is content to leave him to it and take a nap.

"This lowly one is honored to meet you, Pilot-Sergeant. Your Mirawynd as well." The T'irsh-fel fluffs her feathers lightly, sending a cascade of rippling light around the ancient masonry embellishing the natural cave around them. *"This lowly one did not realize that human ships were now venturing to visit Jewel-Eye."* She rather distinctly does not give a name in return.

"Oh, we're not... Wyndi and I just wound up hitchhiking a bit. It's a long story." He flashes her a conspiratorial grin. "If you like, I'll tell it to you while you show us where that surface opening is? Humans are pretty decent climbers, usually. If I can get up that hole you've found, I can let the folks at the outpost know that you're stuck down here and where to come get you out."

Again, the furtive turning of the T'irsh-fel's eyes away from him. It's a longer moment this time before one of them focuses on Potts again. *"This lowly one will do all she can to ensure you and your Mirawynd are able to return to the surface... and would not be opposed to hearing your story.*

It has been a long time since this lowly one had anyone to speak to her."

Potts almost thinks he hears a wistful sadness in her voice this time. He doesn't know why. "Okay, then. Lead the way."

Without another word, the white-feathered T'irsh-fel turns back the way she'd come, keeping one eye turned towards him as she leads him deeper into the passages beyond.

★

POTTS FOLLOWS THE GLOWING WHITE-FEATHERED T'irsh-fel for at least half an hour before he can't stand the silence anymore. The underground ruins and caves go on and on, and his guide is almost eerily quiet. If it weren't for the distinct rustling sound of her thick belly scales sliding across the stone floor, he'd almost wonder if she was even real. He doesn't want to think he's hallucinating, though, and he doesn't currently believe in ghosts. Besides, wouldn't a specter in this place be one of the mysterious Diggers who once lived in it?

"So," he asks, absently studying the rock formation they're passing by, "how long have you been down here?"

"This lowly one has been searching for an exit she could use for some weeks." There's a pause as several of her eye-stalks turn upwards, similar to the human gesture of looking

up to focus on calculating something. *"This lowly one is unsure of the precise length of time."*

"I can see how it would be hard to keep track." Potts walks in silence for several minutes before his curiosity gets the better of him again. "So, how'd you wind up down here, then?"

There's a slight hesitation coloring the T'irsh-fel's mental voice as she answers. *"This lowly one was assisting the honored researchers to study a new section of the honored Diggers' construction in the deep layers of the caverns. There was an unexpected seismological event. This lowly one did her best to secure the unstable roof of the access tunnel as the others exited, and became trapped when it fell."*

Potts can picture it, but does his best to push away the thought of whether that sort of cave-in happens regularly around here. "I'm surprised they haven't been able to rescue you, if they knew where you were."

There's another long pause before she replies. *"The honored researchers have no reason to expect that this lowly one is alive. The falling rocks, from their view, would have crushed her... and her connection with the All had long been severed. This lowly one was surprised herself to have survived. It has been fortunate for her that the mosses in these passages are edible, or this lowly one would still likely have died."*

Potts looks down to her with a curious tilt of his head. The mental projection might come with translation, but the phrasing the T'irsh-fel favor still confuses him at times. "The 'all?'"

The hesitation before she responds this time is even longer. Potts isn't sure if she's just choosing her words carefully or if he's managed to offend her. *"The All. This lowly one's people need line of sight to connect to outside minds, but to each other, a deep connection exists always. The All extends from the bloodline to the greater whole."*

Potts isn't surprised to learn that the T'irsh-fel had some sort of hive mind thing going on. It stands to reason, in a way, that a telepathic species would. What confuses him, though, was his new friend. The way she refers to herself with that reluctant, almost apologetic tone, the fact that she'd been left down here for dead because the other T'irsh-fel apparently couldn't sense that she was alive—there's something off about the whole thing. Curious still, but not wanting to upset his only source of light in the caves, Potts quiets for a few minutes while he tries to find a suitably inoffensive question.

"I should have asked when you found us," he begins, "but what name should I call you?" It had struck him as odd at the time, too, since every other T'irsh-fel he's met has made a point of introducing themself formally with some combination of their titles, name, and preferred pronouns. This one hadn't even done the last, leaving Potts to gather that she was female as she spoke.

The silence of the cavern stretches on for ages before a single one of her long eye-stalks finally casts its gaze back toward him. *"This lowly one has no name."*

"You don't?"

"Names..." The single eye-stalk turns away from him while she seems to be choosing her words. It's a minute or two before she finally looks at him again. *"Names are given to people. This lowly one has been severed from the All... a name is unnecessary for the severed."*

Potts can't believe it. Of all the things he's encountered since *Equinox*, this is by far the most alien. It makes him angry, somehow, deep in the part of his soul that was raised to believe in fairness.

"Forgive my ignorance, but you seem like a person to me."

"It is hard for the honored Prelvee to understand, too," she says, in a sad tone that almost suggests she's had this conversation before. *"This lowly one has been severed from the All. It is a strange kindness of the universe that she survived the severing, and a greater kindness still that the honored Professor Zynn allowed this lowly one to remain and find worth assisting the team here with their work."*

Potts is still struggling to believe this. "You were one of the researchers here before, then? And this 'severing' thing, whatever it is... makes the other T'irsh-fel think you're not a person anymore." He rubs absently at the back of his head, trying to wrap his mind around it. "So they left you for dead down here after the cave-in?"

"This lowly one is not part of the All," she repeats, again with that mental tone of gentle resignation. *"Whatever she might have been before does not matter. It is not a reason to be angered with the honored researchers, that they would assume her dead. To know that those who exited while this lowly one had the strength left to hold the rocks in place for them have survived is enough."*

Potts falls silent for a few minutes. Finally, he lets out a small sigh. "I think I get what you're saying, but it's just... I can't fathom why you'd stop being a person just because you managed to survive some disease or whatever. I mean, the other T'irsh-fel don't think the rest of us who aren't part of your 'All' aren't people, do they?"

"*No, a member of another sapient species is a person, as you would say.*" All of her eyes turn to Potts now, fixing a steady gaze on him as she continues. "*You have misunderstood the situation, honored Pilot-Sergeant. May this lowly one explain bluntly?*"

Potts barely holds back an awkward laugh. "To be honest, ma'am, I'd prefer if you did. I'm not really trained for being diplomatic and catching on to subtle things."

"*Thank you for indulging this lowly one's indelicacy.*" All of her lightly glowing feathers wave in the T'irsh-fel equivalent to nodding one's head. "*The severing is not a disease; it is a punishment. There is none more severe. This lowly one is the last of a bloodline which was dishonored beyond recovery. The actions of the highest among the bloodline led to the deaths of multitudes, and the failure of the others in the hierarchy to prevent this or mitigate the damage was just as unforgivable. A severing is rare, but it encompasses the entirety of the bloodline. From the highest to the lowest, each is cut free from the others and the All in the same moment. It is only done for the most dishonorable of crimes, and it cannot be undone. If one survives the severing, they can never return to the All or their former role. Any life a severed one regains is by the kindness of the universe. To survive at all was long ago seen as a sign that a severed one had been truly innocent of the bloodline's crimes, or at least worthy of a chance to continue to serve in penance for the others. Now, this is called a superstition, for there is no proof that survival is anything but random.*" She pauses, turning all but one of her eyes away again. "*This lowly one understands that the honored*

Prelvee see this as harsh, and you may as well, but it is the truth of how things are."

Potts' eyes widen. "So you nearly died... because of something someone else was being punished for? Harsh doesn't begin to describe it."

She hesitates before responding. *"This lowly one was distant from the bloodline's hierarchy in many ways, but they were her true connection to the All. Perhaps this was 'unfair' as other species would see it, that this lowly one was severed with the rest, but it remains that she survived. If this lowly one continues to survive, perhaps a new life will be found for her."*

Potts has no idea what to say to that. He stays quiet for a long time, trying to process all of it. He wonders if the human diplomats and Fleet officials who've worked more closely with the T'irsh-fel even know about the concept of one of their bloodlines being severed. It's a comfort, at least, that the Prelvee apparently don't agree with the practice any more than he does.

After following her around another turn in the corridors, he comes to a decision. "Well," says Potts, looking over towards his T'irsh-fel companion with a wry smile, "forgive me, but I'm still of a mind that you're a person... and it looks like we're going to be hanging out down here for a while yet. Would it offend you if I give you a nickname? Just until we get out of here, at least—if you want to be nameless after we're rescued, I won't say anything about it."

"The idea of names matters to you that much, honored Pilot-Sergeant?" Her telepathic voice in his head sounds genuinely startled.

"It does." Potts doesn't know how to explain why thinking of her as "her" or "the nice T'irsh-fel who's keeping me from getting lost and dying horribly down here" doesn't sit right with him.

"If it pleases you, honored Pilot-Sergeant. This lowly one will accept whatever you choose to call her."

Potts smiles, looking his new friend over for a moment. The perfect name comes to him almost immediately. "How do you feel about 'Lily'? Like the flowers... your feathers sort of remind me of them."

The feathers in question fluff out softly and then wave back into their former position, gently flowing around her eye-stalks and spreading their odd pale light in shimmering patterns around the cavern. *"This lowly one is grateful beyond measure for such a kindness. You are welcome to call her Lily."*

As he continues following Lily through the maze of the caves and the Diggers' ruins, Potts can't help but be pleased with himself. He has the suspicion that being given a name means more to her than she was willing to let on.

★

AN HOUR OR SO LATER, POTTS IS STILL FOLLOWING Lily through the maze of half-collapsed ruins and natural caves.

"This place really goes on forever, doesn't it?" He stares upward for a moment, trying to spot the ceiling of the cavern they're traversing in the dim glow of Lily's white feathers. Potts has learned by now to stay close to his T'irsh-fel guide. If he gets too far away from her, he inevitably trips on something he can't see. In this massive space, he doesn't dare fall behind for more than a moment.

"*This is the largest room in this section of the natural cave system, yes.*" Lily stops her thick-scaled slither beside him, also turning most of her eyes upward. "*This lowly one has estimated its height at its extremity at a minimum of...*"

There's a pause as her nearest eye looks between him and the direction of the ceiling for a several moments.

Potts feels a light prickle of the hairs on the back of his neck. He brushes it away absently with his hand, forcing the thought of any small multi-legged things that could possibly have caused the sensation as far out of his mind as possible.

"Please forgive this lowly one." Lily makes a small closed-eye bowing gesture with two of her eye stalks that Potts has begun to recognize as some sort of sign of apologetic respect, although he hasn't been of a mind to ask her for confirmation of that. *"The conversion of unfamiliar measurements is difficult even with non-intrusive thought projection. The distance might equate to two hundred meters."*

He whistles softly, still straining to see any further than her light will allow. "That's a big cave. You can see all the way up there and figure out the distance?"

"No. This lowly one has had ample time to survey the accessible parts of the honored Diggers' home. The technique is ancient and rudimentary, but it works well enough for estimates one does not expect to have the opportunity to report or assess properly."

"How do you do it, then, Lily?" Potts looks back down at her. Once again, his curiosity is piqued as to what she must have done before she wound up in her current situation.

"Please allow this lowly one to demonstrate." Lily ruffles her ice-white feathers, shifting the glow of the light around the two of them into strange patterns for a moment as they settle back into their usual positions. She focuses two of

her eyes on a pebble near Potts' feet. *"Observe the rock, please, honored Pilot-Sergeant."*

Potts does so. "Nice rock. You can call me Julian, you know. I don't mind."

If Lily registers the remark, she doesn't comment on it. *"Now, as I lift the rock, there is a sensation of distance..."* As she speaks, the pebble slowly rises up from the floor to the level of her eyes.

Potts refrains from saying anything about how truly spooky it is to be watching his new glowing alien friend levitate the thing in the middle of the pitch black of a massive cave. If he hadn't already encountered T'irsh-fel telekinesis, he'd be back to ignoring the memories of the ghost stories Uncle Earl and Aunt Kit used to compete to tell around campfires.

The rock rises a little higher, pausing for a moment in front of Potts' face. *"With experience, one learns to measure the sensation."* As it floats in front of him, a single gossamer white-lit strand from one of Lily's feathers joins it. The feather strand ties itself neatly around the small stone. *"In this environment, adding a source of light to maintain concentration is necessary."*

"So you just... float the rock around and use it for a marker?" Potts watches as the pebble continues to rise.

"Essentially."

Before Potts can ask any more questions, an abrupt stirring in the breast pocket of his jacket interrupts. Wyndi pops their fuzzy little head out with a yawning squeak. Within seconds, they've climbed out of the pocket and up to the top of his head. With a much more excited squeak, they launch themself into the air and grab onto the stone.

They squeak excitedly as it bobs in the air under their weight.

"Wyndi!" Potts reaches out to catch them. "Come back here!"

Lily's projected voice as she slowly floats both kitten and stone into his hands has an amused, almost giggling aspect to it. *"Do not worry, honored Pilot-Sergeant. Your companion is not beyond the lifting ability of this lowly one. They are quite safe."*

Potts lets out a small sigh of relief. "Thanks, Lily." He lowers his eyes solemnly to meet those of the little Florivan he's holding. "Mirawynd. *Please.* Don't go scaring me like that."

Wyndi squeaks charmingly and tilts their head to one side, then holds up the feather-wrapped pebble and offers it to him. They seem pleased with themself.

Potts has known them long enough now to realize when they aren't going to listen to any lecture on safety he might care to give. "Okay, yes, I see your point. There's no way you could resist something like that, is there?"

Wyndi squeaks again, as if agreeing with him. They wriggle up out of his grip and climb along his arm towards the breast pocket they'd been sleeping in. After tucking their lightly glowing prize into the pocket, they abruptly climb down along the side of his leg. Their chattering running commentary as they climb is adorable, even if Potts can only guess what they must be saying.

He plucks Wyndi back up before they can get into the side pocket just above the knee on his left pant leg. "Yeah, I know, you're awake and you're hungry now, aren't you?" Potts laughs lightly, then uses his free hand to slip one of the pieces of carefully wrapped preserved fruit stick out of the pocket. He sets Wyndi on his shoulder and breaks a bit of the fruit stick off for them. "Here, you can have your snack as long as you stay put. I don't want you to get lost scampering around this maze."

Wyndi lets out a half-squeak as they set about contentedly nibbling down the treat. He takes that as an agreement to behave.

Potts breaks the remainder of the fruit stick in half. He looks back to Lily. "Would you like some? It's some sort of Prelvee fruit jerky—closest thing I could find to the emergency ration bars I normally carry."

"*Thank you, honored Pilot-Sergeant.*" Lily delicately floats the bit of dried and compressed fruit out of his hand. It disappears into the junction of her softly glowing white feathers. "*You are well prepared for supplementing missed meals.*"

Potts swallows his own portion, then stifles a chuckle. "Well, it's more a darter pilot thing." He makes a vague gesture to the pockets on each of his pant legs. "They even designed our uniforms to make it easier to keep emergency snacks on hand while we're flying. According to my Majors, there was this incident with one of the other test pilots when the darter program was first starting where he'd missed both breakfast and lunch for some reason or other before the test flight started... and his blood sugar dropped so hard he ended up crashing on one of the outer islands. Even though he wasn't hurt badly, he had to sit there alone for *hours* without food or fresh water waiting for the recovery shuttle to come pick him up. That was enough for all of them to agree on the pocket policy."

Potts pulls his lightweight flask out of his right-side cargo pocket and pours water into its lid for Wyndi before taking a sip himself. "I'll admit, I didn't see much use for the system until I started flying with Wyndi. They tend to need snacks more often than I do." He holds the flask out to her. "Water?"

"It seems a most sensible arrangement. Perhaps the honored researchers should consider such measures in the future." Lily accepts his offer of a drink, tilting the flask in mid-air and floating a sphere of water away to the hidden place at the center of her feather ruff before returning it to him. *"Come, there is a source of clean water where you can replenish your reserve on the way to the surface opening. This lowly one will be pleased to show you the murals she has discovered there as well."*

Potts takes the empty lid from Wyndi and screws it back onto the flask before slipping it back into his pocket. "Lead the way, then. I'll admit, I'm curious about what you've found."

It only takes a few minutes for Lily to guide him through the next set of half-cave, half-ruin passages. She talks more along the way than she has since she first appeared, telling Potts about the things the research team has learned about the Diggers. She seems to be just as much an expert on their construction methods and culture as anyone he'd met on the surface. He can't help wondering again just what her position with the team was before everything that happened to her.

"And here," Lily says, leading him around a corner into a long gallery where the cavern has been reinforced and divided into a street and a multitude of side chambers

with carefully arranged stone walls, "*is the remarkably well-preserved section of the deep ruins which this lowly one wished to show you.*"

"Wow." Potts whistles softly. The echo of it is far louder than he expected. "It's almost as if there should be people living here still." He marvels at the artwork on the most intact sections of the thick red and white plaster which must once have completely covered each of the stone walls. Rows of blocky hieroglyphs surround detailed images of the jungle above and its creatures, divided into sections by patterns of lines and dots. Figures that Potts can only assume are the Diggers themselves are scattered throughout the murals: frog-like beings with three long, thick claws on each hand and colorful bands of cloth wound around their bellies and legs. Professor Zynn had described them as "amphibian life forms well adapted to moving soil and stone," though, so Potts isn't all that surprised by the images. In the back of his mind, there's a touch of relief that the species who built all of this weren't another insect-adjacent horror.

"*It is regrettable that so little remains as a record of the honored Diggers.*" Lily slips up onto the long, low wall opposite the largest of the murals so she is now closer to eye level with Potts.

On the other side of the wall, the expansive center of this section of cave has been converted into a large courtyard around a central spring pool.

"*Still, this section of the ruins is remarkable for the number of near-complete sections of their script and frescoes. This lowly one is pleased that success in your escape will allow her to inform the honored researchers of this place so it can be studied properly."*

"I'll be glad to get you out of here so you can do that." Potts looks over the alien script. "Can you read any of this, Lily?"

"Regrettably, this lowly one was never part of the effort to decipher the honored Diggers' language. There have not been enough examples of their writing before now to provide context for the individual symbols." Lily pauses, turning three of her eyes towards the image of the Digger in the center of the wall. *"This lowly one is of the opinion that this image depicts one of the honored Diggers engaged in a ceremony to do with the pool behind us."*

"Oh?" Potts turns to look at the spring bubbling gently in the center of the courtyard. "What makes you think that, Lily?"

"Do you see the icon there by the honored Digger's outstretched claws?"

"Yes."

"Come around to the other side of this wall." She gestures with one of her eye-stalks, turning it downward towards the stones she's perched upon.

Potts hops over the wall, the squats down to look at the smoothly intact paintings beneath his T'irsh-fel friend. The whole wall around the courtyard is covered with a sequence of engraved paintings prominently featuring the icon Lily had pointed out. In fact, it's alternated with images of Diggers who seem to be either swimming, dancing, or drawing water from the pool.

"Okay, yes, I see what you mean." Potts feels Wyndi climb down from his shoulder, but at the moment, he's not too worried about them. The little Florivan can see in the dark far better than he can, after all, and they're not usually inclined to leave him alone for long. "So the big fellow over there is either part of this sequence of images... or he's giving the list of rules for safely enjoying the water?"

Lily's eyes fix him with eight matching curious and somewhat shocked stares. *"Your impression is that the mural depicts a guardian of the spring, issuing commands for its use?"*

Potts rubs absently at the scruff that's finally started to take over his chin with one hand. "I mean, I wouldn't even begin to try to guess what all of this actually says. It was more of a joke than anything."

"This lowly one does not understand."

"So, humans—well, *most* humans—enjoy swimming for recreation. The places where we do that all have signs with rules like 'don't run near the pool,' 'children below a certain height must be accompanied by an adult,' 'don't dive into the shallow part of the pool,' 'don't chase your little brother around trying to show him the dead bug you found floating in the water...' things like that." Potts pauses to glance over towards the water and make sure that Wyndi's excited squeaking from that general direction is the *happy* kind of chirpy monologue and not the kind that means he needs to try to learn how to swim to rescue them from some danger he can't see. Thankfully, it seems to be the happy sort, although he can't see what they're so excited about.

"Those are rather specific regulations. This lowly one can understand the need for caution with the first two... but humans need to be told such things?"

"To be fair," Potts says, "that last one was added onto the sign at the pool where my family lived… and Eddie never remembered to follow it, anyway." The thought of the *live* insects that would find their way into the water remains a major reason why Potts avoids anything more than wading up to his knees, not that he'd mention it to his new friend. "But yes, humans have to be told what the rules are, and have reminders posted so we stand a chance of following them. Well, or at least so the person in charge of safety can point to the rule sign if someone gets themself hurt and remind them why there's a rule."

"This lowly one had never considered such a thing." Lily turns several of her eyes towards the large mural. *"It is a truly alien concept to this lowly one for a being to not know and understand all of the regulations from their youngest days so that they may follow them easily. The All makes it rather impossible for a rule to be forgotten. The honored Prelvee require education as juveniles, but as far as this lowly one knows, they do not use such signs either."*

"They don't on their ships, or at least, I never saw any on *Frog*. There are a lot of humans who will know there's a rule not to do something, see the sign reminding them, and then just go and do the thing anyway just to see what happens."

"Truly?"

Potts hides a nostalgic grin under his hand, trying to keep his tone level. "My brother and I *may* have been the sort of children who were too curious for our own good and climbed a few fences we shouldn't have. I've got a scar on my right ankle from getting it crushed under a falling rock when we were on one of those little adventures."

Lily looks him over for a while, then towards whatever Wyndi is doing that now involves happy squeaks and soft splashes. Potts hopes that they're really only pushing pebbles into the water from the shore of the pool and not trying to go for a swim. That's as much as the dim light from Lily's feathers can show him from this distance.

"Forgive this lowly one," Lily says at last, slowly and with a resonance of humor he's not heard so clearly from her before, *"but are the people you tell stories of your youth often surprised that you survived it?"*

Potts laughs. "More often than not. My friend Reba always says she went into medicine *specifically* because she was always the one patching me and Eddie up once she found us and dragging us back to the lodge for her mother to treat."

"And now it is young Mirawynd's task to be your guardian? They seem rather small to render medical aid."

Potts starts to correct her, but he can't help but admit the truth. "Well, I don't know who's the guardian between us… but Wyndi's been good at helping me stay in one piece. I'm looking forward to introducing them to Reba once we're back in our own territory. She's going to love having someone to help her pester me."

Presumably because they heard him say their name, Wyndi chooses this moment to scamper back over to Potts and cheerfully hold up a large green-brown stone to him. They squeak cheerfully.

"What's this, Wyndi? You found something shiny?" Potts takes the stone and looks it over while his little copilot climbs back up to their usual place on his shoulder.

Wyndi squeaks again, pointing toward the water.

"Yes, I know you got it from the waterside. Thanks for not getting in the water yourself. Well, it's a nice little rock. Do you want to take it back to show—Ack!"

Potts flings the stone away and shakes his hand in the air vigorously, trying to get the sensation of uncurling claws to go away. It makes a rather smaller splash than something so surprising should have.

"Honored Pilot-Sergeant?" Lily is at his side in moments, one of her eyes carefully inspecting his hand. *"Have you been injured?"*

"That was *not* a rock." He shudders, rubbing his palm against the side of his leg for a moment. "Rocks aren't supposed to have legs."

"Camouflaged cave crabs do closely resemble stones. Your warmth must have awakened it. You are unharmed?"

Potts takes a deep breath, then nods. "Yeah, Lily, I'm fine. I'm just... not good with surprise critters." He glances over to the somewhat disappointed-looking kitten on his shoulder. "Wyndi. *Please.* If the shiny thing is alive, leave it where you found it. I can't handle having cave bugs popping out of my pockets because you stashed them there while they were sleeping."

Wyndi's ears droop a little, but their squeak sounds like a sincere apology and acceptance of terms—or close enough, in Potts' experience.

"Thank you." He turns back to Lily. "Would you mind if we go on ahead to this exit you found? As neat as being the second person to see all of this since the Diggers left is, I'm ready to get out of this cave now."

Lily gives the impression of a nod with a wave of her feathers and starts towards the long corridor. *"This lowly one shares the sentiment. We are not far from there.*" She pauses to glance back at the large mural and the spring's surrounding courtyard. "*Honored Pilot-Sergeant—*"

"You're welcome to call me Julian, you know. You've seen me nearly lose it over an unexpected alien crab, I'd say that makes us friends."

Lily is silent for a few minutes. "*If this pleases you. This lowly one is in no position to further question human informality. This lowly one meant to ask, will... her honored friend... please tell the honored researchers of the 'rules of the pool' concept when he explains what they will find in the ruins here? It is a surprisingly plausible theory.*"

Potts grins. "I'd be happy to, Lily."

★

QUITE SOME TIME AFTER THEY LEAVE THE PLACE with the paintings and the nice water, Mirawynd is still sitting on their human's shoulder and trying to wrap their young mind around why he didn't like the moving rock they found. Their human usually likes their presents, after all. They like bringing him shiny things like bits of metal or moss, and rocks are still a new and exciting type of thing to them.

Still, the moving rock made a *wonderful* splash when he tossed it into the water. Mirawynd would have liked to stay there longer and play rock-tossing with their human. He seems to be eager to get back to the outside, though, so they're trying very hard to be quiet and not go exploring ahead of Lily's sphere of soft, pale light.

A change in the air catches Mirawynd's attention. It's moving now, and fresh-smelling. There's another source of light, too, growing brighter than Lily's.

Mirawynd can't resist the call of their curiosity any longer. They bounce down from their human's shoulder and scamper ahead, towards the light and the source of the nice breeze.

"Wyndi!" they hear their human calling behind them, "don't go too far!"

Mirawynd squeaks a cheerful acknowledgment even as they continue onwards. They don't have to worry so much about their human getting hurt or lost right now. Their new friend Lily is there to keep an eye or three on him.

Soon, Mirawynd is standing in the center of a wide circle of daylight, staring up through a gaping chasm with nearly sheer walls at the sky above. Everything is bright and warm, although the dirt under their feet is a bit damp. They've liked exploring the caves, but it's nice to see the sunshine again.

Mirawynd's eyes are quick to adjust to changes in light levels. Their human, though, squints when he arrives in their patch of sunlight as if looking at anything hurts his eyes. After rubbing at them for a few moments, he, too, looks upwards. He whistles softly. The sound echoes back from the walls of the hole to the surface.

"Well, Lily, I see what you meant about it being hard to climb..." Mirawynd's human walks over to the least-sheer of the walls and runs his hand across the stone. "How far is it to the top of this?"

Lily slips into the sunlight patch beside him and turns all of her eye-stalks upwards. As she passes from the shadow, the soft glow of her white feathers disappears. Whatever she says to Mirawynd's human, they don't hear it.

"Yeah, I'll believe that," he replies. He's still examining the wall. "So about twelve meters of vertical rock with barely any hand holds... and a near guarantee of injury if I slip and fall. Just my luck."

Mirawynd climbs back up to their usual perch on their human's shoulder and mimics him, petting the smooth stone with both of their left hands.

Their human turns to Lily. "Don't suppose that telekinesis of yours is strong enough to catch me?"

After a moment or two of the silence Mirawynd has come to associate with Lily's half of the conversation she's been having with their human, they feel a sensation of rising. Looking down, they see that his feet are hovering a few centimeters above the ground. Curious, Mirawynd jumps back down to investigate.

Lily's eyes are narrowed, all of them staring intently at Mirawynd's human's feet. Her feather ruff is stiffly slicked back away from her eye-stalks, as if to give her more room to stare properly. After another few tense moments, he rises another fraction higher, then abruptly falls back into place with a heavy thud.

Their human being himself, this throws him off-balance enough that he winds up falling down altogether. The thud when he lands on his bottom right next to Mirawynd is even heavier than the first one. He folds his legs as he dusts himself off, accepting Mirawynd's squeaked offer of a nice safe place to sit on the ground for a while.

"No, no need to apologize, Lily. The gravity here is *not* a friend of mine to begin with." Mirawynd's human turns his head skyward again. "I'll admit, I'm not looking forward to trying to climb that... but we have to get out of here *somehow*."

Mirawynd scampers back over to the wall their human wants to climb and makes an attempt themself. They're usually quite a good climber. They leap up towards one of the few cracks in the lower part of the wall that their little hands can get some sort of grip on, then try to pull themself up higher. The rocks, though, clearly do *not* want to be climbed. Within moments of Mirawynd's weight being applied to it, the surface crumbles away from the crack and drops them in a small mound of dust and rubble at the base of the wall.

Mirawynd squeaks their annoyance at this to their human, then tries again. The result is the same for their next four attempts, leaving them a dusty and disappointed little kitten. They trudge back to where their human is sitting and squeak at him, trying to explain that the rocks are being mean to them.

Their human helps them get some more of the dust out of their fur and then rewards their efforts with a bit of the fruit stick from his pocket. He sighs. "If that wall can't even hold Wyndi's weight... there's no way I'll be able to climb it. I'm sorry, Lily. There's not another place like this we could try, is there?"

Lily's expression says it all, even if Mirawynd can't hear her words.

"Of course there's not." Their human stares back up at the sky.

Mirawynd can see why their human must be disappointed. They know that he must be tired and hungry by now. It's been a long time since they had their breakfast with all of their nice new friends. They're not sure how he plans to get out of this hole. They climb back into the pocket of his jacket to think about things in a more cozy place while he figures it out.

Inside their nice pocket-nest, Mirawynd is just about to settle in for a nap when they find the now-not-glowing feather strand, still tied to the rock that Lily had given them earlier. They like their shiny rock, and decide to bring it back out so that their human can play with them while they wait for him to decide how to get out of the hole.

"What's that you've got there, Wyndi," their human asks.

Mirawynd holds the feather wrapped stone up for him. They squeak happily. Chasing the floating rock sounds like a good game to them, regardless of what he is doing.

Their human looks at the rock for a few minutes, turning it over in his hand and then tossing it up lightly in the air. It hovers above him, slowly rotating. They think he must be listening to Lily talk about something, because he's so quiet for so long staring up at it.

Mirawynd finally loses their patience with their human. They scamper up to the top of his head, then leap up to catch the rock. Just like before, once they grab it, they're floating in mid air. Since it doesn't move, they carefully re-arrange themself so they can sit on top of it.

They look down to their human with a triumphant squeak once they've accomplished this. He doesn't seem to notice.

"Do you think it will work, Lily?"

From their floating perch, Mirawynd sees that all of Lily's eyes are now trained on them. She must be saying something to their human, though, because after a moment, one of the eyes looks past them.

Suddenly, they hear a soft feminine voice talking to them. "*Honored Mirawynd*," the voice says, "*may this lowly one have your permission to lift you so that you can go and find help for us?*"

Mirawynd looks over to their human again and squeaks curiously. Lily has not said anything to them since they first found her. Then, she had asked what they were doing in the cave and they had led her back to their human. They like her voice. It sounds like the soft waving of the white feathers in her ruff.

"The plan is," says their human, "Lily will float you up to the surface. Since she says we can't be that far from where the research tents are, you should be able to find someone and bring them back here to help us out. Do you think you can go get us help, Wyndi?"

Mirawynd thinks about it for only a moment. Their whole purpose is to protect their human. They squeak excitedly and bounce down from the floating rock onto his shoulder to give him a hug. They squeak at their human the whole time they're hugging him, promising in their own small way that they will bring someone back to help him so that he can get out of the hole and get dinner. They don't like leaving their human, but they understand.

Besides, floating sounds fun, and Lily will be here to watch over him while they're gone.

"All right then," their human says, giving their ears a good scratch. "Be careful out there, Wyndi, okay?"

Mirawynd squeaks and nods their head enthusiastically. They look back over to Lily and squeak at her, holding their arms out. They're ready to fly now.

"Be very, still, please, and this lowly one will lift you to the top." Lily's eyes narrow their focus onto Mirawynd, save for one, which turns its gaze towards the sky and the top of the wall. They feel themself held firmly by her invisible grip. After a moment, they slowly begin to float towards the sky.

Mirawynd does their best to be a very still and quiet kitten, but it's hard because floating up and up above their human's head is the most exciting new game that they've encountered since they can remember. They wonder if maybe, after they bring back help and have dinner, Lily will play with them again. They want to try flying around the room like one of the big-winged bugs they saw outside earlier.

Down below, they can see that their human is nervous, for some reason. They wonder if he's afraid to be left alone, even though Lily is there. Mirawynd knows it's been a long time since he didn't have them there to keep him safe.

Soon, they are at the top of the rock wall, staring out into a big cluster of trees. *"Honored Mirawynd, you must go get help now. Please be careful."* Lilly gently sets them down on the ground just beyond the edge of the hole. *"You are facing in the direction of the honored researchers' tents."*

Mirawynd turns and looks back down the hole at their human and Lily. They squeak and wave to the two of them.

"Okay, Wyndi, now go get help," their human calls, "I promise we won't go anywhere!"

Wendy squeaks again and makes their best impression of his special pilot's salute with their upper-right hand. They scamper off into the depths of the jungle in search of someone to help get their human out of the hole.

★

Over fallen trees and stones, and past so many shiny and interesting things that would normally have drawn their attention, Mirawynd keeps to the straightest line they can in the direction Lily had told them to take. They resolve to take their human exploring to show him all of the neat flowers and flying things they've spotted along the way, but for once in their short life, they don't allow themself to become distracted. They're a kitten on a mission.

Mirawynd isn't sure how long it takes them in the end to get to a place where they can see the tents growing out from the dense mass of trees in front of them. They know it's started growing darker, though, and they're certain that it's long past dinner time. They hope their human is doing okay waiting for them back in the hole with Lily. They're tired and hungry themself from their dash through the undergrowth, but that doesn't matter. Their human needs help, and it's *their* job to find it.

When they finally reach the edge of the big tent and slip through its doorway, Mirawynd begins looking for someone who would know how to extract their human and Lily from the hole. It takes them a few minutes to find anyone. They're glad to see that their hard-shelled friends are gathered around the meal table when they check there, with some kind of large shimmery map projected in the air above it. They quickly spot Dr. Goldie and climb up to the tabletop in front of her, squeaking rapidly as they try to get her attention.

"Little one!" She reaches out a clawed appendage to them. "We have been looking for you since yesterday! Is [Pilot-Sergeant] with you?"

Mirawynd shakes their head and takes hold of the offered claw, tugging gently on it and trying to explain about the hole. Unfortunately, they know all too well that she can't understand their squeaks. A flash of a memory crosses their mind—Emerald taught them for this!

Amid all of the rapid clicking and buzzing that the hard-shelled people gathered around the table are making, Mirawynd becomes very still and quiet and closes their eyes. They have to remember the right sounds. When they open their eyes, they tug on Dr. Goldie's claw again.

"Little one?"

Mirawynd looks up at her with their most serious face, even though their tail is waving rapidly. They try twice before they successfully make their kitten-squeaks turn into a chattered, trilled version of the most important word of her language that Emerald had tried to teach them: "Help!"

Before any of the stunned figures around the table have time to react, Wyndi uses Dr. Goldie's long carapace as a ladder down from the table and scampers for the door.

They pause there and turn back to her to make sure she's understood. "Help!"

Dr. Goldie catches on fast, thankfully. She follows Mirawynd out of the tent, catching up to them when they pause just outside it. Dusty is right behind her. "Which way, little one?"

Mirawynd scampers in the right direction for a few meters, then looks back at her once again. "Help!"

She scoops them up as she passes by, skittering far faster on her many, many clawed feet than Mirawynd's two fuzzy ones could ever hope to go.

★

“*T*HIS LOWLY ONE IS CERTAIN THAT SHE POINTED *your Mirawynd in the correct direction.*”

“I know you did, Lily.” Potts stares upward at the rim of the chasm again. “I just worry about them. There’s a lot of big insects out in that jungle...” He doesn’t want to think about what else might be lurking in the trees, or whether any of the local predators would consider a little fluff-ball like Wyndi an appealing snack, but the thought keeps coming back.

“*This lowly one has noticed how deeply you and your Mirawynd care for each other.*” Lily’s ruff of white feathers is beginning to softly glow once again in the growing shadows of the evening. She’s quiet for a few moments before adding, “*they expressed great determination to rescue you.*”

Potts allows himself a small laugh at that. "Wyndi's the most determined little critter I've ever met, yeah. I'm lucky they decided to take on with me."

"May this lowly one ask what sort of creature your Mirawynd is? Their mind is clearly that of a fellow sapient."

Just as Potts is trying to decide on an answer, he's distracted by the sounds of something approaching the hole through the underbrush above him. He stands abruptly and goes to the other side to try to get a better view of what it is. "You hear that too, right, Lily?"

Lily joins him and turns all but one of her eye-stalks upwards towards the sliver of the tree line the two of them can see over the edge of the sheer rock wall. *"It sounds large. It may well be one of the native predatory life forms beginning its nightly search for prey."*

"Let's hope none of those... natives... caught sight of Wyndi." Potts isn't sure he wants to ask just what kind of large life form Lily's talking about. It's the first he's heard of big predators stalking the jungle here.

The sounds come closer, and then suddenly stop at the edge of the chasm. A cheerful series of trilling squeaks heralds the appearance of a distinctly Prelvee face peering down at them, with Wyndi perched atop it.

"I see him, little one!" says Dr. Goldie, waving her facial tentacles at Potts. "I hope you are uninjured, [Pilot-Sergeant]?" She pauses for a moment as her eye turns slightly to the side of him as she looks at Lily. Something about the tone of the translation of her words tells him that she's choosing them carefully as she adds, "and you, old friend. I had been informed of your death. It is pleasing to see that this was incorrect."

If Lily says something to her in reply, Potts doesn't hear it.

"Now, if the two of you will remain still while I climb down to retrieve you?"

"Be careful," Potts calls up to her, "the cliff face is really unstable."

"Not to worry, [Pilot-Sergeant]!" Dusty's familiar face also peers over the cliff now, also waving a facial tentacle in greeting. "My dear older sister is an expert at this sort of rescue." She continues to explain as Dr. Goldie disappears from sight for several minutes and Wyndi comes to sit on her head. "Our home colony has many sea caves with surface openings where an unwary young one could become trapped if they strayed too far. She's spinning a support rope for herself now and securing it to a sturdy tree here so the climb back up will be easier."

Potts does his best not to think about the silk-spinning aspect. "Why do I get the impression *you* were the one she was rescuing from those sea caves, Dusty?"

Dusty clicks the few clawed appendages Potts can see together and makes the sounds he associates with Prelvee laughter. "I wasn't the *only* larva who ever needed to be rescued..."

Dr. Goldie's voice is similarly toned as it approaches the cliff again. "Oh, no, little sister, you were just the one who always found the deepest holes to swim into before the tides changed." She switches back from the heavily accented dialect the two of them use with each other and calls down to Potts again. "I will be descending now, [Pilot-Sergeant]. Please stand clear of the cliff face in case any of the unstable rocks break free before I can secure them."

Potts and Lily back up a little further and wait under the overhang of the tunnel mouth leading into the caves and Digger ruins. It's all he can do just too maintain his composure as they watch the Prelvee physician slowly climb down the sheer surface of the crumbling cliff face. There's something disturbingly fascinating about the way Dr. Goldie coordinates all of her many, many limbs and claws to support the lengthy bulk of her body as she descends head-first. As she climbs closer, it's clear that she's deftly spinning a layer of shimmering pale blue silk across the rocks in front of her. The fact that this seems to be enough to secure and strengthen her path is amazing, even if the visual of it makes Potts a touch queasy.

Soon, Dr. Goldie is standing in front of him and Lily, clearly pleased with herself. "There. Now, are either of you injured?"

Potts shakes his head. "I'm fine, ma'am, far as I can tell. Lily's been down here for a long time, though."

"So I gather." Dr. Goldie leans forward and looks over the white-feathered T'irsh-fel with no small amount of concern in the expression of her large square-pupiled eye. "Lily?"

Potts is amused that Lily choses to let him hear her answer. "*Yes, honored physician. This lowly one has been granted a name by her honored friend the Pilot-Sergeant Julian. He was most graciously insistent that she receive one.*"

"He is good at choosing names, isn't he?" Dr. Goldie's eye turns to him for a moment with an amused wave of one of her facial tentacles before continuing. "It suits you, old friend. Are you well enough to anchor yourself to me so I can carry you both out?"

"This lowly one will do her best, honored physician." That hesitation from before is back in Lily's voice, although Potts can't fathom why.

Dr. Goldie makes a few small clicking gestures with her upper claws. "As an extra precaution, I will spin a securing harness to hold you in case your grip weakens. It is my intention to bring you safely to the surface, old friend."

"If you all want to be out of that hole before dark," Dusty's voice calls from above, "it would be good if you start climbing now! The little one and I are certain your anchor is secure, and I have sent a message to [Professor Zynn] so the team will be expecting us."

A series of impatient squeaks from Wyndi punctuates the young engineer's statement.

"Thank you, little sister!" Dr. Goldie calls back. She turns her attention to Potts. "[Pilot-Sergeant], please do not be offended, but for your safety, it is best that I carry you up in my forelegs as I would a wayward larva. I am not certain you would be able to hold securely to my carapace, and I have the impression you would not be interested in my securing you with bands of silk."

Potts holds back a shudder at the thought of the latter option. "Ma'am, if you can climb while carrying me, I'd really prefer that. Are you sure you can manage both of us?"

"I am stronger than you suspect, [Pilot-Sergeant]." She lets out her species' buzzing version of laughter and then holds out her uppermost clawed appendages. "Come, now, you have my word as a physician that I will not drop you."

As soon as Dr. Goldie is satisfied that she has spun enough of her shimmery pale blue silk to hold Lily securely to the middle of her back, she carefully picks Potts up off the ground. It barely seems to take any effort on her part to do this, even with the gravity levels on this planet increasing his usual weight by so much.

It's a weird, unsettling sensation to be held in the equivalent of a bridal carrying pose, but with dozens of finely jointed clawed limbs holding him close to the belly segments of an alien's bug-like body. Potts is immediately glad Dr. Goldie's eye is in the wrong place for her to see his instinctive grimace as he shuts his eyes and tries to focus on the important fact that she's *friendly* and saving his life. Why that should come with aspects beyond his worst nightmares, he doesn't know. At least she didn't decide to strap him to her back with silk. He's not sure he could have handled that.

As he feels himself lifted higher and hears the scraping clicks of her many lower claws against the silk-covered stones, Potts finds his composure long enough to glance down. Heights, at least, have never bothered him.

Below, he can see Lily stretched out along the Prelvee doctor's back, her eyes narrowed in concentration. Even with the carrying strap around her, she seems to be making a focused effort to hold on with her telekinetic grip. He wonders how *she* feels about heights, considering that none of her eyes are pointed anywhere near the ground.

Potts closes his own eyes again. The growing distance between him and the floor of the hole isn't the problem. The view of Dr. Goldie's many, many centipede-like legs deftly climbing up the river of silk, on the other hand? That's more than he can bear to watch.

In a matter of minutes, though, Potts feels his Prelvee friend's body level out as she finally reaches the surface. He opens his eyes just as she's gently setting him down.

"There!" Dr. Goldie pats him on the head with one of her upper claws in the same gesture he'd gotten used to *Frog's* Captain using to express her fondness. "All safe and sound on the surface. I'll do some scans to make sure you weren't unknowingly harmed once we have returned to *My-Love-is-the-Stars.*"

Potts looks up at her gratefully. "Thanks, Dr. Goldie." He doesn't have time to say anything else before an excitedly squeaking Florivan kitten has replaced her claw upon his head. Wyndi seems to be checking him over for injuries themself, too. "Yes, yes, good job, Wyndi. Thanks for bringing back help."

By the time he has Wyndi settled down into their usual place on his shoulder, Dr. Goldie has removed the silk bands holding Lily to her back. Lily catches his attention with a telekinetic tug on his sleeve. *"This lowly one thanks you, honored friend Julian, for helping her to return to the world above."*

Potts grins. "You're welcome, Lily, but I should be thanking you. *You're* the one who guided us out."

"Now," says Dr. Goldie, "let us return to our friends before it gets any darker. I expect the three of you would like a proper meal."

With a chorus of wholehearted agreement, they follow her back to the tents of the researchers. In the growing dim of the evening, Lily's white feathers shine just as brightly as they did down in the depths of the caves.

★

After a warm, enthusiastic welcome from all the folks who'd been searching for him, Potts finds himself the center of attention all through dinner. Lily, for some reason, makes a point of asking him to relay the information about what she's found down in the caves to her former colleagues. Potts doesn't understand why she can't tell them herself, but it seems as if he and Dr. Goldie are the only folks she's comfortable speaking to at all.

Granted, she's been underground alone for a long time. It must be shocking to suddenly be among people again, even without her odd "severed" condition.

The weird thing, though, is that while the Prelvee researchers clearly know her and are excited to ask her questions about the paintings and everything else directly, even if she continues to ask Potts to reply on her behalf, Professor Zynn and the other T'irsh-fel seem to be ignoring that she's even in the room. Potts suspects that's part of whatever cultural quirks surround Lily's condition, but he still finds it unsettling to sit in the middle of it all.

Wyndi, for their part, seems to be keeping a squeaky running commentary of their own on everything that's being said. No one understands them, but the Florivan kitten seems pleased to participate nonetheless. Their dining napkin is never short of a tasty treat that someone or other has passed to them, too.

Potts can't help but wonder if Dr. Goldie isn't somehow related to his friend Reba's mother. Like Dr. Kiely, she seems determined to set food in front of him until she's sure he's properly fed. The Prelvee physician's version of that is to daintily pluck morsels from the shared platters every now and again and offer them to *Wyndi*, asking if the little Florivan thinks Potts would like to try the treat. Wyndi, of course, immediately seems to agree with her every time and puts a bit more than half of whatever it is onto Potts' plate.

He hasn't had a moment to ask Dr. Goldie why she's taken to addressing Wyndi as something that the translator chip in his ear insists means "Small Pilot." He figures he'll have time later to find out, though.

At the end of the meal, Dr. Goldie uncoils herself and steps to the clear area in front of the table, clicking her clawed upper appendages together in a way that immediately calls everyone else to attention. "Friends, may I borrow your eyes as witnesses for a moment?" She beckons to Lily with one of her facial tentacles, who hesitantly joins her.

Wyndi looks up to Potts with a curious squeak.

"I don't know," he whispers, "but stay quiet and watch. I think this is important."

"Severed one," Dr. Goldie begins, an air of distinct formality coloring the translation of her voice, "I have taken you out of the darkness. I would take on your life-debt. Do you accept?" She leans down and extends one of her facial tentacles to Lily.

All of Lily's white feathers ruffle for a moment, and then relax as she gently sets one of her eye-stalks against the Prelvee physician's offered facial tentacle. Whether Potts is the only one who hears her answer or not, he doesn't know.

"This humble self will follow her dear Lady the Physician to the ends of the galaxy, if asked. Her Lady is her All."

After a momentary silence, Dr. Goldie addresses the rest of the room. She returns to her usual posture and gestures to Lily with several of her upper claws. "Friends, this is [Physician's Companion Lily], who will accompany me from here on. Please welcome her."

Professor Zynn dips his eye-stalks for a moment, clearly addressing his words to the group. *"Thank you, honored Physician. We are pleased to meet your Companion."*

As the rest of the researchers go over to exchange greetings as if Lily has just arrived, Potts looks over to Dusty, who's still sitting near him. "So, what just happened?"

Dusty shifts over so she's next to him and does her best to keep her clicks and buzzes low in the Prelvee version of a whisper. "Did [Physician's Companion Lily] explain that she is Severed?"

"Yeah, mostly... and that your people don't agree with the practice?"

"We dislike it, but we have been friends and allies with the T'irsh-fel since our peoples first gained spaceflight and found that we shared a star system. The Companion's Rite is our way of helping those like [Physician's Companion Lily] who have survived severing. If someone has saved their life, or something equivalent to that, the Severed can be claimed as a companion. They form a telepathic link with the person who's claimed them, and start a new life without any stigma from whatever happened to them before. Being linked to my big sister like that means that [Physician's Companion Lily] is now a *person* again as far as her people are concerned."

Potts grins, looking over to his T'irsh-fel friend. Something about the posture of her feathers and eye-stalks tells him that she's happier now than he's ever seen her. He's not sure if that's his impression or something to do with the translation chip reading her body language for him, though. "Glad to hear it."

Being rescued, Potts muses, doesn't always mean just getting pulled out of whatever hole you've fallen into.

★

Part 5:
My Love is the Stars

It's been nearly a month since Potts' misadventure on Jewel-Eye and his subsequent transfer to the Prelvee starship *My-Love-Is-The-Stars*. He still finds himself regularly waking up from dreams of deep, dark caverns and falling into them. Or, rather, he finds Wyndi waking him up from those dreams with a practiced swish of their fluffy prehensile tail across his nose and a pointed squeak or two into his ear. How the little Florivan kitten knows the difference to wake him like that only from nightmares, he still hasn't figured out.

On this particular ship's morning, he's the one to wake first. He goes through his usual routine of tucking the still-sleeping fuzziness of Wyndi under the silk blanket on his bunk before slipping into his cabin's attached washroom to take care of his morning hygiene needs. *Love's* technicians had enough advance notice of his arrival on the ship to arrange for things to be more human-scaled in his cabin, which Potts appreciates. It's been a nice change to not have to be constantly mindful of whether or not he's about to fall into things that were made to accommodate people several times his size, for sure. After meeting Wyndi, they'd even presented him with a suitably-sized basin for the kitten to safely bathe in separate from the other water fixtures.

He's glad that his little copilot seems to be less fussy now about waking up alone. Potts isn't sure if that's because they've grown more comfortable with the idea of him being unsupervised for even a minute, or if it's just because they're back on a starship where Wyndi knows that he can't stray far. They seem less anxious about his safety in general, at least, since coming aboard *Love*. Potts suspects that this has something to do with Lily, Dr. Goldie, and Dusty generally being around.

He's just finished dressing and attaching his braces when Wyndi opens their third eye and squeaks sleepily at him. "Good morning to you, too," Potts replies. "Ready for breakfast?"

As usual, the mention of one of their favorite subjects brings the little Florivan immediately to full wakefulness. Within moments, they're on Potts' shoulder and cheerfully chattering away in their adorable kitten squeaks.

Potts laughs and pats them on the head. "I thought you would be."

★

Sitting around the small dining table in Dr. Goldie's private office off of *Love's* infirmary, Potts and Wyndi share their usual breakfast with the physician, her sister, and Lily. It's a pleasant way to start the day off, as far as Potts is concerned. In a way, being around the three of them reminds Potts of the meals he shared with the Musketeers back on *Surnia*. His new friends are always full of interesting new tidbits of information about their respective species' cultures that come up in conversation, too.

One of the surprising things he's learned lately about the Prelvee, for example, is that their people are actually made up of four distinct ecotypes. The majority of the folks he's met between *Frog* and *Love's* crews and the researchers at Jewel-Eye have been from the three terrestrial ecotypes, which make up the majority of the spacefaring population. Dusty and Dr. Goldie, however, are members of the more rare "aquatic" ecotype. Learning about that explained some of the stories he'd heard from Dusty about the colony world where she and her sister grew up, for sure. Apparently, the golden speckle markings Potts had nicknamed both of the sisters after are a hallmark of their ecotype—as are special sets of gills hidden beneath the junctions of their uppermost body segments which allow an aquatic-type Prelvee to spend as much time underwater as they like without surfacing.

Potts is pretty sure that he's the first human who's ever found out about any of that.

He's also sure that his physician friend's new plan for keeping him healthy while under his watch is more than a little to do with her aquatic nature.

"No, really," he tries to explain, "it's just... not something I ever took to, even as a kid. I swim like a rock. I can barely manage to keep my head above water."

Lily's slightly amused voice echoes across his mind. *"Perhaps if you practiced with my dear lady the Doctor, you would upgrade your swimming skills to at least those of one of the rock-crabs from the honored Digger's caves."* She's really come out of her shyness since they left Jewel-Eye. Potts never expected her to reveal such a keen sense of how to tease him.

Potts shakes off the memory of the little critter trying to scuttle away from his hand. "I'm not sure that'd be much of an improvement."

Dr. Goldie makes the bright clicking sounds that signify her own amusement. "It was noted in my materials on human health that your species possesses at least a rudimentary swimming instinct. I am surprised that your education did not include the skill, but rest assured that I will teach you. The water will assist in lessening the strain on your fragile body and allow you to stay in good physical condition. Besides, it is pleasing to think that I will be returning you to your people with a new skill."

"Besides!" Dusty chimes in, waving a cheerful facial tentacle, "this ship has excellent water facilities, thanks to [Captain]. You couldn't ask for a better place to learn."

Love's Captain, as it turns out, is another aquatic Prelvee. She's also apparently an aunt of some sort to the other two, although Potts still isn't sure whether the relationship is a true biological one or a cultural one. Either way, Potts has found her a delight, since she was a pilot of sorts herself in her youth.

"I'm sure I couldn't." Potts sighs dramatically. "Well, Dr. Goldie, if you're sure about this... I might as well try." He looks down to Wyndi, who's sitting on their dining napkin beside his plate. "Looks like we're learning to swim today."

Wyndi pauses in their nibbling-down of one of the crisp seaweed biscuits that their aquatic friends had introduced to the menu today. They look at him curiously and then squeak their approval for the plan. Potts is sure it's approval; he knows how much Wyndi likes splashing around in their water bowl, after all. He has the suspicion that the kitten will take to properly swimming far faster than he himself will.

"Now, since that's settled," says Dr. Goldie, "we'll start your swimming program this afternoon. I believe the artificial gravity settings in the water facilities are adjustable, but if not, you will need to keep your braces on..."

★

WITH THE PROMISE OF SWIMMING LESSONS IN the afternoon, Potts carries on with his usual morning routine. That takes him down into one of *Love's* outer docking rings, to the shuttle bay where his darter is currently being stored.

Dusty has been in charge of the remaining work that's being done on his darter, although *Love's* various senior engineers have been popping in from time to time to see how things are going. From what she's told him, Emerald gave her all the instructions she needed to complete what they'd started back on *Song-of-the-Midnight-Frog*. To Potts' initial surprise, Lily, too, has been assisting with the work. She hasn't said one way or the other just what her background is with tech in general, but she seems to be enjoying herself. Having a telekinetic assistant seems to have made Dusty's work run more smoothly, too.

"[Pilot-Sergeant]," says Dusty, looking over the readouts on one of the monitors she has set up with the rest of the equipment staged around the little craft, "I believe we are now ready for a test flight."

"You're sure about that, Dusty?"

"I have confirmed that all of your craft's systems are operational now, and that the repairs made to the structural elements are secure. There is no danger of atmosphere leakage, and all of the communications systems have been tuned." Dusty clicks her upper claws together excitedly. "It will be most pleasing to see your craft flying, considering how long it has taken to complete all of the repairs. I regret that I cannot fit to accompany you for the test flight."

Potts looks over his darter with a grin. "If I could take you up, I would."

The prospect of getting back out into space and *flying* again is enticing. He's never been good at sitting around. He just hopes his darter will cooperate with the idea, considering what it's been through in the last few months.

"I will notify the relevant officers of the test flight," says Dusty, turning to one of her interfaces. "Once we have clearance to begin, I will let you know. In the meantime, it would be best if we did a final systems check."

Wyndi chooses this moment to drop down onto Potts' shoulder from *wherever* it was they were perching. They squeak curiously at him.

Potts feels like he knows exactly what they're asking. He gives his little copilot a gentle pat on the head. "Yeah,

Wyndi, you can come along. It's not like we've got an active battlefield outside this time."

Wyndi purrs happily and nuzzles his hand. Apparently they're just as excited about getting to fly again as Potts himself.

Lily's gentle telekinetic tug on his sleeve catches his attention. *"As the honored Engineer Dusty cannot accompany you, might this humble self offer to do so as an observer in her place?"*

Potts turns and smiles at the white-feathered T'irsh-fel who's peering up from the tool box under the wing that she'd been tasked with organizing earlier. He'd thought Wyndi was helping her, but they'd clearly wandered off at some point. "If you want to, Lily, you're welcome to fly with us." He pauses, trying to gauge her expression. "I know my Majors always tell their stories of how hard a time the T'irsh-fel observers who flew with them had. Do you think you can handle it?"

"This humble self has heard the stories as well." There's almost a giggle in the projected thought. *"Perhaps she will fare better than the honored Hierarchy officials, perhaps not. Still, it sounds like it would be an interesting experience to fly with her honored friend Julian."*

Potts can't help but be impressed by just how far Lily's come since he met her in the Digger caves. Her true personality is turning out to be feisty enough that he's sure she could hold her own with any pilot he's met. "Okay, then. Let Dr. Goldie know I'm borrowing you for an hour or two. We can sort out how to strap you into the back seat before we do the systems check."

✶

Potts doesn't realize just how much he's missed flying until the moment his darter is free of *Love's* shuttle maintenance bay. The sheer joy of flight, of controlling the swift little spacecraft as he pulls her out into a nice wide loop around the massive Prelvee ship, of feeling himself free and mobile and surrounded by open space—he's overtaken by it all at once. It takes a few moments to remember that he's supposed to be out on a properly ordered test flight.

"*Love* Flight Control," he says into his headset, "this is Darter 2-M-4. I'm clear of you and all systems are responding normally. How long do I have to put this bird through her paces?"

"*The Cap-tain has sug-gest-ed an ho-ur at the lim-it,*" the on-duty communications officer replies. She's not as fluent in Coalition Standard as Emerald or Doc are, but she's been clearly happy to have a human around to practice with. Even if the chip in his ear does work over radio connections, it's still nice to hear words in his own language that aren't his own for a change. "*She and the oth-er of-fi-cers are watch-ing with in-ter-est.*"

"Thanks, Control. Tell them I'll answer any questions they have as best as I can when I get back. Darter 2-M-4 out." He flips up the microphone bar on the headset and glances back to his passenger for a moment. "How are you holding up, Lily?"

"*This humble self is...*" There's a long pause, as if his friend is trying to choose her words carefully. "*This humble self is pleasantly surprised by the smoothness of the flight. She had been given the impression that the experience would be more jarring."*

Potts pulls his darter around into another loop, flying along the perimeter of the outermost of *Love's* gyroscopic docking rings. "To be fair, I'm not pulling anything particularly fancy at the moment. From what the Majors told me, they put your people's observers through a mock combat... and Colonel Darcy, at least, was making a game of showing off as much of the acrobatics these birds are capable of as she could."

"This humble self thanks her honored friend for being considerate of his passengers, then. This view of the galaxy and her dear Lady the Doctor's current ship is unparalleled, even at such a speed."

Wyndi pops up out of Potts' pocket before he can reply, squeaking almost demandingly.

Potts laughs. "Yes, you can come out now, Wyndi. Just stay on my shoulder, you hear? I don't want you floating around the cockpit bumping into things."

Once the kitten is perched in their usual place, they nuzzle against his neck for a moment and then settle down into a soft squeaky running commentary as they watch the stars and the ship go by outside the canopy bubble.

Potts is glad they're able to settle like that. It'd be dangerous to take them flying if they couldn't. He readjusts his course with a neat upward spiral to bring the darter in line with the path of *Love's* inner ring. Thankfully, he's not getting any alerts from his readouts yet, and his darter's new Prelvee bio-steel wing seems not to have affected the handling of the craft much. It feels like he's having to adjust his tensions too much when he turns to that side, but he's not sure yet whether that's the new wing or his having been grounded for so long. As long as the wing stays attached, though, he's sure he can get a feel for his bird again without much trouble.

"Well," he says to Lily after a while, "I'm glad you're along for the ride. Let me know if it starts to be too much for you. I know more than a few humans who can't handle darter flight for long."

"This humble self will be sure to alert you if she experiences discomfort." There's a pause, and then a distinctly cheerful note in Lily's projected voice. *"My dear Lady the Doctor wishes to convey her delight that you were willing to share the experience of this with us."*

"Tell her it's my way of thanking the two of you again for getting me and Wyndi out of that hole." Potts is still getting used to the fact that Lily and Dr. Goldie are linked closely enough that Lily can share the experience of being in the darter with him with the Prelvee physician despite the normal line-of-sight restriction to T'irsh-fel telepathy with other species. It's a weird sort of fascinating, really—Dr. Goldie is essentially with them, even though she's back in *Love's* infirmary. "You know, I think she's the only Prelvee who's gotten to experience darter flight at all? I mean, I always teased Doc about seeing if he could fit in the back seat, but we didn't have the bird ready before we left."

"From what this humble self understands, that is probably for the best. In her experience, most Prelvee do not enjoy being in tightly confined spaces."

"They don't?" Potts pauses to switch directions again, this time pulling into a loose roll for a few moments to check the balance of his wings. Test flights are just as much about feeling one's way around the darter's handling as they are about making sure the systems are working correctly.

"*It is one of the reasons the honored researchers at Jewel-Eye's City of Caves maintain a combined crew. Larger females in particular do not typically seem fond of being in an environment where they must keep the majority of their bodies coiled tightly. My dear Lady the Doctor would like me to point out that she is something of an exception to this. She was initially stationed with the honored researchers because of her experience and comfort as an explorer of caves and a rescuer of those who become lost in them.*"

"And I deeply appreciate that experience." Potts stifles a chuckle. Somehow, he's not surprised that Dr. Goldie is not the average Prelvee.

After a few minutes of silence, save for Wyndi's unintelligible monologue of small whispered squeaks, Lily's voice slips into his mind again.

"*In a way, honored friend Julian,*" she says, "*it is surprising that more of this humble self's people do not fly with yours. This is a similar experience to projecting oneself into a larger swarm of protection drones.*"

Potts has heard of the T'irsh-fel drone swarms before, but he's never seen one in action. Somehow, it catches him off-guard that Lily has experience with them at all. "I take it you've piloted those before?"

Lily hesitates for a moment, but not with the sadness she always did when they first met and he asked about her life. "*The lowly one this humble self once was had been trained to manage protection drone swarms, yes. It is a necessary skill taught to all individuals who are raised to a named rank within the Hierarchy, even if their official duties are not to be aboard a ship. For example, the honored Professor Zynn is one who could be called upon to project himself into City of Caves' own protection drone swarms if Jewel-Eye were to be invaded."*

"Huh. Makes sense, I guess. I'd say my view's better, though. I can't imagine splitting my attention between a whole *swarm* of things and not having them crash into each other." Once again, Potts wonders, but does not ask, just how important of a person Lily must have been in her past. Something about her does strike him as officer material, though. He can easily picture her holding her own with the Majors.

"It takes training and practice for one to separate one's mind in the correct way, but the protection drones are automated to swarm together as the officer wills. This humble self will agree, though, that your craft offers the superior experience of open space."

They spend most of the rest of his allotted test flight time absently talking about Potts' days at the Academy and what the different maneuvers he's practicing are called and how they are used. It's difficult to explain some of them when one doesn't have the rest of a squadron flying alongside to properly demonstrate, though.

Lily proves to be a touch of a thrill-seeker, if Potts' impressions of her tone are correct. She seems to enjoy the spins and rolls and tight turns just as much as he does, even if he's not taking them at full speed today. He has to wonder if her resilience to darter flight is somehow to do with her connection to Dr. Goldie, but he's decided to save that line of questioning for another day.

This morning, after all, is about reconnecting with his darter. All he really cares about at the moment is *flight*. Having Wyndi and Lily along to share it with him is a nice bonus.

★

LOVE'S WATER EXERCISE FACILITIES ARE Mirawynd's new favorite playground.

Ever since Dr. Goldie and Dusty brought them for their human's first swimming lesson, Mirawynd has loved exploring the place. The main feature is the big pool, which takes up the majority of the room. It's filled with mildly warm water that smells clean and fresh no matter how many people have been swimming in it. At one end, it's shallow enough to barely reach their human's knees. At the other, it might as well go on forever as far as Mirawynd's concerned. Dr. Goldie had demonstrated the depth to their human by stretching out the whole of her gold-speckled segmented body so that only her head was above the water, and explaining that her lowest pair of appendages could only barely touch the bottom.

Mirawynd is a far better swimmer than their human, but they prefer to stay in the shallower parts of the water.

They also like exploring the smaller pools that occupy the series of alcoves built into the walls at the far end of the room. Each is wide enough for two or three of the biggest hard-shelled people to sit coiled up in it and is only as deep as their human's shoulders in the center, with a shallower bench built into it all around the edges. Most of the time, these are the same as the water in the big pool, but apparently, the water can be adjusted to suit whoever wants to sit and soak in it. Mirawynd's human usually lets them swim a bit while he's soaking and chatting with Dr. Goldie and Dusty after his lessons, which they enjoy because the water is nice and warm then. They only tried to keep *Lily* company in her small pool once, and it was so cold that Mirawynd immediately regretted jumping in. They don't know how their many-eyed friend stands being in water that cold.

Mirawynd has come to look forward to the water time they share with their human and friends each afternoon. It's taken ages for Dr. Goldie to teach him to do anything other than sink or flail about trying to keep his face above the surface. Mirawynd's not the best at keeping track of time, of course, but they're sure they heard Dusty congratulating their human earlier for having survived two weeks of swimming lessons.

Today, Mirawynd is quite proud that he's managing to paddle alongside the safety rope Dr. Goldie stretched across the big pool for him without too much difficulty. He's not splashing nearly as much today, and he's only needed Lily to pull him up into the correct position twice so he could catch his breath so far. They've been swimming back and forth to try and encourage him, but he's clearly too focused on what he's doing to pay attention. Mirawynd doesn't understand why their human hasn't taken to the water on instinct like they did, but they're looking forward to him finishing this part of his swimming practice so that Dr. Goldie will let them play games with him in the shallower water.

Granted, Mirawynd was able to practice their swimming in the nice wide bowl their hard-shell friends gave them to bathe in long before Dr. Goldie brought them and their human to the water room. They like splashing and swimming, for sure. It feels perfectly natural to them. Mirawynd wonders sometimes if their human's problem is that he doesn't take proper baths. If he's only ever stood under a stream of flowing water to get clean, it's no wonder he had to be taught how to float in it.

The game they want to play first today is the one of climbing up into the soft drapery of moss that hangs down from the ceiling of the chamber and dropping down to make a nice splash right in front of their human. It's fun to see how startled he is when their splash is big enough to touch his nose. He doesn't usually let them play the climb-and-splash game for long, though. Mirawynd thinks this is because their human gets sad that he's not small and able to climb up into the moss like them.

Their favorite game, though, is the one Dusty plays with them when she's not needed to supervise their human's lessons. She has wonderful floating water toys that she brings with her to one of the small pools and tosses in for Mirawynd to chase and retrieve. She's been trying to teach them to say the words that go with all of the toys, too, like their colors and shapes. Mirawynd still hasn't mastered any of that, but the game is fun. They don't know how to explain to their hard-shelled friends that they *do* understand most of what they're saying, and have since before their planetside adventure.

Right now, though, Dusty is busy watching over Mirawynd's human because Dr. Goldie needed to step into one of the dry sitting rooms around the water room. Mirawynd's not quite sure why. Usually, she stays in the water with their human throughout the lesson so he doesn't get scared of the deep water.

Mirawynd is about to start another lap between their human and Dusty when they feel themself being gently lifted out of the water. They float up into the air and over to one of the soft, fluffy silk towels beside Lily, who then lets go of them and does her best to ruffle them dry with the towel. They look up at her with a curious squeak.

"Please excuse the interruption, honored Mirawynd," Lily replies. *"My dear Lady the Doctor asked me to dry you off and bring you to her. The honored colleague on the call with her wishes to see you."*

Mirawynd is curious, so they allow themself to be further dried and bundled up into the softness of the towel. Lily carries them into the dry sitting room and sets them down gently into Dr. Goldie's waiting upper appendages, then disappears back into the water room.

"Hello, [Small Pilot]," says Dr. Goldie, ruffling their ears with a gentle claw before setting them down on the table in front of her interface screen. "Say hello to [Physician Star Sapphire], my colleague who's helping me learn how to take care of [Pilot-Sergeant]. They asked if they could see you while they wait for him to be done with his lesson so they can talk to him."

Mirawynd excitedly squeaks at the familiar star-marked face on the screen and waves both of their right hands in greeting. Their still-damp tail sends a few stray water droplets off into the air as it waves happily. They've only met this presumed entile of theirs once before, but they are thrilled to see *family* again.

"*Thank you for indulging me, friend,*" their entile says to Dr. Goldie over the video connection. "*I was very curious about how Sgt. Potts' little companion was doing, since I know they're important to him.*" They pause and make a trill of greeting under their breath.

"[Small Pilot] is a delightful little creature."

Mirawynd does their best to chatter and squeak their way through telling their entile all about their human and the adventures they've had with him. They're very pleased to report that he doesn't abruptly fall asleep anymore, too.

Their entile laughs softly. "*Delightful is the word. Well, Mirawynd, I'm told you do a good job of keeping Sgt. Potts in good spirits and as much out of trouble as one can expect for a darter pilot.*"

Mirawynd squeaks cheerfully and makes their best version of their human's pilot's salute.

Dr. Goldie chimes in with her version of clicking laughter. "[Small Pilot] keeps all of us in good spirits. If [Pilot-Sergeant] had not explained to us how unfortunately rare such creatures are, I would be tempted to adopt one to assist with improving the morale of my shipmates."

Mirawynd notices an odd amused-but-serious expression on their entile's face for a moment before they respond. "*Who knows, friend... perhaps when this dreadful war is over, you and I can get together and discuss that.*" They pause, absently running a hand through a stray lock of their shoulder-length silver hair. "*Although from what you've said, I'd expect you'd need plenty of time to adjust to your more recent adoption first. Remind me to get in touch with your Captain when you've reached Coalition territory so I can see if Asio will be in range to meet up with you after Sgt. Potts is dropped off at Kapteyn. I'd like to compare notes in person with you and Lily about a few things.*"

"I will look forward to that. Perhaps, if you're in range when we arrive, we could meet your ship to deliver [Pilot-Sergeant] and—"

A loud buzzing alarm sounds throughout the room, coupled with a flashing of yellow and red lights from the small sphere above the door. At the same time, a notification of some sort pops up on the screen with an equally jarring tone to announce it. Another one pops up right after it.

"Forgive me, [Physician Star Sapphire]," says Dr. Goldie with an alarmed gesture of her facial tentacles. "My Captain has issued an all-hands alert and requested my presence. We will speak another time?"

"*Of course. Safe journey, friend.*"

The image of Mirawynd's entile disappears. They look up at Dr. Goldie with a disappointed squeak.

She pats them gently on the head and uncoils herself. She carries Mirawynd back to the water room, where their human is already out of the pool and standing over the scary loud thing built into the floor by the exit to dry himself off. Dusty is nowhere to be seen.

"Lily said the Captain wanted me too?" he asks, stepping away from the flash dryer and pulling his shirt back on over his special support braces.

"Yes," Dr. Goldie replies. "Aside from the alert message, however, she did not give me any details."

"Well, then." Mirawynd's human catches them as they leap from Dr. Goldie's head to his shoulder. He plucks his ever-present pilot's jacket up from the bench where he'd left it and slings it over his other shoulder. "We'll just have to go see what she wants. I highly doubt she'd go alerting the whole *ship* to summon me to a surprise birthday party..."

★

Ｐotts can't shake the feeling of déjà vu as he walks into the Captain's study off of *Love's* bridge with Dr. Goldie and Lily. Wyndi's fast asleep in his pocket, but even their soft purring doesn't do much to lessen his sense of unease.

"We have come as you requested, [Captain]," Dr. Goldie says as the door slips shut behind her final body segments. "What is the situation?"

Love's Captain has the majority of her long gold-speckled body coiled behind her curved desk. A set of interface screens are arranged all around her, showing everything from diagrams of the ship to scrolling readouts of text in Prelvee script to views of the stars outside. She gestures with one of her facial tentacles towards the two large mossy-green silk cushions in front of her desk. "Sit, I will explain."

Potts shares the second cushion with Lily, since Dr. Goldie's coiled body segments fill the whole of the first one. Something about the Captain's tone has him suspecting that somewhere, something has gone terribly wrong.

"We have encountered a distress beacon from a T'irsh-fel ship not too far off our course. There are three other Alliance vessels within range to assist, but we are the closest. The message was not detailed enough for us to know the full situation, but it carried the codes to indicate survivors of an attack by Novan forces."

Potts' eyes widen. It's too eerily close to his experience with Equinox for comfort.

Dr. Goldie makes a series of quiet buzzes and clicks that the translation chip in his ear explains as a statement of untranslatable profanity.

"My thoughts exactly, [Physician]." The Captain's voice is colored with a trace of amusement for a moment, but then she turns serious again. "Protocols dictate an attempt to recover any survivors. Your shuttlecraft will be prepared to launch as soon as we arrive, and you may call upon any personnel not on active duty stations to assist as you need them."

"Understood, [Captain]. Do we know the size of the ship?"

"Our ranged scans and the distress beacon indicate a mid-size supply vessel with a standard crew size between two and three hundred. I have already informed [Prime Engineer] to prepare suitable sections of the lower decks to accommodate any survivors you are able to recover."

Dr. Goldie waves several of her facial tentacles thoughtfully. "Thank you, Captain. I will begin preparations of my own at once."

Potts can't keep his thoughts to himself any longer. "Ma'am, forgive me if I'm interrupting... but how likely is it that this ship in distress is bait for a Novan ambush?"

"You are welcome to speak, [Pilot-Sergeant]." The Captain clicks several of her claws pointedly on the surface of her desk. "Unfortunately, quite likely. I expected you would be as aware of that as I am, [Pilot-Sergeant], which is why I asked for you to come with [Physician]. I, too, am reminded of your story of how you came to be traveling with us."

Potts is relieved that *Love's* Captain isn't the sort of person to take things like this at face value. "How can I help, Ma'am?"

"I know that you are a guest aboard my ship, but it is fortunate to have you with us. I would like you to fly out when we arrive at the T'irsh-fel vessel and serve as an escort for [Physician's] shuttlecraft. In the event we are attacked, you will assist with defending [Physician] and her team until they have safely returned. I doubt any Novans coming back for an ambush would expect a human pilot to be aiding us."

Potts nods. "I'm in."

There's a small pause as the Captain looks over the scrolling text on one of her interface screens. "Additionally, [Physician's Companion], I would like you to fly with [Pilot-Sergeant] instead of with the shuttlecraft. I do not trust that our communications frequencies will remain stable in the event of an ambush, and I want [Physician] to be in contact with [Pilot-Sergeant] at all times. Do you consent to this?"

Potts is surprised, in a way, that Lily answers within his hearing. *"This humble self will be pleased to consent and assist with the defense of her dear Lady the Doctor."*

"Thank you." Love's Captain turns her great square-pupiled eye back to Dr. Goldie. "You have roughly an hour before we arrive. Go make your preparations."

★

Just after Potts and Dusty finish going over his final pre-flight checks before launching, he feels Lily's telekinetic grip tug gently on his jacket sleeve. He isn't strapped into his seat yet, so he flips up the microphone bar on his headset and turns around to look at her. "Yeah?"

"As we are about to enter a potential combat situation..." Lily hesitates, then turns all eight of her eyes to focus on him. *"This humble self remembers the stories of how the observers of her people fared when flying with your squadron mates. Although she is quite comfortable with the way you fly in practice, this humble self would like to ask if her honored friend Julian would allow her to form a link with him for the duration of this exercise. This would allow this humble self to be of greater service to you, as well as keeping my dear lady the Doctor informed more easily."*

Potts isn't surprised by the request. He'd actually wondered through all of the test flights he's taken with Lily over the past couple of weeks why she'd never asked him before. He's well aware that Major Ioane was the only test pilot whose T'irsh-fel observer didn't pass out entirely during the combat simulations they did, and that this was because she'd consented to being telepathically linked with her passenger. From what the Musketeers have told him, that somehow is also the only reason the three of them survived the fall of SCV *Athene*.

"I'm fine with it," he says with a touch of a grin. "As long as you don't have any qualms about touching a human's mind. What do you need me to do."

"Thank you, honored friend Julian. If you would allow this humble self to touch your hand?"

Potts holds his hand out to her. "You've got it, Lily. Go ahead."

Lily closes one of her eyes and gently lays its long scaly stalk across his open palm. It's colder to the touch than he expected.

Beyond the coldness, Potts feels the curious sensation of Lily's telekinetic touch all the way up his arm and into his very brain. He has to close his own eyes after that to try to focus as he feels her mind somehow weaving its way along his thoughts. There's a surreal, shiver-like feeling as, for a moment, of being in two places at once and being able to see all around the canopy bubble of his darter even though his eyes are closed.

Not alone—as one.

Thoughts overlay thoughts, intertwine.

The joy of flight.

A moonlight slither over ice paths through a city of spires.

Every neuron lit in sequence like landing lights on a runway.

Memories flashing past without a clear owner.

Thought over thought over thought without end, echoing between void and stars.

Not alone—as one.

All of that dims from his conscious mind as Lily removes her eye-stalk from his hand and speaks to him again. *"The link is complete, honored friend Julian. You may safely open your eyes."*

Potts does so, then rubs at his eyes as he turns around to get himself strapped into his seat. "That felt a lot weirder than the Major ever said it did... but not nearly as overwhelming."

"The honored officer to whom she is linked is a part of the All," Lily says, sounding a lot clearer in his head now. *"This humble self would not be surprised if the immersion into the All was overwhelming for your honored Major."*

Potts goes through his final checklist of the darter's systems. "Lucky me, then. Does this link let you access my understanding of how the rear seat firing controls work, in case I need you to use them?"

"It does. You focusing on the memory of it for a moment like that makes it easy for this humble self to access and copy the information into her own mind without distracting you. This humble self is now prepared to use the rear seat weapons interface upon your order."

"Good." Potts pauses to call in to *Love's* Flight Control officer and let them know he's ready to launch. After that's confirmed, he turns his attention back to his T'irsh-fel friend for a moment. "Let Dr. Goldie know that we've got her back, will you?"

"My dear Lady the Doctor is aware. She wishes you safe flying."

Potts takes the darter out and circles Love until he reaches the docking ring where Dr. Goldie's shuttlecraft is already emerging from its hangar. "Okay, *Love* Shuttle 1, Darter 2-M-4 here to escort you over. Lead the way."

The crisp voice of his fellow pilot resonates over Potts' headset. "Glad to have you with us, [Pilot-Sergeant]."

★

As he flies alongside the shuttlecraft, Potts can't help but wonder just how anyone could have survived what's happened to the T'irsh-fel ship in front of them. It looks even more badly beaten up than *Equinox* did. The oil-slick geometric decorative surfaces of the ship's exterior are scorched away across most of what's left of it. There's a massive debris field surrounding it, too, which Potts and his pilot friend on the shuttlecraft are having to carefully navigate as they approach.

That debris field is a major reason for *My-Love-is-the-Stars* to be hovering several kilometers away from the derelict vessel. The Captain's concerns regarding both the potential arrival of Novan attackers and the T'irsh-fel ship's engine stability account for the rest of the distance. Potts is somehow not surprised at all that there's a chance the remaining fuel in the damaged ship's engine compartments could be unstable enough to explode without warning. It's just the sort of thing he's started to expect to be told about whenever he gets involved with a mission.

"Say, Lily," he asks, banking to one side to follow the shuttle pilot's lead and avoid a larger chunk of debris, "how far exactly does that telekinesis thing you do reach?"

"This humble self can currently grip objects up to ten meters away with ease. To project her hold further requires considerable focus. A ranking member of the Hierarchy connected with the All could be expected to control a range of one hundred meters."

"Good to know. If you see any of this debris heading for a collision with us or the shuttlecraft that's within your reach, do me a favor and toss it out of the way before it hits us." The darter is equipped with the most advanced magnetic repulsion shields humanity has to offer, but Potts isn't keen to test out just how much those shields can stand today. His T'irsh-fel friend makes a good copilot, but having her able to lessen the risks involved in flying in a situation like this is a luxury in his world.

"Understood. This humble self will keep a watch for such objects."

"Thanks." Potts pauses to tap into his com-link to the shuttlecraft. "*Love* Shuttle 1, it looks like we're about there. I'll hover around the docking site until you confirm you're starting the operation, and then pull back enough to keep an eye on things. Let us know when you're ready to head back."

The Prelvee pilot gives him a no-nonsense acknowledgment, then begins her approach to the one spot on the hulking wreck where the shuttlecraft can safely dock. It's right down on the former lowest deck of the T'irsh-fel vessel. The majority of the upper levels are scattered in pieces around the debris field, but Potts has been assured that *Love's* scans of the ship indicate a number of faint life signatures.

He's grateful, in a way, that his part of the plan today doesn't involve crawling through the wreckage looking for survivors. Potts has known Lily long enough now to consider her a dear friend, but he has no idea how one checks to see if an unconscious T'irsh-fel is alive. He wasn't really looking forward to finding out, either.

Once the shuttlecraft is safely docked, Potts moves his darter into the best position he can find that offers both a good clear area to hover and views of both the T'irsh-fel ship and the somewhat distant golden orb-and-rings of *Love*. He's still on edge, with the memory of *Equinox* occupying the tiny portion of his mind that isn't focused on flying at the moment.

Potts has never been good at sitting still, though.

"So, Lily," he asks, "without interrupting her by asking... is it going okay with Dr. Goldie's end of things?"

"The level of 'okay' is subjective, but my dear Lady the Doctor expresses her relief that a viable atmosphere was still present in the remnant of the vessel. The survivors seem to be relatively unharmed compared to her expectations."

Potts nods. "Good. I'll be happy about that once we've got them safely back over to *Love*."

Lily is silent for a few moments, then gentle as she speaks again. *"Forgive this humble self, honored friend Julian, but she cannot avoid glimpsing the memories of your last experience with a situation such as this. You project them rather loudly."*

Potts stares out at the stars between the wreck and Love. "I'm sorry about that. You shouldn't have to see them... *Equinox* wasn't scattered like this ship is, but it was still a mess getting everyone out."

"So this humble self has noticed." She takes on a lighter tone. *"For your reference, since you have also projected your curiosity: you would be best served to check for a heartbeat in one of the major blood vessels which run along either side of one of my eye stalks."*

Potts almost laughs at that, it was so unexpected. "Well, then. Good to know. Let's hope I'm never in a position to need to do that."

Having a friend who's tapped into his mind is *odd*, but he finds he doesn't mind the oddness. Lily is good company, especially since he has to sit around and wait to either escort the shuttlecraft back to *Love* or deal with a Novan attack.

★

Half an hour later, as Potts adjusts the darter's position to stay in a good spot relative to the wreck of the T'irsh-fel ship, Lily catches his attention again.

"Honored friend Julian," she begins with a touch of eagerness in her telepathic voice, *"could you please adjust our position another few meters in that direction? This*

humble self has spotted something in the debris around us which could be of use."

Potts can feel which direction she's indicating, as if there's a mental arrow pointing at a particular cluster of objects just to one side of them. It's a strange sensation, but it's far more convenient than trying to have Lily describe where she wants him to go. "You got it. What are we looking for?"

"Ah! There! Hold your position relative to that large piece of the vessel's former hull, please." Lily falls silent, projecting to him a sensation that she is focusing very hard on something.

Potts does as he's asked. He has to admit he's curious as to what his friend has discovered.

Within five minutes, he has his answer. A meter-wide sphere dotted with glimmering lights and traced over with the same oil-slick geometric designs as the other T'irsh-fel tech he's seen is now hovering directly in front of the darter.

"This is one of the vessel's protection drones!" Lily's excitement sends a prickle down Potts' spine, she's so pleased by her discovery. *"This humble self was able to use its emergency activation codes to bring it online and under her control. It was laying dormant because the controllers aboard the vessel were in one of the sections which no longer exists. In their honor, we can use it to aid us in protecting the survivors."*

Potts grins. "I like it already. Do you think there might be more of those floating around?"

"Almost certainly. Whether they are intact or not is unknown, but there will likely be more which have gone dormant."

"You think we could pick those up too? Or can you just control one at a time?" Potts is getting the beginnings of an idea, and he has a feeling Lily is too.

"Protection drones are designed to function as swarms. An individual controller with experience can maintain roughly thirty of them actively at once, and give instruction to additional swarms to follow the actively controlled ones in a chain if necessary."

"Good. Let Dr. Goldie know that we're going on a little patrol around the debris field, will you?"

"As the human saying goes, 'you are thinking what this humble self is thinking?'" Lily sounds incredibly pleased with herself.

"That I am, Lily, and not just because of your link thing." Potts guides the darter through a loose circle around the remainder of the T'irsh-fel vessel. "Just let me know when you notice another one so I can bring you close enough to grab it..."

★

"Darter 2-M-4," says the voice of *Love's* communications officer over Potts' headset, *"we have noticed a change in your flight path relative to the plan. Please confirm your status."*

Potts is a touch surprised that it's taken most of an hour for Love's crew to notice that he's up to something. *"Love* Flight Control, I hear you. Can you see me clearly if I pop out of the thick of the debris field for a moment?"

"Visual on you is blocked for the moment, but yes. [Captain] asks if you have a good reason for moving out of your assigned position."

Potts grins as he pulls the darter up through a spot where Love should have a clear view of him. Behind him, a whole swarm of protection drones is neatly flying in a perfect formation that could rival the most practiced flock of birds. "Tell the Captain to take a good look at the little birthday present Lily's picked for me. We're heading back to our mark now, standing by for word from the shuttlecraft."

There's a long pause, and then Potts hears *Love's* Captain speaking through his headset instead of the communications officer. "*[Pilot-Sergeant], please convey my appreciation to [Physician's Companion]. We will celebrate your hatching anniversary when you return to my ship. Am I correct in remembering you telling me over dinner the story of how your family typically marks such occasions?*"

"Yes, Ma'am." Potts chuckles softly. The Captain seems to be just as wary of the Novans listening in on their conversation as he is. "But I'd be happy to bring my own surprise to the party this time. Returning to position now. Darter 2-M-4 out."

Lily shares his amusement over their telepathic link. "*This humble self has also conveyed to her dear Lady the Doctor that we are now better prepared to defend her and the survivors. She is pleased.*"

"Glad to hear it." Potts flies back to his position guarding the shuttlecraft's docking site. "Say, can you stash our little friends back among all of this mess so it's not obvious we have them ready?"

"*Yes, that will be useful. Please stand by as this humble self focuses her attention on instructing the protection drones which will be outside her direct contact range.*"

Potts finds himself strangely relaxed as he continues to scan the view of deep space outside his darter's canopy bubble for any sign of approaching Novans. It's nice to be *prepared* to be ambushed for once.

★

SEVERAL HOURS LATER, POTTS AND LILY ARE STILL sitting in the darter near the wreck of the T'irsh-fel vessel. From what Lily's relayed to him, Dr. Goldie found more survivors than *Love's* scans had indicated. This is actually their second trip out escorting the shuttle, since there were more injured T'irsh-fel than could fit into it on one run.

As dull as the extensive lurking in the debris field is, Potts is glad things are going so much more smoothly than *Equinox's* recovery did. He's grateful to have Lily's eyes behind him, too. It's nice to have so much wider of a field of vision around his darter. It's an odd sensation, though, to be aware of her perception even though he can't see it for himself.

Their second trip into the debris field was much smoother; Lily had taken the liberty of nudging the masses of objects out of the way as they flew by on the way out. There's now a relatively clear corridor out, as well as a decently-sized clear area around the shuttlecraft's docking site. Potts has learned a new element to T'irsh-fel philosophy, too: "If one has unoccupied time and a means of making things less difficult for future endeavors, one should take advantage of this." He's pretty sure that means that a touch of his restless energy had projected into Lily's mind over her link with him—or that she's *also* the sort of person who can't stand sitting around doing nothing.

Clearing flight paths and nudging the debris into larger piles that serve as convenient hiding places for Lily's swarm of protection drones was a good distraction from his sense of impending battle, at least. No matter how smoothly things have been going, Potts still can't shake the feeling of being in the middle of an unsprung trap.

"*Darter 2-M-4,*" the shuttlecraft's pilot calls Potts' headset, "*[Physician] has secured the last survivor. We are ready to launch for our return flight.*"

"Roger that, *Love* Shuttle 1. Ready to escort you back. You're clear to launch. *Love* Flight Control, do you copy?"

Love's communications officer responds within moments. "*Control here. We are preparing for your arrival.*"

Potts pulls into position beside the shuttlecraft. One by one, Lily's new protection drone friends come out of their hiding places and join him as he flies out of the stand-by range she's set for them. For a few moments, as they're nearing the edges of the debris field, Potts starts to think that he's been too paranoid for his own good about all of this.

Then, in a quick succession of events, he is reminded that for a darter pilot, "paranoia" is another word for "finely honed survival instincts that shouldn't be ignored."

First, out of nowhere, he hears the all-too-familiar sound of Wyndi throwing a tantrum and hissing in between their rapid, alarmed squeaks. He wouldn't have been too shocked by this, normally, but Potts is certain that he'd left Wyndi back on *Love* where they'd be safe with Dusty. He doesn't even have to glance backward to see that they are, in fact, in his darter. His link with Lily hits him hard with her perception of Wyndi popping out from under her seat and holding onto one of her eye-stalks with their long prehensile tail as they float in the microgravity of the cockpit.

"Wyndi! What in the *stars* are you doing here? Settle down, we're almost—"

Before he can finish the thought, Lily projects the view through her eye that the little Florivan is so desperately trying to point in the same direction that they're aiming all of their squeaks and hissing. "*Mirawynd is correct. Our attackers have arrived.*"

Lily is a master of understatement. There's dozens of bright yellow flashes coming at them from that direction: a whole squadron of Novan strikers, perhaps more than one.

"Let Dr. Goldie know. Wyndi, come get in my pocket—I'll scold you later." Potts keys into his comms and then pulls up to set his darter between the shuttlecraft and the Novans. Lily's remaining protection drones come out of their hiding places and form up around him. "*Love* Flight Control, we've got Novans incoming…"

★

If someone had asked Potts at any point in his childhood what he thought he'd be doing for his twentieth birthday, "flying around defending a Prelvee ship and shuttle full of T'irsh-fel refugees from the most Novan strikers he's ever seen in one battle" would hardly have been his answer. By all rights, he should be back on *Surnia* being teased by Rudy and the Majors over cupcakes or something like that.

His life, it seems, is not so straightforward.

Even with their preparations for an expected ambush, *Love* was still caught off-guard by the sheer mass of Novan forces that descended upon them as soon as the message that all of the survivors had been recovered went out. Potts was alarmed, too, to see a bigger bright yellow Novan craft appear behind the strikers and start firing at *Love*. With the Prelvee ship's defensive shields up and strikers buzzing all around her, there's been no safe window to get the shuttlecraft through and docked so that *Love* can make her escape.

To that end, Potts has the shuttle holding position in one of the relatively defensible spots Lily had cleared. Her swarm of protection drones is tightly surrounding the shuttle, zapping away any striker that tries a run at it with the eerily purple laser pulses the drones use as weapons.

For his part, Potts has been dodging any strikers that try to come after his darter, leading them away from the shuttle and into the thicker parts of the debris field. As it turns out, even with the swarm of protection drones under her control, Lily's still got enough mental focus to fling a sizable chunk of rubble into the strikers' paths on his mark. They never notice fast enough to dodge out of the way.

And still, the strikers keep coming.

Every now and again, Potts catches a glimpse of the ongoing duel between *My-Love-is-the-Stars* and the big Novan ship. He's not sure anymore how long his Prelvee friends will be able to hold out, but he's too busy flying to dwell on the thought.

All he has to do is keep flying and defend the shuttlecraft. Buy enough time, and those other two Alliance ships the Captain had mentioned are sure to show up.

He wishes he had the rest of the Musketeers here. Darter pilots aren't meant to fly solo.

As soon as the thought's crossed his mind, three of Lily's protection drones pull into position alongside him: two on his right, one on his left.

"Here," she says as a sensation of feeling the presence of those four drones crosses their link and settles into his mind. *"We are more compatible than this humble self realized. Consider these your squadron; they will follow your lead."*

With that, Lily's focus clearly turns back to the rest of the swarm. He can still distinctly feel the three drones, as if they're more than just in his peripheral vision outside the polyglass of the canopy.

Potts doesn't have time to question it. "Okay, gals," he says, more to himself than to the drones, "let's dance with these strikers and see if we can't make a dent in them..."

★

It's easy to lose track of time in the midst of a battle. So much is happening so quickly that all a pilot can do is react and focus on flying the mission and not crashing into anything.

Potts can feel himself starting to tire, though. He's only been a qualified darter pilot for two years, and aside from *Equinox*, this is his first intensive combat. As well-trained as he is, it's still becoming all but overwhelming.

"Lily," he asks, pulling the darter into a tight roll to avoid a chunk of debris and the striker behind him, "do you see any path we could possibly clear to get the shuttle back to *Love*? We're at half charge now on our reserves, and I don't want to wind up a sitting duck out here when that runs out."

"Possibly, but the ship is still under heavy attack. It will be risky, especially as they will have to drop a portion of their combat shielding to let us inside the docking rings."

"We're going to have to risk it. See if you can set the drones to form up entirely around the shuttle and let Dr. Goldie know what we're planning, then grab as much of the small debris as you can to take with us to throw at anything the drones and I miss. I'll call *Love* and—"

Once again, Potts is interrupted by excited kitten squeaks, this time from the depths of his jacket pocket. Wyndi pops out of it and climbs up onto his shoulder before he can scold them, squeaking happily and bouncing up and down, their tail keeping them anchored to his collar.

"Wyndi!" He starts to scold them to get back into his pocket, but a thought occurs to them. "Lily, please tell me that's not another big Novan ship dropping in on us that Wyndi's noticed before we did."

Lily's elation matches the kittens when she replies. "*It is not! They are pointing to two Alliance vessels that have just dropped into visible speed and are approaching!*"

"Thank the *stars*. New plan. We stay right here and defend the shuttle until one of the friendly ships is ready to call us in to dock. Agreed?"

"*Agreed!*"

Wyndi, too, lets out a squeak that sounds like an affirmation before they slip back into Potts' pocket. Somehow, the fact that they begin purring almost immediately tells him that the worst of it is over.

★

POTTS SLEEPS THROUGH THE MAJORITY OF THE next few days after the battle, rising from his bunk only to see to hygiene needs and to escort Wyndi to acquire food from *Love's* officer's mess. He's barely aware of his own hunger, but he can't exactly leave them to roam the ship freely right now. There's repairs underway all over the place, and the infirmary is too busy for them to hang out with Lily and Dr. Goldie like they usually do. Even though all of the survivors from the wrecked ship have been returned to their own doctors aboard the T'irsh-fel vessel that arrived at the end of the battle, his friend the doctor still has her claws full with all of the casualties *Love's* crew sustained during the Novan attack.

He'd assisted for a few hours when they first came aboard, but there wasn't much a human could do to help. In the end, Dr. Goldie had wiped her claws off on her surgical apron, patted him on the head, and told him to go rest and take care of himself before he passed out on her. The tired parts of him and the parts that are still instinctively afraid of the Prelvee's insect-like characteristics had agreed that she was right.

It's been a long time since Potts has been quite this exhausted. He knows a lot of it is mental. His uncles and his flight instructors both had warned him at various points in his life that real emergency situations were far more mentally and physically taxing than simulations could ever be. For that matter, he'd been subjected to a *long* conversation with the Defense Fleet's staff psychologist, Dr. Navy, along with the rest of the Musketeers, about combat fatigue, human stress responses, and the need to find healthy ways to cope with the realities of their work as darter pilots. At the time, he'd thought that tea-and-lecture business had been directed at the Majors, what with them being only a few months out from the battle that had cost not only the rest of their squadron, but the starship *Athene* that had been their home and all the rest of their crew. Now, he knows that Dr. Navy was trying to prepare him for the things they knew he was bound to experience flying as the Musketeers' fourth.

This had been Potts' first real sustained combat experience aside from the *Equinox* disaster, and against overwhelming odds, at that—is it any wonder he barely has the energy to function?

The only reason he finally awakens fully on this particular day and goes to the trouble of getting dressed is the squeaky insistence of a certain Florivan kitten keen on the idea of food. Food, and pointing out to him that there's a message flashing on his cabin's interface screen that Wyndi has deemed important. Potts is glad once he reads it that he hasn't overslept so far as to be late for his dinner appointment with the Captain—although he still doesn't remember having made one. The note is clear enough, though, and for the first time in days he genuinely feels like eating.

Wyndi seems rather pleased with themself once they get him out the door. They keep scampering back and forth ahead of him all the way to *Love's* Captain's study.

"Wyndi, will you settle down?" Potts yawns as he lumbers after the kitten. "Some of us aren't nearly as sparky as you are..."

Wyndi scampers back to him and climbs up to his shoulder, nuzzling against his cheek for a moment or two. They're squeaking something he still can't understand. For some reason, the Prelvee translator chip in his ear still hasn't gotten the hang of whatever language it is that Florivan kittens use.

"Yes, yes, I know, you love me and you want me to feed you." Potts carries on the conversation as if he understands anyway. "But you're still in trouble for stowing away the other day, so would you please settle until I'm awake enough to handle you?"

Wyndi squeaks cheerfully and bounces back down from his shoulder, scampering away down the corridor. They sit and squeak in front of the door to the Captain's study, which to Potts' surprise, opens and allows them in. He picks up his pace to follow, but the exhaustion coupled with the higher gravity and heat don't allow him much room for speed. The door's closed again by the time he gets there.

When it opens, he's confused to see that the lights are off in the room. He's more confused, though, when his eyes adjust and find that there's some sort of a soft glow coming from behind one of the larger seating cushions on the far wall. There's barely enough illumination from that to allow him to make out the familiar shapes of the other furniture.

Before he can say anything, Wyndi appears out of the darkness, squeaking excitedly at him and tugging on his pant leg.

"What in the *stars* is going on, Wyndi?" He follows the insistent kitten to his usual seat, even though somewhere in the back of his mind he has the distinct sensation of being watched. He keeps thinking he hears some sort of sounds around him, too, although he can't see the source of them.

Wyndi hops up onto the table beside him. In his peripheral vision, he thinks he sees that dim light source on the other side of the room move. He's about to turn to look, but then Wyndi is on top of his head and doing their best to cover his eyes with all four of their tiny hands and their tail. They squeak something that he almost thinks is a word in the Prelvee language, although his translator chip doesn't seem to agree.

All at once, the lights come on. Wyndi gets all of their appendages out of his face with a cheerful squeak.

Potts finds that he is surrounded by people he hadn't seen in the room at all. *Love's* Captain, Dr. Goldie, Lily, Dusty, and two other Prelvee he doesn't recognize are all clustered around him. All of the Prelvee click their upper claws together happily.

The suddenness of it all nearly shocks Potts out of his skin. He manages not to give in to the instinct to faint, but only barely. "What in the—*Why*—"

It's Lily's soft voice and presence returning to the back of his mind that brings everything into focus. *"Belated fond wishes on the occasion of your hatching anniversary, honored friend Julian. Did we perform the ritual of surprising correctly?"*

It's at this point that Potts realizes that sitting in front of him on the small table is not only his little scamp of a Florivan kitten, but a feast suitable for the whole lot of them. In the center of it all is a large platter bearing the largest version of the steamed fruit buns he's ever seen. Its outer layer is the deep green that signifies the filling is the apple-ish Prelvee fruit he likes best, and over this is drizzled a thick, creamy sauce of some kind with thin slices of candied fruit stuck into it as decoration.

"You... really surprised me, yes."

"Excellent!" says *Love's* Captain. "If my understanding of human custom is correct, this means you are to be blessed with good fortune. Or does your breath need to pass over the celebratory dessert? I must apologize that our ship's safety protocols will not permit us to set it on fire first."

Potts finds himself trading his fear response in for laughter. A birthday party—and with the Captain of an alien ship which was nearly destroyed in a battle only days ago as a main conspirator in the surprise, at that. Somehow, this is the final absurdity in Potts' life that makes everything else he's gone through since he left Teegarden fall into place as a grand hilarity of the universe.

It takes him a minute or two to stop laughing long enough to catch his breath, although he can hear Lily assuring the rest of the group that his response feels like a positive one rather than an insult to their efforts. "Sorry about that. I…" He pauses, wiping a laughter tear out of his eye. Somehow, all of the exhaustion and tension he didn't know he's been holding is gone now. "Well. I wasn't expecting this at all. And no need for fire, Captain—I never was good at blowing out candles anyway. Thank you, everyone."

Dr. Goldie's tone says she's amused at it all herself. Since she's coiled up right next to him now, she reaches out a claw and gently pats him on the head. "We are delighted to celebrate with you, [Pilot-Sergeant], especially after we had to postpone our plans to do this."

Potts is beginning to wonder just how long his friends have been conspiring to throw this little party. He tries to think back on all of the conversations he's had with them over the last few weeks. When had he mentioned that he was about to turn twenty? He can't remember right now.

"I'm glad we're all here to celebrate." He looks over to the other two Prelvee. They're both a purple-orange sort of iridescent. Judging by their size, they're likely female, although one of them is clearly younger; she's about the same size as Dusty. "And it's nice to meet both of you, too."

Love's Captain waves her facial tentacles almost dramatically. "[Pilot-Sergeant], this is my colleague [Captain of *Mind-Over-Dark-Matter*], and her student and chosen daughter [Junior Physician]. Their ship arrived this morning to assist with the last of the emergency repairs that must be done before *Geese-of-the-Wild-Wind* and *Tz'zyr'ik* can tow my vessel back to one of our bases." She turns her great square-pupiled eye to the two purple-toned Prelvee officers. "My friends, this is [Pilot-Sergeant], whom you've heard so much about."

Dark Matter's Captain dips her head nobly. The younger Prelvee next to her extends a claw towards Potts in what he's come to recognize as a polite greeting gesture but not an invitation to shake hands. "It is most plea-sing to meet you, Pi-lot Ser-geant Potts," she says in crisply accented Coalition Standard. "My grasp of your lan-guage is small, but I will be pleased to prac-tice with you."

Potts raises his hand towards her in acknowledgment. "It's nice to meet both of you," he repeats, unsure what else to say.

Love's Captain breaks any awkward silence before it can properly manifest. "[Pilot-Sergeant,]" she says, gesturing for the others to take their proper seats around the table and picking up her eating hooks as a signal that the meal may now begin, "although we are here to celebrate your having survived another year as your people measure things, we are also in a way bidding you a fond farewell."

Potts makes the appropriate polite gesture with his own set of eating hooks as he accepts the morsel that *Love's* Captain has picked up from the nearest serving plate and offered towards him. "Farewell?" He is starting to get an idea of what she means, but he's not certain.

"Unfortunately," she continues, "my ship is too badly damaged to continue on its intended course. We are to be towed back to our nearest base for reconstruction and an exchange of personnel so that those who were more severely injured may recover in a more suitable setting. With the understanding that you would prefer to be returned to your people as soon as possible, I have made an arrangement for your transfer to *Mind-Over-Dark-Matter* for the rest of your journey. If you wish to stay with us instead, it will be several additional months before my ship is bound in the correct direction once more."

"You are welcomed, [Pilot-Sergeant]," says *Dark Matter's* Captain. Her clicks and buzzes sound strained and somber, as if talking is somehow difficult for her. She turns to the younger Prelvee beside her and makes a series of gestures with her upper claws. Potts suspects this must be some form of Prelvee sign language, but his translator chip doesn't seem to be able to help him understand it.

"We go to Kap-ty-en's Star an-y-way," says the Junior Physician, "to take one of our am-bas-sa-dors to meet with your Ad-mir-al."

"I will be accompanying you, [Pilot-Sergeant]," Dusty adds, her tone saying that she's pleased about this. "It's been decided I should because I am the engineer most familiar with your little spacecraft."

Potts nods, still trying to take everything in. "Thank you, then. I'm grateful to be heading in the right direction."

The meal carries on, with the others cheerfully discussing various bits of ship's business, the recent battle, and some sort of obscure Prelvee sport that both of the Captains played in their youth. The latter topic reminds Potts far too much of listening to Major Albright talk about hoverpolo with any other martian she encounters.

Apparently, the Captains support teams with a history of friendly rivalry.

Potts finds himself quieter during the meal than he normally would be. He should be happy that this arrangement will shorten his journey back to *Surnia* and his squadron. Still, after everything he's gone through with *Love's* crew—and with Dr. Goldie and Lily in particular—it's all colored with shades of melancholic regret to be leaving his friends. It's nice to know that Dusty, at least, will still be around.

"Honored friend Julian," he hears Lily say in the gentle tone that somehow makes him certain that only he and Dr. Goldie can hear her words, *"please understand that we also regret that you must depart sooner than we expected. In the short time we have known you, you have become a most honored and precious friend. You will always be as a part of this humble self's All, even if distance prevents us speaking. My dear Lady the Doctor is certain that our paths will cross again."*

Potts smiles, hearing that. A few months ago, the idea of being telepathically linked to an alien he'd found by chance in an ancient cave would have seemed like the wildest of his Aunt Kit's tall tales—much less the intensity of combat making at least some degree of that link permanent. He does his best to project a replying thought to her, and is pleased to note a sense that Lily is receiving it. *"Thank you, Lily. I did need to hear that. I'm going to miss you both."*

Dr. Goldie, presumably being passed this message from Lily, sets her eating hooks down beside her plate for a moment while she leans over again to briefly pat Potts on the head with a gentle claw. "It will be hard to adjust to not having you with us, [Pilot-Sergeant]." After a moment, she lets out a warm buzzing sound that equates to a Prelvee chuckle. "[Captain of *Mind-Over-Dark-Matter*], has my colleague told you yet how [Pilot-Sergeant] assisted me to acquire [Physician's Companion Lily] while we were at Jewel-Eye?"

After a series of claw-gestures from her Captain, the Junior Physician is the one to reply. "No, but my Cap-tain would like to hear."

Potts shakes his head. "At least that's not the *most* embarrassing story she has to tell you about me... it's a long one, though." He's reminded again how much Dr. Goldie is like his friend Reba's mother—good-humored gossiping about all of the odd ways her charges have found to get themselves into trouble is one of her favorite things.

Dr. Goldie is clearly pleased with herself for changing the subject so deftly to something more likely to bolster Potts' morale. "I shall tell you, then! We'd gone down to Jewel-Eye to visit my old colleagues at the City of Caves..."

As his friends cheerfully explain how he and Lily found each other, Potts shares bits of seaweed and fruit delicacies with Wyndi and lets them do most of the talking. Lily's right, he decides by the time they come to cut slices out of the big fruit bun "cake": friends find their way back to each other, sooner or later. Being passed off to *Dark Matter's* crew for the final leg of his journey is exactly what needs to happen.

It's time he found his way back to the Musketeers.

★

EPILOGUE:
THE PILOT, RETURNED

HUMANS HAVE NEVER BEEN ABLE TO COME TO A satisfactory conclusion about the nature of choice and destiny.

Some argue that one's choices are all self-determinate, and that there is no inevitability of any one thing happening over another. Others claim that there is—must be—some greater force at work, directing people towards some specific path. Many highlight the concepts of probabilities and natural laws, and on every conceivable side of the argument. Still others try to combine the two concepts, saying that each person makes the choices that are inevitable for *themself* at the time given their personality, history, and circumstances.

Chance encounters and seemingly random occurrences tend to throw all sides of this argument into chaos looking for an explanation which falls in line with their position. Is it fate which leads two people to meet, or simply the sum of each of their choices? Is it *destiny* which informs the course of history, or the cumulative effect of one single atom having formed and acted according to its nature?

These are the sorts of questions which drive philosophers and mathematicians mad. In any case, whatever their root cause, personal whims and chance encounters have more to do with the paths a person takes than not.

In the case of one young human who has just arrived at the Horizon Prime Station in orbit of Kapteyn b, no amount of foresight would ever have been able to tell him that stopping to re-tie his bootlaces before getting on the lift down from the Station's upper docking ring is the latest thing to place him on a collision course with destiny.

The young human in question is no stranger to odd twists of fate, although on this particular day he is under the mistaken impression that having finally been returned to his own people is a conclusion to the latest turn his life has taken. He is, after all, quite ordinary as far as humans went—in his own mind, if not in truth.

Potts could easily have been mistaken for any number of humans with business on the Station.

Darter pilots like him are far from an uncommon sight, since it's the Defense Fleet's base of operations in the system. If anyone might chance to consider Potts as something other than a single ant in a large anthill, though, they would doubtless notice both that he has the particular spring in his step characteristic to a person who has spent rather longer than they'd have liked in a higher level of artificial gravity than the Earth-normal variety found on the Station.

Potts walks with the carefree gait of a person who's just had both literal and metaphorical weights lifted from them and the directed cheerfulness of someone coming home from a long journey, eager to be reunited with his friends—if he can only manage to find them.

"Well, now, Wyndi!" Potts says with a satisfied chuckle as he stops to take in the view of the large atrium level he's just entered from one of its many overlooking balconies. "We're finally back where we belong. I *told* you I'd get us home to my outfit sooner or later, didn't I?"

The atrium spreads out before him like a vast marketplace courtyard. Tall reinforced polyglass viewports stand all along the curving exterior wall, while doors to a wide variety of recreational spaces and other facilities line the interior on three vertical levels. The open space in between is enhanced with hydroponic plantings of small fruit trees and dotted with semicircular benches— the closest thing a place like this can arrange to simulate a planetside environment. All of this, of course, had been originally built as a civilian spaceport. It wasn't all that long ago that all passengers and commerce going between Kapteyn's original colony planet below and Humanity's other five star systems came through here. Now, Horizon Prime Station leads a different life altogether.

Having taken in his fill of the view, Potts wanders down to the courtyard level of the atrium to take a look at a directory-information holoscreen floating between two of the trees.

"Do you see it up there, Wyndi?" he asks, lightly patting the larger breast pocket of his jacket. "We're looking for SCV *Surnia*. That's our ship! They should have beaten us here by a week or two at least…"

To anyone who might happen to hear, he would seem to be talking to himself. He is, after all, standing seemingly alone in front of the directory screen. Wyndi had decided almost immediately upon being introduced to the Station's climate that it was time for them to take a nap and let Potts handle things. If he didn't know how much being cold bothered them, he'd be concerned that the irrepressible little Florivan kitten isn't eager to explore everything around them. As it stands, he can feel their soft purring in his pocket—he suspects they're also a bit sulky from saying goodbye to Dusty and all of the friends they'd made during their time on *Mind-Over-Dark-Matter*. Wyndi never likes saying goodbye to people.

After a few moments, Potts finds the information he's looking for. SCV *Surnia* is docked on one of the Station's lower levels, as are two of the Defense Fleet's other large carrier-class vessels and the Admiral's flagship. It's about as far as one can get on Horizon Prime Station from the upper-deck priority berth where *Mind-Over-Dark-Matter* had docked. Somewhere far above him, Dusty is busy arranging the transfer of his darter to *Surnia* with the Station's transport tow team. He'd have loved to take his friend with him to explore today. Unfortunately, *Dark Matter* is only here to drop the Ambassador and his guard off before they head back out on another mission.

"There we are, Wyndi!" Potts pats his pocket again and strides off excitedly. "Just you wait, the Majors are going to be *thrilled* when we show up and surprise them."

As he approaches the crew lifts for the lower levels, Potts isn't paying much attention to where he's walking. He's too caught up in his one-sided conversation with his pocket and with trying to remember which corridor marking to watch for once he gets to the right deck. This is, as it turns out, distraction enough that he doesn't notice at all that he's put himself on an intersecting course with an officer heading in the opposite direction.

Unfortunately, this particular officer's eyes are *equally* distracted with the holoscreen of their pocket-com. They don't see the pilot walking towards them any more than he does them.

"Now," says Potts, still talking seemingly to himself, "once I report in to Colonel Bell and make sure my darter's been delivered to her, we'll find *Surnia's* jumper and see if they—"

The inevitable collision cuts him off mid-sentence.

Both Potts and the officer fall to the floor. He instinctively twists his body to ensure that nothing impacts with the breast pocket of his jacket where Wyndi is still sleeping.

Uninjured, Potts is the first to get to his feet. He dusts himself off and pats his the pocket lightly. He knows Wyndi's unharmed just from the fact that he can still feel their nap-time purr vibrating through the fabric. After a moment, he realizes that he's run into a person and looks down to the officer.

They're still on the ground.

The officer is unmistakably Florivan, with skin of an unusually pale blue-green color compared to the other members of their species whom Potts has encountered. Their long silver hair is tied up in a complex braided bun woven through with semi-sheer ribbons which match the colors of their Defense Fleet uniform and drape partway down the back of their neck like a veil. Under the long forest green and ivory officer's jacket they're wearing like a cape, the Florivan has both arms on one side of their body encased in slings and medical casts.

That last detail, Potts assumes, is the reason they haven't stood up yet.

"*Stars*! Are you alright, sir?" Potts offers his hand down to them.

"I'm fine, really," the Florivan officer tells him with a genial laugh, once he's helped them get to their feet. "Gravity's just out to get me lately, that's all—especially the artificial sort." Just like Wyndi, their lightly accented voice carries after-tones like wind chimes in a gentle breeze.

"That explains the..." Potts gestures vaguely at the Florivan officer's injured arms.

"Yes," says the Florivan officer, "I suppose it does."

"Well, anyway," Potts says, sheepishly running a hand through the back of his hair, "I am sorry for crashing into you, sir. I suppose I need to learn to watch where I'm going."

"I probably need to learn to do that *myself*." The Florivan officer shoots him a wry smile as they pick up their dropped pocket-com with their tail and tuck it back into one of the pockets of their jacket. "I'm fortunate my Navigator wasn't around to see this little incident and get overly concerned about whether I've gone and hurt myself again—he makes such a fuss over me, anymore."

Potts nods. He's sure the Florivan officer's Navigator worries about them just as much as he does about Wyndi. "I'll be on my way, then, sir," he says, feeling awkward for no apparent reason. He gestures vaguely towards the crew lifts. "Sorry again for running into you."

"Oh, it was my fault as much as yours for walking while preoccupied." The Florivan officer dusts themself off as best they can, still sounding more amused than anything. "I'll wish you a less eventful walk to wherever you're going, though."

Potts smiles broadly. "Thank you, sir—and I'll wish you the same, then." He turns to go, but then a soft, sleepy squeak from the kitten curled up in the depths of his pocket makes him hesitate. He looks back to the Florivan officer, having barely taken more than three steps away. "Actually, sir, do you have a minute? I've been needing to ask one of you—a Florivan, that is—some questions for a while now, and it's... well, kind of important?"

"Hmm..." The Florivan officer is silent for a moment, then smiles at him. "I'm on leave and my Navigator's busy. I have plenty of time to spare... but depending on the questions, I can't guarantee that I'll have any answers for you."

Potts breathes a small sigh of relief. "To be honest, sir? Anything you could tell me at all would be helpful."

"I'll admit, young human, I'm curious. Come, sit with me and ask your questions." The Florivan officer strides over to one of the nearby benches with a beckoning swish of their long tufted tail.

Potts follows, giving his pocket another reassuring pat.

"So," the Florivan officer asks, arranging themself into a comfortable sitting position with one leg tucked up under the other and their whole body angled toward Potts, "what sort of questions do you have that you needed one of my people to answer them and couldn't find out for yourself on the relays?"

"Well, it's... kind of a long story, really, sir." Potts plops down beside them, similarly angling himself for ease of conversation. "The short version is that one of your people kind of... well, gave me something to take care of a while back—but they didn't have time to give me any real instructions for how I was supposed to take care of it."

"Oh?" The tuft at the end of the Florivan officer's tail waves curiously.

"Yeah..." Potts hesitated, awkwardly rubbing at the back of his neck with one hand. "I've been doing my best, sir—but to be honest, I have no idea if I've done anything right... or what I'm supposed to do now that I'm finally back with the Fleet."

The Florivan officer raises all three of their eyebrows. "Perhaps it would be best if you showed me what it was you were given?"

"Right! I probably should have done that first." Potts gently reached a hand into the pocket of his jacket, speaking softly to his little copilot. "Come on out, Wyndi, I know you must be awake by now. I have someone for you to meet."

Wyndi makes a pointedly unhappy little bell-like squeak and seems set on not coming out at all.

Potts looks back to the Florivan officer. "Sorry, sir, Wyndi's a little shy today—probably because it's colder here than they're used to? We've been hitchhiking with Prelvee ships for a while now."

"I see." The Florivan officer nods, still with a curious tone in their voice. "I've been on Prelvee ships briefly here and there for conferences. I can't say I care for the higher artificial gravity, but your species could certainly learn a thing or two about comfortable temperatures from them."

"Somehow, I'm not surprised you'd think that, sir." Potts goes back to cajoling the stubborn inhabitant of his pocket. "Really, now, Wyndi, at least poke your head up and say hello to—" He pauses, looking back over to the officer. "I'm sorry, sir—I completely forgot the introductions, didn't I?"

"I believe we both did." The Florivan gives him a small nod and a slow three-eyed blink of amusement. "I'm called Celadon."

Potts dips his own head briefly in return. "Pilot-Sergeant Julian Potts, sir. And my friend here, if they will ever cooperate and come out—"

With a small, thoroughly unimpressed squeak, Wyndi's furry little silver head pops out cautiously from under the pocket flap. Their three sleepy golden eyes halfway glare up Potts.

"Ah! There you are! Now stop giving me that look, I woke you up for a good reason." He tickles them under their chin briefly, then turns his attention back to the officer. "This is Mirawynd, sir."

All three of the Florivan officer's eyes widen for a few moments, and then their expression softens. "Well, now...

hello there, little one." They reach out the long fingers of their free upper hand towards Wyndi, making a soft wordless trilling sound.

Wyndi stares back at them curiously and then halfway mimics the sound—although it comes out more as something between a small bell chiming and a kitten's mew. They allow a brief stroking behind their ears, then yawn and dive back into the warmth of the pocket.

The Florivan officer meets Potts's eyes with a curiously serious expression. "I think you'd better tell me from the beginning, Julian."

"Yeah…" Potts leans back against the bench and stares up at the atrium ceiling for a few moments. "I had a feeling you'd say that…"

Appendix

Timeline of *Strange Space®* Adventures

The following timeline lists all of the published *Strange Space® Adventures* and Short Stories in roughly chronological order. Where stories feature major time skips, they have been placed based on the earliest events of that story.

Short Stories marked with *[1] can be found in *Tales of the Navigators: Volume 1*.

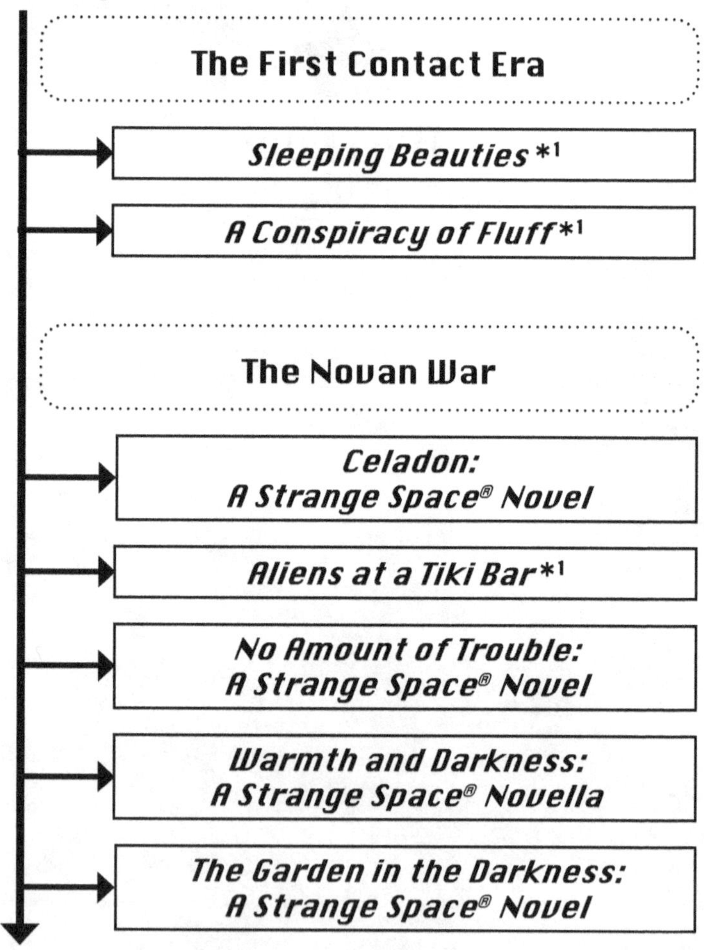

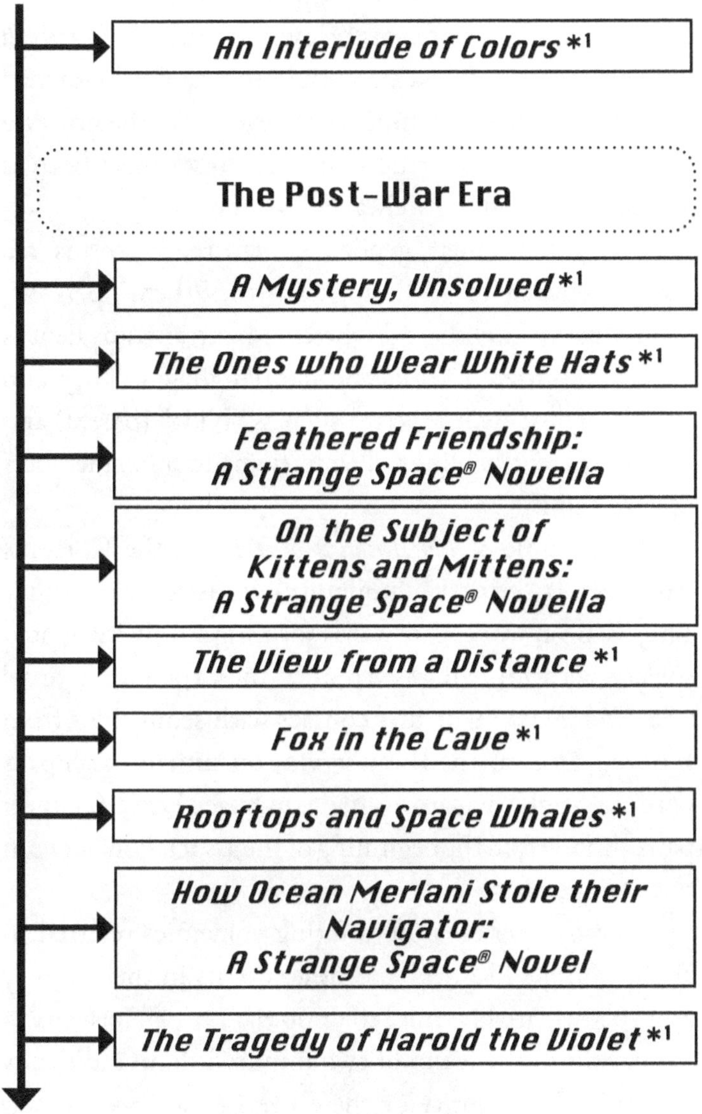

An Interlude of Colors *1

The Post-War Era

A Mystery, Unsolved *1

The Ones who Wear White Hats *1

Feathered Friendship:
A Strange Space® Novella

On the Subject of
Kittens and Mittens:
A Strange Space® Novella

The View from a Distance *1

Fox in the Cave *1

Rooftops and Space Whales *1

How Ocean Merlani Stole their
Navigator:
A Strange Space® Novel

The Tragedy of Harold the Violet *1

On Florivan Kittens

The Florivans are a curious species by nature.

Roughly humanoid in form with silver-striped blue skin, a second pair of arms below the first, a long tufted prehensile tail, catlike ears at the top of a head crowned with silver hair, and a third golden eye above the first two in the center of the forehead: it's easy to see them both as "human-like" and "entirely alien" all at once.

In light of their genderless nature, Florivans are always referred to with singular "they/them" personal pronouns in English and whatever neutral equivalent is most appropriate in other human languages. They also exclusively use neutral terms such as "Nida" (parent) and "Entile" (parent's sibling) when referring to other members of their family.

In the time of *No Amount of Trouble*, the Florivans have been friends with humanity for just over a century. They've been working towards forming a fully integrated society with humanity ever since the exploration vessel LSS *Hulthemia* made first contact with scout ships from Procyon. Florivans had been serving on human starships as part of Astral Navigator/Quantum Space Drive Engineer pairs almost from the beginning of the association between the two species.

Due to a series of devastating epidemics referred to as the "Jungle Plagues" and other events in their history as a species, at this time, the population of Florivans as a species is in the realm of two hundred thousand adults in total. The majority of these live in the Procyon star system on a planet known as the Sanctuary. Roughly one thousand Florivans live at the human colony of Luyten's

Star in an area called the North City Sanctuary, and another thousand or so currently serve with the crews of different starships, either as Quantum Space Drive Engineers or apprentices. Although the Jungle Plagues are mainly to blame for the current "endangered species" status of Florivans, their unusual biology is a core factor in their rarity and the slow rate at which their population can recover from any significant losses.

Florivans reproduce asexually, but only perhaps one in ten of them will ever undergo the metamorphosis to become a reproductive individual. Everything about the process is shrouded in secrecy, as far as humans are concerned. What *is* known, though, by the humans who find themselves as close friends with a Florivan with a reason to tell them, is that even the Florivans themselves cannot control or predict just *who* will undergo the metamorphosis or when it will happen to them. It is well known that both the metamorphosis itself and the process of going physically into the Strange and "catching" a litter of kittens are potentially deadly.

Usually, a Florivan reproductive individual is between thirty-five and fifty Earth-Standard years old at the time of their metamorphosis. They are considered an "Elder Candidate" after their metamorphosis is recognized, and an "Elder" after their second litter of kittens is old enough to be formally introduced to Florivan society.

The families of reproductive individuals are very protective of them because of this, as is Florivan society as a whole. Only Elders who were in active space service prior to their metamorphosis are permitted to live outside of one of the Sanctuaries. Similarly, a starship whose QSD Engineer has become an Elder will *always* have a second Nav/Quan team assigned to it. A ship whose QSD Engineer becomes an Elder Candidate may delay acquiring this second team, depending on its mission and size.

Kittens are caught in litters of two to five, and start their lives as adorable silver-furred things about the size of a sugar glider. The Florivan parent carries their kittens in a pouch on their abdomen analogous to that of a kangaroo, although they aren't technically marsupials. The kittens typically grow to about the size of a red squirrel before they begin to mimic words and language understandable to anyone other than Florivans. Notably, Florivan kittens are known to rapidly pick up an understanding of any language spoken around them consistently, even if they are not yet capable of repeating the words.

As kittens continue to grow, they shed their fur and reveal their unique shade of silver-striped blue skin. Around the same time they shed the last of their fur, Florivan kittens go through a series of growth spurts, after which they are similarly sized to human children and adolescents of the same age.

Occasionally, one kitten out of a litter will be smaller and develop more slowly than their littermates, having a more fragile constitution as a result. Referred to as "survivor-smallest", kittens, those who live long enough to open their eyes tend to take several additional years to grow to maturity. Despite their smaller size, these kittens typically show the same level of intellectual and linguistic development as their larger littermates. In some cases, a survivor-smallest kitten may even prove to develop their linguistic abilities more quickly than average.

Although few such kittens prove strong enough to survive to adolescence, let alone adulthood, those who do are notable for their higher sensitivity and greater skills in working with Quantum Space. Notably, survivor-smallest kittens never undergo reproductive metamorphosis, but if they do reach adulthood, they are also known to live longer than the average Florivan by several decades.

On the Prelvee and T'irsh–fel Alliance

At the beginning of humanity's involvement in the great Novan War, two of the myriad member species of the Greater Galactic Commons introduced themselves directly to Admiral Jennifer Marvin of the Sol Coalition Defense Fleet and her ambassadorial counterparts in the Sol Coalition Diplomatic Corps. These were the T'irsh-fel and the Prelvee, two highly advanced species who had long been close allies and were the primary force preventing the spread of the Novan Armada.

The Prelvee are the larger of the two species, and have something of an insectoid cephalopod appearance. A Prelvee has a long segmented body supported by an armored exoskeleton, with each segment bearing up to four jointed appendages with claws. Their heads are unarmored, and feature a single massive square-pupiled eye with five fleshy tentacles hanging over a beak-like pair of mouth-parts. Male Prelvee reach an average of eight to ten feet long at adulthood, while females are typically twice as long at the same age. Females never cease growing throughout their long lives, and are typically the more socially dominant members of the species.

A number of different sub-species or ecotypes of Prelvee exist. Most of these are terrestrial varieties from different regions of the Prelvee homeworld, but the aquatic ecotype is particularly notable both for its rarity in the spacefaring portion of the population and its innate differences from standard Prelvee anatomy. Aquatic Prelvee can be recognized by the gold speckles which cover both their faces and the armor of their carapaces. They have a set of gills beneath the junctions of their uppermost body segments which allow them to breathe underwater. Interestingly, aquatic Prelvee do not show any distinct preference between fresh or salt water.

Prelvee are able to exude and spin silk via glands at the junction between the head and carapace. The natural texture color of silk varies by ecotype, but an individual Prelvee can develop the skill to produce a wide variety of fabric types and textures. Prelvee in the medical field are particularly notable for their abilities to create bandages and antiseptic silks. Similarly, it is common practice for Prelvee artisans and engineers to use shed exoskeleton components as a base material with a surprisingly large range of applications.

The T'irsh-fel are a relatively small-bodied species in comparison. An adult individual's thick-scaled, slug-like body is three feet long on average; the scales of their hide vary in size and are bony in composition, with general brown-to-grey coloration. At the 'head end' of the body, a T'irsh-fel sports eight long, stalked appendages, each bearing a single large round eye at its end. The eyes are capable of independent movement, allowing the T'irsh-fel individual a full 360° view of their surroundings at all times. They will often direct several eyes towards one object to bring it into sharper focus as needed. Surrounding the point where the eye stalks connect to the rest of their body, each T'irsh-fel has a thick ruff of long, fluffy "feathers". These structures are brightly colored, usually in reds, oranges, yellows, or purples. T'irsh-fel feathers are poorly understood by humanity's science, although due to their mobility and certain observations made by those who work closely to them, it is suspected that these decorative structures are more akin to the appendages of certain crinoids.

T'irsh-fel are also notable for their telepathic and telekinetic abilities. They are line-of-sight telepathic both with other members of their species and alien life forms. The T'irsh-fel telepathic projection is generally one-way with members of other species, unless a significant personal bond exists with the alien in question. Their line-of-sight telepathic projection functions over visual communication feeds. While the T'irsh-fel do possess organs analogous to ears and can perceive the spoken words of others, they cannot project their thoughts through audio-only communication media.

The telekinetic abilities of the average T'irsh-fel individual are also based within their immediate line of sight. This ability, however, is not transmissible over visual communication feeds. The strength of the individual's telekinetic abilities is tied to their age and position in the T'irsh-fel social hierarchy. The average T'irsh-fel adult is able to telekineticly lift and manipulate small to medium-sized objects. They can also split their attention between such manipulation and other tasks like movement and telepathic conversation.

Socially, the Prelvee organize themselves into systems of clans led by matriarchs, which are then assembled into a greater regional assembly. Each ecotype has its own way of organizing these clans, as well as its own dialect. Prelvee culture centers around concepts of respect, duty, and politeness.

T'irsh-fel social structure and culture is somewhat strictly hierarchical, and organized through the semi-hive-mind "All." The component parts of the All are made up of individual T'irsh-fel bloodlines. Because an individual's connection to the All is made through their bloodline's hierarchy, if the bloodline's leaders are cut off from the All as a punishment for wrongdoing or negligence, every member of the bloodline below them is simultaneously "Severed" from all other T'irsh-fel. Those who survive the physical and mental trauma of severing are no longer considered living persons by other T'irsh-fel. As the Prelvee do not agree with this practice, it is not uncommon for one of them, usually a medical professional, to arrange to formally adopt a Severed T'irsh-fel as their companion and assistant.

Needless to say, T'irsh-fel take matters of personal and bloodline honor very seriously. T'irsh-fel telepathic speech patterns reflect this. When speaking to those outside their own clan group or with whom they have deep personal bonds, the T'irsh-fel always refer to themselves in the third person, usually in the form of "this humble self". They will also tend to call others by their full titles as a sign of respect, and may take it as a deep offense if their own are ignored.

The Prelvee and T'irsh-fel Alliance has existed for more than a thousand years by the time of *No Amount of Trouble*. The ancient friendship between these two vastly different peoples stems from their having each evolved on one of the bodies in a binary planet pair. The Prelvee originated on a terrestrial world twice the size of Earth with a generally warmer climate resembling Earth's Carboniferous period, while the T'irsh-fel's planet was an Earth-sized rocky ice world similar to modern-day Europa or Earth during the Cryogenian period. Both species reached a rudimentary spacefaring cultural stage at a similar point in time, and had made contact via advanced telescopes relatively early on in their history.

Although both the Prelvee and T'irsh-fel continue to have their own cultures, their greater society is far more of a blend than it would appear on first glance. The primary reason that the spacefaring component of the Alliance is separated into species-specific ships is biological: the majority of Prelvee ecotypes cannot function at low temperatures for long periods of time, and T'irsh-fel are at risk of over-heating and suffering organ failure at temperatures in excess of 20°C (68°F). Additionally, while the T'irsh-fel are remarkably resilient to shifts in gravitational forces, both species prefer to keep the artificial gravity on their starships close to that of their origin planets. In a similar vein, both species tend to build colonies on worlds similar to their origin planets, although if a single world offers suitable environmental conditions, it is not unusual for combined colonies and outposts to form.

Individuals of either species who spend time in the others' preferred environment typically wear specially-developed protective garments or technology to keep their bodies at the correct temperatures. For the T'irsh-fel, this takes the form of a backpack-like structure anchored along the scales of their back. Prelvee forms of protective garments are usually thickly padded tube-like coats, which may have heating systems incorporated into them, depending on the circumstances.

On the Defense Fleet's Darter Squadrons

The Sol Coalition Defense Fleet's squadrons of darter pilots are either legendary for their bravery or infamous for their love of danger, depending upon whom one asks.

The technology for small, two-person craft capable of maneuvering both within a planetary atmosphere and in the zero-gravity environment of outer space was already in development prior to the beginning of humanity's involvement in the Novan War. At that time, the inherently pacifist Florivan Council of Elders was still restricting the use of their all-important Quantum Space Drive to civilian and Ranger Corps vessels only. Without the Drive to allow their ships to use the veiled dimension of Quantum Space as a shortcut around the physical distances between planets and stars, the Sol Coalition Defense Fleet was left to come up with other means of protecting the eight star systems in its charge.

The concept of short-range fighter craft serving as a mobile force which could be placed on individual inhabited worlds or space stations as a final line of defense against potential invaders was the Defense Fleet's best option at the time. The danger of invasion was primarily theoretical at the onset of Project SnailDarter's development, as the only alien species humanity had thus far encountered were the neighboring Sol-based Europans (who were unable to leave their moon of origin without assistance) and the charismatic and friendly Florivans who had become humanity's closest ally and begun a process of peaceful societal integration.

When humanity found itself suddenly in the middle of the ongoing war between the Novan Imperium's conquest force and the Prelvee and T'irsh-fel Alliance, the development of Project Snail Darter was sped up in order to provide a serviceable defensive and expeditionary force.

Notably, the representatives of both senior member species of the Alliance were reported to be "horrified, but thoroughly impressed" by the demonstrations held for them of the capabilities of the "darters" and their pilots in combat scenarios against long-range particle weapons and unmanned drones. While the Alliance's strategists were familiar with the live-piloted "strikers" used by the Novans to overwhelm their enemies with seemingly endless waves of disposable attack craft, neither species had ever *dreamed* of placing live pilots at the controls inside similar spacecraft themselves. The idea of a single human being responsible for operating an object operating at the very limits of what the laws of physics and understanding of human science would allow and sending them out to attack the enemy directly was as completely alien to them as humans themselves were. Nevertheless, the Alliance quickly recognized the value of the Defense Fleet's darters as a counter to the Novan Armada's striker forces.

Initial plans for the use of these unique small fighter craft centered around forming squadrons of darters to be stationed as the defense of individual inhabited worlds within the Sol Coalition's territory. Additionally, a number of these squadrons would be selected to serve as an expeditionary force on the Alliance's ships in nearby battle sectors. The so-called "defection" of the Florivan Elder Celadon Toreval and the arrival of their household as the Fleet's "Florivan Volunteer Corps" made several changes to the Alliance's core strategies possible. The newly formed squadrons of darters were instead posted on the Defense Fleet's brand-new QSD-equipped starships, where they could more easily be mobilized to defend the Sol Coalition's territory and aid the other members of the Alliance when possible.

The first nine darter squadrons were formed by the time the Fleet's ships were ready, and each was placed under the command of one of the veterans of the Project Snail Darter test pilot program. While eight of these squadrons were immediately assigned to starships, the 9th remained stationed at the Teegarden Shipyards to defend the base there and assist in the training of additional pilots.

At the time of *No Amount of Trouble*, there are a total of eighteen darter squadrons in service. Each is composed of sixteen pilots, divided into four "wing teams" during maneuvers. The wings of a squadron are subdivided into patrol pairs. Each wing is led by one of the squadron's most experienced pilots, with the "lead wing" being that of the squadron's commanding officer. A darter squadron also includes a number of maintenance technicians responsible for repairing and updating the darters as needed. Typically, there is one of these technicians assigned to each wing, with a "chief mechanic" overseeing all of them.

The 2nd Darter Squadron is a notable exception to this standard personnel arrangement. The 2nd began as a typical squadron, albeit as the only one with more than one former test pilot in its ranks. After its commanding officer and the majority of its members were lost along with SCV *Athene* during the first Battle of the Teegarden Expanse, the decision was made to allow the remaining three pilots to reform their unit as a single-wing squadron retaining their initial designation. At the time of *No Amount of Trouble*, the resulting smaller 2nd squadron is assigned to SCV *Surnia* as an attachment to the ship's own recently-formed 18th Darter Squadron.

On Character Identities and Pronouns

No Amount of Trouble takes place in a far future setting in which human society has long since reached the stage of accepting and celebrating all varieties of diversity. This is a sort of world that I, personally, would like to live in. I don't claim it to be a *perfect* setting, but I do take an optimistic view of our potential as a species.

Several of the human characters presented in this story would, in today's terms, likely identify with one or more communities under the LGBTQIA+ umbrella. While the narrative of this story did not call for these characters to specifically state which labels they would use, and I like to imagine that a lot of who they are can be inferred through their interactions, as a member of the LGBTQIA+ community *myself*, I'm aware of the importance of clear representation. Seeing characters like ourselves in stories where they are valued for who they are and able to live without being marginalized for their nature is, in my opinion, *powerful*, and a big part of my philosophy as a writer.

Please note that at the same time, it is impossible to represent an entire community in the form of one character. My characters are simply themselves, and while they draw on my own experiences and those of people I know, they are not meant to be "perfect" renditions of one thing or another. Just like every human, their various identities are *aspects* of them, rather than the entirety of their personality.

That all being said, the following characters central to this story would like to "come out" to you and share this aspect of their lives:

Pilot-Major Abigail Ioane would describe herself as asexual and aromantic.

Elias Rudolph would describe himself as homosexual/homoromantic. (In his words: "a man who happens to be attracted to other men." Rudy has never been all that interested in labels of any sort.)

On behalf of all of my characters, I'd like to thank you, dear reader, for being accepting of them and respecting their preferred sets of pronouns.

I hope that we all will one day live in a world like the one these characters inhabit, in which a person can openly be themself without fear. I do believe it's possible for us to get there, too; every small step we make in the right direction matters.

—*Katie Silverwings*

Katie Silverwings is an award-winning author, illustrator, and stained glass artisan originally from Texas and now a nomadic creative spirit. She holds a BA in English and History from McMurry University in Abilene, Texas, with minors in Art, Arts Administration, and Biblical Greek Translation, as well as a BA (Hons.) in Glass from the University for the Creative Arts in the UK. Silverwings identifies as aromantic, asexual, and genderfae; "she/her", "they/them", and "fae/faer" pronouns are all welcome.

Long fascinated by nature and space, Silverwings' speculative fiction work centers around notions of optimistic futurism, friendship, found family, and adventurous journeys into the known and unknown. Her characters do most of the driving, and she does her best to keep up and negotiate pleasing stories with them.

Silverwings' two cats are commonly found staring over her shoulder while she's writing. The small cloud of dark matter with eyes likes to sit in her lap and interfere with typing, while the calico makes operatic editorial comments from across the room.

www.KatieSilverwings.com
@KatieSilverwings

Official Podcast

Come along for the adventure as author Katie Silverwings reads her award-winning *Strange Space*® *Adventures* books one chapter at a time!

The *Strange Space*® *Adventures Podcast* is available wherever you listen to podcasts, including Spotify, Apple Podcasts, and YouTube.

More Books
by Katie Silverwings

Celadon

✦ A Strange Space® Novel ✦

The Novan War has just begun. All that stands between Humanity and utter destruction are the ships of the Sol Coalition Defense Fleet.

The only problem? None of those ships are equipped with the all-important Quantum Space Drive which allows humanity to travel between planets and stars at a reasonable scale of time. The Drive needs Florivan QSD Engineers to run it, and Florivans are pacifists. Their Council of Elders has never allowed service on military vessels.

The Fleet can do little more than sit at the edges of the Coalition's seven member systems and *wait* for the Novans to attack.

Celadon Toreval is the Youngest of the Florivan Council of Elders. If anyone can come to Fleet Admiral Marvin's aid and help her save her people—and theirs— it's them.

Celadon, though, has their own reasons to get involved...

Warmth and Darkness

✴ A Strange Space® Novella ✴

Admiral Jennifer Marvin used to think she'd seen everything the galaxy had to throw at her. That, though, was before she met the Florivan Elder Celadon Toreval. She can sum up this Quantum Space Drive Engineer and dear friend of hers in two words: *cryptic chaos*. Their preference for the company of the most troublesome humans they can possibly find in the Fleet's ranks doesn't make matters better.

These days, Admiral Marvin is just grateful that the galaxy occasionally sends her a sign that something unusual is about to upset her carefully laid plans. Whether she manages to see those signs in time to do anything about it, though, is always a gamble.

Join Admiral Marvin's crew aboard the starship SCV *Aegolius* as they face the next chapter in the tales of the Novan War, and find out what new adventure waits for them in the darkness.

Even in the depths of space, you can find warmth...

Available now from Amazon and Barnes & Noble and at
www.KatieSilverwings.com

The Garden in the Darkness

Adventures happen when you least expect them.

In the time of the Novan War, the pilots of the 2nd Darter Squadron "Musketeers" are no strangers to peril. Even the little Florivan kitten who serves as their mascot has a tendency to get into trouble. When two of the Musketeers and their mascot find themselves stranded on a seemingly deserted mining colony, though, they find themselves in a situation none of their previous adventures could have prepared them for.

With no way to contact the rest of the Defense Fleet, they'll have to find their own way to repair their darters and get back to their starship. To make matters worse, enemy forces are lurking in the nearby asteroids.

The Mayview outpost was abandoned at the start of the War, but the Musketeers aren't alone here. Someone is watching them from behind the overgrown vines...

How Ocean Merlani Stole their Navigator

✦ A Strange Space® Novel ✦

Every starship wanting to use the veiled dimension of Quantum Space as a shortcut around the physical distance between planets and stars needs a Florivan to run the Drive.

Every Florivan QSD Engineer needs an Astral Navigator to orient them and keep them anchored to Normal space. Finding the *right* human to be their life-long counterpart is one of the most important choices a young Florivan ever makes.

What happens, then, to someone like Ocean Merlani Barker, who can't seem to click with *any* of the highly qualified Navigator prospects their instructors have to offer? Ocean themself seems content to spend their second year in the Nav/Quan training program alone and taking extra classes for their secondary degree in geosciences.

Content, that is, until a chance encounter with a certain graduating student from the Security/Tactical program changes the course of their life forever...

Available now from Amazon and Barnes & Noble and at
www.KatieSilverwings.com

Feathered Friendship

On the Subject of Kittens and Mittens

Ranger Captain Taimri Hämäläinen loved playing in the snow as a child. Now, on a vacation with her family in the snow-covered mountains of a certain planet in the Beta Centauri sytem, she has a chance to share all of her favorite winter games with her own children.

Taimri's three adopted Florivan kittens, of course, have never seen snow before; they live on a space station with her husband, George Barker. That only makes it more fun to dress Sky, Storm, and Ocean up in their warmest clothes and take them out into the frosted wonderland, in Taimri's opinion.

While her Florivan counterpart, River Myrval, stays behind in the cozy comforts of the lodge, Taimri and her kittens are in for a bit of an adventure they hadn't expected...

9 781959 922452